Critical acclaim for Helena María Viramontes's fiction

Their Dogs Came with Them

"The novel will no doubt—like her other work—break ground and enrich the range and vision of our American literature. I hope you, too, will feel the enthusiasm and faith in her work that I do."

—Julia Alvarez

"In her most ambitious book yet, Viramontes makes the private property of her characters' stories relevant to us all."

—*Poets & Writers*

"There are certain books—and I'm a pretty good judge of this—that are going to become, over time, the books of their time.... This is one of them."

—Michael Silverblatt, host of KCRW's *Bookworm*

"A profoundly gritty and moving portrait of everyday life . . . highly rewarding."

—*Ithaca Times*

"The novel draws us in with Viramontes's hypnotic prose.... Unflinchingly . . . tells the story of the conquered people from the point of view of those conquered and displaced."

—*San Antonio Express-News*

This title is also available as an eBook.

"To fully appreciate it, approach it like a mural. While the grandness of a mural is what first commands attention, the viewer enters through its image details. After which, the viewer can then step back and reflect on the whole. The same is true of Viramontes's startling second novel."

—*The Austin Chronicle*

"A novel carved of both cruelty and sensitivity. Viramontes is a writer of immeasurable spirit."

—Alex Espinoza, author of *Still Water Saints*

"Viramontes's power is in her heartfelt observations about the forgotten poor . . . the despised and reviled: the homeless, the immigrant, the cholas and cholos. She is as compassionate as John Steinbeck, as sweeping as the unflinching camera of Sebastião Salgado."

—Sandra Cisneros, author of *Caramelo* and *The House on Mango Street*

"With elegance and poetic precision, Viramontes has captured a humanity that will not stay down, no matter what the odds. Like the characters in this novel, her prose is a warm breath of the real thing."

—Ernesto Quiñonez, author of *Chango's Fire*

Under the Feet of Jesus

"Adds another important chapter to the existing body of literature about the Mexican-American experience. . . . Working firmly in the social realism of Steinbeck's *The Grapes of Wrath* and Upton Sinclair's *The Jungle,* she paints a harrowing . . . portrait of migrant laborers in California's fruit fields."

—*Publishers Weekly*

"An exciting read. . . . Throughout this rich novel, Viramontes brings us into her world and we fall under her spell."

—*Los Angeles Times Book Review*

"Blends lyricism, harsh realism, and a concern for social justice . . . stunning."

—*Newsweek*

The Moths and Other Stories

"Most of the stories in *The Moths,* Helena María Viramontes' debut collection, are tense, direct, and powerfully imagined . . . she both reveals the invisibilized group and invents a way of seeing that's absolutely true to its own experience and wonderfully attentive to the incalculable beats of personality."

—*The Village Voice*

THEIR
DOGS CAME
WITH THEM

A NOVEL

HELENA MARÍA VIRAMONTES

WASHINGTON SQUARE PRESS

New York   London   Toronto   Sydney

Washington Square Press
A Division of Simon & Schuster, Inc.
1230 Avenue of the Americas
New York, NY 10020

First Washington Square Press trade paperback edition September 2008

WASHINGTON SQUARE PRESS and colophon are trademarks
of Simon & Schuster, Inc.

For information about special discounts for bulk purchases,
please contact Simon & Schuster Special Sales at
1-800-456-6798 or business@simonandschuster.com.

Manufactured in the United States of America

10 9 8 7 6 5 4 3 2 1

The Library of Congress has cataloged the hardcover edition as follows:

Viramontes, Helena María.
    Their dogs came with them : a novel / Helena María Viramontes.
        p. cm.
    1. Mexican Americans—Fiction. 2. Mexican American neighborhoods—
Fiction. 3. Express highways—Design and construction—Fiction. 4. Los
Angeles (Calif.)—Fiction. I. Title.
PS3572.I63T47 2007
813'.54—dc22   2006047982

ISBN: 978-1-416-58834-4

To my son, Eloy Francisco Rodriguez,
and for his father

In memory of
Ann Sunstein Kheel,
who believed in neighborhoods

They came in battle array, as conquerors, and the dust rose in whirlwinds on the roads. Their spears glinted in the sun, and their pennons fluttered like bats. They made a loud clamor as they marched, for their coats of mail and their weapons clashed and rattled. Some of them were dressed in glistening iron from head to foot; they terrified everyone who saw them.

Their dogs came with them, running ahead of the column. They raised their muzzles high; they lifted their muzzles to the wind. They raced on before with saliva dripping from their jaws.

—*The Broken Spears: The Aztec Account of the Conquest of Mexico,*
by Miguel Leon-Portilla

1960–1970

1960–1970

PART I

PART 1

ONE

The Zumaya child had walked to Chavela's house barefooted, and the soles of her feet were blackened from the soot of the new pavement. She swung her tar feet under the vinyl chair as she stacked large, empty Ohio Blue Tip matchboxes the old woman had saved for her into a pyramid on the kitchen table. Throughout the house, scraps of paper, Scotch-taped reminders, littered the walls. Cardboard boxes sat nestled like hungry mouths of birds wide open for wrapped tumblers, cutlery, souvenir ashtrays. Bulk-filled pillowcases leaned against the coffee table, tagged by the old woman with words so scratchy they could have been written by the same needle used to pin the notes to the pillowcases: **cobijas,** one note said; **Cosa del baño,** said another. **No good dreses. Josie's tipewriter. Fotos.** The child swung her feet as she stacked sixteen then eight then four then two then one hollow matchbox until the shadows lengthened in the kitchen. Before the lightbulb had to be switched on, before the old woman Chavela ordered, Go home now, listen to me, it's getting late.

Chavela continued packing tin cans from the pantry into a box on a chair opposite the child. The old woman was toothpick-splintery like her writing. Her hands trembled from the onset of Parkinson's. Rhubarbs faded from the print of her housedress. She padded across the kitchen wearing neatly folded-down cotton socks and a pair of terry-cloth slippers. She barely whooshed the air whenever she passed the child.

Are you deaf? It's getting late. Chavela's croaky words floated from a distant place to the child's ears like yanked strands of seaweed beached on the shore. The child held a matchbox in midair and looked at the greenish flame flicker under the iron comal and waited for the old woman to say something else. The chair was hard, lumpy and stuck to the child's thighs. Chavela shook out a cigarette from a cellophane package, propped it between her stitched crunch of lips, grabbed a matchbox and shook it, rattled another, then another in search of matchsticks until she had scattered the pyramid about the table.

Chavela waxed the shiny temples of her forehead with her tobacco-tarnished hand. The child could see the milky film of her eyes scanning around the kitchen in search of matchsticks and finally the old woman said, It's not right, I'm telling you. Chavela raised the flame on the stove and hunched over the spurting fire under the comal. The heat splashed on her face and then she lowered the gas, inhaled and coughed and returned her gold bunched package to the pocket of her rhubarb dress.

The child had dreamt of lizards, and it was because of the dream that she had listened to the smaller Gamboa boy, who had caught a tiny lizard from a mound of bulldozed earth. The earthmovers, Grandmother Zumaya had called them; the bulldozers had started from very far away and slowly arrived on First Street, their muzzles like sharpened metal teeth making way for the freeway. The Gamboa boy had hidden behind her grandfather's toolshed, and psssted at the child to join him. His face tar-smudged, he held it and at first the lizard clawed the thin air. In his other hand, the Gamboa boy held a pair of rusty scissors. He reassured her that the tail would grow back. It's not right, she knew, even if they witnessed a miracle. The lizard turned to stone, stiff and silent. They both waited. He made her touch it and then he made her touch the rings of wrinkled skin. The cold sensation never left her fingers, his clamp around her wrist as he pulled her behind the toolshed never left her, his dirty rough clasp where the lizard's head poked in and out never left her. That feeling— it's not right—never left her.

The old woman had taped scribbled instructions all over the walls of the house. **Leve massage for Josie. Basura on Wetsday. J work # AN**

54389. I need to remember, Chavela had told the child when the child pointed a matchbox at the torn pieces of papers clinging on the walls. **Water flours. Pepto Bismo. Chek gas off.** It's important to remember my name, my address, where I put my cigarillo down **Call Josie. Chavela Luz Ybarra de Cortez. SS#010-56-8336. 4356 East 1st** or how the earthquake cracked mi tierra firme, mi país, now as far away as my youth, a big boom-crack. The dogs and gente went crazy from having the earth pulled out right from under them. **Cal Mr . . . Lencho's tio sobre apartment. Shut off luz.** The earthquake's rubble of wood and clay and water yielded only what was missing; shoes without shoelaces, flowered curtains without windows, a baby rattle without seeds in its hollow belly, an arm without a body; and how the white smell of burnt flesh choked. **J work # AN 54389. Smoke outside.** That's why I began to smoke cigarettes, to hide the white smell even over here in El Norte, even after seventy-seven years, so don't complain about my cigarillos.

But Chavela forgot to smoke her cigarettes outside and the tobacco made the child's nose itch. She smoked in front of the kitchen sink where the linoleum floor was scuffed with so many years of standing to scrub metal pots or pour a glass of tap water. The old woman inhaled quietly, and stared out the window at the lawn of her small yard to see the lemon tree that yielded lemons every other year, to memorize the potted ferns hanging from the shanty arbor built by a married man she had once loved. As she exhaled, the cigarette smoke resembled coiled earthworms without the earth, and she studied the shrubs of bursting red hibiscus bushes that bloomed lush and rich as only ancient deep-rooted hibiscus shrubs can do. Chavela squinted to keep the fumes away from her eyes and then rested the cigarette on the cigarette-burnt windowsill where she had rested hundreds of cigarettes or saved little discoveries such as safety pins or loose Blue Chip Stamps or buttons. The old woman returned to her task at hand and placed another cardboard box next to the child. Chavela's shaky fingernails ticked against the cardboard lid like the rooster clock on the wall.

I'm trying to tell you how it feels to have no solid tierra under you. Listen to me! Where could you run? The sound of walls cracking, the ceiling pushed up into a mushroom cloud. Do you need Drāno to clean out those ears of yours?

But the child heard it, a long rip of paper.

It just wasn't right. Nothing was left, I tell you. Nada. I cried for so long that if my grief had been a volcano, it would have torn the earth in two.

The child gazed at her, imagining an egg cracking into two jagged halves.

My tears could wash away mounds of clay, a flood as dark as blindness pouring from my eyes.

The child imagined a river of molasses.

And under all the rubble, under all that swallowed earth, the ruins of the pyramid waited.

The child knew the end of the story and continued stacking the matchboxes.

Pay attention, Chavela demanded. Because displacement will always come down to two things: earthquakes or earthmovers. The child stared at Chavela's cigarette smoke coiling as thick and visible as the black fumes of the bulldozer exhaust hovering over the new pavement of First Street.

Now go home! the old woman said abruptly, packing a set of newspaper-wrapped plates in the box. At least you have one.

Saturday morning barely stretched against the skies. The dull gray doused the glow of the yellow porch light. The child lay buried under a heavy fleece blanket imprinted with a lion roaring. Someone had given the orange blanket to Grandmother years before the child came to live with them, and though she tried to be a good girl humming under the weight of the animal heat, the rigidity and the goodness became impossible. She poked her head out, saw morning light, relieved.

She yawned almost as earnest as the lion, and then swallowed a few times to clear the ocean waves in her head. Her hearing sometimes reached and sometimes connected or sometimes didn't connect to the waves of sea. Fever-sweaty, she wrestled one leg then the other from beneath the tight hot compress of the blanket until she was free to jump on the lion's incisors. The springs of the mattress squeaked and the headboard bounced and the pillows spilled to the floor and then Grandfather's thundering threat, Renata will get you! followed from the next room and she froze.

For weeks he had engaged the child's attention with the story of Renata Valenzuela, a local schoolgirl who had vanished, abducted one afternoon. Grandfather once pointed to a derelict house claiming it belonged to Renata's parents to show the child what could happen if she was bad. The neglected grass burnt to coarse pricks under the carnage of dead leaves heaped everywhere. The windows were draped in straggly black curtains. Tongues of paint curled from the rotted wooden door and whispered to the child of horrific grief.

At night the child refused to succumb to the long harrowing blankness and fought sleep in order to keep at bay the menacing Renata. Finally, the morning light arrived entirely, inviting. Her feet itched to walk against the cold hardwood floor and she slid off the bed and began to tiptoe to the window. She kicked aside a pillow and stubbed a toe on the doll that Mrs. M. of the Child Services gave her last Christmas. At the window, the child puttied her hot cheek against the rain-cool glass. On the other side of First Street, Chavela's blue house looked as empty as a toothless mouth.

The rows of vacant houses were missing things. Without hinged doors, the doorframes invited games. Shattered windows had been used as targets. Chavela never would have allowed her yard to weed wild, never allowed cans of trash to be scattered by the street dogs or left to the crows who pecked at coffee grinds and cucumber peelings. The earthmovers, parked next to the row of empty houses, were covered in canvas tarps and roped with tight-fisted knots to protect the meters, ignitions and knobs on the dashboards from the weekend rainstorms. Already the child viewed the two Gamboa boys sawing a butcher knife through the thickness of hemp knot.

The child wasn't allowed out of her room until her grandparents had awakened, until Renata's story disappeared temporarily, but the wait seemed as endless as the coming of morning. The honey-yellow floor was biting cold and her toes sprang up in resistance. She peeked out of her room into the long hallway. Sharp white light escaped from between the venetian blinds and then escaped from between the palm tree drapes, and the light stenciled distinct angles on the plasterboard walls. The child waited until the shadow became a chair and the wall became itself and the light became one morning slicing through the quiet dark of the house.

Her grandparents slept under thick hand-sewn quilts, the overhead fan chopping the still air. Their bedroom door was slightly opened, and the child remembered an aching floorboard that always groaned somewhere nearby. She breathed in as if she had sunk underwater, glided in and out of the shadows, around the chair, over the noisy floorboard and out of the hallway, and breathed out.

Except for a border of blue tile framing yellow windmills, the kitchen was austere and functional and smelled of bleach and bacon fat. The child reached over the counter and grabbed a single spoon and the lingering scent of honey made her hungrier. Still in her flannel nightgown, she pinched the uncomfortable elastic of her underwear, then jerked open a drawer and the spoons and forks bumped into one another. She selected a butter knife and then gingerly picked the aluminum handle of the porch door. The door hinges protested but did not prevent her from stepping out into the morning.

The clouds had shapes of squashed gum and the breeze that forced them to float above her tossed about her choppy-cut hair. She sat on the cool concrete steps of the porch, placed the butter knife beside her and scratched the bottoms of her feet. The eyelets of Grandfather's steel-tip leather boots stared at her as she slipped them on. They were clumsy, damp and sawdust-rough against her bare feet but she knew to return them to their rightful place before Grandfather awoke, his hunchback stuffed with endless scolding.

One of the Gamboa boys mouthed off to the other, and the smaller one punched and shoved the taller one. A milk truck passed and the udders of the cow looked too pink, too plastic fake, and this fakery irritated the child. The child yawned and swallowed. Then the ocean waves stopped in her head and the volume of sounds connected: the cawing ruckus the crows made while pecking the garbage, the milk truck bottles rattling, the boys' curses, the church bells clanking a summons, the dogs barking in response. She even heard the clouds that sailed across the light brush against each other like sandpaper.

The child thumped down the stairs and to the middle of the yard and then twirled a few times like a top. The flannel billowed above her knees until dizziness overwhelmed her. The shells of houses and fences and morning blurred when she came to a staggering halt. Light-headed, she wound herself up again, tripping on the laces and falling on the well-groomed lawn. Her mouth opened in laughter.

First Street seemed deserted. The cars were held back by a new traffic light at the intersection, and the child padded across the Bermuda grass. She waited for the cars to pass and then decided to clunk across the wide pavement. The loose laces of Grandfather's steel-toed boots trailed behind her.

Get outta here! yelled the lizard boy, the smaller but meaner Gamboa brother. He knelt on the canvas tarp, stopped his sawing and held the butcher knife straight up. He had worn the same T-shirt for five days.

Leave her alone, said the bald-headed Gamboa brother, the other one who was really a girl, but didn't want to be and got beaten up for it. She's just the Zumaya kid.

So what?

She don't talk.

She better not. And then he said to the child, You better not. The lizard boy pointed the knife at his brother who was really a sister and continued:

She better not or else.

The child had heard people like Mrs. M. of the Child Services say she was deaf; but she wasn't—was she?—if she could hear them say she was deaf. It seemed fortuitous to the child, an option she commanded early on—to have the ocean's sob and then to decide the noise, the external reverberation of language and landscape, until she demanded the silence again.

The lizard boy severed the knot, the bald-headed one pulled and finally the tarp flew up and then whipsaw-slammed, slapping the concrete. The Gamboa boy who was a real boy cursed the child, blaming the noise on her, and screamed that she better make like a tree and leave. His voice boomed and the child hoped the lizard boy had not awakened Grandfather. She pictured him shirtless, hunching over the kitchen sink to wash his face, the bony spine of his bare back full of anger like the hump of a camel full of water. The child saw it all so clearly that she put her two palms up together in prayer, pleading, Please oh please oh please don't wake Grandfather.

Unwanted, the child clunked her boots toward Chavela's house. The outside stucco swirled under the blue paint where glitter specks glistened. Once the child entered the house, sunshine flooded the empty rooms. The linoleum bubbled on the screen porch and exploded like popcorn and the child did a little hat dance to the wonderful sound because by now this was all a game to her. Every room, as hollow as it was, smelled of Chavela's burnt tobacco and the child sneezed. The cigarettes had left stains on the windowsills and the child rolled a finger in each brown notch.

She looked out at her own house and all the other houses on Grandfather's side of First Street; the houses on the saved side were bright and ornamental like the big Easter eggs on display at the Segunda store counter. Some of the houses had cluttered porches with hanging plants or yards with makeshift gardens; others had parked cars on their front lawns. Some built wrought-iron grate fences, while others had drowsy curtains swaying in wide-open windows. In a few weeks, Chavela's side of the neighborhood, the dead side of the street, would disappear forever. The earthmovers had anchored, their tarps whipping like banging sails, their bellies petroleum-readied to bite trenches wider than rivers. In a few weeks the blue house and all the other houses would vanish just like Chavela and all the other neighbors.

Ten years later the child becomes a young woman who will recognize the invading engines of the Quarantine Authority helicopters because their whir of blades above the roof of her home, their earth-rattling explosive motors, will surpass in volume the combustion of engines driving the bulldozer tractors, slowly, methodically unspooling the six freeways.

She will be a young woman peering from between the palm tree drapes of her grandparents' living room, a woman watching the QA helicopters burst out of the midnight sky to shoot dogs not chained up by curfew. Qué locura, she thinks. The world is going crazy. The chopper blades raise the roof shingles of the neighborhood houses and topple TV antennas in swirls of suction on the living side of First Street. The young woman has waist-length hair and wears a nylon underslip pasted to her sweaty back. She pushes the sun-bleached drapes apart with her uninjured hand. The other hand, swathed in gauze and dappled with antiseptic and blood, tingles from the dog bite. Above the woven arteries of freeways, a copter's searchlight sweeps over the roadblocks to catch a lone stray running out of the edge of light. The bitch zigzags across the pavement of First Street, its underbelly droopy with nursing nipples.

I gotta do something soon, the young woman thinks. The wheeling copter blades over the power lines rise in intensity, louder and closer and closer and louder, just like the unrelenting engines of bulldozers ten years earlier when the young woman was a child.

And from Chavela's kitchen window, the child saw Grandfather's avocado-green roof and her own square front door. A group of kids circled the Gamboa boys. The child propped her head on her elbow to watch a third tarp being liberated as if the broken window were the cherrywood-box television. A few of the kids, Tudi, Memo, Diko and Chula, worked at placing stones on the tarps so they wouldn't smack like tattling lips.

The child embedded a finger on the last notch of the last cigarette burn and then she remembered that Chavela had laid the cigarette down on the windowsill to lift a cardboard box to a chair. The old woman had resumed packing plates while the last cigarette burned the last brown notch on the white paint of the windowsill and when the child placed her fingers there to remember—boxes, tin cans, scribbled notes, pyramids and cigarettes burning—she rolled each finger back and forth.

She never confessed her disbelief in the resurrections of lizard tails or the smell of death wrapping around you as if you were a piece of meat laid on butcher paper. The smoke coiling from the resting cigarette simply disappeared into thin air like everything else.

The last night they spent together, Chavela had said, It doesn't matter a little bit if you believe me or not, as if she read the child's doubts. The old woman always looked at the space above the child's head. Because it's all here, she continued, pointing her toothpick finger to her chest. Everything.

But everything was wrapped in a whirl of dust and floated up somewhere beyond the clouds and so the child continued to search, exploring the vacant house while she picked crusted snot from her nose. She raised her arms, twirled again, this time spinning gracefully. In the bathroom, she discovered the toilet seat up, the washbasin bone-dry. Crumpled balls of newspaper tumbled across the floor. She walked cautiously to the bedroom; shattered glass shards from a broken window crackled under Grandfather's boots.

The bedroom closet of the blue house was the emptiest room of all. Without the shoeboxes and impenetrable thickness of coats, dresses, hats and stacks of telephone books, the grungy carpet seemed solemn. A lone hanger swung from a hook when she opened the door. The back wall revealed a patch of brittle old wallpaper. Horses bucked the cowboys in a rodeo. Who would have thought there were cowboys in the closet?

The child touched the saffron paste of old glue behind the peeling cowboys. A pair of wooden beams held up the ceiling and the child tried to memorize them because Chavela told her it was important not to forget. Her ears remembered and she fished an ashy corner of curling wallpaper and then ripped it, cutting the horses' hooves, leaving the spurs behind, nipping the hats waved in the air by the cowboys. She crumpled the paper into a tight ball.

The shouts of the children blatted a trumpet reveille. The Zumaya child startled and ran through the vacant rooms as fast as the clunky boots would permit. Her grandfather's boots flip-flopped through the wild and muddy yard. A few crows raised their wings and fluttered aside. Not far, a timid cat backed off and sat on its tail patiently observing as the child stomped on the garbage and crossed the street. Casually, the cat returned to gorging on chicken bones.

When the child reached the living side of First Street, Grandfather held the screen door open. She could see Grandfather's nose long and straight, two perfectly round black nostrils vacuuming the air between them. The skin under his chin slung like a loose hammock. The child was out of breath, heaving deeply, and her throat felt as dry as dusty potato skins. His rough hand, as rough as the boots she was warned not to touch, had the capacity to catapult against the side of her face whenever she wasn't a good girl. His glare singed the top of her head. He held a forgotten butter knife.

The child glanced upward. Who was it that told her all she had to do was look up at the heavens to see the shapes of things missing? Was it Mrs. M. of the Child Services or any one of the three foster parents? Everything went up into thin air but didn't go away. The child swallowed and disconnection occurred. Her foot slipped limply out of one boot, then the other, and her bare feet were embarrassingly ticklish against the concrete. If it wasn't Chavela of the Ohio Blue Tip matchboxes, who was it, then?

Grandfather's hand came forth like a swift strike of a sulfur match. The child made a symbolic attempt to block his slap and the fistful of Chavela's cowboys fell. Her eyes glazed with hot welling tears. She didn't want to ask why everyone disappears because it seemed to happen all the time; what she wanted to know, what she wanted to ask, was where. Renata Valenzuela and Chavela's last cigarette and the kitchen table and the photographed faces of her mother and her father and all the other ghosts of all the other houses were wrapped in tinfoil; up in the blurry sky, bulky metal sheets of block, stone, wood, and voices floated like scattered clouds, to where, the child could only dream.

TWO

The name skittered. *Turrrtle,* someone screamed, wrenching the name out of thin light and hurling it into the street like the metal lid of a trash can. How could Lote M Homeboys know where she'd been hiding? She jerked back into the crevice between the warehouse wall and the Dumpster, her heart hurried and apprehensive. The Quarantine Authority helicopter gunfire had ended at dawn and she closed her eyes to a stillborn morning, until the hollow clang of her name spooked her awake.

It wasn't the name Antonia María, tenderly whispered into the ear of a Mexican movie actress Turtle's mother had admired from the balcony of the Million Dollar Theater and which came immediately to mind as soon as she filled out the birth certificate at the General Hospital. And it wasn't the nickname Tony Game, which had been given to her by a friendly Lucky Strikes–smoking gym instructor at Belvedere Junior High. The name was her *For Real* one. She had been christened Turtle—always and por vida till death do us part—when she joined the McBride Boys with Luis Lil Lizard hasta la muerte. The two were known as half-and-half of the cold-blooded Gamboas.

Known as "them two." Were them. Once upon a time.

Turtle perspired and waited, feeling the warm air vent against her leather jacket. Daylight slowly whittled away a new morning. She stretched her cramped legs, one and then the other, and slugged her thighs to arouse her muscles, make her legs spark into a run if need be.

Once she stood, she shook out her cramps hokey-pokey style and slipped the large Workman screwdriver into the back pocket of her khakis, all the while listening. Hunger became unbearable, and she ambled to the end of the alley.

Turtle scouted both directions. The intersection of Hastings and First was just beginning to noise up. Above the volume of morning traffic, Turtle was sure she had heard her name, a wake-up call. A pickup truck carried a refrigerator harnessed with ropes. The weight stressed the muffler into an unusual rattle as it passed. Feeling secure, Turtle eased to the street corner, strutted an attitude to say, No worry in the world. She stood behind a mailbox, yawned and the sour of her mouth hung tight.

A morning chill teased her exposed midriff. She hitched up her khakis and pulled down the waist of her leather jacket. The city roadblocks were racked up and trucked out for one more day but the barricades were the least of her worries. Curfew had landed her in the alley and she slept with her knees bunched to her chest, the screwdriver at arm's distance for protection. Patrol sirens and gunshot reports of the helicopters shot through her thin veil of sleep, and she had dreamt of Luis Lil Lizard crouching in the jungle somewhere in 'Nam, clinging to an army-issued rifle, his fingers trembling just as hers had been.

To the left of the mailbox, a young pimply man read a brick of a paperback and didn't even look up to notice the woman who sat at the bus bench and rustled a grocery bag between them. Turtle guessed the scar-faced man was a Che Guevara wannabe, a brown beret flopped on his head like the mural on the wall of the Ramona Gardens housing projects. Who did he think he was fooling? Che crossed his knees. He seemed small against the large expanse of bench. Oblivious to the woman, to the morning and to Turtle, he continued to read.

What a loser.

Potholes the size of hubcaps near the street junction made tires dip. Flecks of loosened gravel pinged the drain grates. Years ago, the city developers came in with plans for freeways and had erected bright traffic lights. First Street had been newly paved with hot tar as black as fire-treated cast iron. Turtle was five feet one inch by the time she was eight years old and she stood exactly on the same corner as now, tall and awkward, crunching on a pickled pig's foot while she watched the men shoveling the smothering asphalt to feed the steamroller. The dense stench of tar hung tight in the air. Turtle remembered how deflated and lanky she was at eight, wearing her father's T-shirt, a knotty kid sucking on the rubbery skin of a pig's foot while crossing the intersection. At eight or eighteen—it was just like her—never paying attention to the safe harbor of space between two painted fluorescent white lines on the pavement.

Traffic lights changed and people crossed. The Black Cat TV Repair Shop remained closed but El Zócalo Fine Meats was opening and a sullen butcher who wore a bloodstained apron wrapped around his bony hips dragged a soggy mop across the storefront entrance. Turtle knew to stay alert. The scent of pork rinds escaped from the opened doors and the leafy tops of carrots peeking out of the woman's grocery bag agitated Turtle's hunger. Turtle needed to eat before she could think and she jerked the jacket over her empty stomach and then studied the passing vehicles as if breakfast seemed just as fleeting. Every move had to be calculated to avoid the inevitable gang crossfire. Being half of the Gamboas meant holding her own, for Luis's sake.

Turtle wondered where Luis Lil Lizard was on the day she munched on the pig's foot, transfixed by the newness of the asphalt, before the hot summer sun heated the pavement and it became painful to walk barefooted. A few Mexican laborers gathered on the steps of the Sacred Heart Church searching eagerly for possible employment. By their thrift-shop looks, their desperate pleading faces, Turtle knew they were migratory and their faces elicited contempt in her. Turtle became embarrassed for them, their low-casting eyes, their soiled shirts and dirty hands, their *begging* for a job.

What losers.

The church bells chimed seven times. Yesterday, Turtle had gulped her only meal, lukewarm broth at the Little Brothers of the Poor Rest Home. She sat next to a man wearing a raggedy army jacket and halfway through her third bowl his cauliflower smell became overwhelming. If Turtle hadn't been so hungry, she would have left her bowl and white bread right on the table. The day before, she had sought out Cross-eyes and banged under the apartment number 303 until her knuckles drained white. Cross-eyes was a junkie and whenever he plugged himself he was a shotgun type of guy, watching your back, helping you spend your money, ready to take action.

But when he was clean and dry and straight as the dashes of the Interstate (as he was now, and he had raised the radio volume to deaden Turtle's rapping), Cross-eyes became a model of unreliability—his only offering to Turtle a cereal box from between the crack and chain of his door. Turtle smacked it out of his blue-veined hand and for that she had heard him slap the three bolts and hurl a hard Fuck off! She backed away, buying time, and waited at the end of the anteroom to see if Cross-eyes would retrieve the box. One of the tenants had burned chiles so bad the scent tattooed the air around her for hours. Fuckin' hell, Turtle had shouted, giving up and kneeling to scrape up some of the Kellogg's cereal flakes that spilled on the trampled carpet.

Fuck you too.

The Val U Mini Mart would be displaying the fruit bins outside just about now. Turtle considered the double risk of walking down the eight gang-disputed blocks to get to the market and then making a fast food break with some oranges or pears. The immediate moment provided the best opportunity. Would Lote M Boys be out for a jump this early in the morning? Turtle yawned and then leaned over the mailbox, playing with the slat while she tried to think.

The 26 halted and Che rolled away while Turtle fisted her jacket pocket to search for a Lifesaver, maybe a Juicy Fruit stick or if she was lucky, a frajo. Leather creaked from the strained seams, and her jacket rode up again. More laborers appeared on the church steps, some with baseball hats, some twisting the neck of their lunch bags, others bare-handed, hatless, searching deep into the streets.

The carrot tops and the woman and another bus disappeared while the exhaust and confining jacket pressed against Turtle's lungs. The jacket and the high-top tennis shoes were already so tight she became conscious of every resisting stitch. When she turned to check out the corner, her jacket rode high, allowing a chill; when she leaned on one foot to offer the other a break, her damp toes pushed up against cool rubber. Every edge of cloth, leather and shoe canvas squeezed against her flesh like shackles.

Turtle was large, and her mother had once said her largeness was bequeathed from a father they called Frank, though his real name was Francisco. Her size gave the impression that Turtle was all muscle, a birthmark of luck in a neighborhood where might makes right. But in Turtle's head, there seemed no end to the charley horse cramps of growth spurts. Her bulky mass of marrow and flesh ballooned beyond her bones, beyond her outgrown clothes and spilled way too large into the streets the McBride Boys like Palo, Santos, Lucho and Luis Lil Lizard had once claimed as their own territory. Limited to a few city blocks which surrounded McBride Avenue and which provided a safety net of fences and alleys, it seemed, at least in Turtle's head, that their dominance, their ownership of those precious city blocks was now thrown into question by their rivals, the Lote M Boys. Consequently, when she walked the streets, she loomed as inviting to them as a bull's-eye target.

The curfew roadblocks were the least of her worries. Turtle knew how to work the streets, how to avoid the Quarantine Authority who enforced the curfew, how to hide from the Lote M Homeboys and mostly how to keep away from her own McBride Boys. Prior to today, her street savvy had been sharp and crisp and unrelenting.

More people crossed the intersection. Turtle kept an eye out for the grocery baskets and glass box carts of the fruit vendors, saving her the trip to the Val U Mini Mart. A few days ago, she had solicited a corncob, a slice of watermelon, a cup of hot atole with a promise of guarding the cart whenever the vendors went on a pee break. Usually, there were two or three of them out by this time, staking a corner, cracking coconuts with a machete, squeezing lemon, sprinkling chile pepper on pieces of mango. This morning they hadn't appeared; the vendors knew something she didn't know and this thought began to worry her. She continued slapping the mailbox slot.

A man in a straw hat jogged across the street. Holding his hat in place with a hand, he hopped onto the curb and toward her.

Perdón, the man said. He held on to a tissue envelope. Por favor. He urged politely, wanted Turtle to move. The way he said it made her stomach turn in disgust. Taller than the man, she barely inched, and the man excused himself again and she barely inched a second time. The man slipped his envelope into the mailbox slot and when he brushed past her, Turtle threw her leathered shoulder forward, pushing the man to one side with such force his sweat-wrung hat snapped back. Astonished, the man stared up at his perpetrator. He jutted out his chin, gestured angrily with his two hands, answered the challenge with another one.

¿Qué traes pelón? The man straightened the rim of his hat. Pedestrians barely glanced at the two ready to square off under the awning of El Zócalo Fine Meats. Turtle caught herself. Someone had keyed the padlock and pulled back the accordion gates of the Black Cat TV Repair Shop and she caught sight of her prismatic reflections in the blank monitors of the display televisions inside. In another life, Turtle had kept her head finely shaved, razor-skinned scalp shining. But as the days living on the streets turned into weeks, her hair had grown out unevenly, and she looked coffee-stained like an old kitchen sink. The studs stapled on the curves of her ears at first to disguise the Turtle in her but later to disguise the Antonia in him no longer had the glint of steel. Worse, she looked rumpled, sleepless and old for her eighteen years and the televisions inside the Black Cat multiplied this feeling. From the ache of bone to the bags under her sleep-deprived eyes, Turtle felt God Almighty shitty.

A solid punch broke her gaze. Although she had no reason other than to harass the man in the straw hat, she now felt compelled to be left alone. He suddenly was not worth the effort. The man shoved Turtle's chest again to prompt a reaction, and said with jackknife sharpness, ¡No te 'toy molestando, pendejo!

An immediate hot temper pitch surfaced on Turtle's face. Her gut reaction was to crush the jaw of this small, worthless loser because no one, not one body, had the right to touch her. Turtle straightened her shoulders. With an abrupt flick of a hand, she flipped up the black collar of her jacket and the gesture made the man flinch. Turtle returned her attention to Hastings and First because she had learned the hard way that to render someone invisible was more painful than a cracked skull. And so she listened with great concentration to the flap of canvas awning, the hum of the wind between people passing. She jammed a chafed hand in her pocket and fished out a few gum wrappers, a matchbook and a quarter and dismissed the presence of the man as if he were transparent.

The challenger waited, determined to prove her cowardly.

Turtle lifted the quarter and squinted at Washington's silver profile with exaggerated scrutiny. In her peripheral vision, she was aware of the man.

Got another one? Turtle rattled the tense silence.

¿Estás loco o qué?

You know, got a quarter?

Turtle boldly pushed the coin close to his face. If he smacked her again, she would have to do the honorable thing; she would have to finish what was started. She didn't make the rules. The man, more confused than angry, delivered a wanton wave of his hand to banish the request.

Bótate chingado, he snapped. He pressed his hat again, and ran across the street against the light with the speed of a man eager to arrive at his destination.

Well fuck you too, ése, Turtle whispered without malice. She fingered the coin and returned it to her pocket. She breathed out and then waited. As the clouds drifted in like shifting sands from a sand dune, Turtle massaged a palm over the stubble of hair. The city park was not far from the Val U Mini Mart and the wooden awning of the picnic tables provided temporary shelter if it rained. As the clouds began to gather into a contemptuous mass, she tried to remember if Luis was with her the day she watched the steamroller, the day she sucked on a pig's foot. The darkened morning slowly became the gray color of a burned-out bulb and the hunger in her belly rumbled thunderously.

Someone had turned on all ten televisions to the same station. All this action happened without her knowing, alarming her. Fatigue had begun to wear thin her street sense and this was bad news. Turtle punched her chapped knuckles into her pockets. None of this would be happening if the other half of the cold-blooded Gamboas were around. Till death do us part. That was the rule. She wasn't supposed to be left behind with the daily tallies of the Vietnam War casualties broadcasted like sports scores.

Hey, lady! Turtle called to a woman. Yea, you.

Holding her little son's hand, the woman stood close to the mailbox to inspect the price of a television. You, what time you got?

The volumes of the televisions were lowered and the sizzling blue-green images all mimed the same Alka-Seltzer commercial. Behind Turtle's back, someone pulled out Luis Lil Lizard's draft number, someone stole him away to another war, someone tallied up the body counts and someone silenced the television voices and all this had happened without her permission. It pitched a rise in her so bad Turtle needed to listen to someone speak.

Come on. Yea, you. What time you got?

The woman released her son's hand and abruptly clamped her large handbag to her chest, a familiar move that usually had no effect on Turtle until today; the gesture made Turtle lose respect for her. Unleashed from his mother's grip, the boy straightened out his Superman cape.

Time. Time, sabes? Turtle tried to remember her Spanish, words that were boxed in storage. Pan, mantequilla. Ven pa'cá. But what was the word she couldn't find? The sound escaped into a deserted labyrinth of midnight street corners and padlocked doors. She felt as if she had to burglarize her own memory in order to get to the Spanish words. Turtle pointed to the woman's watch. You know, hora. ¿Sabes que hora?

The woman held up her wrist. Turtle returned her attention to the intersection while the woman whisked the boy away, his cape fluttering and disappearing into the pedestrian traffic.

Well, fuck you too, Turtle whispered.

She breathed out and waited. A cramp clamped on her right leg. She used the mailbox for support, jiggling her leg to relieve the pain, and tried keeping a poker face. It angered her to hurt so badly. The knot of dirty shoelace dissolved and she labored to ease the shank of her leg. It hurt so badly. To miss her brother this much.

Them two. The almighty.

Were them. Once upon a time.

A few years back, when they were just kids, they devised a plan to invade the Val U Mini Mart. Luis Lil Lizard played lookout, kept his eyes on the convex mirrors which hung from the corner aisles of the market, nodded when all was clear. Turtle had it down; she'd lift a can and pretend to check the price while her other hand worked hard to grab sticks of candy or bags of macaroni, hiding items beneath her mother's thick winter overcoat. They had it down, them two not knowing that wearing a thick oversized winter coat during the summer heat wave was a dead giveaway.

But they were just kids then, and eons away from the draft, or from the McBride Boys being fingered out for a gang jump by Lote M. Them two knew to eat when they got hungry, to warm themselves when they got cold, to do what needed to be done in order to rule their world.

The bagman who caught her was not a kid. Maybe one, but older, maybe not more than nineteen or twenty, maybe as old as the pimply Che reading the paperback. The bagman followed her out of the Mart one late afternoon and before she reached the drying concrete freeway on-ramp, he grabbed the collar of her mother's overcoat and the candy and tins of black olives and tomato sauce rolled to the overpass.

He forced her to stand spread-eagled. Disregarding the traffic, his big man fingers began to frisk her legs and poke into her cutoffs' back pockets. At first he believed what he felt on her chest were not breasts but stolen apples, hard and concealed, and he clamped his big man fingers on her flesh under her loose T-shirt to make sure. This boy had tits, this boy was really a braless girl with growing, firm chi-chis, her big brown nipples just there, under the shirt for him to pinch in utter disbelief. Then he did it again. The bagman groped her body under the draping wool coat again to make sure they weren't stolen produce, and then he slowly dug his metal-cold fingers between her thighs again, this time pressing harder, palming her buttocks, swirling his two hands much slower and slower to make himself believe.

She inhaled, tried to deflate all her flesh into the hole of her belly button, as she had seen cartoon characters do.

Not one driver from all those cars zooming on the new freeway bridge, not one driver driving the overpass of the 710 freeway construction, not one stopped to protest, to scream, What the hell do you think you're doing, motherfucker, pinche puto, get your fingers off her tits, baboso! Turtle had closed her eyes to shut out the cry as the swift wind of the cars bathed her face. She should have booted the bagman hard in his wobbly pink purses and run for dear life, taken her chances; but his gripping big fingers fastened, loosened, tightened, loosened, tightened. Finally, when she opened her eyes, Luis Lil Lizard appeared.

He was smaller than Turtle, even smaller than the bagman, but he wedged himself between the two of them without a semblance of fear because fear for Luis was a proud conquest.

Like the time Amá had yanked and yanked Turtle's hair in an argument over her choice of boxers under her cutoffs, of her erasure of breasts and dresses and all that was outwardly female, over her behaving like some unholy malflora. What the hell do you think you're doing? Luis Lil Lizard challenged Amá, and shoved Turtle into the bathroom. Luis slammed the door on Amá's curses, latched the metal hook into its eyelet and the metal hook chinked in resistance. Luis took a pair of manicure scissors and sat Turtle down on the toilet seat and cut Turtle's hair, asking, What she gonna grab now? Over her arched shoulders, Turtle's chestnut curls fell like commas on the tiled floor and then Luis took the dull razor from the soap dish in the tub and rasped it against her scalp.

Luis convinced Turtle to believe they could reach a place called New Mexico where you awoke banging your head against the sky or sucked on sweet cactus pulp for lunch or watched lizards transform into alligators in the afternoon. To escape, all them two had to do was bulldoze a tunnel through the hill on Eastern Street, Luis explained, and the country awaited their arrival. Turtle helped him because she loved the way her brother watched Zorro on television, one leg stretched out, the other bent at the knee and shaking with a nervous tic; her other half, her real brother whom she loved worse than herself, this homeboy who always appeared without a semblance of fear and yelled, Leave my sister alone.

Turtle could think of nothing to say except, Luis, and then she began to cry.

Shut up, Luis snapped, because he had a girl for a brother and he profoundly resented it. No matter how many asses she kicked after that, or how bad, how really bad she was, he learned not to care. Luis knew, when it came right down to it, when the correctional officers conducted strip searches or the draft number came in, she wasn't there for him. She could never hang as tight as the other McBride Boys. Hey, he once said, I didn't make the rules. The boys all vowed to be there for each other, always and por vida, hasta la muerte, because that's what it's all about. About loyalty. About tightness. About protecting and serving. About shoving the bagman in the belly and saying with firm conviction, I'll kill you if you don't leave her alone. Luis Lil Lizard fisted a red can of tomato sauce and it looked like his hand bled between his fingers.

What a piece of shit, the bagman replied. (How dare he call Luis Lil Lizard a piece of shit!) I oughta call the cops and lock up your ass. The bagman spat to prove to the two dirt-stained brothers how disgusted he was.

Next time, the man continued, bending to collect the cans on the concrete, if I see you in my market, I'll be the one doing the killing.

They had broken the cardinal rule: never get caught.

But they did, the tarps banging and whipping against the concrete to no end. Amá demanded they leave the bulldozers alone, threatened to spank them all with the wire hanger she held. The children scattered faster than scuttling roaches, including Turtle. But Luis clasped the steering wheel with two fists and refused to let his dream go while Amá ripped his T-shirt and the wire whipped air between her and his flesh. She tired of the beating before he did.

No tunneling Eastern Street, and New Mexico remained a region undiscovered, and they would never know what it was to be somewhere else, be someone else. And if the bagman said he was gonna kill you, wouldn't you believe him? Wouldn't you have done the same? No reason for Luis not to believe, wouldn't you? But what he had to do to the bagman later that night, he had to do himself because he had a girl for a brother.

It shamed them both.

After the bagman's warning, they walked home sullenly, neither one saying a word. The hem of Amá's bulky winter coat swept the sidewalk as they passed the junkyard, the houses, the dead end, the hospital building, and more houses, and another dead end. Luis Lil Lizard retrieved a deposit RC Cola bottle from a patch of weeds near a stop sign and then they cut across the Zumayas' thick Bermuda lawn, where they ignored the Zumaya kid who waved to them, and finally reached the porch of their small rented house. Luis slammed the torn screen door shut, leaving Turtle on the porch. She knew he needed to be alone and so pressed her shoulders against the screen, and felt the perspiration between her breasts, too ashamed to remove the winter coat. Woozy, Turtle stared at the long bending metal rods jutting out of the semi constructs of overpasses, on-ramps, bridges and interchanges being built across First Street. The thick, choking stench of blackened diesel smoke rose from the dump trucks, and bulldozers blew carbon exhaust into a haze. Her eyes were so tired, they squeaked as she rubbed them.

Out of the pulverizing dust of heaved-up dirt and cement, the old neighbor woman appeared, smoking one of her beloved cigarettes. The frajo stuck to the corner of her wrinkled lips in the same way Turtle's Tío Angel smoked while he sat at the kitchen table with Amá and Aunt Mercy, which was the same way the old woman smoked while cracking a tray of ice cubes on the porch railing of her blue house. Since lemons came every other year, the old neighbor woman froze ice trays of lemon juice.

Across the jackhammering blasts and cacophony of earthmovers and over the sound of passing cars on First Street, the old woman dropped three lemon cubes in a cupful of water, spooned sugar and stirred and tweaked as the water and sugar and cubes created lemonade so cold the aluminum tumbler beaded. Turtle was about to place the cool rim of the tumbler to her parched mouth but the swift force of door, the swing of screen, pushed her awake from a stupor, and Luis Lil Lizard's deep man voice said, Get outta my way, you pussy.

He clutched the neck of the RC soda bottle and began walking to Ray's store. Sweat-drenched, Turtle waited for her brother to turn and say to her, What are you waiting for? Come on! But her brother dissolved into the cold shadow of the hot freeway like the lemon ice cubes in water.

Turtle's fingers were stiff cold and she wove them together, then cracked her knuckles. Several schoolchildren crossed Hastings and First, protecting their heads from the drizzle by wearing triangular newspaper pirate hats, jovial at the blustery gusts of wind. Rushed pedestrians whooped and cursed and ran under the El Zócalo Fine Meats awning. Turtle sought shelter under the awning as two women crossed the street. One was short and plump, and the other one, her younger companion, was taller and hunched under an umbrella, cradling a package wrapped in white paper. Was it possibly a white bag containing bolillos or pan dulce from La Pelota Bakery? Turtle saw an opportunity: simply bump her and run with the package. God-sent easy. Certainly, the clumsy rubber boots, the long black shirt she wore would inhibit a chase. Even her red poncho trimmed with black tassels became a matador's cape taunting Turtle to lunge.

But then she leaned over to whisper in the short woman's ear, and the short woman burst out in laughter and the taller one emerged from under the umbrella and ran ahead like a schoolgirl as the light turned red. When the taller one reached the corner first, she stopped momentarily to lift her arms and open the wings of her poncho. While the winds pinched up the corners of the poncho, and the clouds clacked with terrifying force, the taller woman turned and smiled at Turtle with incredible delight and then rewrapped her flapping poncho to nestle the package once again in the cradle of her arms.

She was way too easy.

Large raindrops cackled above her and the awning darkened like puddles of tar. A man wearing a shirt of pink flamingos stood next to Turtle and the shirt seemed ridiculous, absurd, deserving of provocation.

What you looking at? Turtle challenged the man in the flamingos. She wiped her runny nose on the leather of her sleeve, ready to strangle those birds.

No one, the man replied, surprised, unsure what the question meant. I'm not looking at nothing.

At nothing? You calling me nothing?

Hard pebbles of rain pelted, and she eyed the man, who seemed sincere when he asked, What's your problem, carnal?

Got a quarter?

The man shook his head no while his flamingos tottered on their one-legged stances. Others under the awning gradually made space between themselves and Turtle. A bus arrived. Within minutes, deserted sidewalks.

Turtle brushed her palms together for warmth, then returned them to her jacket pockets. Indecisive, cold and hungry, she knew not to stay in one place too long. The loud clamor of thunder sounded like a wrecking yard and the awning already sagged heavy with water. No wonder the fruit vendors stayed indoors. Cars passed and fast-beating windshield wipers melted the faces of the drivers under sheets of water. She supposed now was as good as any time. Turtle shrank her neck in the valley of her shoulders for protection against the downpour.

What you waiting for? Come on, no one said, and Turtle jumped over a flooding gutter and into the wide intersection. At eight or eighteen, it was just like her, never paying attention to the safe harbor of space between two painted fluorescent white lines on the pavement. The rain was immediate and unmerciful and whipped her face. At the end of the storefront block, a bloodied dog's carcass from last night's search littered the street, ground raw into the pavement by car tires. Rust-colored water surrounded the carcass. It must have been female, Turtle judged, because purple droopy teats fell to one side. Black veils of flies swarmed every inch of flesh. Sorry, bitch, she thought, I didn't make the rules. The flies hung tight together, even in the rain.

THREE

Have faith, Mama said with a slight slur, didn't I say?

Amen, Tranquilina replied. They waited on the corner for the light to change. Amen to that.

The two women had convinced the new butcher of El Zócalo Fine Meats to donate a five-pound chuck roast for the after-services meal. In previous years, the former butcher, Obdulio, never hesitated in donating pork rinds or stew bones for their ministry; however, since his departure to Jerez, Zacatecas, he had been replaced by a skittish, nervous man. Lacking more in the ways of butchery than in generosity, the replacement butcher had discreetly and without his jefe's consent promised the two women the chuck roast on the one condition that they never come to him for another donation.

After mopping the front of the shop, the butcher had placed a roast beneath the overturned bucket near the employees' entrance and then weighted it down with an industrial mop in order to protect it from the roaming dogs. Tranquilina removed the soggy mop and discovered the muscle of meat wrapped tightly in white butcher paper. The find was a revelation, a blessed fortune. Mama put down her umbrella and placed her hand over the package. Bluish remnants of jawbone swell strained her ability to speak; yet she voiced profound gratitude by praising God, Thank you, Lord, right in front of the huge trash bins.

More than the meat, the kept promise had made Tranquilina optimistic. The rigorous traveling, the endless list of hostels, the constant flow of pitiless doubters and forever larger supply of ravished believers had worn on Tranquilina, though she refused to admit this to Mama and Papa Tomás, even to herself. Her vigilance of years past had somehow corroded, dedication buried in layers of decaying convictions. She had allowed this to happen almost organically, over a period of time, and thus Tranquilina blamed herself for fermenting such anguish, which arrived one late night in the form of a man smelling strongly of manure.

The manure man had assaulted all three of them after a prayer meeting outside of Cuero, Texas. Although it was the manure man who grasped the shovel with both fists and swung with the might of a scythe against wheat to tumble them and force them to fall, Tranquilina blamed herself for Mama's face swelling twice its size in bruised weight. Although the man pushed Tranquilina down face first, her mouth grit-full of soil, it was she who felt culpable for infecting Papa Tomás's thoughts so that he now slept only in seizures of anxiety.

Mama had wanted to return to the Eastside, to Tranquilina's birthplace, and said so, holding her daughter's head under her own broken jaw in a grove of Texan pecan trees, ready to immediately dispose of the assault like garbage heaps outside of Cuero, no stars or full moon to pour gentle blue light on the fertile earth. While in the two-room police station, Papa Tomás spoke against vengeance, and then spoke against returning to the Eastside. Fragile in health, he knew there was no returning to their beginnings. Time never stood still, and no routine or familiarity, no wishing to return Tranquilina to the safety of her womb, would erase the assault.

Nonetheless, it was Mama's decision to return and that was why at this very moment Mama popped up her umbrella and the two crossed First and Hastings undisturbed by the rains, their spirits lifted by the butcher's kept promise. The winds picked up and a man's hat tumbled just in front of him, and he dashed for it and just when he reached out for it, the taunting currents buffeted the rim of the hat again, out of reach. Tranquilina elbowed Mama and they laughed because the two were not above finding humor in the folly of men.

The butcher's package felt chilled against Tranquilina's chest, and she ran to the corner and readjusted the bulk, the cloak of her poncho raised to shield it from the rain. Then she turned to Mama; but instead her gaze locked with the razor-cut head of a cholo under an awning. Between them a fence of lashing rain, Tranquilina recognized his glassy yellow-eyed hunger. The same crazed intent of the Cuero man who smelled of deep fermenting dung, the cyclops gaze that ushered a fore-warning—robbery in its cruelest form. She held the package tightly.

The storm fractured his face. Tranquilina tried to revive the compassion she once had for those with such hunger, when hunger meant empty bellies or an overflowing desire for a better life. Hadn't she learned? Hadn't she realized that experiences teach, and if God loved the meek enough to deliver them from evil, and if God loved the poor and the broken and the worst of men, then it stood to reason that Tranquilina's brokenness, her dismembering, should only bring her closer to God? And as a way for this gangster youth to forgive her immediate condemnation, her abrupt suspicion, she lifted the corners of her mouth (just as she had lifted the corners of her poncho seconds before), delivering upon him a broad, toothy smile. She turned away but her backside grew rigid, almost expecting the repeat of the shovel against her shoulders.

Tranquilina followed Mama through a weedy lot between two vacant buildings and passed a tower of abandoned tires stacked up in a way as to suggest a child's game. The two women wore rubber boots once worn by men who worked at the city incinerator and their boots tramped broken amber shards of glass, hypodermic needles, frajo butts and gum wrappers on soil as muddled as a swamp.

Mama slowed, and Tranquilina, not paying attention, bumped her. They reached a concrete sidewalk and stomped the clumps of mud off. The wind continued to bend sheets of rain.

Kern Street is over there, Mama said and leaned her umbrella to the right. This time, Tranquilina understood her.

The two women struggled through the rain in a maze of unfamiliar streets. Whole residential blocks had been gutted since their departure, and they soon discovered that Kern Street abruptly dead-ended, forcing them to retrace their trail. The streets Mama remembered had once connected to other arteries of the city, rolling up and down hills, and in and out of neighborhoods where neighbors of different nationalities intersected with one another. To the west, La Pelota Panadería on Soto Street crossed Canter's Kosher Deli on Brooklyn Avenue, which crossed Pol's Chinese Kitchen on Pacific Boulevard to the east. But now the freeways amputated the streets into stumped dead ends, and the lives of the neighbors itched like phantom limbs in Mama's memory: la Señora Ybarra's tobacco smell and deep raspy voice; the Gómez father's garden of tomatoes; Eugenio's pennies taped on envelopes for their ministry; Old Refugia, who had two goats living in her cluttered backyard and who took the goats to graze at the edge of the Chinese cemetery before opening hours.

The city of Tranquilina's birth was hardly recognizable. They crossed puddles so deep, rainwater covered the ankles of their liver-colored boots. Papa Tomás had warned Mama, You can never return to the same place twice unless you discover peace in its transformation. The two women rested here and there, their anxiety growing, leaning against a bus bench, stopping to ask for directions, the rain hammering. On the corner of Humphreys and Floral, Tranquilina pointed to the concrete freeway walls splattered with gang graffiti. The solid slab of endless cement looked as cold gray as the rain-filled sky.

Mama yelled over her shoulder, but the rising wind spirited her words away. She had to shout it again, ¡Otra tormenta! The rains percolated into puddles, glutting the gutter grates. Paper plates, yellowed newspapers, condom wrappers began to lift and whirl beside them. Mama used the umbrella as a shield and her plastic raincoat crackled like burning wood. They seemed to be the only pedestrians on the sidewalk. The winds pressed the cloth of their long, black skirts against their legs. Tranquilina lagged behind, holding the white bundle, the black tassels of her flapping red poncho grasping at thin air.

Tranquilina halted, footsore, a blister caused by the friction of rubber edges and she studied the intentions of the clouds. Her drenched, short brown hair helmeted her head and her poncho was sopping wet. If the downpour continued, it was best to stay under a storefront awning. She caught a glimpse of city geese cutting a large V across the folds of gray sky, a few stragglers struggling to keep within the flock.

Tranquilina winced at brilliant veined lightning. Blinding light sizzled and dazzled just as metal often sparked brightly against a pumice wheel. Though she stilled for a moment to regain her sight, Tranquilina felt the deadening thunder strike like a sledgehammer banging wobbly sheets of armor steel. The pulse of her blood surged, a mad, black water swell poured over her skin as if her body were a great Amazon tributary, its rising torrents flooding structures, breaking windows, drowning church benches, reaching rooftops, tipping steeples and then bursting into the ocean of skies. She felt carried away by the currents of vastness.

Tranquilina heard the receding sound of Mama's rubber boots, barely audible, a losing crunch of weeds, mud and debris until no sound remained except for the whistling transmigration of pumping wings gliding in the mist. Hollow, her boots dangled. Light refreshing drizzle sprayed against her face. She was close enough for the fluttering feathers of the city geese to brush her cheeks delicately. Tranquilina's feet were incredibly cool, and her toes tingled. A wisp of vapor escaped from her astonished lips. She opened her eyes slowly.

Mama often spoke to her of Papa Tomás's legacy. In the short hiatus of youthful innocence, Tranquilina once believed in her birthright, coconspiring with Mama to transcend the stories of levitation into familial fact. Though Mama planted its incubation in Tranquilina's life, the actual experience arrived without warning. Or had it really happened? Tranquilina could no longer make that leap of faith, levitation ascribed only to saints who proved too holy for a world that didn't deserve them. And Tranquilina knew she deserved this upside-down world where the peaceful love of nonviolence was reciprocated by sharpshooting hatred. Even with assassinations, assaults and the slaughter of planet and people, Tranquilina's love for this world remained a conflicted, loyal love. Because everything happened here on these sidewalks or muddy swamps of vacant lots or in deep back alleys, not up in the heavens of God. Lost souls roamed here, and Tranquilina stomped a tingling foot on the ground as evidence. Then, embracing the package as if it were an anchor, she muttered a prayer of contrition for doubting Mama's stories. The geese remained in full view and she scurried to catch up to Mama like the last of the stray geese. Unsure of her experience, Tranquilina pressed a palm to her forehead as if to squeeze some sense back into her brain.

She asked her mother, Where do I go now?

The rain battered the flowered fabric of Mama's umbrella. The rubber soles of her boots shuffled against the slickness of unfamiliar sidewalk. Mama wished out loud that wherever the disappeared neighbors were relocated they had lemon trees outside, where long garden hoses on summer afternoons were permissible and goats were not prohibited; where the sun took forever to descend between the telephone poles. She thought of them in a vagueness that unbridled her attention. She stepped off the curb and didn't notice the bumpers of speeding cars until Tranquilina yanked her by the collar back to safety. They decided to wait in the Cruz Azul Farmacia until the rains eventually turned from downpour to drizzle, until there was space between the cars, until their hearts calmed.

The storm subsided, a brief, powerful tormenta, suddenly turning into a misty shower. Mama and Tranquilina passed a small boy, proud and elevated, his Superman cape fluttering high.

Now let's find the main boulevard, Mama instructed clearly, without slurring. It's shorter.

Soon after their trek resumed, the sunshine wrestled and tentative shadows appeared. Mama closed her umbrella, insisting they make up for lost time. They stopped once more to ask for directions at a patio table where a group of noisy girls laughed loudly. Mama became grateful again for the smallest things: a man who chased his hat in the wind, a boy wearing a red cape, a sun-laden day, the fine youthful laughter of girls, a bundle of meat, a recognizable house.

Mama shouldered a leather bag under her raincoat, which was soft and worn from years of use but still held the scent of brine when dampened. She pulled a few quarter-folded mimeographed leaflets and handed them carefully to Tranquilina since the purple ink stained their hands. The bilingual flyers announced the return of their ministry and Tranquilina distributed them in mailboxes or door slots while they headed for the main boulevard. With the last of the leaflets delivered, Mama regained a feeling of revival.

Once they passed the wrecking yard, Mama knew them to be close to the Val U Mini Mart, and her boots drummed the sidewalk. They arrived at a familiar block of storefront shops and Tranquilina said, Let's talk to Horacio again. The morning manager of the Val U Mini Mart proved to be a miser of the worst kind.

It can't hurt, Tranquilina continued.

Horacio refused to give them discarded produce and instead dumped it in the bins to spoil rather than hand it over to the two women, who could resuscitate the old vegetables into a consommé that at least filled the stomachs of the less fortunate.

The Health Department don't let me, Horacio had explained. On this, Tranquilina was more forgiving than Mama.

Go rot with your vegetables, Mama had replied.

You're all the same, he had said.

Same what? Mama asked.

You're all freeloaders.

Just free, Mama said.

Get out.

Go rot.

Mama locked arms with Tranquilina and they continued walking.

Tomorrow was Friday and the pan dulce not sold on Saturday at the Panadería as day-old bread was promised to them on Sunday. Tranquilina waved to the baker's son as they passed, and he nodded, his hands gripping a tray of sugar-caked sweet bread. In Mama's eyes, the baker was only one notch kinder than Horacio.

They walked through a tree-lined path of the Little Brothers of the Poor Rest Home; the sunlight interwove through the clouds once the wind and rain quieted. Mama used her umbrella as a walking stick. The rain had rinsed the few trees of ashy smog residue from the freeway traffic and the green of the trees sheened brilliantly. The two women continued to their destination, their muddied boots marching over the humps of sidewalk uplifted by the twisted roots of trees so old, their canopy shaded the path.

How are you? Tranquilina asked an ancient man who sat under a dark alcove of the convalescent home, his spindly legs as ropy as his hospital-gown ties. Here was a man, she surmised, who waited out the long, worn day by recalling the speed by which his own life had passed. How are you doing? she repeated, genuinely concerned as was her way, and the inquiry derailed his reminiscences. He looked up from his wheelchair, his face pleats of shriveled copper skin.

I had to do it! he replied, spearing the air to show her. It was him or me, so I had to do it! And he shook his wrinkled chin in shame, the rings of his neck quivering. Shaken out of his memory, the man seemed intent on trying to recognize her face.

Finally, he said, you've returned!

Crazy rains, added Mama. Raindrops clung from the roof gutter above the alcove, which resembled cake icing.

You've come back, the man said, clenching Tranquilina's thin wrist. His translucent skin shone like prayer-candle wax and his jagged fingernails scratched into her wrist bone. Tranquilina glanced at Mama as if this happened time and again.

Now, now, Mama said and slowly pried open his cold grip as Tranquilina patiently waited to be released.

Now, now, the old, old soldier repeated, at once devastated but resigned. He let out a sigh so sorrowful that Tranquilina bent down and whispered a defrosting warm breath of a prayer in his ear.

Against the concrete graffiti walls, sunlight broke and the shadow of the tree canopy eclipsed the old man's face. A group of kids appeared in the distance and began a stickball game in a schoolyard. The chatter of a home run shattered the monotony. The old soldier smiled. When she had finished the prayer, Tranquilina stroked his liver-spotted hand. She commented on the shouting accusations of a foul ball. They were angels, these kids. Tranquilina now understood why Mama wanted to return to the Eastside. This is why their ministry returned. The angels were never lacking here, and thus explained the name of the city.

You've come back! The old soldier lifted a saluting palsied hand to his forehead.

Amen, Tranquilina replied. Amen to that.

Mama had made a promise right before Tranquilina's birth. Her belly swollen, she had pressed her two palms together above her heaving chest. At the bottom of the canyon, up against a stone wall of tall granite, she stared at Papa Tomás's bruised bare feet, punctured and blood-crusted. After having run for three nights, they rested, breathless, licking their parched lips, and Mama prayed "like a woman bartering in front of a firing squad." The weight of the pregnancy hung so far down in her body, she thought the child in her "had turned into the same stone that made up the mountain." Recounting the action to Tranquilina, Mama explained how she went into a prayer trance while the huge vultures circled the white sky above them. She whittled at her only hope: "God help us. God receive us," she asked, now biting her knuckle. "Save us," she begged, now wet from the explosion of lactating breasts. "Deliver us from evil." The details changed with every telling, though the essential elements of the story remained the same.

Sometimes it was sunrise, sometimes it was sunset; sometimes the day was cloudy, other times it was clouds parting, but nonetheless, Mama promised her baby to God. "This child is Yours," she proclaimed without hesitation or forethought as to what she was actually doing. "Save this baby, for it is Yours and Yours alone."

And then, according to Mama, that was when "the light" occurred, and this was when "we became Messengers of God."

They had almost reached their destination.

Tranquilina was as tall as the beginning of her name and just as thin, and Mama always worried for her daughter as any mother would. She tried to shield her from sudden storms and misguided people who were compelled into unforgivable transgressions. When the force of wind and the city's debris rose like flecks to blind their vision, Mama worried she had done her daughter a great injustice. The child of God who was not of this earth, this child she had bartered away for their safe escape. And she would look at Tranquilina in times of otra tormenta, in times when the assault at Cuero stayed forever, and would want to defy her promise to God. To take her daughter back. But the defiance and doubt would soon calm like all storms. People slowly returned to populate the streets of the earth once again, and the shouts of the children playing and old soldiers confessing reminded Mama that she and Tranquilina belonged as much to this earth as they did. The puddles of rain on the misty asphalt created mirrors and their reflections were reassuring.

Their church consisted of a small boxlike kitchen attached to three other rooms that doubled as their living quarters by day, their ministry services by night, and all the rooms smelled of lard. Once they reached the church, stubborn mud clung to Mama's boots, and she rubbed them against one another before entering. She slipped them off, removed the plastic raincoat and shook it, then grabbed a hanger and hung the coat inside the crowded closet where the collapsible chairs were stored. She pulled out a pair of flip-flops, slipped them on, then hung her leather bag on the inside hook and then closed the door. No movement was wasted, no action taken without purpose. A slab of light appeared from the small window near the table, and Mama's hands passed the light as she immediately began to boil potatoes in a huge steel pot.

She turned for a moment to admire her daughter's face, which appeared square and pure, like a plank of unvarnished wood. Mama smiled at Tranquilina, who raised up her long skirt to pull off her dampened socks, obviously enjoying the liberation from the thick rubber boots, and spread her toes against a floor chipped by the scrape and weight of kitchen chairs. Tranquilina had inherited Papa's way of walking barefooted and Mama stared at her daughter's bare feet padding to the closet to hang her dripping poncho, then watched her grab a cotton apron and tie it over her white blouse. She walked to the kitchen table where the wrapped package sat. Tranquilina's unpolished toenails peeked out from under her long black skirt.

Let's see what we have here, Mama said and Tranquilina slowly unfolded the butcher paper on the small Formica table. The meat with its big stewing bone gleamed bright red on the white of the paper. And the meek shall eat and be satisfied.

Amen.

Beautiful.

What do you think?

Maybe two pots.

And the bone?

Amen to that.

Maybe half a pot of broth. Hard to say.

Tranquilina dragged a hairnet out of her apron pocket. Rather resentful of having to wear it as a promise to the health inspectors, she pulled it over her wet, short hair and swept her brown bangs under its nylon rim. If Mama and Papa Tomás taught her one thing well, it was keeping her word, because promises were the cobblestones of their faith. Mama's hair, on the other hand, made a hairnet unnecessary. She wore her long graying hair completely pulled back tight into a neat roll plugged by bobby pins and only because of the storm did a few strands tumble loose.

How do I look? Tranquilina asked mockingly, offering various poses in the ridiculous hairnet. Mama was so pleased that Tranquilina was her daughter.

Let's get to work, beautiful!

Mama sliced the fat off the chuck roast. Above her, loose wires dangled where a ventilating fan had been removed. Without resting her knife, Mama instructed Tranquilina to fill the sink with water, pour a dash of salt. Tranquilina turned the spigot on and then began to dismember the limp stalks of celery, letting them soak in the salted water before scrubbing them with a vegetable brush. Mama's pudgy fingers tossed the chunks of meat into the simmering pot, added four onions, lowered the flame. The salt and pepper shakers on the table trembled from the vigor of Mama's work.

At fifteen or seventeen years of age, Mama held high a woven frond basket containing ripe mangoes. Rows of wooden vats soaking green pelts stretched and layered in salt were lined up in the corner of Papa Tomás's workstation. The brine tainted the girth of the vats blackish gray and the scent irritated Mama's nostrils into a potential sneeze. If a sneeze erupted, an explosion of spit and mucus upon the oval mounds of Horseback's beloved fruit, she'd be punished harshly, no two ways about it, and so she bit her lips not to sneeze.

Her bare feet itched, ached, and her upper arms throbbed from holding still the weight of the mangoes. The basket's palm edges cut deeply into her hands. Already too old for his age, Papa Tomás's face resembled the rough pelts he soaked in brine as he punctured holes with a harness awl, tracing Horseback's foot on a patch of leather hide. Horseback was a short man, his stockinged feet flat on the floor, his legs spread apart. Tomás marked Horseback's foot arch in precise measurements. The arch bones were as important to a body as a heart, Tomás told her later. Because there were seven bones in the foot arch alone, and that meant a great deal in supporting the weight of a man's life.

The date palms that lined the entrance to the hacienda brushed against one another with a drowsy summer breeze, and an unlocked corral gate creaked open, then slammed repeatedly. Mama rubbed one bare foot against the other discreetly and her callused heel felt like the rasp of the shoemaker's tool. Tomás's fingers worked the map of Horseback's feet, counting the arch bones, while Horseback bit lustfully into the flesh of a mango and then sucked white the yellow bone of the fruit until the syrupy juice slid down his stubby fingers. The shoemaker knelt before him, punching holes, feeling the splat of wet slide down his sun-wrinkled neck.

They were told they were free to go where they wished. But their families had signed promissory notes to Horseback, to Horseback's father, and before, to his grandfather. Thus the kneeling shoemaker, the peasant girl holding up a heavy basket of mangoes and the other hundred and five men, women and children living and dying penniless at the Rancho Paradiso were indentured servants, obliged to pay historic debts, because one had always to be accountable to history.

Papa Tomás took pride in his shoemaking and Horseback recognized true value when he saw Tomás trace the frontal area of the instep with a rusty awl in concentrated artistry. Horseback discarded in the pig trough the bone and skin of the mango and then wiped his sticky fingers against his dusty trousers. Horseback's small, stubby fingers twitched nervously, as if his fingers compensated for their smallness with the jittery rapid way they moved. Specks of brilliant mango clung on Horseback's black mustache as he smiled at Mama. He reached over and fondled another mango from her basket and Mama felt the frond basket cut against the flesh of her open aching palms.

She wanted shoes. After Horseback left, she desired tiny boots that fastened with button and hook and lace, buffed so fine, they shone like mirrors. She wondered if the shoemaker recognized her footsteps approaching, the thumps of her walk against the worn dirt road, the rustle of weeds near the barn, the loud steps of a woman heavy with possibility, because he seemed always alert though feigning indifference. He worked very hard to make the point that her appearance at his workstation had little significance in his life. She came each day after the morning milking to convince him otherwise.

I want to walk away with pretty boots, she had said, swiveling the toes of her left foot in the dirt. She used a touch of lard to slick her hair and braid it tight. She pricked a finger to bleed some red on her lips, pinched her cheeks to blush.

I'm too old to make them pretty. His leather apron flaked like fish scales, and he placed the cobbler's hammer on the counter with the hardened skin of his hand.

Shoes I can run away with.

It's the feet that do the running.

Papa stepped from behind his counter finally. The best shoemaker on Horseback's rancho stood barefooted. She scratched one foot behind the other but kept her eyes on him. The late afternoon light filtered through the gray gauze of clouds. Tomás nervously rolled a clinching nail between his dye-stained fingers. They looked at one another.

Shoes are good, she replied.

If you say so.

I say so.

The first rough leather Mama felt was the leather of his hand tenderly inspecting the seven bones of her foot arch.

What was wrong with wanting a pair of shoes? Tranquilina asked.

This is not a story about shoes, Mama replied.

At night and on top of his straw-stuffed mattress, Tomás whispered, Weight of a man's life. The mattress smelled of yeast and prickly hay, and the words were damp and misty as he slipped his sucking lips from the mound of her nipple to the nape of her neck. But this was much later, and Mama left this part out of the story.

Papa Tomás got wind of Horseback's plan to take away the child Mama carried.

We don't have a chance, Mama wailed and buried her face in her hands.

Have faith, Tomás replied. It's not the shoes that do the running.

Tomás wrapped beef jerky and tortillas in cheesecloth, filled a barro with well water and packed one pair of leather scissors, harness needles, hog thistles for thread, awl, hammer, rasp, stabbing knife and clinching nails he had made himself into a leather shoulder bag he had sewn together in haste. He wrapped all his tools in strips of leather so that they would not clink and bang into one another.

Mama met him where the mango groves began and in the light of the full moon. She held her rounded belly, readied in the thick-soled sandals he had made for her. And then they began to run; to escape to a place that existed only in stories, in gossip, in letters, in hearsay. While dawn blanched across the sky, doubts of the homeland's existence rattled her bones because freedom was as inaccessible as her dream of fancy boots.

By the fourth day of their escape, they confronted the impermeable mountain range, and she staggered to a mesquite. Centuries of compressed, crusted plates of limestone rose layer after layer in front of her like a fortress and she tilted her head to see what they were up against. Indeed, the desert range was so high, she could not manage to bend her neck that far backward. The sun glared. Shadows of the carnivorous vultures circled above. Mama prayed feverishly, bartering for their lives to a God who, up to this point in her young life, remained eternally silent. No moisture left for tears, her thirst endangering the placenta's health. Three nights, four days. It would take centuries to climb and reach the mountain ridge, to cross the border of the sky. Centuries. To the left of her, the vultures landed at a safe distance.

Mama prayed, God help us. God receive us, she asked, now biting her knuckles, Save us, she begged, now wet from the explosion of lactating breasts, Deliver us from this evil. The pleas called for a milagro more powerful than the sun. Under the mesquite, Mama admitted defeat. The will was in her, pulsating like her heartbeat, but the body collapsed. Mama rubbed her belly, a still and fisted hump of child, tight and dry, like dead hot air. Then Mama rolled and moaned, the mesquite tree providing splotches of shade, while Tomás swatted away an army of desert flies. He fiercely studied the terrain, and then he bent to kiss her forehead and stood up.

She pleaded not to be left behind, but Tomás hushed her, hobbling to a clearing. In her delirium, Tomás became a blur, a rigid saguaro as he forked his fingers to the heavens and waited for the gusts of winds to glide him off the ground. He didn't turn into a bird or bat; didn't even need wings. The wind took hold and a strong current whipped him up and Tomás rode it with measured speed. Her chin dropped and gourd seeds pinged and rattled crazy in her veins. He rose in a spiral, dust billowing, barely nipping the tops of mesquites, over the saguaros until the bloodied bare soles of his tattered feet slowly shrank, then disappeared into the clouds.

The kitchen stuffy, Mama rested her knife, and dabbled her forehead with the corner of her apron. Potatoes and onions bobbed in the boil of the pot and the steam fogged the window glass. Mama eyed the loose wires above her, and then instructed Tranquilina to open the window, mija, por favor, and Tranquilina used a hymnal book to prop it up. The fresh breeze was greedy. Taking a large wooden spoon, Mama skimmed the fat and bone chip surfacing in the simmering broth. Then she scraped out a chair and collapsed on it, her knees falling open. Her ankles had a tendency to swell.

According to Mama, Tomás was a man strung together by iguana bones and wire. Fine, slender bones and wrists so thin, Mama could wrap her two fingers like a bracelet around them. Since the first sun, she told Tranquilina, the Azteca priests singled out men like her father to be voladores. Strong but balsa-wood light, the chosen men held hefty faith in the wind to cradle their bodies on the breath of its sighs. Long, long ago, they wore feathers carefully woven into silk cloth wings and claws that attached to bracelets. Artisans selected plumes from the bravest eagles for their breastplates and reinforced the plates with wax. Their breechcloths were spun from gold and fitted tightly around their upper thighs.

The magnificent half birds emerged, attaching their waist harnesses to a hemp rope interwoven with women's hair and already spun around the tallest of poles. Beginning from the top, the voladores would jump, spinning and gliding with the grace of a bird, the ropes slowly unwinding as they used the crown of their heads, the drum of their human hearts to direct their flight. Loose feathers sometimes wavered down to the earth, and it was good fortune if a child discovered an eagle's plume underfoot. After centuries of ritual, who needs harnesses and wax when hemp spun of mighty, willful faith can hold you up to the wind just as strongly?

Tranquilina washed the celery in the salt water. She submerged her hands, kept them underwater. She tested Mama: If Papa Tomás could fly away, why didn't he just escape the Horseback's ranch?

I don't know, Mama replied, rubbing her swollen ankle. Your papa didn't want to leave me behind. Maybe because humans have little control over the divine. Maybe because miracles happen when they choose. Mama perspired. Maybe we need a fan.

In the distance a dump truck moved sluggishly between the warehouse buildings. The struggling engine roared, spilling black exhaust in the air, lifting the trash bins with a forklift and catch. An acid stench of unflushed toilets entered their kitchen through the open window. Flustered, Mama stood up, bumping into the table and spilling pepper from the shaker. She lumbered over to the sink counter, let the water dribble out of the spigot and then pressed droplets against her fleshy cheeks to make the sign of the cross. The remaining celery drifted like lashes in the water.

It was all that walking in the heat and rain, Tranquilina offered, holding a celery stalk and vegetable brush.

Mama didn't know much about hot and cold fronts clashing, but recognized a thickness in the air that made breathing difficult. Her full bosom rose and fell, struggling. Texas weather stuck in her skin just like the word "Cuero," like the bruises stuck on her jaw. Mama gripped the counter.

Where's Papa? Mama asked, as if it were crucial she know his whereabouts.

He's resting.

Good, yes, Mama replied, nodding.

You better rest too, Tranquilina said.

I better rest, Mama told herself as she leaned under the shade of the mesquite, searching the clouds. The child in her, once dead still, suddenly pushed against the muscles of her belly. Mama clasped her belly, terrified the baby would break out, and she groped for some clumps of weeds to brace herself, to keep her knees pressed together. Another cramp seized her. Keep back, stay back, she warned the baby, digging her face into the branching embrace of the mesquite's bark roots. Not here, not now. She wrestled her own body, turned on all fours, then knelt, belly down, while her spine thrust her pelvic bones apart with such force, she yanked clumps of nettles from the baked earth. No. No. No!

The vultures no longer concerned her. She talked to her belly, begged it to be quiet and patient. But the child wrenched her pelvic bones again, causing Mama to fold over so tight she could almost hear her backbone snap in two. Mama fell to her side, an ear to the ground, rolling tears over the bridge of her nose, down the slope of her cheek, to the earth, beading into obsidian pebbles. Even the lapses between the labor cramps provided little relief. Ants crawled, thousands of little legs twitching, hurried with purpose, before the shade shifted, before the full eruption of the sun, their marching trail closer and closer. From the grate of hot gravel against her cheek, Mama heard whispers striking like waves of a desert quake. Her head was on fire. Weakened, Mama grasped the mesquite, pushed her face against its thin trunk to force herself upright to better hear the inaudible humming.

The thick row of black ants moved in dizzying speed, passing the talons of the waiting vultures, crawling around Mama's sandals, over a cluster of spineless cacti buttons, passed jumping chollas. The ants continued to slither around saguaros and opuntias and sage bushes and kept flowing like an endless stream of water.

Where was she? Mama wondered. On what side of this earth did she sit struggling to angle her body to shut its door to the baby? Mama squeezed desert soil through her fingers; the cacti buttons hummed. What accounted for this miracle? Cacti beckoned her. Not for one second did she question the sound of trapped, sobbing wind, instructing her to eat some.

Mama inched closer. The jumping chollas guarded, prepared to prick spines at intruders, but they seemed of little consequence. Her fingers trembled as she plucked a handful of buttons. In the palm of her dirt-smudged hand, the buttons balled small, a pale green seeming to be both harmless and lethal. To bring a button to her cracked lips, to chew one, took immense faith that the gummy bitterness didn't indicate poison, but medicine of some sort. Immediately Mama felt nauseous, the uprising of emptiness eager to spew, and so she chewed another, and another, until her desire to vomit vanished, along with her hunger and thirst. The sobbing of the captured winds thrashed about faintly, lulling the baby beneath her belly button to slumber once again. Mama rested, her tears refreshing though the gravel she lay on inflamed her body.

No accounting of time, shifts of light and shadow, rustling of footsteps, snapping of fired, crusted ruts. His feet swollen purple—poor, leathery bare feet. She reached to touch the bulbs of his toes to make sure it was him. Tomás's embrace was so strong, she felt the sharp nubs of his rib cage. The iguana man held her, brushed away the sand from her face and then he pressed his lips to hers, a passionate wild kiss, jagged stones chopping a waterfall rush, his tongue feeding her a mouthful of clouds, and after this day, he would never give her a kiss like this one again. No need to as well, because Mama knew they would die together, not alone anymore, she, the baby and Tomás, together rather than ever returning to the Horseback's Rancho Paradiso. And to die would be all right too, because there were bigger magics on the other side of death than the ones on this side. Her resignation reassured Tomás.

You ready? he asked, and she answered yes, the terror gone. From the skies, Tomás had viewed where the range valleyed, knew the location of the dry riverbed where they could cross and perch themselves in a cave until nightfall. He hauled her on his back, hooking her wobbly legs, and then he began to trot between the cacti and thick, forked saguaros. Mama weighed more than a rain cloud, but no matter. The vultures scattered, a few electing to follow Tomás's breathing, a long, unbroken chain of grunts towing them slowly to a new beginning.

The celery stalk, once whole, now a clump of diced green, spilled into the broth with a swipe of a hand. Tranquilina envisioned the pair: Papa Tomás like a centaur thirty-three years ago, his hoof feet thumping, carrying Mama, and her belly packing in all that rain.

The dump trucks roared outside their window. Mama glanced at her beefy fingers, didn't like their stillness. Immediately she rose from her chair and stirred the cocido. She tested a spoonful for taste. Shook some salt in for added measure. It was all coming together.

Now, that's something! Making a meal out of nothing, like loaves and fishes, Mama said, pleased and ready to be quiet over the sound of the dump truck's hydraulic pumps.

Tranquilina didn't look up from the cutting board. Long after Mama's voice had trailed off, Tranquilina tried reconstructing Mama's stories. An iguana of a man who raised his chin to the sky. Against all odds for their salvation, he cast out their old lives, threw off the leather of their skins and thus eliminated the borders between human and nonhuman. Every breath of every ancestor, every ash of every wind, every dead volador of every century lifted him, raised him to a renewed vision. Papa flying, seeing the cracked, dried riverbed below; succumbing to the pull of gravity, returning to the towering saguaros. The medicine plant, coaxing Mama to take it. The brutality of an impatient baby in the boiling liquid of her mother's womb, the selfish knees-to-chest center of Mama and Papa's universe, the medicine anchoring her drifting body and creating patience for the right time, right place.

Tranquilina chopped stalks of celery on the cutting board. If only her future and the future of the ministry could be revealed as clearly as the fog on the glass window. If only she possessed the spirit to deeply love once more the diseased and the despised that fell from the great constellations for no reasons other than poverty or illness wearing thin their adhesiveness. If only she could fill the vast empty room of doubt, fill each tiny nook and every corner with the lives of their parishioners, like the scar-faced, studious Ben or Mary of the tumor or Bebu's wife and all the other deserted ones whose elliptical lives shed little light on a world that had nothing in return to award. If only Tranquilina could promise to be their nourishment, their milk and muscle to all that entered the ministry doors for evening service, she could cast away, from ashes to ashes, from dust to dust, her fear of God's extinction.

Tranquilina diced with increasing haste and absorbed volition. She tried to hear Papa Tomás's galloping hooves like the chops of the knife against the cutting board, and then she attempted to feel Mama's steely will keeping the baby simmering and bobbing inside the broth of her belly. It was right and just that she, their child, should now hear the heartbeats, clopping of hooves, learn to repeat the journey of her dear Papa's shoeless life. Running, running, always and forever after, carrying more weight than one man's life.

FOUR

Ermila Zumaya and her three girlfriends walked into the merchandise-cluttered liquor/hardware/grocery store when school ended. By three in the afternoon they knew that La Bootie's son, a middle-aged man nicknamed Going Bananas, maintained a potent alcoholic buzz. Two of the girlfriends, Rini and Mousie, pinched a flask bottle of Sueño rum while the other two leaned on the counter distracting Bananas, giving him a little T&T (tits and teeth). Ermila, all brown doe eyes and dimpled smile, played coy. She flicked her long, shampoo-scented hair over her favorite mohair sweater and bummed a cigarette; Lollie, the champion in bra size, swept her breasts against the glass counter, studying the batteries, extension cords, clothespins, tapping a fingernail for a price check on this or that.

Treacherous winds, the freaky rainstorm struck, the streets coursed into navigable rivers. Consequently, the planned student walkout at Garfield High became impossible, a huge disappointment for the girlfriends. Not that Ermila and the girlfriends viewed themselves as politically active; they had attended one meeting of the Young Citizens for Community Action at Garfield, where they were given copies of a newsletter with the bold words **Demand, Protest, Organize, Grievances or Grief. You decide!** After the meeting, Ermila and Mousie rolled the flyers up into party horns, tooting and yelling, joyriding with Alfonso and his McBride homies in his newly customized Impala. Regardless of their detachment, the girls had participated in the initial blowouts, the student insurrections for the fun of it, ditching school, rabble-rousing, everyone else thinking they held up banners or raised fists to demand a better education, declare Chicano Power.

Now stranded at school the entire day, the girlfriends sighed and looked out of the cracked windows to see the hurried rain, the winds bending the maple trees, their branches whip-slapping the tables of the quad. While Mrs. Flint measured sugar in home economics, Lollie suggested the rum and cola to salvage the rest of the day.

The four girlfriends convened under a patio table umbrella at the Top Hat Hot Dog & Pastrami Eatery, which faced Whittier Boulevard, the main cruising drag of the Eastside. Lollie poured equal amounts of rum into four Royal Crown Colas as they waited for Ermila's boyfriend, Alfonso, who had agreed to give all of them a joyride home. They nursed their drinks for over an hour, their white paper straws going limp. The rum sedated Ermila's agitation and she dolloped more ketchup onto a center napkin for the large communal order of onion rings they all jiggled their coin purses to buy. Her turn came to recall her earliest childhood memory.

Ermila remembered Mrs. M. of the Child Services, who drove a big moss-green Buick and always styled her coiffure into an amazing puff of hairspray and tease. Because Ermila couldn't look out the rear window, she surmised that she was probably three or four years old. Bored, she sat in the fluffy backseat of the car, right behind Mrs. M., and had nothing better to do than gawk at the rust-colored hairdo resembling a mannequin's wig like the ones at Newberry's.

Wait up! Lollie quizzed. If you're so young, how could you know it's a Buick?

Buicks are bitchen cars, Mousie said. Shortest of the four girls, Mousie wore huge false eyelashes, which her mother forbade and which she pulled off right before going home. Even the church held its mysteries sacred and the girlfriends would die first before ratting on Mousie. The storm began to loosen its grip and the wide orb of the umbrella protected them from a misty drizzle.

My cousin Lucho gots a tuff one, Mousie continued. You know, gold and red one and it gots an eight-track with four speakers. Bitchen.

Lucho, the one who don't talk good? asked Rini.

Yea, him.

He gots a Buick? This from Lollie, incredulous. She pushed up her long sleeves, then rubbed a spot near her elbow and then pulled her green pullover sleeves down again.

I dunno for sure if it was a Buick, Ermila replied, suddenly doubting her memory. She hated liars, especially those who fueled the tanks of truth with alcohol. Mrs. M. had backed out of the driveway of the foster family and Ermila sat in the backseat of the car studying the giant woman's vibrant coiffure. She flipped open an ashtray situated on the armrest and it talked like a squawking mouth.

Don't do that, honey, Mrs. M. had said from the front seat. Please!

Let it be a Buick, offered Rini.

Yea, let Ermila got a Buick.

As the girlfriends talked, a few Buicks paraded by, showy hydraulics bumping and dumping. A few detailed Chevys cruised as well, one of which was a deep purple bomb '57 Chevy, Rini's dream car, bulbous and polished smooth and round like an eggplant with tangerine-and-sweet-potato-colored flames scorching the sides of its doors in spontaneous combustion. In between the Chevys, Buicks and Plymouths, a few classic Pontiacs appeared, glistening gold rims and whitewall tires famous for airbrushed portrayals of buxom women who wore sombreros and smiled flatly on the hoods of engines or the trunks of the cars.

Were you the model? Mousie asked Lollie, who flipped the bird at her.

Junkyard parts welded into beloved showboats, dismembered then lovingly remembered part by screw by bolt by piston, into another wholeness, into an art so hot, it ignited fire. Radiant colors glossy and wet, shiny as canned beets on a Thanksgiving table, or streamlined bright pinks on blinding new customized paint jobs. Almost every make and model of car passed them by on a Thursday late afternoon cruise except for one sky-blue Impala.

The sunshine sifted from between the clouds in small increments, making shadows. Ermila's long, straight hair fell like a steep cliff, and she flipped it over her shoulder as she dipped a finger in the puddle of ketchup, then looked for Alfonso down Whittier Boulevard. She sometimes plaited a thin braid to defy what she felt was limited fashion capacity, but mostly wore her black hair free of pins, barrettes and hair bands. Lollie peeled the breaded fried crisps of the onion rings, sloshed the crusty breading in ketchup and then discarded the droopy onion. Rini alone ate the bare onion because she said it was a sin to waste food.

How weird that we like onion rings but not the onion, huh? Mousie observed. She preened the gummy dried glue off her spidery eyelashes and placed them safely in their clear plastic box until tomorrow. You think Nacho likes onions? she inquired, feigning innocence.

Who cares? Lollie replied, crunching up her green pullover again. The girlfriends never mentioned Lollie's repulsion to her own body hair. Lollie pushed up and then pulled down her sleeves because she shaved her arm hair, thick and black against her pale skin, with her father's Gillette blade razor. She plucked her haystack eyebrows into pencil-thin lines, then bleached them a shade lighter and wore her curly walnut hair closely cropped to her head, plastering her bangs with globs of Deb Gel. Even now, as Lollie crunched up her sleeves, she rubbed the black stub dots on her arm, then pulled her sleeves down again without the slightest awareness that she did this regularly. The girlfriends glanced at one another, refusing to comment on the bad habit or wonder about how Lollie dealt with her pubic area.

Sounds to me like *you* care, Lollie Loop de Lou! Rini teased, pushing a finger at Lollie's busty chest, chuckling.

Nacho? Fucken no. The Tijuana retard? No way! Are yo' nuts? Lollie crunched up her sleeves again. He's FOB, fresh off the border!

Cold shot.

Don't cap on 'Mila's cousin.

He's not my real cousin, Ermila added listlessly, half listening to the conversation. Her hearing sometimes reached, sometimes connected and sometimes didn't connect to the waves of sea or sound. Someone had said she was stone-cold deaf and dumb by the age of five, but she wasn't, was she, if she could hear them say it? Ermila looked down Whittier Boulevard. The wet had slashed through her mohair sweater, her T-shirt and her bra and she sat stewing in damp chill. Alfonso was probably hanging with the McBride Homeboys at the Silver Dollar Bar, the bastard. What balls, to do this to her again.

Kissin' cousins make good lovin'.

How gross, Rini opined.

Nacho's kinda cute. Mousie regretted the indiscretion and then added, For a Tijuanero, I mean.

Anyways, Ermila sighed, was I saying something?

'Bout hair spray or sumthin'.

The foster house had been permeated by a dirty laundry smell. The foster mother had worn plastic bracelets, which clinked up and down her wrists as she pulled a lemon-and-lime cotton summer dress over Ermila's head. The foster mother left papaya lipstick smudges on cigarette butts and tumbler rims. She wore her hair with shellac Aqua Net like Mrs. M.

Two women in long black skirts and rubber boots stopped at the table to ask for directions. The shorter one, wearing a clear, lame plastic raincoat that came in pocket-sized folds and sold at the First Street Store for a dime, did the talking. Mousie shrugged because giving directions wasn't a strong point, and Lollie didn't know because she took the buses and knew only the bus routes.

No matter, said the taller one.

Creepy, huh? Rini asked after the women left.

I keso.

Lookit! Lollie said, displaying her bare arm. I got goose bumps!

The intimacy of their conversation continued in exaggerated gestures, in laughter unusually loud, in hosting a captive audience around the patio table. A horn beeped, and the girlfriends turned their attention to a Roadrunner car polished to such sheen that the lime-green reflection wavered on the passengers' faces making it hard to recognize them. Hydraulics on the back end lifted up like the hind legs of a spider readied for attack. But then something happened; pressed tightly against the back window, a flash of fleshy, pale bare ass. The girlfriends were being mooned straightaway, bare-ass mooned. Then the car sped off, its tailgate splashing a pothole of water on an unsuspecting pedestrian.

Did you see wha' I did? Did you see that? Lollie shouted, blinking hard several times. You stupid fuckers, she barely shouted in fits of convulsive laughter. Mousie covered her blushing face in the blindfold of her hands while Rini's rum and cola spurted through her nose. Ermila was beside herself. In a minute, she'd have to go pee.

Did you got the license plate?

No way. It had to be Julio.

You recognize his ass?

Forget you.

I gotta go pee.

The sludge of clouds left by the storm vanished in the two and a half hours they waited, but curfew tarnished whatever sunshine escaped. The ketchup stayed a dried blot of an island on the napkin. Mousie counted the orange and green trucks rumbling down Whittier Boulevard with greater frequency, stacked roadblock horses weighing their trunk beds down.

That makes eight, Mousie observed.

Shit! Lollie said bravely, rubbing the stubs of arm hair. We can't wait no more.

The girlfriends lived within the shaded boundaries of the map printed in English only and distributed by the city. From First Street to Boyle to Whittier and back to Pacific Boulevard, the roadblocks enforced a quarantine to contain a potential outbreak of rabies. Back in early February, a pamphlet delivered by the postman read: *Rising cases of rabies reported in the neighborhood (see shaded area) have forced Health officials to approve, for limited time only, the aerial observation and shooting of undomesticated mammals. Unchained and/or unlicensed mammals will not be exempt.* A quarter of the pamphlet described rabies symptoms, untimely deaths, rabid squirrels and other urban rodents, city fines. *For limited time only,* a curfew enforced. The mayor had signed the brochure with such a spectacle of a signature, Grandfather Zumaya had judged the man incapable of ignorance or wrongdoing. *Let's work together to keep our families and our city safe,* the end of the message urged.

Yea, Mousie added. You know some culero will be, like, "You got your ID or INS or SS card wit you?"

For sure, like, "Hey, let me see your IUD?" Lollie joked, opening her knees wide and then saying, "Yea, wanna check it out?"

How gross, Rini replied.

Ermila accordion-folded a paper napkin. The city officiated those in charge as the Quarantine Authority, but Ermila and her girlfriends referred to them as culeros. Four months of waiting in lines longer than the devil's tail only to be interrogated by the culeros for *valid gov-*

ernment documentation, from eight in the evening to six in the morning. In a suspicious tone, the QA examined the girlfriends from sneakers to earrings, studied their IDs, long pauses of distrust to unnerve them, to convince them of some guilt. Except for the troublemakers, the neighborhood people bit into the quarantine without question. Lollie translated the pamphlet to her parents, who spoke little official English, and they had reacted like everyone else: they believed and obeyed. Ermila's own grandparents were convinced that the curfew and the shooting and the QA all *contained the rabies epidemic.*

Thirteen trucks, Mousie counted. Bad number.

If you stay, Rini said to Ermila, fingering a bra strap that slipped from her shoulder, I'll stay with you. The bush and tangle of her childhood hair had thinned out, ironed into honeycomb waves.

We'll be screwed, Ermila said. She knew, however, that she was undisputedly screwed already. Last Sunday morning at three a.m., she arrived without her shoes, her hair full of sand, at her front door, wasted and painfully dying to pee. Homeboys laughing and giving her shots of tequila until she vomited in the Impala, and then Alfonso said, Fucken no, get out of my ride. It was Mousie's cousin, Lucho, she vaguely remembered, who gave her a ride home, who had to deal with the QA, and just left her on the porch, barefoot, swaying and rattling the screen door with enough noise to wake up half the neighborhood. Grandma Zumaya's punishment was another desperate curfew accompanied by such horrible screams they reduced Ermila into a disgraced and inconsequential child.

However, by Thursday of the same week, Ermila felt smothered, full of herself again, wanted a smoke, thought to buy herself some freedom with her girlfriends and asked Alfonso for a ride home, to make up. But close to three hours later, what possible story, what alibi could she conjure, without flinching under Grandmother's suspicious vigilance? Lollie pulled her green sleeves down to her wrist, then slipped her purse strap over her shoulder, readied for departure.

It's not your fault, 'Mila. But I gotta split, Lollie said. If we don't got the bus, the QA curfew'll fuck us big time.

Maybe Alfonso got here already, Mousie offered.

Whatta you mean?

You know, the butthole in the green car.

Cold shot.

Don't cap on 'Mila's boyfriend.

Let's wait for a little while more, Rini pleaded. Rini saved her lunch nickels to pitch in for the onion rings she disliked. Her girlfriends knew Rini frightened easily and the airy back house her mother rented after the divorce reminded her of death. To Ermila, it resembled the so-called house that once belonged to the parents of Renata Valenzuela. The house gave Rini the creeps until her mother's boyfriend, Jan, came into the picture. He was creepier than the house. He scared Rini more than ghosts.

Nah, Ermila replied, no longer looking down Whittier Boulevard. I keso, it's late. Her black hair draped her profile, masking her humiliation. Worse yet, she would have to confront Grandmother Zumaya. The girlfriends understood.

Silence confirmed the general consensus, and yet there still lingered a great reluctance to leave one another. Mousie peeled off the cooled crisp and handed the last soggy onion ring to Rini. Eventually the girls followed Lollie, who, in another gesture of departure, rested one bent knee on the patio bench. They began balling napkin fans, collecting trash, and returning the fry basket and empty RC bottles back to the Formica counter. Then the three of them loitered as Mousie, the smallest of the four, went to the restroom to change her sanitary napkin.

They stood around the table, dressed in various shapes and sizes of the same brand of blue jeans they had purchased together at the First Street Store. Though flared bell-bottoms raged in the fashion world, the girlfriends stuck to straight-legged Levi's blue jeans in order to make a statement about togetherness and nonconformity. Lollie thought the Levi's made her ass stick out like a shelf and said as much to her friends to show the sacrifice she made for their benefit. Ermila buttoned the brassy buttons of her canary-yellow mohair as Rini closed the umbrella.

Bitchen sweater, Rini said, petting the mohair. The sweater was a larger size, long-sleeved and fuzzy, with shoulder pads that added more mass to Ermila's one-hundred-pound frame. The sweater molted and Rini caught a yellow fuzz floating.

Did you got it from Alfonso?

Salas Used Cars paycheck.

How lucky you got that N.Y.C. job. The Neighborhood Youth Corps ran out of jobs and Rini had to babysit almost every weekend.

Does the viejo still have the pitchers? Lollie asked, fumbling inside of her bag purse to look for her wallet. The nudie cuties?

Yea.

Whatta horny dog.

Who's a horny dog? Mousie returned. Whatta miss? Don't talk when I'm gone.

Cheeze, man.

Who's the horn dog? Lucho? Nacho? Come on, don't be like that.

Mousie handed out squares of Bazooka bubble gum, to cover the scent of liquor. When it was time to disperse, the girlfriends departed with considerable gravity and in different directions. Of them all, only Ermila took home geography and algebra texts for homework. Lollie carried a paperback and diary in her purse but no binder folders; Mousie's only book was a pocket address book. Ermila glanced one last time down Whittier Boulevard as Rini, who secretly loved their home economics class with its orderly, measuring cookery, blew a bubble and waved good-bye to her before turning the corner.

Close to seven, she was dead meat for sure. Ermila caught sight of two more orange and green trucks entering the right-of-way. Late, the Kern bus opened its flush of doors. Ermila onboard and pressing her books to her chest, clinking a token in the glass box, finding a seat in the rear. The Kern bus rumbled past pedestrians, jerked to a stop, resumed, passed the church with its quatrefoil flowers on the painted glass windows, jerked to a stop, resumed passing storefronts and houses, stopping and starting again and again. The binder and texts idled on her denim lap while Ermila flicked her hair over her shoulder. She inspected her reflection on the glass window. The plush mohair sweater she wore was an expensive indulgence (a layaway plan that took months to pay off), and her jet-black hair starkly contrasted against its bright yellow color.

Grandmother had rejected Ermila's hair as if it were a personal affront. Raven-black and as straight as an arrow, her hair was proof of her father's mestizo blood. Ermila knew little of her mother, but even less of her father. Grandmother couldn't even utter his name without trembling, and yet, in Ermila's bedroom, Grandmother had hung a photograph of her parents, so young and eager and blurred, before they ran off like thieves in the night, before becoming communists, before they disappeared forever, leaving only a child. Hung on a triangular wire above the light switch for years, the photo in the picture frame was cracked and lined on one splotchy corner where the sepia had rubbed off from someone's fingerprint. The father stood next to a vegetable cart and looped his arms around the mother's waist. Taller, he hunched a playful chin on her shoulder as the camera shutter snapped. The mother's mouth froze in such a break of laughter, such an uninhibited moment of startled joy, she could have easily slipped out of the frame. It was Ermila's father who pulled her back in by the waist with the tight belt of his arms.

Ermila never smelled the soft fragrances of this father or that mother who lived wickedly crazy, never tasted their kisses or listened to the nuances of their voices, never touched their sepia skin. Nonetheless, without fail, whenever Ermila switched the bedroom light on or off, the mother pointed straight at her with an accusation that did not escape Grandmother.

Passengers exited at the rear, others boarded, then found a seat. A few heads tilted back in deeply sound sleep, gaped mouths, their lips pumping and compressing like the pistons of the bus engine. The grind of bus gears and clinking fares—ten cents one-way, three tokens for a quarter—bled into a memory of Chavela's voice insisting that Ermila pay close attention. When no one was looking, Ermila pulled her glob of gum out of her mouth and pasted it underneath her seat. The bus rode on until an abrupt stop forced Ermila's algebra text to slip from her lap and fall. She hated dropping things and so excused another of Alfonso's no-shows.

Despite the small opening of the Buick's rear windows, the heat stifled and the child floated lazily on top of the dead, hot air. The asphalt beneath hummed with the tautness of rubber, sang her into drowsiness. Before Mrs. M. delivered her to Grandmother Zumaya, she promised the child a visit to "the ocean." For this reason, the foster mother packed a suitcase, pulled a freshly ironed cotton dress over her head and embraced her enough to crush the child's ribs into powder.

The child sat in the backseat, smoothing out the wrinkles in her lemons-and-limes-printed dress, then studied her walnut knees. She dozed off again, and when she awoke, she saw the shiny tips of her new black patent leather shoes. As she pointed her toes one way or the other, the child discovered that sparks of light darted on and off their tips. Finally, Mrs. M. said, Here we are, honey!

Grating brakes halted the Kern bus. Ermila pressed her binder and texts under her arm and she stepped out onto Fourth Street. The clouds, quartz-brilliant against the blue, were suspended so low that her wish to touch their edges did not seem absurd. Orange traffic cones on display diverted traffic in preparation for the curfew. On the other side of the crosswalk, tall palms bordered the boulevard and housed the cemetery bats that thrashed about the fronds.

Ermila crossed against the light, a long protesting blast of horn, trailing yellow mohair behind her. She trotted the four neighborhood blocks netted together by thick overhead wires, which dipped and lobbed from telephone pole to pole to house to pole in an endless cat's cradle until she arrived on the living side of First Street. The orange and green trucks lowered the last of the roadblocks. Wearing puffy orange vests, the Quarantine Authority officers distributed the orange traffic cones. The freeway bridge interchange swelled, tires slapping the steep asphalt curves. Ermila hid a churning apprehension under her smile while waiting in line.

Rows of pigeons dotted the multiple wires like musical notes on a scale, undisturbed by the hot flow of telephone conversations. Which of her girlfriends would call later to carry on the talkstory? Would it be Mousie, who had told her friends while chewing Bazooka bubble gum about her older brother YoYo and how he smelled of Brut in junior high, or how he used to punch her arm? YoYo stories were regularly showcased and the girlfriends glanced at one another, never registering a complaint.

He hated grape soda, Mousie might say on Tuesday, maybe at lunch period or maybe during typing drills. On a dare, he drank four straight up, and *here Mousie holds up four fingers*, just like that, he got wasted sick. Purple lips for five days *and here she spreads her palm in front of Ermila's face.* Can you believe it?

YoYo returned from Vietnam in so many pieces, Mousie's mother decided on cremation, which went against the practice of the Catholic church. Everyone warned her of blasphemy.

The casket transforms the soul, Father Germán explained, opening his gnarled, cocoon fists into butterfly wings. Without it, what you are saying, what you are showing God, is that you do not believe in the promise of Resurrection. And, he said, holding a finger up, his clerical collar resembling a single bucktooth in a vacant mouth, the living need this promise much more than the dead. Mousie's mother stared at him blankly, her face eroded into one red, featureless swell of grief.

After all these days, Mousie had hoped her mother's moaning and noisy wailing moved toward closure. But her mother sat motionless on a wooden bench in Father Germán's office like a mountain well versed in the flow of ancient rivers. Mousie had accompanied her to the rectory, and sat on Father's wooden deacon's bench. Though the bench accommodated three people, her mother opted to sit close to her. Too close, so close, Mousie felt her mother's heat blistering from under her white cafeteria uniform.

Father Germán realized his arguments had failed, and so he lowered his voice as if to share a secret. It's necessary, he whispered, wedging his head between theirs, his musty black gown smelling of muffled sins and stale tobacco, for the living to lay prayers beside the deceased. Mousie felt her mother's body ignite.

Like if he's some cedar chest? Her voice quavered and she punched her forehead with tight-fisted punches. He's my boy, my only son, Padre, not some box.

Of course! Yes, then honor him, Father Germán replied, reaching to catch her avalanched chin. Yes, he repeated with the reassuring smile of a man about to make a sale. It's not fair to honor a soldier by burning him up in the fires of hell like his murderers. Imagine it, he said, one strike of a match, puff, and where would YoYo's daring soul find peaceful rest?

What if Father Germán was right? Mousie had asked her girlfriends. Would it be too late to stop the fire as it charred and blazed the body? Mousie became inconsolable at her mother's decision. And her girlfriends rallied around her without an answer. At what point is the soul no longer redeemable? At what point can it not be resurrected? What if, she kept thinking, as they waited for the ashes at the cremation services Mousie's mother had found in the Yellow Pages, what if Father Germán's words were true, and YoYo's soul wandered around homeless for eternity? Oh, God, what if?

Full of bone chip and particle but empty of his soul, YoYo was buried at the military cemetery without ceremony. It'll be okay someday, Rini reminded, her Kleenex in shreds. The trees randomly rubbed against one another with such indifference, their slightest swooshing offended Lollie. Ermila's cheeks, aglow with rage at the injustices that mothers force on their daughters, squeezed Mousie's quivering shoulder. The girlfriends swore against allowing YoYo to vanish into a number on the Cronkite evening-news death tally as they walked out of the cemetery. Mousie took it upon herself to cross-stitch him together to recapture his soul. Her friends understood. She mentioned him at least once a day, so that no one, least of all her, forgot that he lived until his nineteenth year, and punched arms, went to school with purple lips, reeked of bargain cologne, made her feel special because she was his sister.

On Thursday afternoon, around the patio table, Mousie told of the day YoYo received his induction papers, and they all wondered about the draft lottery. Whose number was high? Why was Alfonso's number low, and what about Nacho?

Yea, what 'bout him, Mousie?

If Nacho don't got no immigration papers, they won't take him, right?

I keso.

They took Bootie's son, the one with the tiny ears?

You lie!

Going Bananas?

Nah, the younger one.

Gone to Fort Ord, maybe.

How weird that his ears were so small, huh?

Big ears or no, all the good ones got the walking papers.

Like Sparky. Not him, his cousin, I mean.

No way!

Do you think he'll come back?

Why? You gonna wait?

The only things they cherished, their only private property, were the stories they continued to create and re-create in a world which only gave them one to tell. And so they never tired of one another's company; they listened to Rini rewrite accounts of her phantom father by proclaiming a gift package or a funny postcard arrived in yesterday's mail addressed to her with a return address, and the girlfriends nodded but never asked to see his handwriting. Or Ermila's single-sentence stories of foster homes, half memories of the Child Services or half truths about Alfonso, wording his name like the punch line of a joke. At the Top Hat Hot Dog & Pastrami Eatery, Lollie continued her ongoing saga, a daily revised life detailed in letters and slipped into her girlfriends' lockers about her imagined marriage to the Monkees guitarist, Peter Tork, the goofball who wore a bowl haircut. She wrote lists of what she cooked for him, described the house in Beverly Hills that she redecorated. The account was followed by her adulterous late-night dinners sipping Lambrusco wine with news anchorman Bill Bonds, who admired her soft hands as he kissed each fingertip, which was, Lollie wrote insistently, as far as he got. It's Vaseline, she reread out loud to the girlfriends from one of her letters, rum-fueled and giddy, and wearing gloves for when I sleep.

They met behind the gym, before homeroom, at the lunch benches, after school, at Concha's not-really-a-beauty-salon, in the back of the bus, and if they had the privilege, they phoned one another at home because a few hours without conversation were insufferable. With conviction, they designed escape routes, rehearsed their breakout and hurled their futures over the roadblocks of their marooned existence. Lest they forget that silence is destructive, they pitted each other against the sorrowful and infinite solitude, each and every hour, because that's what friends por vida are for.

Ermila waited at the First Street roadblock, behind five children all clinging to one woman. The woman, a stalk of branchy bark and bones, reported to the QA how her purse was stolen, not a dime left, her grandmother's miniature scissors—an heirloom—vanished with the rest of the contents, arguing with increasing intensity to be allowed to fetch her rent receipts to prove that she did live at 3151 East First Street, rear house, and had lived there for all five births of her children. As Ermila listened, she wondered if she was the only person to doubt this peculiar situation or had found it as confusing and crazy as she.

The city officials demanded paper so thin and weightless, it resisted the possibility of upholding legal import to people like herself, her cousin Nacho, her girlfriends and all the other neighbors with or without children who had the misfortune of living within the shaded designated areas. Didn't the QA know that in the Eastside getting a valid ID was more complicated than a twelve-year-old purchasing a six-pack from Going Bananas? A neighbor's idea of validity was totally incongruent with the QA's norms or anyone else's, for that matter. Business was done differently in the Eastside. In need of a dentist? Wait for Dr. Padilla from Tijuana the first of each month, home visits with a leather bag full of clanging metal tools and novocaine injections. What about a loan? The lending was done between two men, one of which had a reputation for breaking bones. Need legal status? For those without papers, legal status became a shift in perspective, a matter of dubious demarcation, depending on who the border belonged to.

No one in the Eastside believed in paper. Most of the Eastside stores didn't even give paper receipts. Ray, the Japanese owner of the Friendly Shop, calculated sums on paper bags. La Bootie had an adding machine that she punched and cranked with amazing precision. No one questioned the calculations as long as all agreed that the poor didn't cheat the poorer, and, of course, your word was your word.

But there they lined up, behind Ermila, these unquestioning neighbors leaning on their canes as the thinning colors of twilight made them nostalgic for their cluttered, coffee-smelling kitchens, or their delicious beds readied to nurture sleep. They clutched grocery bags or parcels that grew into heavy buckets of gravel in their arms as hours passed and the slithering line of people either shrank or lengthened against the curb. They fisted gas company bills, birth certificates, bogus driver's licenses, anything to get themselves home. The longer the wait, the larger the nervous obsession with the handled paper. Shifting weight of bodies, hushing children, hours passing, backs aching, only to be told certain papers were unacceptable as proof of residency, including rent receipts, the QA officer yelled back.

The woman persisted as the evening became hot and muggy, earthquake weather. Her arms waved in the air indignantly, while her children whimpered, obstinately refusing any requests. The QA officer pulled the woman aside, her frantic children misbehaving, and flashed their teary faces with his baton flashlight as twilight turned into night.

What might happen if the line of people simply wrapped themselves around the QA officers like a python? **Demand, Protest, Organize.** Before the words infiltrated her thoughts, Ermila was cleared from the roadblock and suddenly found herself running to her house, repeating her alibi. She had to work an extra afternoon at Salas. She earned her due, learned her lesson, magically became what her grandmother now knew to be impossible—a good girl.

Three afternoons a week, Ermila worked as a part-time bookkeeper for Salas Used Cars. Though the N.Y.C. job was relished, the monthly paycheck promised less than the aggravation. Salas hung calendar pictures of bikini-clad women aiming their double-barrel chests advertising El Zócalo Fine Meats right above the thick accounting books where Ermila recorded sales figures. To complain of this offense to the likes of Salas, who lied through his teeth about a car's odometer, would be useless. So useless that for three afternoons a week, and for three hours, she stomached both the heavy smell of Pennzoil, the constant buzz of drilling and the obscene comments uttered by Salas and his mechanics, who regarded the semi-nude, egg-yolk-blond models as major entertainment.

As the weeks passed, and as Ermila recorded figures into the green accounting grids, she secretly dreamed of hanging a bare-bottom man with a cannon of an erection and balls of iron advertising La Pelota Bakery. Con safos, back to you, baby! The thought would distract her into miscalculations. Nonetheless, the fantasy was worth the mistakes and made the three hours fly by.

Lollie, the brave one, had advised her: Tell Mr. Horn Dog you hate the pitchers.

And then? Mousie might retort.

No job, no money, Rini would add.

The risk of dissent was too costly. There's the door, Salas would say, removing her fifteen-year-old ass before he would remove his pinups. A paycheck somehow reassured Ermila that she took care of personal business like an adult. The fear of homelessness, perhaps, of roaming the neighborhood like some old crazy street woman collecting bottles, guaranteed her silence. So at the end of her three hours, Ermila would close the accounting book gently, sharpen her dull pencil lead and brush away the clumps of black eraser from her assigned desk. In doing such, she rolled the fantasy of the cannon and iron balls up for another day.

She opened her compact to check her blooming rose lips, and then waited for Alfonso outside the garage. Like someone well schooled in the knowledge of survival, Ermila appreciated that Alfonso's gang-banging reputation was known by the mechanics.

Alfonso, a.k.a. Big Al, owned a fine pair of wheels, a hydraulic powder-blue Impala he had purchased from Salas himself. Salas never asked how such a young man acquired hundreds of dollars so withered that the faces of the presidents were cracked and veined. It was not his role as a car-lot proprietor to ask how a nineteen-year-old man whose signature revealed he had not made it past middle school could proudly display various bills from a crowded billfold and spread them across the cashier counter like a winning poker hand. Salas saw his role as a service provider to the community where he grew up, and thus successfully distinguished himself as (1) an asset to the Eastside, which was why he was awarded an N.Y.C. job slot; and (2) someone who never pursued any line of inquiry, for his own good. In upholding these two business rules, Salas successfully exchanged keys for cash, while Ermila dutifully recorded the sum of his mounting success.

After the purchase, it greatly pleased Salas to see Big Al gunning his engine whenever Ermila slipped into the front seat, an explosive vroom of exhaust from the vibrating muffler. Salas would stand before his showcase window to watch Ermila press her books as thick as cinder blocks against the delicate yellow mohair sweater and then be sped to places unknown. He was compelled to think that he contributed to the young couple's deep cozy nights by having offered Big Al a bargain, once owned and odometer-reversed by his own used car lot. The sight of the couple's cumulus black exhaust evaporating as he puttied his palms on the glass window reinforced Salas's satisfied smile.

And unbeknownst to Salas, the couple parked on Laguna Cliff, behind the dented **No Trespassing—Private Beach** sign. With a glove compartment of maps and condoms and can openers, Ermila's thighs opened enough to accommodate Alfonso's bony hips, enough for him to bump and grunt inside her with such frenzy, he wheezed and struggled for air, like a man drowning in an ocean. Drowsy with Strawberry Hill and in the buoyant backseat of the Impala, Ermila closed her eyes and imagined herself an empty wine bottle being jammed with a note and then tossed out into the ocean, roiling on the spume of the sea until someone discovered her. Her long fall of hair cascaded to the floorboard as she lay in the backseat of Big Al's car, her thighs cradling open like a finely carved canoe, an offering for their survival in the uncertain sea in which they trespassed.

The car door clicking open aroused the child. A giant of a woman, Mrs. M. clamped the child's wrist, then lifted her with one hand. The child felt the skin of her thighs rip from the vinyl seat. The brisk salty chill was immediate. Mrs. M. dangled her in midair, then whirled her body and then planted the child on the sodden shore like a seedling, shutting the rear door with a hip.

Lord, it's cold, Mrs. M. said. She held her elbows. Her nylons brushed when she walked. Can you hear the foghorn, little one? Say yes or no. Nod your head, hon, yes or no.

The child's shoes sank into the slushy beach sand. The ocean melted into rippling silver against the cut-and-paste of sky. Seabirds perched on the gray bloated wooden pier. The backs of her thighs pained her greatly, and she rubbed them while looking down at the yielding sand. As she twisted her shoes this way and that, the sand dulled their shine. The child looked up again to see the pelicans. Mrs. M. discovered an ear-shaped shell.

Hear something? Mrs. M. asked, pressing the conch against the child's ear. The child's interest moved away from the pearly shell.

Why are you playing this deaf game? Mrs. M. whispered. Will I ever know? She spoke in stiletto Spanish, tap tap, tap over the child's muffled, low-pitched hum. Amazed the ground beneath her was so pliable, the child rooted her new shoes deeper into the dampened shoreline. Mrs. M. instructed the child not to do this with her shoes, but the child squirmed in her clasp, then pointed to a wooden pea pod boat. Mrs. M. spied her wristwatch instead of the silvery nips against the boat that caught the child's attention and waited another ten minutes.

Sorry, bunny. Your Grandmother's waiting for you. Mrs. M.

dragged her, the child digging her heels in the sand, long snail trails, her lips mouthing protests. She turned once more, to the ocean's color like the chrome bumper on the Buick. Mrs. M. gently pulled her into the backseat and strapped her seat belt. Angered, the child kicked the front seat, toes reaching.

Don't do that, honey, Mrs. M. said. Tucked between her socks and shoes, the child felt stowaway beach sand. The grainy lumps comforted her enough to calm her.

The two wended their way to the Zumaya address. Holding hands, they discovered the steps to Grandmother's house were too high for the child to climb without Mrs. M.'s assistance. Mrs. M. knocked for a very long time and the child noticed someone peering from the screen porch window. Finally, Grandmother Zumaya cracked the door and her only daughter's only child would never know what fire lit inside her when she looked down for the first time at her own flesh and blood hiding like a frightened and threatened stranger. The child held on to Mrs. M.'s skirt tightly and waited for Grandmother Zumaya to grab on to the papers Mrs. M. held out to her, reeling her grandchild's life in with the loops of her stringy signature. Mrs. M. revved her inflections taptaptap but the child wanted to hear Grandmother's voice trembling that flabby chin.

On the porch steps of her grandparents' home, Ermila hesitated, nausea overwhelming her. She placed her books on the top step and then she pulled her long hair back like a thread through the hole of a rubber band and wrapped it into a tight and slick ponytail to keep her hair quiet against Grandmother's constant complaints. Years ago she had arrived a frightened child with the starch of her lemons-and-limes dress peeled away by the long car ride, and she remembered standing on these same steps, so small and inconsequential, beneath the paper-packed envelope suspended between Grandmother and Mrs. M. Now a young woman, Ermila could only imagine what went speeding through Grandmother's thoughts at the crucial moment when Grandmother stared down at her not seeing a granddaughter but a female with such wicked potential that even her hair—sheared as choppy as the seashore—boldly defied bobby pins. That was why Ermila wore the ponytail even if it spread her headache. Ermila poked a finger to scratch under the taut rubber band.

On the first day of her arrival, Ermila remembered a group of kids played baseball and lobbed a tennis ball across the street and into the yard. It rolled under a sprinkler tish-tish-tishing arcs of overlapping water. The blue swirls of Chavela's stucco house glittered beneath the trellis of hibiscus flowers blooming. The bald-headed Gamboa boy ran to retrieve the ball, and then stayed under the sprinkler, laughing, and then the other children quickly followed, abandoning the stickball game for the sprinkler. All that water teasing, all that anticipation sloshing around in her belly, Ermila had wanted to pee. Her bladder pressed its limits, and she tried to plug herself between her legs and jiggled this way and that, her knees locked together.

Lord, Mrs. M. had said, why didn't you say you had to potty?

Ermila finally remembered why Grandmother was so angry at three a.m. Barefoot, her sight so blurred she couldn't find her pocket to find her key and couldn't find the ground to put her foot down, her drunken body hitting the screen door, causing the dogs to bark and the porch light to turn on. And then she did the unthinkable: Ermila relinquished and peed, released the warm bleachy liquid that gently rolled down her legs, puddling beneath her. She reeked. Care and trust fell through the thin ice of Grandmother's glazed look.

What was happening to her? How could she have been so trashed that she peed on herself like she had as a five-year-old child, both times in front of Grandmother? Inserting the key into the lock of the door, Ermila deeply sighed. Humiliated again, she prepared for Grandmother's wrath.

Grandmother removed the child's shoes, and the next thing, beach sand spilled all over the swept floor of the screen porch. Grandmother's loose chins trembled, nervous ice-burning hands peeling off the child's wet, warm undergarment, then placing her in the laundry sink. She drove her fingernails into her small scalp, attempting to scrub away the coarseness of the child's hair, uprooting the tangles like tumbleweed with a big green bar of Lava soap. The child basted in her own watery juices as Grandmother poured water on her head over and over again. Grandmother's own hair was spumy around her swirling ears, which seemed needfully big to the child, as if they were fish gills breathing in noise.

Somewhere between blotting the child with a sun-dried towel and tugging her drumstick legs into a fresh pair of shorts, Grandmother decided she would have to do something about the child's hair. Grandmother brushed her hair into a ponytail so tight, it strained the temples of her forehead into a dull annoying headache.

A streetcar later, Grandmother hauled the child to Gene's barbershop to get a haircut, since hair salons existed to cheat her out of every penny, every time. The dull peppermint neon bristled when it spun, little bells ushering in a customer. Beneath the caked cigar smoke and Brilliantine or Tres Rosas, specks of blinding metal clippers and tall radio speakers, one barber held a bowl of sudsy shaving soap. Dipping a fat brush, the barber painted the lathered clouds under the peak of a customer's nose.

Gene stacked telephone books on his majestic burgundy barber chair. The child sat royally, resting her palms on the vinyl chair's chrome armrests, a white wraparound for a queen's cloak. Gene snipped the rubber of her band, it flew off and she rubbed the relief of her scalp, thankful. Tug and clip of shortening hair, the scissors sharp cold against her ear. The child tried to keep her neck rigid, her body motionless, which took an incredible amount of energy, and she flinched. Gene gently scolded. In the next chair, the barber shaved his reclining customer and the child studied the lumps and mounds of his relaxed body.

On the high nest of telephone books, the child noticed the customer's missing limb. She tried to avoid looking at the space where the man's pant leg neatly creased over at the knee. She wanted someone to mention it, but everyone acted normal. The child's growing discomfort made her fidget several times, forcing Gene to stop. Grandmother warned her, Hold still or get your ear cut off! The child whimpered. Grandmother demanded she speak up, Now, what is it?

The child's voice moved out of the basement of her belly and climbed the passage of her esophagus to a high-pitched shrill that ripped through the eardrums of the adults in the small shop. One barber jiggled a steaming towel like a hot potato, while another almost snipped his client's nostril instead of nose hair. The one-legged man jerked up, his face towel yanked away, causing her shrieks to become deadening. Grandmother panicked. Though the haircut was incomplete, Grandmother pulled the child into the stinking bathroom and walloped her bottom red for wasting hard-earned money on half a haircut.

Later that afternoon, the child sat on a kitchen chair, half her head spiky and uneven, her chin crestfallen. Her lungs breathed in grief, and she sat shameful and quiet in front of a heaping bowl of oatmeal, without a trace of hunger. Grandfather entered, placed his tin lunch pail on the counter, took one look at her and began the argument, heated, boiled to a spill, ripped paper words firing back and forth and back and forth, nose to nose catching flecks of spittle.

Stop it, Rogelio, Grandmother demanded, her voice deep, as if the words had to twist and bump from the depths of her entrails.

Hide her; hide her so that I won't have to see her! His graying mustache bristled like the spine needles of the opuntia cactus.

She's our flesh and blood, Grandmother said.

I said hide her.

No! Her eyes were glassy.

The child eyed the lump of hardening oatmeal. When was Mrs. M. coming back, nylons scratching, to take her home? The kitchen filled up with the scent of incense, faint odor of old wood ash, light vinegar, a scent that would remain with Grandfather always. There was no control of the table's edge, no frozen air to halt the tipping bowl, no hand quick enough to stop it from tumbling to the floor.

The two turned to her. Grandfather punched all his patience into the hump on his back, no room left. He kicked the broken bowl aside with such force, specks of gray oatmeal splattered the wall just as his spittle had Grandmother's face. He threw himself at her, hands swinging in aping gestures, looming big and unforgiving, and leaned close enough to hurl words at her with a blast of breath that smelled of cough medicine. A mess of coarse hair, the child melted from the chair and quickly hid behind Grandmother, tightly wrapping a trembling arm around her bony leg.

If she goes, I go, Grandmother said in an exhausted murmur, pulling on a handkerchief tucked in the sleeve of her knitted salmon-colored sweater. She wiped the tears under her glasses, then turned to her own flesh and blood and pinched the whimpering child's runny nose with the same handkerchief. Unable to breathe, the child twisted her head to push the hankie away while firmly clasping Grandmother's thigh.

The hammering, someone hammering, and how could Grandfather in his La-Z-Boy recliner snooze through the noise of the hammering and the evening news? Grandfather had suffered a mysterious stroke that left him sleepy a greater part of the day, and he mostly slept all the time now except at night. He slept over TV voices and over the hammering. Fluorescent greenish tint flickered on his face while her cousin Nacho sat bored on the couch, flipping randomly through the latest issue of ¡Alarma!, a magazine of lust and murder filled with sordid police photos and mug shots that turned up in her nightmares. All he had to do was cock an eyebrow at the sight of her, an abbreviated warning to Ermila of the inevitable eruption.

Nacho had been sent by his family five months ago to come live up north and help out since Grandfather had been disabled. Coming to the Eastside would be a good opportunity for him to learn English, have a chance at learning a trade and earn money to send back home; but Nacho thought otherwise. Two weeks after he began his ESL classes, he dropped them; laid off from a car-washing job, he felt busing tables to be below him. He informed his parents via a letter that he proposed to paint—which was well and good, until his family found out that he intended to paint murals, not houses. Nacho boasted of painting La Virgen de Guadalupe floating above the great pyramids on the side of a corner tiendita—a strange request for the Chicano owner, who seemed prouder of being Mexican than the Mexicans. Nacho dreamt of following in the footsteps of the three great Mexican muralists, Rivera, Siqueiros and Orozco.

However, there was no end to their bitter correspondence. Her grandparents felt the same and waited for a time when Nacho was prepared to embark on his artistic career outside of their time and dime. Grandfather's complaints were no secret and he took every opportunity (and opportunities became as abundant as sunrises) to reprimand Nacho for his lack of ambition, and worse yet, his downright laziness.

Surprising to Ermila now that Nacho and Grandfather could share a peaceful evening together in the same room, Nacho sat at the end of the couch, a sense of doom contained in his gaze. Ermila flipped him the bird. Lights out in the kitchen, Grandmother not in the living room. Let's get it over with, Ermila hoped. Bathroom light out, main bedroom vacant, but from the hallway she spotted Grandmother standing on her bed. Grandmother's pale skinny legs waffled on Ermila's lion blanket as she held the steel nail with pincerlike precision against the drywall above her headboard and hammered.

Oh, Grandma, what—

Ermila muffled her words, rolling them back up in her tongue. What? she shot out. Whatta you doing? When Grandmother noticed a blistering Ermila, she swung the hammer with greater force, tilting the photograph above the light switch. The two-inch tough nail had to be gunmetal-strong to hold the weight of the crucifix that Grandmother carried in the pouch of her apron pocket.

Fall down and break into tiny pieces, Ermila wanted to say, but immediately regretted the wish because Grandmother just might fall on purpose to say, See? See? More tears are shed for answered prayers, her little shriveled body poofing like dust particles of ancient wall plaster, just to teach her granddaughter a lesson.

Maybe this will protect you, Grandmother said, slipping the wire hoop of the bulky metal and wood crucifix onto the nail, because I can't anymore. I can't. The worn mattress springs crunched underneath.

Oh, Grandma. . .

There's the door, Grandmother replied. This conversation had already been blueprinted in Grandmother's mind, grievances piled so high, their tumbling inevitable. The shrill of the telephone, the muffled male voice of the television news, the mattress springs, these were the indistinguishable sounds Ermila heard, not her Grandmother's rants about Alfonso, her urine-stinking body, the risks and dangers, the lying, skipping merrily into the paths of hell like a foolish, reckless idiot.

To Grandmother, each strike of the nail held the repeated expectations of an insidious performance by her daughter whose DNA chain-linked doubly to her granddaughter. Ermila was fated, punto final. And Grandmother was too exhausted by her age and Grandfather's ten years of constant nagging regarding her sole decision to bring Ermila home to rear her own "flesh and blood." A big mistake, he had predicted. Ermila's fate was something Grandmother could not challenge, and it wearied her to the point that, though she was not a churchgoing woman, she sought out God's assistance, a thing she should have done, in hindsight, when her daughter first showed signs of femaleness. All of Grandmother's rational thoughts were absorbed in preventing Ermila's sex from entering their decent household. She also knew too well that this prevention was absolutely impossible; her efforts seemed as feeble and futile as raising her palm to halt the coming of a hurricane.

Grandmother's mouth collapsed into a well of wrinkles so deep her condemnations were endless and her thready bare feet smashed some of Ermila's prized carnival dolls. Ermila made her bed each morning and leaned Alfonso's gifts carefully on her pillow shams.

I said I was sorry.

I can't believe how stupid women can be!

This is all—

Ermila hesitated because this wasn't a good time to say what she really felt but said it anyway—Bullshit! Bullshit to the second power!

You're just like your mother, and look where it got her! As if Grandmother knew from experience, as if Ermila's mother had been that wickedly crazy. Using her old rubbery arm, Grandmother lifted the hammer again and pointed to the photo, which had tilted so badly, another blow would have forced it to fall.

I'm me, Grandma, not my mom.

No more, Grandmother repeated, shaking her head. Ermila freed her waist-length hair from its rubber band and shook it loose. There's no use trying. The incessant peal of the phone, and still Nacho too lazy to answer it. She raked a few puffs of mohair in her hair and then offered a hand to help Grandmother off the bed. Grandmother's hand was bony-thin and ice-burning cold. No words of promise, no exacting behavior would ever please Grandmother again. What was the use of even trying? The ringing of the phone ended abruptly.

Grandmother slid into a pair of slippers and skimmed the floor, her old back bent from the burdensome agony of repetition. Before Ermila closed her bedroom door she watched Grandmother sadly carry the hilt of the hammer down the dark corridor of the hall. For a few generous moments, Ermila felt pity for her. It was like that from the very beginning; she loved and hated Grandmother at the same time.

Ermila tossed and turned between her sheets, unable to sleep. Drifting sinews of steam slowly entered her room from her open door. Nacho had just stepped out of the bathroom and the steam floated out and layered the ceiling, a halo of fog surrounding the hall light. Grandmother forbade them from walking around in their underwear, but since Ermila's lamplight was off, Nacho assumed she slept. His lapse of judgment and the crack of open door afforded Ermila a glimpse of the bulbs sacked in his elastic underwear briefs. He plugged his head into the hole of his tank top, and before he covered his torso radiant from the hot shower, she saw his nipples, chocolate discs that resembled the ones she used to buy at Ray's for a penny. Blushing, she turned her face.

She had never known Alfonso fully naked except for his cock, a small anomaly of flesh that seemed strange for people to have in the first place. How it hid, then surfaced like a one-eyed pirate, the commanding growth looting, then retreating back into its own collapsible cup of flesh. The first time they did IT, it burned, harsh and bloodied. He drove her home, his arm over her shoulder as a token of recognition, his old lady, she looking out the window, surprised everything remained unchanged. Like a border crossing, sex promised a different, uplifting life and yet all she encountered was intolerable guilt, a filthy feeling that bathing couldn't cleanse and the fear that her body would someday call for mutiny. Her girlfriends knew, could see it, smell it, but never point-blank asked her and so she told no one and all of this grandly disappointed her. If Lollie could believe that her pretend marriage to the Monkees' Peter Tork was real, then why couldn't Ermila believe that her real sexual involvement with Alfonso was simple fantasy? She turned again to face the vertical light from the door and tried not to think of Alfonso or his cock and then she lay on her back. Not even self-deception could force her eyes to shut and Ermila stared up at the bulk of the crucifix for a long time trying to figure out what motivated her to do the things she did.

After the first ring, Ermila bolted out of bed so that the phone in the hallway would not wake her grandparents. She listened to the litany of Alfonso's lies, struggling to pull her arm into the sleeve of her thick chenille robe. You sound high, Ermila said, you sound wasted. She turned away from Nacho on the couch, under a floral iris-printed sheet. I never want to see you again, you asshole! she said, louder than usual, and then proceeded to whisper into the mouthpiece a time and suggest a place for Friday's date. She said she loved him, which was also a lie, and then returned to bed, immediately regretting having arranged the clandestine meeting.

The freeway bumble across First Street and the sporadic spray of bullets, too faint in the distance for concern, lulled her into a fidgety sleep. In and out of dreams, floodlights jetted through the drawn blinds, drone of engines in and out of the hours. Restless, inspired heat in the room overboiling, Ermila sensed that something wasn't right. The blind slats rippled and then settled and then rattled again and again until a force of wind billowed the pair of curtains and the hem of the curtains rose, then fell upon a small curled-up dog.

A sleepy Ermila gazed at the shadow. Huh? The shadow of the dog yawned wide, rose on all fours, then leisurely arched its back. Ludicrous on its sausage legs, the small dog seemed clownish. Grandmother had threatened her with something like this, *to protect her* because Ermila was the daughter of a mother who fled like a war refugee in the choke of night. Convinced Ermila would do the same, Grandmother must have laid a guard dog atop a rumpled pile of clothes near the open window. What other explanation would there be for the dog that raised its comically long snout to track a scent? Ermila kicked off her sheets, planted her feet on the cool hardwood floor. The dog withdrew into the shadow of the open closet door. Ermila heard paw-clicks on the floor.

Hey there, she cooed, holding out her hand. Nice doggy, stupid doggy. The dog growled low and steady as Ermila approached. The curtains camouflaged the dog's movement and it remained partially hidden in the shadow of the closet door. Nice doggy, nice. A gesture of a hand held out, an offer to the darkness.

The dog gnashed its fangs, striking her, a mighty sting. Ermila cried out, the wound throbbed around the break of skin immediately and she cracked the blind slats for light, held her bleeding hand up to inspect the bite. The beads of blood were so lacquered red she was astonished the color belonged to her. Both the pain and surprise contributed to her bitterness. If Grandmother did things like this, little wonder why her mother had escaped into the night with her father.

Ermila backpedaled through the threshold of her bedroom door and bumped into the swelling humid heat of the hallway as if it were a low ceiling. Grandmother believed that sleeping with open windows invited burglars, and so all the hot, steamy soup of air stirred in the hallway. Nacho's floral sheet tousled about the floor, uncovering his tank top and his briefs. He lay on his back in sound sleep, one knee bent, the other stretched on their creaky couch. In order to get to the bathroom, she had to tiptoe past an arching floorboard somewhere near her grandparents' bedroom and she peeked in on the two sleeping like arthritic parentheses under the thick hand-sewn quilts, the overhead fan whumping the air.

The iodine bottle was absent from the medicine cabinet, so Ermila settled for antiseptic. With her good hand, she palmed cool tap water on her neck and water beads necklaced her breasts. How else would the dog have gotten in her room if not for Grandmother's suspicions? Ermila rinsed her injured hand, applied some antiseptic, which burned and foamed, and she winced and then awkwardly swathed it with gauze.

Back in the hallway, Ermila thought to check for unlocked doors, to give Grandmother the benefit of the doubt. Okay, so Grandmother was crazy, but a dog in the house? Perhaps Nacho had left a door open and the dog wandered in to escape the helicopters. Her absentminded cousin never thought about the rhythm of her grandparents' lives and seemed forever out of sync with their set patterns. Nacho paid dearly for this: every time Nacho left water running in the sink, drawers pulled out, lights on during the day, windows opened, toilet seat up or water boiling to evaporation, Grandmother wanted to pull his ear because this irresponsible, ill-bred young man was incapable of completing one fluid act—to open, then close a cabinet, to turn on, then off a faucet. As Nacho slumbered, a hand pillowing the back of his head, his thin lips parting to breathe, who would guess him careless enough to leave the door unlocked and open? Or could Ermila have been at fault herself for having left her own window open? Her window faced First

Street and was screened, barred with wrought iron. Barely open, it was almost impossible to get a decent breeze in, much less a dog. No.

One by one, Ermila eliminated the possibilities. She gathered her hair up from between her slender shoulder blades, and cat-padded delicately to the kitchen. She jingled the handle of the screen porch door, locked, and then returned to the living room. The main-entrance door was locked and securely bolted. Perspiration beaded on her skin. Her bandaged hand hung lead-heavy and tingled from the dog bite and she used the other to pull back the aged sun-bleached drapes of the living room, taking a peek down First Street at midnight.

Ermila watched the Quarantine Authority helicopters burst out of the midnight sky to shoot dogs not chained up by curfew. Qué locura, she thought, the world is going crazy. The chopper blades raised the roof shingles of the neighborhood houses and toppled TV antennas in swirls of suction on the living side of First Street. Ermila's nylon underslip was pasted to her sweaty back. Above the woven arteries of freeways, a copter's searchlight swept over the roadblocks to catch a lone stray running out of the edge of light. The bitch zigzagged across the pavement of First Street, its underbelly droopy with nursing nipples. I gotta do something soon, Ermila thought, her hand swathed in gauze and dappled with antiseptic and blood. The wheeling copter blades over the power lines rose louder and closer and closer and louder, just like the unrelenting engines of bulldozers ten years earlier when Ermila was a child.

Once the copters completed their second sweep, bits of moon glistened in First Street's oil-moistened tracks. Ermila tiptoed from the window. Before going into her room, she approached the couch and bent to retrieve Nacho's sheet. In the dark, the irises looked like wine spills. He swayed his bent knee and touched his belly as if he sought out his blanket. The copters returned a third time. The walls trembled, disturbing the framed old magazine picture of John F. Kennedy, shattering a glass in the kitchen. The epicenter beneath her, the eternal moment waiting for the quaking to cease, but Nacho's abrupt movement roused her, and she felt her uninjured arm snarled in a grip. For a second she recalled how Luis the lizard boy had clamped her wrist and forced her to do something she didn't want to do. The memory of it infuriated her now.

Stop it, Nacho, she whispered angrily, I wasn't comin' on to you! Nacho propped himself up on an elbow and took the sheet she held, unfurling the flowers on his legs.

¿Qué te pasó? he asked, referring to her bandaged hand. His lengthening hair parted like dried wisps of kelp over his sweaty forehead. Did tu novio hurt it?

Let go.

Sssh, he whispered, pressing a finger to his lips. He arrived five months ago from Reynosa to torment her, and he glanced over at the grandparents' open bedroom door. She could barely see his eyes.

Leave me alone. Her words dissipated. By the fourth sweep, the vibrations crescendoed, making the walls and floor unsteady.

The slant of counterfeit light coming from the helicopter poured into the small living room, flooding everything around her. Light splashed on Nacho's face and the floorboards rolled beneath her bare feet once again. Ermila panicked, her slip billowed upward to her thighs. The photograph of her parents floated toward the ceiling; the stuffed dolls won in dime tosses at the church carnivals danced and dipped as buoyant as the beer caps Alfonso threw in the sea. Her slip lifted to her bare belly, and finally swelled over her two firm breasts. Her nipples felt the pinch of chill. This was happening because the world was going crazy. She could feel his moist palms inside the cool nylon of her underwear as a faint succession of bullets continued. Nacho buried his face, his lips against the slant of her belly, and she inhaled, closed her eyes because she wanted nothing to do with the light.

She exhaled. The copters lifted the floodlights and immediately the room grew gray once more. She broke his grasp, made sure her nylon slip reached her knees again.

Nacho whispered a word or two she couldn't hear and then she heard him say he planned to return to Reynosa on Saturday. In the morning.

Who cares?

What you do to me, he whispered in a concoction of English and drowsy seduction. The light in Grandmother's room flipped on. Ermila fled, slipping on a throw rug in the hallway and bumping into the phone. The large crucifix nailed above her headboard still swayed as she closed and locked her bedroom door.

The gunfire continued until dawn.

PART II

FIVE

The ubiquitous woman pilfered through the oil barrels outside the garage of Salas Used Cars where the mechanics sat at noon on the rims of open-hooded cars, their cheeks as grease-shined as the sparkplugs they replaced. For lunch break they throttled bottlenecks of Cokes or washed down bites of meaty burritos with cold squat bottles of Pabst Blue Ribbon that they tossed inside the barrels. She uncovered nine, eleven, fourteen, sixteen empty bottles, but when compared to the numerous captive hungers battering inside the caverns of her intestines, the number was insignificant. Nonetheless, she packed the findings in the belly of her rainbow straw bag and the bottles rolled and chinked to her nimble, sliding steps. The woman trekked across the concrete bridge, the deposit bottles clamoring for food.

Midway across the bridge, she stopped to consider directions. Years of open exposure resulted in skin flaked, dry and as papery brittle and strong-smelling as Spanish onions. She wore three knitted hats, a pair of ill-fitting shoes, which produced tiny wine-grape blisters on the veins of her soiled feet. The bridge she crossed didn't have the familiar flamboyant arches of the Third Street Bridge. In fact, it resembled an ugly bandage of cement suturing together two boulevards. She turned a whole circle compass around, then placed her bag down and pressed her parchment hands and face against the metal girds of the foreign bridge. Her scaly fingers hooked the girds tightly. Instead of the slow-moving rackety rock of the railroad cars, the woman felt the wind-blast speed of freeway traffic vibrating the metal girds. The velocity traveled right through the marrow conduit of her fingers, straight through the thin veil of her onion skin and down to the glass bottles in her bag. All this new construction altered the city into a beast alien to her and she castigated herself for standing on the wrong bridge.

The woman furiously wrestled with ideas of what to do next. The only thing more obnoxious than hunger was thirst, and the only thing more obnoxious than both was being lost at a time when her legs refused their function. She released the girds, hesitated, then grabbed hold of the worn straw handles of her bag and, after a few cautious paces, stopped again, indecisive. The late afternoon clouds above her soaked up the sunlight slowly until the darkness expanded, pulling her farther away from her destination. She rubbed her flaky birdlike eyes hoping to get a reading. Below her, perfect gold coins of vehicle headlights shot across the freeway.

The woman's favorite restaurant stood near the Red Pagoda in Chinatown. The cooks kept live chickens in wire coops against the alley wall, out of sight of customers. She often visited the row of cages secretly, salvaged a handful of eggs from the shedding mounds of feathers by using one finger to flick the wire hook of the cage door, reaching in with a steady, firm arm. The intrusion often caused the chickens to stomp on their own eggs in an infanticidal frenzy. They blinked their thin blue eyelids, pecking her arm until their beaks drew blood, their tattered wings beating as violently as their little rock muscle hearts.

Painted brilliant red and gold-trimmed, the Red Pagoda could be seen from city blocks away. Find the Pagoda and the woman would kill two birds with one stone: get her directional bearings and eat a meal of warm and soupy uncooked eggs. Then she deserved to claim her secret place where she peeled away layered pairs of three: three housedresses, three undergarments, three hats, three overly used brassieres, three sweaters with pockets bulging from tiny and mostly unimaginable, useless personal treasures. Most prized, a ratty-looking beaded coin purse empty but for a few copper pennies and an assortment of unknown pills, some of them so small, they disappeared inside its torn seams. Considered items of discarded trash to some, to the woman her possessions represented a thousand precious ballads which made up one whole operetta worthy of protection and her secret place was more private than any county shelter. Clasping the handles of her bag, off the woman went in search of the Red Pagoda.

Purely by accident, she trespassed the gang member's funnel of lamppost light, a grievous breach, and their silhouettes collided. On a night so destitute there were no stars, she read the presence of the cholo as a premonition and her chest heaved under her three sweaters. He must have been there all along like a crack on the sidewalk, standing near the metal bridge grates. Oblivious, he remained fixated on a spray-can graffiti lizard until the tinkling of glass bottles forced the spiky-headed cholo to jolt. The area was vacant of people except for the two of them, and he stared her down under the post light, his eyes like slits as thin as silver dimes. Was he capable of anything her mind or experience could conjure in moments of clarity? The woman recognized his smell of the streets and looked into the slits of his eyes and she raised a trembling finger to her parched lips to hush any thoughts of him hurting her. Somehow, his eyes didn't fit his face, his face didn't fit his eyes, but he was soon gone, rolled out of perfunctory light, vanished. She scratched behind her neck and then resumed her search, all the while wondering if she had imagined the haunted soul.

The storm left the night bleak and all raw nerves. The bottles chink-chinked as she continued her aching walk. The run-in with the cholo chilled her into a wintry mood—she felt the loneliness of a last leaf awaiting its fall from a bare sprig. Her mental compass gone awry, she resolved to depend on her instincts. The woman found herself following a slavering dog that suffered a rash on its flanks. Sniffing and pawing around the storefront doors, parked cars, abandoned metals and throwaways, the dog resented the intruder, looking over its shoulder periodically to make sure she kept her distance from any edible discovery.

The panting dog passed Fred's Furniture & Income Tax, passed La Malinche Passport Fotos/Yerbería, lifted a hind leg to urinate, continued its prance to the end of the alley and stopped at a door. It clawed and whined, then barked and whined until an arm appeared to toss out a beef bone bare of meat but otherwise chewable and the dog snapped it up in haste as the door closed. Never removing its cautious eyes from the woman, the dog awkwardly dragged the jawful into a corner and instantly gnawed at the bone with lustful bites.

A lightbulb illuminated the small window. The woman saw shadows floating about, some indication of commotion inside. The bone person didn't slam the door with the necessary force to make it stay shut, and thus the rusted lock slipped from its rustier doorjamb and the door yawned open. The light sliced into the dark alley, sweeping the tips of her worn Salvation Army specials. The woman became anxious: aside from her back pain, there was much to consider before entering. But the scent of simmering beef cocido and toasted corn tortillas recalled a distant memory of a very decent meal and so she forgot the Red Pagoda and entered the shabby rooms willfully, the door creaking shut behind her.

She placed her bag of complaining bottles down gently so as not to make too much chinking noise, and sat in the last row of chairs to listen to the preacher. Empty of idols, crucifixes and candles, about two dozen children sat in front, their small heads bobbing. A few of them turned to investigate the noise her entrance created; behind them, a teen sat by herself, an unspecified tumor the size of a Granny Smith apple bulging in the nape of her neck. To the left of the teen sat a couple so emaciated, they leaned on one another, their heads joining together, and to the right, a derelict who mumbled to his thumb. A young man tucked a book tightly under his arm and seemed out of place between a few people, and an older woman with leathery jowls, who had the quirky habit of shaking an empty prescription bottle, looked familiar. All, including the children, sat well behaved.

The weight of search off her feet, the woman slipped out of her shoes and felt contentment bathe over her like childhood summerlust. She couldn't tell if the scent of cocido deceived, or if the ancient preacher speaking in a recognizable tongue was trickery, but the untold of the situation demanded she remain seated, demanded she pay attention to the sense of her arrival. She had fallen, cushioned by a heap of autumn leaves, and experienced a comfort she thought she was incapable of ever maneuvering again.

Wiry, Papa Tomás preached in a gray crumpled suit, the knot on his orange tie dented to one side as if he released the tight noose for breathing. He swayed in front of his small congregation like a worn, rusted weather vane barely able to withstand an exhaustive wind of sermon. Tranquilina and Mama bookended him, on the edge of their seats in case they needed to catch him, to keep him propped up until the sermon's completion. Papa opened a tattered Bible, its corners and leather cover blotched black by the deep oils of fingerprints. His stubbled gray cheeks puffed, he raised the book two inches from his nose, and cleared his throat. Quoting Psalm 22:16, he recited in a voice as groggy as a sun-melted eight-track, for the dogs have compassed me. The assembly of the wicked have enclosed me. They—

Papa inhaled deeply and then closed the book, incapable of another utterance.

As the children in the front row held their palms upward, Papa scraped his throat of one last word, hauling it up with all his strength. He uttered, Amen, for which the parishioners returned shouts of hallelujahs. Papa limped painfully back to the middle chair and sat, his gnarled fingers grasping his Bible as if its pages were made of stuff that kept him afloat.

The woman thrust her palms high, at first shyly, and then with shamelessness, imitating the congregation. Hallelujah, she whispered through the hollows of her missing teeth. Amen! She strained between the bobbing heads to see the cause of Papa's limp. The woman realized the preacher belonged in a postcard just like the Chinese emperor of yesteryear she had seen on the glass window of a curio shop. Papa was barefoot, yellow clumps of flesh caked with calluses, toenails branched out into twisted, browning and unclipped appendages like the claws of a wild bird ready to scoop down and snatch its prey. Consequently, the woman stretched out her arms farther, reached higher, hoping to be taken away.

One of the children sneezed and was hushed by an older one.

The congregation murmured prayers loudly. In this room, there was no secrecy to feelings, no request left solely to God's ear. The woman let her chin fall to her sweater-thick chest. Amen. Let them come across safely. Amen. The tumor is shrinking. Amen. We get stayed wit job. Amen. Twenty cents more for my Thunderbird wine. Amen. Pepe—you and your cousin—please don't find us. Amen. In hopes with the grace and mercy of the Lord, that medical research continues its advances on a cure for this most dreadful disease. Amen. For the war to end. Amen. Sweet Bebu, come home to me safe. Amen. Oh, Daddy, Daddy. Amen.

Her arms ached from holding them upward. Number 10. Tranquilina and Mama resembled a number. Ten had a special meaning to the woman, but why, or to what extent, she couldn't remember. Ten toes, ten fingers, ten bottles? The woman winced, determined not to succumb to the muscle pain of her raised arms. The number kept her mind ablaze until the zero of the number stood up and raised her hands as well to receive the healing power of God. Everyone in the room relinquished complete control, moaning in trancelike absorption of the grace and mercy offered by the sheer invisible electrical force, which zapped the parishioners into trembling flesh. Contorting her mouth, the teen wept and grieved, her tumor slightly breathing, or so it seemed to the woman. Someone coughed. All the women, including the small female children, wore long black shirts or black wraps, and the woman felt conspicuous and hoped no one would notice her exposed ankles.

Tranquilina asked for the congregation to rise and the children jumped up all at once like good soldiers, relieved to be able to move without a scolding, their hands at their sides. The woman pinned her arms down to show how obedient she could be. Tranquilina had asked Mama to say a few words about the quarantine and the roadblocks, but Mama shook her head because their church had no room for a discussion regarding government rules. Her only concession to Tranquilina was to select a song describing lambs in the valley of wolves and so in a burst of deep patriotic furor, the congregation sang "Somos ovejas en el valle de lobos," which was also the refrain the children rejoined. The woman mouthed the words enough to make one believe she knew the song by heart. The service ended and a murmur surfaced like a communal sigh of relief. Not even the sporadic applause woke Papa, who pressed his Bible over his pigeon chest, his bony beak chin falling downward into sleep.

A big pot of steaming cocido, huckaback towels wrapped around the pot handles. The parishioners knew the drill, lined up, children first. Delighted, Mama tied her apron around her thick waist and opened her fatty arms. Come along, Come along, she said, a limp in one corner of her lip. She embraced her faithful brethren, invited them to grab a thick-lipped bowl. Mama ladled the broth, Don't be shy! The clattering metronome of spoons to reach the bottom of the bowl, a lovely rhythm. Rabid with hunger, children lifted their bowls to slurp up the last drops, and then scrubbed the remaining moisture with bits of tortillas, and finally licked their fingers as they rushed to get in line again. Mama motioned for the woman to come closer, and the woman grasped her straw bag and approached the line. Mama mentally raised the total of the congregation by one.

Tranquilina and Mary of the tumor helped the emaciated couple to a table, talking politely across the unhealthy pallor of their faces.

I can feel the Lord's hand on it and it gets so hot, as if it's melting, Mary said, referring to what at first the interns at the General Hospital thought was an unusually large goiter, but turned out to be a mysterious growth, a mutation of cells, the results of its potential malignancy unverified until next week. The teen cupped a jaundiced elbow of the woman-half of the couple, who delicately pinched her skirt so as not to trip on its hem.

Praise God.

Like fire burning it out.

Amen, the man-half added. He wore white spongy shoes and his steps shuttled silently.

Like I'll wake up one day, and it'll be gone.

Yes to that, Tranquilina replied. Here, sit. She pulled out the chair and invited the raspy man-half of the couple to sit. Tranquilina noticed that Ben the student stood away from the meal line and politely refrained from eating.

Mary, can you get their meals?

The children were permitted to eat first, first to ask for seconds, second to ask for thirds until their bellies were fueled with mischief and fearlessness. A few circled around Papa's toenails, trying to poke his bare foot with a spoon. Tranquilina slowly slipped the utensil out of a child's hand.

Out of a habit of convenience that became a necessity, Papa Tomás slept on a folding chair. Because of the crazy burrowing keratin length of his toenails, Papa was incapable of resting in a horizontal position, and slept upright, his callused undersurface of heels so dead-hide tough, Tranquilina actually heard his clicks like hooves on cobblestone when he ambled back to his seat during service.

Tranquilina gently lifted his chin and pressed an enamel cup of broth to his lips. With thousands of lifetime hours clocked in, Papa could barely support the weight of another minute. Erosion burned so that his joints rusted to a standstill, his muscles vanished into threads of flesh and then next to nothing, and the warranties of his functioning organs had expired one by one. Papa fluttered his crusted eyelids. His waxy eyes glossed over his daughter, as if he hadn't seen Tranquilina, but Remedios, a name he wanted to give her at birth. A secret: he held hatred for names beginning with the letter T, his own included. The letter T reinforced the cross they had to bear. Unable to see his daughter as tall and as crucified as the first letter of her name, his head fell heavy on the tips of her fingers.

Tranquilina rustled a pair of children's heads away from Papa by asking for the help of God's little soldiers and immediately the children stood at attention. At her request, the children began collapsing the unused folding chairs. They dragged them noisily, then, finding a game in everything, they began to compete with one another as to who could get the most chairs to the wall. Their excitement crowded out normal conversation.

The derelict asked for seconds, this time for his thumb, and Mama served him extra potatoes, cabbage and squash, saying to him, Help yourself to the tortillas. Her healing jaw soaked up the warmth of the steaming pot. Last in line, the woman held out her bowl. Over the rows of empty chairs, in the corner of the room near the kitchen door, there she stood while Mama ladled broth and filled the woman's bowl, and Ben stared at her, a piercing glance needling in and out of people. He pulled out his beret like a handkerchief from his back pocket, and slanted the leather rim across the overlapping scar tissue of his broken brow line, a remnant of a severe childhood accident.

She could be anyone's mother, Ben said when Tranquilina approached him, his paperback novel clamped under his arm. Over the hubbub, he jutted his chin toward the street woman, who stood in line again. A child, almost tripping on her long black skirt, dragged a folded chair past him, touched the wall and ran to get another.

Where have you been hiding? Tranquilina said, careful not to arouse his suspicion. It's been a while, Ben.

Has it? He acted surprised.

It feels like it.

Hi, Ben, Mary said, carrying a tray with two side-slapping bowls of soup. Either the condensation of the hot soup or Ben's nod of hello swelled a refreshing color to her cheeks. Had it not been for the growth, which caused the lopsidedness of her head, and had it not been for the lopsidedness of her head, which caused the angle of her body to dip and bank as she walked to the couple's table, Mary would've recognized the origin of her ruddy flush as youthful yearning, the source of her uncooperative legs.

Ben glanced at his filthy fingernails. He attempted to clean his thumbnail and then noted how utterly nasty his sticky dregs of palms were. Dressed in dirty blue jeans and brown beret, he seemed thinner than the last time he attended services. Tranquilina would call his sister Ana to let her know he had reappeared.

Just a month before, Ben's condition had deteriorated. He had stopped answering his phone, stopped coming to services and stayed in his apartment day and night. The landlord, being concerned more about the rent past due than Ben's welfare, complained to Tranquilina, who called Ana, who asked that Tranquilina please accompany her to Ben's apartment.

Unlocking his door, the two women realized they were in over their heads; Ben's condition was beyond love and prayer and beyond a cocktail of experimental medication, even beyond the saving grace of poetry. He cowered in the corner of his bedroom, an army blanket wrapped around his shoulders. Within the apartment gunk, Ana uncovered the phone and dialed the Psychiatric Emergency Team to come and rescue her brother. As they waited for the team to arrive, she and Tranquilina cleaned his apartment as best they could.

When PET entered, they bound him and rushed him to the General Hospital, where the two women walked the long winding halls of paperwork and waited as Ben was being "evaluated." The hospital lighting offered the deepest gloom, and beneath the veiled aroma of rubbing alcohol and ammonia in the waiting lounge, a burning pestilence lingered. Ana had recognized the waiting room because it hadn't changed from the time Ben was first rushed into the emergency at the age of eleven. Hit by a cement truck, Ben had remained in critical condition for weeks. She told Tranquilina, Even the magazines are the same. Ana chipped away at her chalk-white nail polish, scanning the dreaded lounge, ready to jump up from her cold metal chair and grab someone, anyone, and strangle them until they begged for dear life.

When the head RN finally called their last name, Brady, Ana sprang over to the cage surrounding the nurses' station. Already agitated, Ana's voice strained through the grids:

Let me get this straight, Ana repeated. Ben can only stay here for seventy-two hours? Tranquilina rested a palm on Ana's padded shoulder to calm her, but Ana jerked away angrily. One earring missing, Ana leaned her open palms on the grid caging the hospital station and stared at the concoction of graveyard-shift tired faces. Listen, you motherfuckers, he needs full hospitalization! Tranquilina gently whispered, Ana. After all the industrial cleaning she had done back at Ben's apartment, Ana's business skirt was dishrag-wrinkled over long rip stretches in her nylons. Are you all crazy? Ana yelled, her voice pushed to the ledge of a ten-hour wait and ready to fall off its edge. Are they crazy, Tranquilina? Old mascara gummed around her eyes. He's suicidal, what more do you need? And with that, Ana had rattled the grids enough to spill a LVN's cup of coffee. Call the fucking police, you do that!

Miraculously, Ben had now returned, standing before Tranquilina, and except for the shadowed half-moons under his eyes, he appeared safe and reasonable as far as she could tell. Tranquilina was genuinely glad to see him.

Go on, Ben said, not listening. I'm listening.

I said, what are you reading?

Ben fumbled the paperback. Oh. This? This is your basic trash. Because he hadn't used his voice consistently, vocal irregularities occurred, audible or inaudible malfunctions like a radio needle in pursuit of a clear station, and Ben sometimes shouted or sometimes swallowed his words, always amazed by his inconsistencies.

One man's trash is another one's treasure, Tranquilina said with a smile. A pause hung awkwardly until the children's work chimed in, giggling and slamming chairs while the parishioners sipped with such haste, one would think they feared the broth would evaporate.

Your name, Mama repeated, holding the full ladle over the woman's bowl. If you want us to know you, what's your name? The question overwhelmed the woman. Mama could as well have asked her how the planets formed or why water was the skin of the earth. Suddenly feeling a wet, dripping sensation on her face, the woman looked up at the ceiling, forgetting that she wore three hats.

I'm sorry, Ben said, his composure slipping, go on, I'm listening.

I said, when will we see you again?

Oh, he said. Okay. I understand. Not for a while. Exams are in two weeks.

What exams? Tranquilina asked. I thought you had taken a leave of absence from the university.

Oh, no. No, Ben replied, shaking his head gravely at the very thought of it. Who told you that?

Tranquilina hadn't a single desire to trip the land mine of rage in Ben's faulty wiring. Ben was nearly comatose the last time she saw him, and Tranquilina assumed he would have taken a leave of absence from school. As an afterthought she said, I must be mistaken.

One child jumped up and snatched the paperback from under Ben's arm and retreated to a quiet corner to flip the pages for pictures. Another kid attempted to grab the book from the first and a tug-of-war ensued.

Give IT back, Ben shouted, annoyed by the child's boldness.

Con cuidado, Tranquilina warned. Now! she demanded, pointing to Ben. The bigger kid, who won the tug-of-war, returned the book reluctantly.

Ben, let's move out of harm's way.

The two moved closer to the table where the couple sat. A long pause.

I better get going.

Tranquilina didn't want him to go quite this soon. So much to query: his health, school, books, medication, disappearances, hallucinations. She cleared her throat: Why the hurry?

In answer, Ben took hold of her hand. Her hand seemed small for her gangly body, and her fingers fell light on his palm. He tightened his grasp, his fingernails unclipped and jagged, and the two stood there among the chatter of the children and the generosity of fellowship and he sandwiched her palm between his own two slush-sweaty hands, without a clue as to why he acted so impulsively. With their mated hands, Ben felt so close to her, so intimate and loving, it took all his reserve not to lift her hand to his lips, not to inhale the scent of godliness he knew he would never achieve. He loosened his grip because he had absolutely no reason to touch her except for his desire to do so, and he instantaneously fell into an old routine:

Posterior dorsal view, Ben recited, turning Tranquilina's palm up as if inspecting it, as if this were the purpose for holding her hand. Now it's the anterior palmar view. Ben pinched the tip of her finger: Distal phalanx. He touched the second joint: Middle phalanx. And this, this is proximal phalanx. He turned her hand again to the posterior dorsal view, studied the swarming skin of her finger knuckles. This is called . . . Do you know what this is called? Ben said, turning up the volume in his voice, though Tranquilina stood only a few inches away.

You tell me.

The knuckle.

Just your basic knuckle, Tranquilina replied, delighted, amused enough to ignore a child who tugged at her black skirt. His own palm was pancake color. Wherever his joints bent, as in his elbows or knuckles, the folds resembled deeply tarnished pennies.

Clanking metal chairs, voices rising over the volume of children. Tranquilina leaned in close to Ben's ear. She glanced over his shoulder at a young boy inspecting Papa's yellow and blackened and tangled toenails from a safe distance. One moment, Mama, ladling the broth and addressing the woman, her lips mouthing in slight spasm; the next moment, the man-half gingerly feeding the woman-half of the couple. Under the light of the room the hurrah of the children high-fiving at the wall of chairs, screaming winners, debating losers. Ben, here, standing before her. A haze of contentment meandered like an aroma thick and sweet and overpowered Ben's smell. So exquisite, so wondrous, Tranquilina fell into despair at how easy it could be destroyed.

Have something to eat before you go, she whispered in his ear and offered the enamel cup full of the soup Papa Tomás had been unable to drink. She leaned close enough to Ben to notice the thin folds of grime on his neck. The manure man had shoved sand, stuffed gravel in a way that was painfully difficult for her to forget, and Tranquilina didn't want to associate Ben's scent with his. Ben didn't specialize in decay and she repeated this to herself; he was not molded in the rot she detected from the rank of his clothes. She knew better.

Tranquilina's childhood forked two memories: heat and prayers. Barely six, she had escaped under houses where temperatures dropped ten degrees less and where the earth, for some reason, had the consistency of gold talc, finely sieved powder with a cool silky texture that was, at once, liquid and solid. Her fidelity to earth, or better, her understanding of miracles came not from Mama's fanatical prayer session, the frequencies of full-throttled worship taking place right above her—a dozen black-clothed women chiseling away sin—but from spent silence in the dankness and dampness of unvisited spaces. Forbidden places teeming with life she could not see. Miracles demanded faith in the unseen, and good earth, handfuls that ran through her fingers, was filled with minute worlds of it.

Tranquilina slowly wrested her hand away from the press of Ben's. Feeling a sense of awkwardness, Ben busied himself by pulling the beret over his forehead again to camouflage the scar.

It's a delicious meal, the man-half of the couple said to Ben, spooning the broth into the mouth of the woman-half. You should take Miss's advice and have some nourishment.

Ben shouted no. Startled, the man-half dropped his spoon, spilling soup on the woman-half's lap. Oh, man. I'm sorry, Ben said. Oh Jesus, I'm SO sorry. A pancake palm grabbing a paper napkin, brushing lightly, briskly, the woman-half's skirt. I'M terrible. This is AWFUL.

It's nothing, really, Tranquilina said, moving close to the table to get more napkins. When she set the cup down, she noticed her fingers trembled and flexed them to halt their disclosure.

Over the table Mama stood grasping her ladle while the woman thought for a minute and realized she had forgotten her own name. How could that be? Had it been that long since anyone asked? Her sole credential, a Social Security card, had her right name, or was it the one she found in a county trashcan? The woman thought to unravel years and shut her eyes from any distraction that would interrupt the memories already sparking like fireflies. Even though water pebbles continued to drop on her head, an annoying warm wetness, the woman's concentration delivered somewhat. She heard a faint voice calling her from between clotheslines of a distant foggy past, but couldn't make out the name.

Finally, the woman shrugged her shoulders. Mama poured another helping of cocido into the woman's bowl.

God bless you.

Ben worked himself into a terrible mood. Another chair slammed shut in the small room and Ben jumped. What have you done to deserve this? he asked, balled napkin between his two hands. By "this" he meant at first his own thoughtlessness, but then realized what he really meant was why were they the ones chosen to suffer such a disease? Did they ever wonder? The man-half replied, Honestly? In all honesty, I no longer ask. Smiling weakly, the man-half turned to the woman-half, dabbed her dribbling lips. The upright chairs piled hastily by the children slid like clattering dominoes to the floor, making loud booming repeating noises, and the parishioners turned from ripping bites of their tortilla to glance at the children, who now stood shamefully alert as if they were in a criminal lineup. The resounding racket hadn't succeeded in waking Papa.

You little weasels, Tranquilina said. You little nutty squirrels! One hand on her waist, the other holding a few napkins, she inspected the mess of chairs, her bare feet kicking out from under the long black skirt. The children shifted on their feet, sullen expressions of remorse on their faces.

Mama, a full ladle of soup extended to give another serving, would have managed to spill the hot broth had it not been for the woman's quick reflexes. The woman kept the bowl under the ladle at all times, chairs clattering or not. She looked deeply into the thinning soup in search of eggs, and then gulped it down, right then and there, and wiped her mouth against her sweater sleeve and asked for more. By the time Tranquilina tended to the fallen chairs and the children assisted in stacking them one by one in the closet (struggling to contain their energy, their faces perspiring with the effort), Ben had vanished.

You all did so good! Tranquilina addressed the children, clapping her palms together. She thought of rewards and went into the bedroom and returned to the children, embracing a cardboard box of clothes, and opened the flaps slowly to raise the anticipation of the children. The children lunged, rummaging through the box just as they had their soup, with urgency and hunger. One child, who moments ago had grown sour at the task of chair duty, discovered a green sweater, and the other children surrounded her to admire the white ducks lined in a row by the front pocket.

Name or not, are you ready to receive the Lord? Mama asked. The woman became anxious over directions: the direction of questions, the direction of her secret place, the direction of salvation; the direction of Mama's plump arms ladling up the last of the limp cabbage, a couple of carrot ends, a few grains of rice. The woman wanted to ask Mama for directions on how to rewire the electricity of her veins to cease the ache, how to put together the children who resembled ripped pieces of paper, how to avoid the wrong someone on the wrong bridge and then how to avoid fear.

The woman began to cry, a tearful quiet wailing, and flakes peeled off her oniony skin. She groped for the tattered remains of a tissue she saved in the pockets of her three sweaters for occasions like this. How could she explain? She felt loose buttons, paper clips, bottle caps, safety pins, but no tissue. How could she tell Mama that chickens and their blue beady eyelids succeeded in making her miserable? Chewed pencil ends, tinfoil folded as neatly as origami. What message did the gang member on the bridge want to deliver before she hushed him and he rolled away? The woman ended her search for tissue and looked up at the ceiling. The drops of water bleeding from the ceiling and pelting her head were, in fact, the tears she could not shed and she gratefully allowed them to roll down her cheeks.

Mary of the tumor tilted her body to keep perfectly balanced in an imperfect world and handed the woman a handkerchief. The whole of her body turned to Mama, always Mama in the hopes that she could arouse a response to shelf the woman's sadness at least temporarily.

I invite you into the Lord's home, Mama said, a banging thump of her ladle inside the empty pot. Give me here. She pulled the bowl gently from the woman's grasp. Mama wiped her hands on her apron, took the woman's hand and grasped it tightly against her own ample breasts, dropped the folds of chins into her chest. In recognition of Mama's prayer work, the children stopped their rascality and circled the two women, a prayer circle, ring around the rosy, their eyes wide and round and somber like black cups of coffee.

Mama's head lowered, extra rings of fleshy chin, she thundered, Dios poderoso, shutting her eyes with such compression, her crow's-feet wrinkles fanned out. This girl's a sinner. I say *You* are merciful! And in *Your* mercy, let her lay her sins at *Your* feet. (Each time Mama emphasized the word *Eres*, her *r*'s drumrolled.) I say she needs a home, and the home is *Yours*.

Well trained, the children raised their palms. Dios poderoso, they shouted like a pledge of allegiance. One child wiggled a tongue nervously, while the one who wore the duck sweater asked, She stink, don't she? Her respondent wrinkled his nose in agreement.

Tranquilina commandeered a high stack of used bowls into the small kitchen, porcelain vertebrae between her two hands. Each trip back to the main room to collect the bowls, she flexed her fingers. Absorbed in the utilitarian purpose, pursuing God's practicality, the cleanup, Tranquilina clasped her hands to hold another collection of bowls, hurried steps back into the kitchen and out again to the main room, gathering the bowls from the tables, then stacking them on the kitchen counter. Returning to the main room, Tranquilina covered her mouth, not in a gesture to behold surprise, but to stifle a gasp at the sight of the woman collapsing like a heap of thrift clothes on the floor, the straw bag emptying of bottles that sprawled and rolled and rippled across the linoleum floor. Or was it the unsettling sight of little girls wearing lovely little deadly black skirts covering their bony knees; of the young boys layering items of clothing like hopeful armor from the box she had just opened? The insufficient light cast shadows on the face of every parishioner, who seemed to be at once bewildered and curious and bored at the woman's convulsions. Suddenly all their faces faded like an indecipherable number on a claim ticket in a pawnshop.

Three children broke the prayer circle to fetch the bottles.

Tranquilina! Mama shouted, shattering Tranquilina's rapt stance. Mama needed assistance, knowing all too well these types of conversions. This was no epileptic seizure. The Holy Spirit entered, forcing evil to spew out like spittle from the mouth of the convulsing woman. The woman's body expelled all her past sins while the rest of the children let their hands fall to their sides and stared blankly at the disheveled figure contorting into a fetal position. A boy tried on the woman's hats and the hats resembled an oversized bell on his small oval head.

Tranquilina believed that boundaries didn't exist between her life and their lives. As a result of this conviction, their ministry affected her and her parents in a big and small way. But she was losing it, letting it slip through, and she flexed her fingers, to grasp, to release, to hold on to handfuls of good sod as a reminder of miracles. She watched the drunken swagger of the derelict, who gulped from the mouth of his paper bag without so much as a glance at Mama, who labored to kneel, one knee, then the other. Her roundness made it so difficult, her chest drew in great wafts of air. Another soul saved, and Mama grabbed on to the woman to restrain her floundering. Tranquilina knew right then that their ministry was no better than another bottle of Thunderbird wine, a quick fix of heroin, another prescription drug for temporal relief, and she stifled her impulse to laugh because she couldn't judge which was more hysterical: the parishioners who had no intention of entering salvation—they simply sought another drug—or the wondrous innocence of children. Having retrieved the bottles, the children lined them up in a battalion of bowling pins.

Wake Papa up! Mama barked at Tranquilina. And make some coffee! Mama barely contained the woman with a bear hug, her lips tightened in serious joy. Tranquilina obeyed, her stamping pads of fast-paced footwork to the end of the room.

Papa was not stirring. Tranquilina pressed her hand over Papa's chest and his heart bolted with astonishing power—enough to dent her palm. But things were not what they seemed and his breathing was shallow; full seconds passed between his inhale and exhale.

Wake him! Mama shouted. I've had a healing!

Papa, gaunt, was lighter now, as thin as bending light gliding from one dream world to the other. Tranquilina touched the darkened discoloration, which remained on the bridge of his nose from the assault. Seconds later, Papa exhaled. Such a small, quiet expiration indignantly dwarfed against the enormousness of one lifetime.

Tranquilina didn't know it was his last until it was. As long as her feet stood grounded, Tranquilina felt the wounds of the earth widening beneath from hairline cracks into gorges of open sobbing pain and her knees buckled. She laid her head on the desert-hard knees of her dear father's lap. When she tilted her head skyward, she saw the children's eyes like spinning orbs, their celestial bodies big and small orbiting outward and away from her, so very far away.

SIX

Ben's father dropped him off at the First Street Store to buy himself a new pair of tennis shoes for gym class. Thinking that eleven was old enough to start a different middle school in September, his father ordered Ben to go shopping alone. Handing him a five-dollar bill, his father gave him one hour, no more, no less, to buy the shoes and meet him on the corner of First and Rowan after his purchase.

Do it or else, his father wanted to say, a sink-or-swim philosophy, a lesson of survival he developed from the army. Instead he ordered:

Don't dillydally.

Ben stood under the newly installed traffic light to watch the black exhaust of his father's pickup muffler as it sped away. Cars and people crossed the streets without paying much attention to the new traffic signals, unaccustomed to having green to yellow to red lights telling them what to do. Ben didn't move until the red pickup and his father disappeared down the First Street hill and then he loitered a few minutes more.

One hour. Ben never went shopping by himself. As his father had slipped out the five-dollar bill from the wrinkled lips of his wallet, Ben wanted to confess his inexperience. He always shopped with his mother, or his older sister Ana, or both, but never ever alone. Nonetheless, his father felt he was old enough, and so Ben finally walked to the department store shoving the Lincoln bill into his faded denim pocket because his father expected results.

Ben's plan was to walk around the store for an hour until he rendezvoused with his father. They were too expensive, he'd say when his dad returned in less than fifty-three minutes. Even before his father slipped money out of his wallet while the pickup idled and forced the pennies to clackety-clack in the metal ashtray, Ben had not felt like himself. Even before Ben begrudgingly opened the squealing rusted scab of door to do as his father commanded, he somehow knew this was only the beginning.

Don't dillydally, his father said and lowered the radio broadcast reporting on Renata Valenzuela, pennies clacking.

They didn't have my size, he'd say, rehearsing the line as he got out of the pickup cab and slammed the dented door shut. They didn't have the shoes, he'd say, even as he stared at the cracked taillight patched with duct tape. And in no time, Ben stood in front of the First Street Store, his lungs pumping air to inflate his courage. The Saturday noonday sun, the bargain **BACK TO SCHOOL** sale, beamed against the thick glass doors. Ben felt gently tossed about and buffeted between the arriving and departing shoppers, between the push of rustling bags, the pull of jovial money-savers.

Inside the large department store, the cash registers jumped and tallied, an intercom carried the nasal voice announcing a sale on Hoover vacuum cleaners and the noisy hum of shoppers to-ing and fro-ing made Ben feel anxious. He seemed incapable of moving and squinted downward to see if his old comfortable Converse sneakers were buried in the nibbling water-blue carpet. All he had was a five-dollar bill to plug up the sinking feeling in his chest. Ben's first desire was to stand right there for the next forty minutes until he could say, They didn't have my size. His second desire was to go home and sit at the kitchen table with a glass of buttermilk dotted with pepper while his mother made tortillas.

You're old enough, that's for sure, Ben's father said, before inserting the key in the pickup ignition, before slipping out the five-dollar bill. And since Ben seemed old enough, he decided to flow into the labyrinthine world of racks and bargain sales and layaway plans, just like everyone else. His hands deep in his pockets, Ben strolled between the racks of dresses, skirts and blouses, shirts. He sidestepped for a wheeling baby carriage and then made room in the main aisle for a string of whining children being dragged by their shirt cuffs.

The denim hem of his father's blue jeans dragged against the carpet. Money had to be saved (wear my jeans) and shoes had to be purchased (you're old enough) while on sale. Cuffs and sleeves and whirls of skirts jumped and bumped him. Ben evaded a tall salesman with a gray whisk-broom mustache by pretending to inspect the folds of men's slacks. Once the mustache brushed past, Ben moved on in search of a face clock.

In Housewares, pots and pans hanging on hooks gleamed as new and shiny as Christmas ornaments. Dish sets, spoons, glassware were on display over a polished dining room table whose legs were thickset and varnished as smooth as his mother's razor-shaved legs.

Ana can't go with you, his father had said, forking a mouthful of steaming scrambled eggs in the hole of his beard. You're on your own. Ben's father learned self-reliance from the Oklahoma flatlands, where he spent his first seventeen years and then because he was on his own, he joined the army. An important survival lesson in case a wife disappears and a man is left with two children to raise in foreign territory. Ben glanced at his breakfast, cold and shriveled and untouched on the plate and he shivered his leg until it was time to hop into the pickup.

Ben sat at a dining room table display to rest. The table and the dishware reminded him of his mother and he thought of her tamarind hair, her gelatinous embraces. A man wearing a bow tie and who couldn't have been much older than Ana asked him to leave the display alone.

I'm waiting for my dad, Ben said, shivering his leg to such an extent, the dishware on the table chinked.

Yeah, well, if you break it, you buy it. The man hooked a finger at the collar of his tie and tugged. Your dad will like that just fine! he said in a tone to suggest it was all Ben's fault for his tie fitting so tightly.

Ben felt unwelcome.

I'm looking for shoes.

This is Housewares, the man replied, thinking Ben was too slow to know.

I know, Ben said and got up to leave. The man's eyes rode heavy on Ben's back. He perspired inside his baggy pullover sweatshirt. Ben moved about in the aftermath of the **BACK TO SCHOOL** sale, where looted racks were now empty of merchandise. His hands in his pockets, he wandered aimlessly, his head down, trudging between the aisles. Blotches of old gum, spilled drinks, specks of leftover peoplewreck drifted on the sea-blue carpet.

Ben ended up in Cosmetics. Eye shadows and nail polishes and lipsticks and blushes and brushes were on display in a mosaic of colors that exploded on the wall. Some of the colors were subtle in shades, while others were so bright, they shouted at him to stop, look and admire the technicolors. He realized that he shouldn't be standing in Cosmetics admiring the colors unless he stood with Ana or his mother or both, because his father or the Mexican boy would find out. And he didn't want that to happen again.

Ben knew he was an easy target to hate. In the lunchroom there was always someone who hated him. Somehow, by the way he wore his T-shirt, the way he bit into his sandwich, the way he pronounced his last name, there was always someone who needed to hate him. That was why his father had enrolled him in another middle school.

As Ben dressed that Saturday morning, he laced up his faithful sneakers and didn't think a new pair were necessary. He wanted to say as much, challenge his father, who was not accustomed to challenges, but there seemed to be no way out of his dad's order. Though the shades were pulled down over their bedroom window, the sun broke the edges into thin lines. He heard Ana's hum of sleep as he knotted his laces. Bacon fat and coffee wafted under the bedroom door and then his father shouted to hurry up.

He wanted to hurry out of Cosmetics, but his sneakers slogged through the aisle and by the time he arrived in Fabrics, his sneakers anchored behind the large multicolored panels of patterned fabric. Above the wide cutting table, he checked the big face clock nailed to the wall—Ben had thirty-one minutes left of his hour. A half hour ago his lungs felt overpumped and ready to burst like the inner tube of his bike tire. Now he was deflated, flat, fixed and watching a saleswoman measure yards of blue flannel by extending her arms over her chest. She then grabbed a pair of sharp shears. The broad-shouldered woman began the deepening cut and parting of the flannel's deep blue sea, the mouth of metal severing the silence of cloth. Her fingers were as heavy and accurate as the metal shears. The rhythmic blades' severing sounded deep and sorrowful to Ben.

What can I do for you? the scissors woman asked, pleasantly but without looking up. Ben had been positive no one had noticed him. Just as he was about to ask where the Shoe Department was located, a rumpled customer to his left replied.

Can you tell me how much? The older customer held up embroidery threads as stringy as the thinning hair on her head. The smiling scissors woman stopped her shearing to check. Ben fingered the wrinkled Lincoln bill and then shoved the bill way inside one pocket, and the money felt as unimportant as a gum wrapper. Only after the woman returned to work did she realize the pair of shears was nowhere to be found. She lifted boxes containing cones of laces, pushed aside racks with spools of thread, then checked below the blanket of the flannel, her face becoming flustered in the hunt. Finally, as the woman investigated under the cutting table, Ben's stomach unhinged. He wished for the courage to reveal to her the location of the missing shears. It unhinged him to see her determination turn into annoyance, however, and he sought out the men's room.

In the stall, he released runny stools and stayed seated, reading and studying the graphics carved into the door, until he was sure the entire bathroom was vacant. Opposite the stained urinals, he washed his hands in one of the sinks and dried them on his jeans. He was always startled to see himself in the mirror, the round nut-brown face, the black military crew cut his father razored every four weeks, his thick neck protruding from a bulky gray sweatshirt washed too many times. Ana resembled his father, but Ben took after his mother. His body didn't seem to coincide with the way his entrails felt—pinkish and raw and gummy—and sometimes when he hurried past the lockers at school, he didn't recognize his reflection.

After exiting the bathroom, Ben caught sight of wooden racks that exhibited the plastic legs of bodiless women in the Hosiery section of the department store. The shapely legs stood above the packets of suntan or soft black or burnt ash stockings and were lined up in a neat row, reminding Ben of the ﹖ Sullivan dancers sticking their legs out from heavy velvet drapes. ﹖ ﹖mach bloated. Ben tried not to think of his mother walking th﹖ ﹖l by herself. Since the beginning of

June, his mother had disappeared and Ben had spent the summer sleepless over her. Then, in August, a maintenance worker who was pitchforking trash in the city landfill discovered the remains of a body.

Don't dillydally, his father had instructed, turning down the news update of Renata Valenzuela of the Maravilla Projects while idling on the street corner, the pennies in the ashtray clacking unmercifully. It rattled Ben not to know the end of the report on the investigation into Renata's disappearance.

The police had interviewed her classmates, and Ben regretted hardly speaking with Renata throughout the years as they passed in the playground or shared a table in the school cafeteria. Both were sixthgraders, but assigned to different rooms. The last time he saw her, it was photo day and she wore punctuated curls. Renata's ponytail could not restrain the kinkiness of her hair. Her bangs curled up into tight zeros.

The day of the school photos, most of the kids wore starched white shirts or Sunday dresses and played with restrained calmness at recess to keep their clothes looking crisp, their hairdos from undoing. After the photographs, the kids went berserk, sparkling in their own bliss on the playground, unbuttoning skirts, kicking off good shoes, a roiling, toiling commitment to the games they were now allowed to play. Ben called a tetherball court. Renata held second.

Before Ben found his father in the living room and before his father simply said, Mama's gone, his blue eyes looking for a place to settle down, and before his father turned on the television again, Renata and Ben played tetherball near the four square. Renata swirled her hip delicately to fist the tetherball and the hem of her plaid skirt slogged back and forth. When she fisted the ball, he noticed that she wore a thin wristwatch. Ben was impressed—she was his age and worried about time! She also won two out of three games. Barely five words spoken between them as she glanced at her watch and said she was late (to what, he should have asked and regretted this too) and grabbed her satchel, her ponytail swaying on the back of her white blouse. In fact, everyone remembered the blue pleated skirt, white blouse, Brillo curls because the photo was published in the front right-hand corner of the *Eastside Tribune.*

Ben convinced himself that any d   His st   streets a   'd discover his mother's mutilated body, a victi   ng people.

Somehow, the dead man found in the dump and his mother and Renata fell together so that Ben drilled himself into a well of anxiety, conjuring up the kidnapper hacking away at his mother's legs, Renata's arms. As each class period at school passed, Ben could not think of anything other than his dismembered mother until lunch period when the Mexican boys would start jeering him.

First it was his last name, Brady, in a roomful of Rodríguezes and Pérezes and Holguins. Who the fuck did he think he was? White, did he think he was white? And then it was his sandwich, the way it looked to the Mexican boys. Ana made him a peanut butter and jelly sandwich, and it was all smashed, strawberry bleeding through the white bread. It got stuck on the roof of his mouth when one of the Mexican boys pushed him hard in the lunchroom.

Shit, your mama is darker than dirt, man, dirt on my shoes.

I don't care.

You ain't white! said the bald-headed one, keeping watch.

I know.

He don't even care.

Whatta tub of lard.

You know whatta pendejo is, pendejo?

Get off my foot.

You don't even care.

I don't care.

Fucken girl. The lizard boy sneered so close to Ben's face he could smell his words. Lime Jell-O.

Fucken pinche puto.

Let go.

Your mama's a chingada. What 'bout that?

So what?

Whatta you gonna do 'bout that?

Nothing.

Yeah?

He ain't worth it, said the bald-headed one. Let's make like a tree.

By the end of the school day, Ben ran, his Converse sneakers pounding up and down the hills of the Eastside to get home, knowing in his heart his mother would be dead because in the lunchroom he had done nothing to defend her. White? Did he think he was white?

Couldn't they see he had the skin of his Mexican mother muddied all over him? But at night he prayed dearly, consistently, ferociously for her forgiveness.

I'm sick of this bullshit, his father said. I'm up to here with you! And he slashed his forehead with his hand. Mama's not coming back, he yelled the night before Ben went shopping alone. We make do or die, hear me?

Ana followed Ben to the roof. He lay on his back, the sandpaper shingles scraping like granules of salt through his thin cotton T-shirt. He hid his tears by turning toward the sky and trying to figure out which were city lights and which were stars on the tar-dark Friday night before his father had ordered him to get rid of his old shoes. Looking up at tiny stars between the crisscross of wires, Ana said they were really God's little eyes guarding you.

Prove it, he challenged, because no one had been guarding Renata. Ana pretended she didn't hear him. Ana resembled Father and her ginger hair spun around her neck with a rising breeze. His dad even said it once. She reminds me of me, he said, proudly pitching his thumb to his heart.

Jewelry, Ladies' Accessories, Watches. Ben ran his sweatshirt sleeve under his nose. When his mother spoke, Ben saw them hold her in contempt. God's little eyes not guarding his mother when she had asked for extended credit at the Friendly Shop and the Japanese owner studied her face. Or when she went into the dry cleaner's to pick up Father's Sunday suit without the whole amount, the clerk had threatened to call the police. Like God, they all remained unkind and undeserving of her. And his father was no different. Before his cheeks turned the color of rage and he informed them of her disappearance, before he resumed watching television again, Ben's father had referred to her as a slut.

Ben pressed his face against the cool case housing the assortment of watches, and noticed that another ten minutes had passed. Time was now running downhill. There was no space left for excuses, and he seriously considered going to the shoe section in the northeast corner of the store. Gas swirled in his stomach. Conjure the words to say size eight, bring the vocal cords to vibrate a sound. He wasn't himself, though he should try, try and take a look, ask for a size, try on a pair, just in case, so that his father wouldn't hold him in contempt.

Ben's father forbade him from sneaking into Ana's bed, but he did anyway and she smoothed his hair with the brush of her fingers. She tried to explain, once again, in her wise and maturely incomprehensible way, that Mama left because, well, she needed to leave and, well, you know, everything's gonna be okay. Prove it, he said and lay next to her in the darkness of their small bedroom trying not to fall asleep for fear his father would find him in his sister's bed. Outside, a new lamppost shone, and the window of their bedroom resembled a boxed sun. It's all a game, his older sister Ana said as she turned to the wall, her solid curve of back a warm mass of blue flannel. Like hide and seek. Only Papi lost her this time.

No blisters, mister, Ben practiced, among the rows of headless and armless mannequins in the Lingerie aisle. Mutilated torsos as pink as a puppy's belly and fitted with fine black cobweb lace and cat's-eye bras made Ben swallow hard, and he touched the cool metal hardness of the shears in his pocket for reassurance.

Can I help you? a brassy voice asked. Two big brown eyes magnified by a pair of bottle-thick glasses peeked over the tall stacks of bras and garter belts and girdles. The voice startled Ben, and his hand flung loose, bringing down a stack of boxed Playtex bras. The gaping head belonged to a saleswoman too old to be working anywhere, much less on the main floor of a department store. She stood behind the rack and all he could see was her head. Extra folds of skin hung on her cheekbones and her face begged to be touched when she smiled.

He shook his head no. No, she couldn't help. Ben looked downward. Spread across his sneakers, he discovered an array of beaming white-coned breasts returning his stare with gratifying smiles. Feeling not like himself, he needed to go to the closest men's room before he exploded again.

My, my, my, she said at the fallen boxes, at Ben's hot cheeks. Her hair massed like clumps of cotton balls and her bobbing head seemed to float in the air as she moved between the plastic torsos. Her slow fragile body materialized from around the rack. Ben pictured her sitting at a kitchen table, just like the one on display in Housewares, her old lady's feet resting in fuzzy slippers. Instead, the elderly woman began to pick up the boxes. To steady herself, she held on to the wooden rack and Ben heard her joints snapping like twigs from her laborious bending. Ben felt suddenly saddened by how cruel the world could be.

On Saturday morning, before they walked out of the house, before Ben followed his father into the pickup truck, Ben thought of God's little eyes. Groping in the vague light for his favorite pair of sneakers, Ben wondered what happened to the stars and moon once night was over.

Ben said, I'm . . . I'm looking for a new pair of shoes.

Oh, she said, not disturbed by the snap and crack of her knees, the shoe department is in the back. Her gold locket fell between the wrinkly bark of her chest when she straightened. Tell Nicky it's Doreen that sent you. He'll treat you good.

Miss, what time is it? The words strained from between his teeth. The woman opened the gold locket.

Twelve of, she said. Already? My, my, she said.

Twelve minutes left, just twelve, and Ben realized he hadn't even tried to get his new pair. Just a half hour ago, time was so slow. Now it seemed too rushed, too crazy fast for him to think clearly, and he bit his thumbnail.

He tried jogging to the back of the store but the shears stuffed in his pocket bounced bulky and stiff and he could feel the metal slap against the flash of his thigh. One rapid swipe to steal the shears, one, and the thievery made Ben stop short of transgressing the carpet demarcation of the shoe department.

The shoe trees exhibited clogs and pumps with heels as thin as carpenter nails, and yellow shoes and fuzzy slippers, which were hooked onto racks and hung like animal pelts, and there were new Beatle boots and feathery mules and miniature shoes for little children.

You're old enough, that's for sure, his father had said while jingling his jacket for the sound of his truck keys.

Ben caught his breath and willed himself invisible behind the luggage, purse racks, wallets and briefcases. Mr. Nicky, Doreen sent me, he practiced as he fondled a price tag on a briefcase. He studied prices on the tags haphazardly, zipped and unzipped in an attempt to behave like a shopper, to feel himself normal, to walk up to Nicky and say Doreen—or, wait, was it Dora?—sent him. But the shears pulled him down with gravitational force, a reminder of an irreversible action, and sweat, reams of it, singed the sides of his cheeks.

Ben assumed the one salesman was Nicky. He wore a wrinkled cotton plaid shirt and a loud floral necktie, which competed in global color with the centerpiece on the display dining table in Housewares. Nicky shoehorned a black and white oxford shoe on a grimacing young girl who sat beside her mother. It seemed obvious to Ben that the necktie was too obnoxiously long and Nicky kept flinging it over his shoulder to get it out of the way.

Don't dillydally, his father had said. And yet, that was all Ben did, with only a few minutes remaining. What was he thinking? There was absolutely no way he could face his father without holding a pair of new sneakers. What words would his father say to punish him this time?

Across the bench from Nicky's two customers, Ben spied a small boy waiting patiently for his five-year-old sister as she tried on her oxfords. He rocked his rubber sandals back and forth, rearranged his buttocks on the bench, yawned to break the boredom of waiting. Three, maybe four years of age, the boy seemed greatly content, and Ben suspected his contentment was due to what he clutched by the neck of his paper bag. Except for his active little piercing eyes, he didn't move from his bench.

Ben watched him watch.

The small boy scanned everything, studying the movement of a body passing, the hem of a dress, the bow of a shoelace. What caught Ben's attention was the boy's intense fascination with little unimportant things like the way Nicky's lips dipped when he spoke, or the way the paper sack creased when he tightened his grasp, the way his mother's fingers robotically moved in rhythm to create a loop that wove into a bow that tied his sister's new shoe, all this while rocking his sandals back and forth.

Nicky reappeared from behind a counter balancing three more shoeboxes. Unfolding the tissue of the top box, he brought out a black shoe, then flicked his tie back to lace the shoe, and Ben watched how the small boy studied the flick of necktie, lacing of shoe. Both the mother and Nicky huddled around the girl, opining on the fit and style.

Ben realized the boy studied him. Ben had thought himself invisible until he felt the boy's charcoal eyes burrowing through his musty sweatshirt. Dead-set eyes right on him, X-raying him, skinning him.

The raspy wheeze in his breathing sounded like the very old woman when she picked up the bra boxes. Ben's sneakers were unable to move from behind the construction boot display and luggage, to run away, even if it meant running back to his father empty-handed.

In the spark of impulse, a rapid swipe of one hand, Ben coaxed the small boy with a hooked finger. If the boy had turned to tell his mother, if the boy had pointed at Ben, Ben wouldn't have known what to do. The boy's forehead frowned in query; baffled, he continued gazing. Then, just before Ben had to meet his father, just before disappointment set into his father once again, Ben saw the boy's small cherub face light up. The boy's lip drew a smile and he turned to his mother and then to his sister, who was busy scrutinizing a mirrored reflection of a third pair of shoes. And then, angling his head in thought, he suddenly turned to search out Ben.

Ben, queasy and frightened, released a handle of the Samsonite, unaware that he had been clenching it. The heaviness of the shears had torn through the cotton lining of his pocket, and the sharpened ends of the scissors scratched against his thigh like a seismic needle scribbling on a Richter scale. The boy slowly climbed off the bench, the sounds of his rubber flip-flop sandals absorbed by the carpet. Clutching the bag for dear life, the small boy quietly joined Ben.

Ben took the boy's plump, moist hand. It was a generous hand, soft and giving and damp. How easy it was for the small boy to slip his sweet hand into Ben's, and then tighten his grasp with unquestioning devotion. He looked up at Ben, amazed, delighted at the invitation for adventure, enjoying the secret they shared. Ben tugged up his father's jeans, and then the two began to run.

At first they trotted through the racks of clothes, light-footed, as if they ran to catch the ice-cream man, then shamelessly gathered speed, whipping by the racks of phantom dresses and legless slacks. The shears snipped violently against his flesh and the rhythmic sound of his breathing was deep and exhilarating as they reached the front of the store.

Ben pushed open the glass doors with an incredible one-palm thrust. He turned to the idling red pickup at the corner of First and Rowan, its cracked taillight patched with duct tape, and then ignored the pickup's exhaust, and turned his back. He began running in the opposite direction to the chaos of the new traffic light that no one obeyed. Ben and the boy ran, scissoring their legs on the newly paved streets, little awkward bodies receding on the pickup's rearview mirror like brief sparks of sunbursts. Tumbling downhill to the intersection, no turning back, bang bang of the hollow drum of the small boy's bag, his sandals clackety-clacking against the cement sidewalk just like the pennies in the ashtray of the pickup waiting on the corner of First and Rowan.

The boy slipped and whimpered, rubbing his knee, and Ben tried to catch his breath, and only for a second, because they should never dillydally. God's little eyes watching, Ana had said, running her fingers through his hair, before he was ordered to get rid of his old pair of Converse sneakers. The boy called out, Mama, and Ben wrapped the cloth of his own mother's skin around the tired weight of the small boy. Calmed by the glossy red to yellow to green traffic lights that shone like wet, slick, colorful lollipops, Ben hoisted the child up and leaped off the curb into the tar darkness of the starry night, their bodies like splitting atoms of white sunburst against the chrome steel bumper grille of a speeding cement truck.

God's little eyes guarding them from everybody, except themselves.

After the church services, Ben hobbled along the concrete ravine of the city's riverbed for a few miles. A narrow rivulet collected from the freakish storm, and the low-riding level of rancid water allowed the full viewing of the spray-painted placazos tagged on the ravine walls. His bad leg pained him as he reached a boulevard of small novelty stores and Chinese restaurants. In celebration of something Ben wasn't privy to, snapping, popping strings of Chinese firecrackers floundered on the pavement like fish out of water in front of the Red Pagoda. The noise and firecracking sulfur forced him to cross the street and his skull swelled against his beret. He widened his stride, a compensating drag of one leg, to reach the other side of the Interstate freeway. He crossed the Friedman Bag Company parking lot and headed for Fifth and Crocker, to the five-story redbrick apartment building, number 501. By the time he got to his door, he arrived with a full-blown migraine.

Even as he pushed the key to unlock his door, he resisted entering his apartment. Against his craving for daylight, he needed darkness for his migraines and accumulated stacks of books, newspapers, dishes, cassette tapes, clean and grubby laundry mounted together to create blockades for this purpose. Avoiding the light switch, Ben stumbled through the path of unoccupied space, felt a slip of magazine under-foot, a misstep sending a tumbler against the wall, his hands groping to reach his easy chair. His body conformed into its familiar cushions. Ben flipped off the tourniquet of his beret, and then tilted his head in the darkness to let the pain run its dazzling course.

Ben suffered the first of his headaches following the traffic accident. In the orthopedic ward he regained consciousness, slowly fluttering his eyelashes until he saw the light of dawn. His neck felt embraced in a tight, muscular headlock of bandages and surgical tape. His left leg was suspended above him in a hospital sling. A metal rod pierced be-neath his kneecap.

His nostrils flared to inhale the scent of warmed-over coffee. Through the turban of gauze, he heard the faint music of the radio from the neighboring bed and knew that this was not Ana's bed. Ben opened his eyes wider to see that parts of his body were braced or in warm shells of plaster of Paris casting, and then just as he became aware of the sling's chink of chain, the smell of coffee, the itch on his nose, an excruciating pain shot out from the crushed kneecap and zoomed like the speed of light all the way up to his mangled skull. A commotion of unbearable agony, the train of curtain rings crashing open STAT, nurses puncturing his vein with a steel-cool syringe.

Before his eyelids fell into a heavy drug-induced sleep, Ben called out for his mother.

Days passed as nights and vice versa for weeks. His body became a junkyard of parts. He could see his headache sparking, hear his bones denting, feel the burn-chill of steel braces welding into his skin. His body was so noisy it kept him awake. He tried to be very still. The metal bedpan was always too cold.

One day or one night Ben heard a man's voice: Do you copy? the voice kept asking. Ben strained through the bandages to listen. He opened his eyes and nodded slightly. The stranger had borrowed a chair from another patient and straddled it like a horse, waiting for Ben to wake fully.

Benny boy, you hear me?

Underwater audible.

The man told Ben he was a reporter for the *Eastside Tribune*. Not much pay, the reporter reported, but he liked the work because it gave him an opportunity, you know, to give back. The reporter asked him if he was thirsty and Ben didn't answer, and then he asked Ben if he believed in luck. He told Ben about luck, about how his editor boss sent him to the hospital to cover a story of an Eastside Mexican woman who gave birth to her eleventh child when Ben had been wheeled into emergency. Just by luck, the reporter watched the action, and decided right there that Ben was the bigger story. The reporter really hoped Ben could hear him, because he wanted to be the first to congratulate him.

They were both lucky men.

The reporter proudly displayed the clipping of the accident published in the *Tribune* almost three weeks earlier. Ben winced his crusted eyelashes and then focused on his school photo placed on the front page of the newspaper, next to a photo of a Marine killed in the line of duty. That's what the reporter told Ben. Gilbert Durán was the Marine's name. From City Terrace Flats, from just down the street where Ben lived. A hero killed in the line of duty by the Viet Cong.

Gilbert Durán was not a lucky man.

You remember anything? the reporter asked. Ben's head pulsated. The reporter slipped a stick of Spearmint gum into his mouth, chewed and snapped and then recounted the events leading up to the dramatic accident. The reporter had an exclusive with a butcher, his name started with an O—now, what was it? The butcher was walking to El Zócalo Fine Meats and saw it all. Snap of gum, jaw muscles ribbing on his cheeks, tight like heartbeats, and then the reporter paused before recounting the butcher's story in one sentence.

Ben had courageously attempted to save a small child from the dangerous traffic, the butcher related, only to be hit by a cement truck. Bigtime hero, the reporter said, chewing jawbones churning over the gum. Groggy, Ben wanted the reporter to stop, to shut up, wanted to say the facts were all wrong. What happened to the kid? Ben wanted to ask. The reporter rolled his gum in his mouth slowly, contemplating Ben's reaction. As if he read Ben's mind, the reporter looked down at his shoes.

The kid didn't make it.

Ben's tears stung his asphalt-grated cheeks. What had the boy done to deserve this? Poor, poor little kid.

Now, now, the reporter said, tapping Ben's wrist where the cast ended. You're one brave young man.

The reporter began to read from the news clipping. He reminds me of me, the reporter read his father's quote. His neck in a brace, Ben could barely turn his eyes away from the hypocrisy of his father's pronouncement. Ben could hear his father saying, He reminds me of me, could see him reeling his thumb to his chest. The thought became as draining to Ben as the blood-drawing syringe the nurse administered while the reporter kept chomping his Spearmint in earnest, reading out the printed lies.

Finally, Ben closed his bloodshot eyes and faked slumber. Nauseated at finding himself a hero not killed, he shut his eyelids until he heard the vinyl wheeze from the lifted weight of the reporter. By the time Ben opened his eyes again, it was after midnight. He saw the gauzy light of the hospital corridor via the nylon curtain, and for once he became grateful for the deliverance of peaceful dark.

Convalescing at the General Hospital's "Broken Bone Ward" involved equal parts of boredom and pain. Some patients brought TV sets or radios from home, while others languished in their metal harnesses, lucky to have a visitor, luckier to have a candy striper volunteer available to roll a bed down the hall to the pay phone. Ben remained suspended by slings, which kept his bones in place for another two months. Once his head bandages were removed and replaced with smaller portions of gauze, Ben could read, oblivious to the noise-making, steel-grinding, bowel-grimacing and pain-whining of the other ten patients in the room.

One day Ben awoke to find Renata Valenzuela.

He remembered that his father had turned down the radio news update about Renata, and Ben never learned the end of her story. She sat next to his bed. As always he found it difficult to converse. She smiled the same school photo smile, curls punctuating her forehead, a lovely girl who had seemed inconvenienced by the disruption of her tetherball playing. Having an appointment she was late for, she ran off, only to stop for someone who psssted her into nothingness.

She kept Ben occupied, and thus kept his pain under control.

During the long hospital days that turned into weeks, then into months, Ben and Renata played the memorization game with *Life* magazines gift-wrapped like Tootsie Rolls and brought by his sister Ana. Ben memorized advertisements, prices, sales, telephone numbers and then turned to anatomy texts that were readily available in the doctors' lounge and readily delivered by the nurses, who didn't want to be called on so often. With Renata's help, Ben compiled, filed and stacked towers of information so high in his mind, only those thoughts that had the bold consistency of invading sunlight could enter, only those with the capacity of sneaking into the thinnest of crevices could materialize.

Remarkable, Dr. Gale said. Ben practiced on Renata daily, reciting the anatomical names of the bones he memorized from the *Gray's Anatomy* book. Dr. Gale examined Ben's bloated and bruised face between the swaths of gauze, shone a beam of light into the pupils of his eyes as if searching for the root of such brain power. Renata became his scaffold, the bars and clamps that kept Ben from collapsing completely like the buildings being pulverized one block at a time by the iron wrecking ball making way for the Interstate freeway. But once the braces were removed and the gauze snipped with the cool, sorrowful sound of hard steel against his tender, shielded face, Renata disappeared again. Her looming smile, her kinky hair coiling on her forehead, all gone, and her lace collar rumpled deeply under the crease of the folded and unfolded newspaper clipping he had saved in his wallet. Sadly, all of her was gone again and Ben doubted he could survive her disappearance a second time.

Do you remember Renata? Ben asked Ana a few days before his hospital release. The bandages had left his skin pale and moist and doughy. He studied Ana's silhouette against the pea-green hospital wall. The crowded hospital room smelled faintly of feces. A soggy-edged straw gaped from the spout of a lukewarm carton of milk on his bed tray. Ana had a dazed expression, her mind not present in the conversation. She poked her head out from her shorthand steno book.

What?

Renata Valenzuela, do you remember her? Ben asked.

Who?

The one who disappeared.

Whatta you mean?

She's been visiting me.

Ana wondered about the visitors' book and the blankness of the page. Not even Father's name appeared.

You had a visitor?

It's nothing.

No, tell me. Who visited you?

Forget it.

Their futures were already set in motion. Resting his head on the hospital-issued pillows, Ben turned to Ana's slouched body, her pencil point urgently scratching against her practice steno tablet, trying to make sense out of the curves and curls of shorthand.

Ana looking up from her steno tablet to see her little brother welded together, but not holding up well. And she touched his hand.

Father, nowhere in the room, plowing their futures: *Webster's Collegiate Dictionary* and a *Roget's Thesaurus, Gray's Anatomy* for his son; a typewriter for his daughter. A new desk awaiting his son's return, a pair of flat heels for his daughter. Moneymaking career for his brilliant, brave son; a job for his daughter. In the years to come, Ben's father would push Ben as someone whose intelligence would raise the Brady family to levels of professional respectability while Ana would be relegated to being the gatekeeper.

The contestant clock set, Mama hid and Father sought. In the Brady family, only one child would swim, the other sink.

As dusk approached through the large wired windows of the room, Ana's silhouette faded into the green hospital wall. Only the sound of her pencil scratching gray whirls on lime paper remained as darkness swallowed her. It fascinated Ben, how cruel the world could be.

By the time Ben graduated from James A. Garfield High School, he had become an Eastside celebrity a second time for his near-perfect SAT scores. In a community rife with conflict and upheaval, Ben's story was a lapse, a breather, a burning reminder of individual accomplishment against all the odds. Demonstrators who protested for a better education held Ben up as an example of someone with the capacity to achieve because of Chicano alma and corazón. To those who believed protesting was a waste of time, Ben exemplified hard work and no excuses. While others, like Father Germán, proclaimed the scores a miracle, and another photo flashed of the priest, handing over a green leather Bible to the high school senior. NOT A MIRACLE, JUST LATE-NIGHT STUDY read the headline of the *Eastside Tribune* written by the same reporter who had discovered Ben at the hospital, now with a girth, salt-and-pepper hair and obviously distrustful of Father Germán.

Renata should have been the one to receive the pat on the back from the school board, should have been recognized as a wunderkind from a modest pool of barrio genes, the promising bright star against the bleak statistics of dropout rates. Instead, it was he who received a full scholarship awarded by the University of Southern California. Benjamin Brady, who moved like a junkyard of clunky body parts, who shook hands with a nameless superintendent while the photo bulbs flashed him blind, it was he who registered without question and without desire.

On good days, Ben attended classes. His knee joint was not painful, nor his limp pronounced. Light speared between the stacks of books on good days. He stored a collection of stories about his scars in case someone asked. On good days, Ben phoned Ana to let her know he maintained adequate medical supervision, ate a hamburger at the cafeteria without an anxiety attack and once even mustered the courage to inform the attractive cashier that the prices for Tuesday's menu were incorrect. On these days, Ben was really who he was meant to be.

On in-between days, Ben wondered about leading a life not his own, yet could never imagine another. Walking through the campus quad on in-between days, a parade of protesters, a tornado of discontent, made contact on the lawn, touching down on the university premises and flinging his thoughts in its swirls. As he rushed to class from one building to another, a wheelchaired look-alike of Gilbert Durán scooted alongside of him, asking about his limp, his scar, and when he answered no, he'd never been to Vietnam, the unisex protesters distributed pamphlets with instructions on how to be a conscientious objector, and when he said he wasn't going to any war, the braided Chicano Power militants brandished clipboards pushing a petition on him that contained signatures demanding admission policy changes. And finally, when he said he wasn't a Chicano, they replied that if you're not part of the solution, you're part of the problem.

Confused and terrified by the antiwar salvo of chanting and pro–civil rights demonstrations, he rushed to pass the tables that flanked the front of the Doheny Library and only halted in answer to his bad leg. He'd stopped to rub it, and as his backpack slipped off his shoulder to the floor, a young toned woman asked him, Are you okay? And then she touched his toasted brown arm to assist him.

The woman said she studied pre-law. A Chicana, she pointed to the MEChA table, and wore a brown beret over hair so long it reached the folds of her buttocks. She touched Ben's arm gently, and rubbed the slit scars with her thumb as if reading the Braille of his childhood accident. She smiled and then released him and Ben glowed with embarrassment because this was the closest he had ever been to a woman other than Renata, and because the Chicana stared shamelessly at his face scar.

Thank you, he said. Being late for class, Ben said he'd better get going because seats became scarce in his Intro Soc class. But the young woman shouted to his back, A gift for you, hermano. And then ran up to him, removed her beret and placed it on his head. And at that instance when he looked directly into her eyes, Ben would've given his life to walk upright without hobbling, to push his chest out, to brave the mental eye of the tornado and be absorbed by something larger. The woman cocked her head to read his stunned expression, and he turned to mask it. His leg plagued him like his fear. He resisted being lifted up into a gathering mass of swirling political storms. He refused to be clearly defined as a Chicano, and for that, he refused to belong to a fluid movement, joining her, joining them, joining other Chicanos to become a part, to become a whole and not just stay forever in between.

To avoid bad days, Ben meekly attended church services. It was a plan that ordered his time, travel time, preparation time, sitting time, recuperating time. While the preacher administered, Ben dreamed himself poised in some smoky café sharing Ginsberg with Renata, her two tetherball-playing hands on the table. On bad days, his cramped apartment broiled. Depleted of energy, Ben sat on his chair, staring at the open crack of the closet door until the night obscured the corners. The irony struck him; he was not crazy enough to live alone in such squalid surroundings, and yet not sane enough to live outside it.

On bad days, he didn't even deserve sunshine. His paranoia was such that he became convinced Ana was jealous of him and secretly plotted to sabotage their relationship. He lost things: keys, wallet, library card, books, money, letters, countless pencil sharpeners, bills, eviction notices. He could not sit still because of his knee, could not walk because of his limp. Bad days passed as worse nights and vice versa, blurring. In the timeline of Ben's life, the past melted into the future and erased distinctions or bent boundaries. Each hour of the day was remarkably the same and yet unremarkably different. He ran out of food and panicked every time he went to the market, and the more he didn't go, the more of a trial it became when he had no other choice.

At some point in his timeline, he simply became incapable of fulfilling all those little details that made people conduct their lives. He forgot simple things others took for granted. He forgot how to expand his lungs to breathe, how to swallow, how to sleep, how to speak, how to put water to skin, soap to clothes, Pine Sol to floors. To eat a meal sitting down, enjoy a song on the radio. Sip iced tea with a sliver of lemon. Forgot how to love. Every movement was a remarkable challenge. His heart bled constantly, draining him of any vitality. Even tilting his head produced a splintered skull full of migraine. It seemed indescribable except to say on bad days, the days were indescribably bad.

Telling no telling what. Several nights passed into days, which passed into nights, and hours smashed together like handfuls of beach sand. The fecal odor had been reported to the landlord, who reported it to Tranquilina, who reported it to Ana. Tranquilina, tired of knocking on his door, and Ana, tired of the unanswered calls, marched to his apartment together.

Or were there four of them? Eight legs, one pair of liver-colored galoshes, and his sister's legs parted, those thick stump thighs pressed against her secretarial skirt, breaking and entering, trampling on his brown beret, pleading for him to play fetch peacefully with the two Psychiatric Emergency Team workers. His arms shielded his *cerebral hemispheres* and the PET workers clasped his pencil-thin wrists and forced him up, stole *his frontal lobe; principal speech area, precentral gyrus or primary motor area,* took him howling like a scribble off the page of white paper, *I can't stand my own parietal lobe, temporal lobe, occipital lobe,* all the way back to the dim institution, where the walls were as gray as brain matter. Where sharp pencils were forbidden.

The migraine's viselike throb dissolved into a manageable ache and Ben opened his eyes cautiously. Near the paws of his chair, empty Bayer aspirin bottles were piled high, and he dipped his hand looking for the bottle-rattle of remaining aspirin. Discovering some, he poured a few into his mouth and chewed. The hour, the time, his time, was the kind of late of late-night movies, of Cal Worthington Dodge or Salas Used Cars commercials, of public service announcements on television. Ben had lost his paperback and it killed him not to know the end of the story. He switched on a reading light, and the small bulb poked a hole in the brackish night.

Ben set his weapons, knife-sharpened pencils and a spiral notebook, on the card table with neat precision. The rotors of helicopter motors shook the loose windowpanes as if someone rapped on the glass. The floodlight vanished and someone shouted, and someone else shouted back. Ben heard a child's congested wailing. The old building ached and grunted and its bony framework pinged and banged in its plumbing. One man's ceiling was another man's floor. Boxes and clothes and piles and other piles made his living space limited, but he paced between its boundaries to revive the blood circulation in his bad leg. Ready, he sat at the card table and then stared at his weapons. Why had he set them out like a dinnerware setting? Ben glanced out to the lonely elongated night ahead.

He focused on the blank perimeters of college-ruled paper and cracked his knuckles. His basic knuckles. The street woman could have been anyone's mother. Over the rows of empty chairs, in the corner of the room near the kitchen door, there she stood, and he stared at her with a piercing glance needling in and out of the crowd.

She could be anyone's mother, he said to Tranquilina. Over the clink and chatter of the room, Ben jutted his chin toward the street woman, who stood in the food line.

She who was not old, Ben began to write. The old woman was not old. If one stopped to look while pressing a quarter in her filthy hand and stare at the smile the donation created, one would see she was in her late forties. Her family in Mexico had lost track of her many years ago; the woman who was not old had planned to venture north, seek employment to feed her younger brothers and sisters, abandon her suffocating and restrictive life of poverty to find a future, against her father's objections. He assured her that she would leave his house over his dead body; and soon after, his dead body they found, a heart attack—the townspeople said—caused by the sheer vein-bursting anger her plans had inspired. Her desire to leave vanished just as suddenly as his death and although she yearned to stay, now she could not; for the stones of silent accusation of murder befell a woman unable to repel them. In the end, her future became as irrelevant to her as the clothes her father would be buried in.

She had no choice but to leave. All of her was summed up in the contents of a rainbow straw bag that she carried: a dress, perhaps a red sweater (she heard it was very cold up north); a dry pair of socks, items that she stuffed with enough cash to get her to the border. She rode the midnight trains that rolled and rattled and cleaved through lonely stretches of blinding night, hearing the buzz and whisper of people sitting not far from her, people involved in building this big thing called life. They made noises like a busy workshop, hammering, planning, sawing and sanding until they slept and in their dreams built even greater futures.

The woman rode through endless stations that appeared and disappeared, never once disembarking; she bought vendors' trinkets of food from the train window for fear of being left behind, rarely bartering the prices; passed the repetition of homes, watched thatched roofs and open entrances where children slept peacefully in hammocks. Things, small and large, colorless and colorful, fled like memories except for those lingering clamped in her chest. Nevertheless, she accepted the ascension of the railroad ties like a ladder, climbing the rungs of ascension, her destiny roaring northward bound for the U.S.

Somewhere along the ride, the rail bolts spiked against her. At the Palladium Ballroom in Hollywood, she met a man in uniform, an Anglo as tumbleweed-harsh as the Dust Bowl farmlands he sprang from. Derailed, she married him for respectability, for citizenship, perhaps to have a roof over her head, food on the table. Perhaps she tried to marry someone very unlike her father, or perhaps it was love—who knows what that word meant to her—and with this Anglo, she birthed two children in the city where she had imagined God's little eyes protecting them.

What can one do when an economy is based on capital, and one has so little currency in her pockets? Never, never lose a coin, never ignore a penny on the floor. Save and save. Saved for a birthday gift of Converse sneakers, a promise to her boy, because the advertisement promised that children could fly in these sneakers. And that was one thing she wanted for her children. Flight. But it was she who flew and after her escape, hard times befell the woman. If one stopped a minute from the frantic trot of daily life to ask her while she sat on a park bench, her rainbow straw bag filled with discarded redemption bottles at her feet, and if one knew how to speak Spanish, for she knew little English, if one asked what her wildest desire would be, she would reply, I want to hold my boy and girl again, and then her eroding composure would give way to a flood of tears.

Her shoulders would quake with sobs, and her legs would quiver her deposit bottles. Her fingers, once intertwined and resting properly on her lap, would resist working her hands into a ball of mud. Bottles tinkling, fingers kneading, the crying would then abruptly halt. *The sadness clamp would loosen a bit with the oil of her rushing tears and she was thankful that one person had enough courtesy to ask.*

Ben's hands surprised him. In a bewildering sort of way his longish and dirt-encrusted nails had the capacity to mold a mother's life. He inspected the length of his fingernails. His ears became alive over a muffled conversation, a television volume high somewhere in the building. The black window sealed him off from the rest of the world.

Someone like him tried to survive the body-bag blankness of the hour by watching television.

She would sigh so deeply, one would think the pit of her soul was as far-reaching as the molten core of earth. Relieved to be breathing without asthmatic-like pain in her chest, the woman would snort and sniff until all she could hear was the buzz saw of her own wheezing. This made her feel an electrical vitality, as if she had now recaptured the responsibility for building her life once again. Regaining a certain amount of confidence (after all, one sat on *her* bench), the woman would ask for loose change with such a poker face, one could not guess that a few moments prior to her panhandling, *her life seemed a fragile coral reef in a sea of pollution.*

Ben's writing hand cramped. The dull lighting in his room tired his eyes. He had written a long letter about the lighting to his landlord but like all his other written work, the folded pages remained entombed somewhere in the apartment. Though he wondered about time, he didn't dare look for the clock because it always disappointed him. He cracked his knuckles over the scribbling of his notebook.

Ben read what he wrote. Stories, like life, had no logical conclusion and it made Ben angry at the uncertainty of it all, and it was this uncertainty that kept him an insomniac. Ben couldn't remember the last time he slept well. He stretched, pulling his limbs, and then walked to the bathroom, where he urinated a fountain's gurgle into the toilet. In the grubby mirror, he inspected a chin dappled with unshaven growth, and he mulled over his monster stitches, making him extremely self-conscious. He returned to his card table, slumped onto his chair and then picked his pencils up and drummed them on the table, Bible, Bayer aspirin bottle, transistor, old dictionary, until the monotony bored him. He rubbed his hair, discovered a thinning spot and returned to the bathroom mirror to investigate. How could this be? Truly, he wasn't that old. When he tired of worrying over his hair, he returned to the card table and switched his transistor on. Static chewed, and he turned off the radio and tried to think of something else to occupy his mind.

Next to his foot was the phone outlet. Ben wondered what day it was. He picked up the cord, followed it like a loose skein on a carpet, and pulled it from under a stack of newspapers, toppling books sloppily piled, unburying a scattering of unwashed cups where cockroaches had the misfortune of hardening into trilobites with the last traces of black drink.

The phone. One night like any other, like this one, Ben had scraped off the numbers for no reason at all. It left the telephone looking shamefully naked and cold. He rang up Ana's number on the rotary dial and hung up when she answered in a dazed, four a.m. voice. He redialed, then slammed the phone before Ana answered once more. Ben touched his thinning spot. He couldn't believe the loss of hair. Time was thinning. All that time working out good days amounted to nothing. Who was he kidding? Each day, each day continued with the reckless speed of a cement truck, no stopping for him.

Back at the table, Ben pulled the corner of his T-shirt to polish his sweaty forehead, swiping and swiping as if his skull bone were a magic lamp. The one wish he would wish if asked: protection against this aggressive loneliness.

The woman who was not old had stumbled onto the church while searching for a safe and warm place to sleep for the night, where her collected bottles would not be stolen nor her breasts threatened by the fondling sharp edge of a switchblade. The city buildings, once brightly speckled with fashionable, neatly creased people, were now deserted as night fell on the streets of downtown and more people like her squeezed out of the crawl spaces and crevices of the alleys. At sundown, war was declared between the haves who abandoned their office buildings for home, and have-nots who pushed their portable cardboard homes in shopping carts to reclaim a place in the streets denied them during daylight. Dogs emerged, packs of them gathering in number as they roamed the streets to scavenge, to challenge the have-nots.

If one would pass the woman while driving home from the office after a crinkled day of work, one might acknowledge her disorientation with a merciful sigh, but rushing home nonetheless to retrieve the child, make a quick stop for groceries, pick up a bucket of chicken. If the woman stood on a pedestrian bridge overlooking the Hollywood 101 Freeway, let's say, one would think the woman who was not old entertained the idea of suicide and the driver would maintain a diligent vigil from the rearview mirror. Could the driver know what the woman thought? In order to envision her life, one would have to think of her with greater generosity. It would be too easy to simply imagine her existence as horrendous, and therefore think of suicide as the only option left for such a pitiful soul. Yet life is stratified layers of time, a complex gut of pulsating mystery. One would need much more than obvious assumptions in order for the driver to turn off the ignition key, set the parking brake right and ask after her. One would have to be close enough to look into her eyes, jump into the trunk of her heart, lift the stage curtains to see behind her props. It was one thing to assume, another to conjure, and yet another *to feel for her. One would need metaphor to love her.*

Slumped over the notebook, Ben awoke to morning, his cheek imprinted by a folded page. Elated at surviving the night, he proudly flipped through the crumbled pages of his writing. He reread the last intelligible paragraph of his exhaustive scribbling. *Into the trunck of hr hart . . .* The writing had left him famished, and after gulping three cold wieners, he resolved to walk over to the nearest Jack in the Box, two city blocks from his building. He patted his hair, resisted looking for his so-called thinning spot, angled his beret over his scar. He checked his shirt to make sure he was buttoned correctly.

Once down the stairs, Ben realized he had forgotten to brush his teeth, but the new morning, compassionate in its sheer lightness, greeted him and made him smile. He walked briskly, feeling the dampness of the early-hour condensation. It was good to know that other life outside his existed. He joined a wave of people going about their morning business and entered the Jack in the Box. When it was his turn to order at the counter, he cleared his throat and, in a modulated, even voice, ordered a large black coffee. He sprinkled coins and thanked the clerk.

The day slowly unraveled. Ben sat in the fast-food booth until he finished his coffee, until the morning rush ended, until it was close to noon. He ambled another ten blocks to the public library, where he took a nap in the California History Room while three teens chatted and giggled across the table from him, presumably working on a history project but really working on plans for a hot Saturday night. Once outside, he walked to Pershing Square, the city's main quad of trees, which was located in the middle of downtown, and sat on a bench in the soothing warm sun and watched the comings and goings of people, fast-forwarding. Ben wondered how it felt to be normal like that suited man eating an apple or that woman pushing the baby stroller. These people who he greatly admired also scared the shit out of him. They made him nervous because he knew good and well that they loathed people like himself. They read his thoughts, smelled his dirty laundry smell and thought him less than the scum he had under his fingernails.

He didn't even deserve to share their sun.

Hungry as he was, he returned to his apartment unable to bring himself to walk into an eatery where decent people ate. Instead, he loudly sipped from a can of Campbell's soup and then shook raisins from a box into his mouth. Like a horse, he ate standing up. He dialed Ana's number. No answer. Ben had forgotten to take his medication and searched for the bottles, lifting couch cushions, plates, balls of paper. Convinced he didn't need the medication anymore, he stopped searching and instead ate an old, stale, half-bitten Twinkie he had found between the folds of the couch.

The phone rang, jolting him from a light sleep. As it continued its hollow and angry ring, Ben debated whether he should answer it. There were maybe three people who knew his number.

Hell-O, Ben said, dragging the word out like a heavy ball.

Ben?

Yea?

Is that you?

What do you mean?

I mean . . . I mean it doesn't sound like you.

Well, yea, it's me. Ben.

Didn't get much sleep?

Well, yeah, Ben sighed deeply. Yea, I was able to. A few hours. What makes you say that?

Did you call me last night?

Say what?

It doesn't sound as if you've gotten sleep, that's all.

Go on. I'm listening.

It doesn't sound like you, that's all.

No.

No, what?

No, it's not me.

Come on, Ben.

You have the wrong number. And with that, Ben hung up.

He went over to the kitchenette, where he had an old toaster oven surrounded by bread crumbs and a hot plate pressed against a grease-splattered wall and a sink filled with unwashed dishes. Guilt-ridden for his impatience with Ana, Ben began to dislike himself, and then began to dislike Ana for making him feel this way, and he tumbled towering dishes, and banged pots, clinked silverware in unrestrained carelessness searching for his good knife. Finding it, he sharpened the points of his pencils, whittling and blowing off the curling chips to see if the point was fine, the way he liked to have his pencils.

The phone rang again. Ben hoped it was Ana, and then hoped it was not.

Yea? Ben answered, this time annoyed. He could not remember the last time he'd received two consecutive calls in as many minutes.

Who's this? he responded. The caller had a squeaky voice. Whom may I say is calling? Ben cradled the phone between his shoulder and ear as he finished whittling his last pencil.

How come? What kind of name is that? You answer my question and I'll answer yours. Where did you get the nickname?

Ben sat at his card table and began doodling a mouse on the margin of his notebook, complete with diaper.

Okay, then. Wrong number. I'm a wrong number.

Ben left the phone off the hook. He wanted no interruptions and stared out the window into the gentle reams of twilight lavender dabbled with rows of dissolving clouds. The devastating fumes of freeway traffic, and not the natural course of things, affected such beauty. He pricked his thumb with his pencil. It had to be sharp to cut deeply into the paper. He waited whole seconds for the blood in his thumb to rise like dark sacrificial ink.

SEVEN

Grandmother Zumaya didn't think to inform the child. After washing the dishes, she placed the rack in the direct sunlight, untied her apron and hung it on a hook inside the pantry door. Though it was early still, the sun had already begun to press on their heads as they walked down First Street to a cluster of nondescript stucco buildings. Grandmother and the child proceeded into a hallway and through a door and stood on the other side of the pine counter. Grandmother inquired about the child's admission to elementary school. As she waited for an answer, the bold, fat clock on the wall above the principal's office door had the gloss of a gawking eyeball. Without her apron, Grandmother noticed a quarter-sized button of her housedress missing, an embarrassing circumstance, and the child, who by this time cowered behind her, pinched her housedress on the spot where the apron strings should have been. Grandmother swatted away the child's hands, irritated by the eyeballing clock and the child's nervous pinches.

Since the school secretary was running an errand, it was Nurse Hamilton who assisted Grandmother. The nurse's manicured fingernails sprinted through a shoebox file of white index cards, jumping hurdles over the typed names. This must have been a tiresome exercise for her fingers to do because Grandmother heard her breathing heavily.

It's gonna be a scorcher today, Nurse Hamilton said, sucking up more than her share of air for a second wind. At one point, she lifted an index card and fanned herself.

The clock on the wall blinked loudly.

Here! The nurse finally pulled out an index card attached with a blue paper clip. Grandmother debated whether to ask about the meaning of the blue clip near the child's name. The nurse whistled through her nostrils as she read the card and then instructed Grandmother to take the child to Miss Eastman in Bungalow Three.

No apron strings to cling to, the child sucked her fingers while she followed Grandmother through the long hollow corridor between two more nondescript buildings. Grandmother was not accustomed to her hands hanging like washed gloves teased into stillness on a laundry line. Having been born with one arm slightly longer than the other, she maintained a lifelong habit of constant motion to hide her shameful defect. All the child ever saw was a shapeless blur of working until today. Grandmother's hands, a pruny pair of gloves, hung like temptation, almost inviting the child to slip her own spit-sticky hand into one of them.

Radiant morning sunshine burst at the end of the dark corridor and the child scrunched up her face as if the fingers she sucked on were sour. Grandmother used her longer arm to shade her eyes to better see the numbers on the classroom doors. (What is a bungalow anyway? Grandmother mumbled. What does the blue clip mean? Where is the missing button?) Only twenty of ten on Monday morning and already the sky was a flat canvas of smog haze pulled taut to its combustible edges as far as the eye could see. The air was too thick to filter through her lungs and the heat clamped down on their necks. Like everyone else watching the evening news, Grandmother knew the approaching summer was not going to be a kind one. Record heat waves were already forcing people out into the beaten, dusty streets. She saw as much on the cherrywood-box black and white television, except everyone on television looked green-tinted and alien and not black and white.

Grandmother swabbed hot confusion off her forehead, the child a heel or two cautiously behind. They passed the school playground, passed the equipment shed, passed the bathrooms and low water fountains to Bungalow Three, a box of a room located adjacent to First Street and surrounded by a tall mesh fence.

A pair of parakeets in a cage on the other side of the room responded to the creaking door hinges by puffing their small blue and green chests with molting, excited screeching. A Negro teacher approached her guests and introduced herself as Miss Eastman, and Grandmother took an immediate dislike to the chaotic classroom, where thirty-one heads turned in their direction. The swampy air made her lungs plunge into heaves.

Miss Eastman nimbly balanced a king-sized Kellogg's box with one hand while gripping a gallon of milk with another, a thing that seemed incongruent, Grandmother thought, for a real teacher to be doing. She wore a welcoming apron patterned with puffy bell peppers of various bright colors, and the apron made Grandmother miss her own, which waited on the hook inside of her pantry door. By way of explanation, the teacher told Grandmother the children learn better with a full stomach, and her meaty, discolored cheeks held only a resemblance of color that once was, against the blackness of her neck. All of this, the apron, the cereal, the parakeets, or perhaps none of this, shaped Grandmother's belief that her granddaughter was getting a facsimile of a teacher.

Miss Eastman, still holding the milk and cereal, spoke to Grandmother, and the very visible mole on her chin trembled under her plum lips. Grandmother nodded an annoyed smile as she attempted to follow Miss Eastman's words over the screeching pitch of parakeets, over the jumpy jitter of the children. How was Grandmother expected to understand all this rat-tat-tat fast English? The child huddled behind Grandmother, plucking at the thin air for the missing apron strings, and this annoyed Grandmother even more. What kind of real teacher would have crazy birds, talk too fast and serve cold cornflakes in school? Don't these huercos have hot oats at home?

Over the birds' chatty noises, Miss Eastman asked Lollie García to guide the child to the empty desk. Later, Ermila would retell the memory, the way kiss-ass Lollie shot out of her chair, almost in anticipation of the request, her long braids knocking against the shoulders of her aquamarine sweater, its gold buttons barely constraining her self-importance. She grabbed the child's sticky hand and marched her to the vacant desk that sat next to the teacher's. The child allowed herself to be led and sucked on two fingers so as not to whine.

A restrained silence followed the pair to the desk. Once the child realized Grandmother had disappeared into thin air, she buried her head in the nest of her folded arms and sobbed.

¡Llorona! Ya no llores, you understand? Lollie threatened up close. The child smelled bologna from a mouth fuzzed with a slight mustache. Lollie crossed her sweatered arms to show authority as the Bungalow Three official translator. She raised her haystack eyebrows when she spoke and the child reeled back, tried to be a good girl and cried some more.

Lollie would deny this. Years later, sitting under the patio table umbrella at the Top Hat Hot Dog & Pastrami Eatery, Ermila would recreate Lollie's mischief while slurping RC Cola drink and sharing some french fries splattered with Tabasco sauce. Lollie would deny it all, saying she didn't remember anything before the third grade, and Rini would say, Woolly Bully, Woolly Bully, sounding like one of Sam the Sham's backup singers, I was there so don't be singing that song to us.

Miss Eastman resumed serving whole milk and cornflakes to her thirty-one students plus one. Wide, a flourish of bell peppers gazing through the space between the rows of long tables, the teacher gracefully moved, hovering over the heads of the children to shake and pour and shake and pour, the warm shade of her breasts brushing the tops of their combed or uncombed heads.

For the rest of the morning, the Zumaya child sat alone, a clean beige sheet of paper and a carton filled with thick crayons in front of her. At recess, the students played outside in rips and roars, while the child stayed behind at her desk, feeling an incredible sense of sadness unlike any she had ever experienced. She hunched on her wooden seat like an old lady. Her heart felt so weighed down it seemed too heavy to lift and carry to the playground and her sighs were so deep they quivered her chin and shook her shoulders when she exhaled. She found an eraser clump on her desk and barely had the energy to roll it back and forth with her finger.

Her apron tucked away, Miss Eastman pulled up a child-sized chair and sat and her hips spilled over.

My dear, Miss Eastman said, can you give us your name? She had an aroma of fresh-baked bread. After a pause, the child gave a secretive sideways glance. The teacher kneaded one doughy hand with another, a gesture Grandmother did to get the warm rush of blood flowing into her icy hands. Powdery maps of fine chalk or flour remained on the lap of Miss Eastman's dress. Finally, the child dragged her face up. The teacher's forehead glistened beads of sweat as thick as resin. The child could hear her breath snuffing through her nostrils as she spied the mole on the teacher's chin. Black hairs sprouted from the mole like a clump of weeds. The child burst into another round of sobs.

Without telling Grandfather, Grandmother Zumaya had asked the courts to return the grandchild to the family. And so, partly out of revenge, but mostly because it was common practice in the Zumaya family, Grandfather Zumaya had purchased a previously owned television set from the Black Cat Repair Shop without consulting Grandmother.

When the deliveryman untied the cherrywood box from the flatbed truck, Grandmother stood on the porch steps, her arms tightly crossed. On this sunny Saturday morning, the child squatted near the cemented path to mash petals of hibiscus flowers with a brick.

Finally, her longer arm cupping her mouth, Grandmother yelled from the porch, It's bad luck to buy some poor soul's pawned furniture.

At this, the mention of a poor soul, the child looked up and found herself between them.

Grandfather was as hardened as fossil in rock, and he embraced the black and white television and slowly grunted its weight from the edge of his finely trimmed lawn to the porch steps and yelled back that the television was a done deal.

The only done deal here, Grandmother replied, feeling a sense of one-upness since she stood on the top step looking down at her husband, is death.

Who the hell do you think you are, telling me what I can or can't do? Grandfather yelled back, though she stood in such close proximity he didn't have to raise his voice. And he tipped the corner of the television onto the first step triumphantly.

The whirling heat of her grandparents' exchanges above her head, the child's hands shone reddish with flower and sprinkled with yellow pollen as bright as bananas.

Grandmother knew everyone had heard and uncrossed her arms and placed her fists in her apron pockets. The delivery-truck driver busied himself with cords and ropes in an exaggerated manner to cover the act of listening. The children who were once playing stickball in the street had stopped and stared at the commotion. Even one of the Gamboa brothers, the one who was really a girl but didn't want to be, poked her bald head out from the torn screen of their rented house.

The marriage contract said nothing of public humiliation. The small humiliations, thousands of them, were contained within the four walls of their well-kept home, between the sheets of their bed, in privacy. But Grandfather redrew the line and tossed aside whatever fragile civility they had mutually agreed upon in order to live as man and wife and Grandmother felt the full crimson flush on her cheeks. She straightened up to show everyone she was unmoved by his public and stupid outburst, and turned and waited for the door to slam behind her before she began to bite her knuckle.

In Bungalow Three, the students fell into rotating groups of math and art. Then recess came and went and the students returned to their desks in riotous moods, settled in silence by a carton of milk, a paper straw, and a cookie the size of their hands, set out in front of their name cards.

They ate cookies smelling of joyous birthdays, of sleepy summer nights, of melted ice cream, of Miss Eastman's hearty embraces. The cookies were baked by a nameless baker, sight unseen, but the students knew he baked for them, as Miss Eastman's fingers hooked the wrap-around strings of a pink box and carried it across the playground right before recess ended.

In Bungalow Three, the parakeets groomed one another, or swung on their little pink swing, or took baths in their water dish, their wingspans fluttering phantom flight. In Bungalow Three, the blue-clipped index cards included the four-fingered girl who had a finger blown off by a firecracker, and thus scratched the stump of her missing finger constantly. There was Rini, with a head full of bush and tangle, who could send the kickball all the way to the other side of the playground; the boy named Hortencio, with big pink gums and breasts; Milagros too, whose mother died and so she stopped caring about recess and stared into vacant space so intently that the other children too would stare at the space in hopes of seeing whatever it was Milagros saw.

There was Stella, tall and scaly and the oldest student in Bungalow Three but who had a heart as big as a wide-open door. The new student Bertha, with embroidery threads pierced through her swelled and hurtful-looking earlobes, and who just arrived from a place called Rosarito, Baja California. There was Moses, who simply couldn't read and couldn't read and couldn't read, and Lollie, who found herself misplaced and wanting prestige for the role of translator she so very well thought she deserved. There was Jose, chewing big wads of gum until he pulled it from between his lips, rolled it into a taco, then jabbed it back into his mouth, after which Miss Eastman would ask him to feed the trashcan. And then there was the child who refused to speak.

Obdulio the butcher had made Grandfather Zumaya regret his television purchase, and it was a regret he would never admit to Grandmother. Why, oh, why, Grandfather lamented, had he not waited for the color models like the one that Obdulio the butcher owned? Back up—why, oh, why had he given MISFORTUNE the opportunity to dance on his hunched back by passing El Zócalo Fine Meats on the very night that Obdulio was locking up the front doors of the butcher shop? Worse yet, pour more salt in the wound—why was the moment fated for two tired souls to cross paths just when the streets emptied of people and the dusk cloaked the neighborhood blocks?

Genuinely relieved to see one another among condemned, wind-spooked houses, they greeted each other as if they had grown up together, though their familiarity extended no further than polite banter over a tray of twisted pork rinds once a week, if that.

The two men shook hands while inquiring after each other, laughing, elbowing in jest at how the ball of gathering age had begun chaining them to its weight. Obdulio looked vulnerable, disarmed without his huge machete cleaver splitting open a goat's skull or the smaller knife that was sharpened enough to slice flank steaks so thin they were translucent. Eclipsed half-moons set under his eyes and it seemed that all that fleshy muscle he sliced and split and gutted inside the butcher shop did little to contribute to his own. Only now did Grandfather realize how skinny the butcher was; his narrow, pointy shoulders and milky eyes made him out as old, though Obdulio was a man in his mid-forties.

Grandfather bade him farewell with another pumping handshake. Obdulio's fingers were long, thin, almost girlish, and his light handshake was judged by Grandfather not to be a confident one. The intersection was oddly quiet, and Grandfather turned to cross it when Obdulio suddenly proposed that they have a few beers to close out the evening. Grandfather dismissed the invitation, but Obdulio wouldn't hear of it and slapped him on the shoulder like an old acquaintance.

Just one beer, compa?

Grandfather tried to come up with an excuse to say no, but his brain was flaccid with hunger and the excuses that suddenly surfaced weren't credible enough for even him to believe, so he reluctantly said,

Just one, compa.

They walked over to La Bootie's store, where Obdulio emerged with a brown paper bag. The streets were strangely absent of cars, and there were only a few people, headed for home, something Grandfather had planned on doing had he not been abducted. The thermos banged forebodingly against Grandfather's tin lunch pail as he followed Obdulio.

The butcher rented a room from Don Gallo in the back of the old man's bakery. Grandfather had imagined that Obdulio's home would smell of the pan dulce, glazed horn pastries or yellow pan portugués of the bakery. Instead, as Obdulio opened the door, the dark room stank of rancid lard, of old shoes kept shut up in the closet. As he flipped the switch, the room transformed from scent to sight and the light and shadow from the one bulb filled the space with a yellow glow. A long cot stood against one wall, a tumble of balled blankets on top of a foam mattress so thin it invited napping rather than committed sleep. Beside the cot, there was a door where Grandfather could see the toilet seat up in the bathroom. Across from the bathroom, a small table stood with large chairs, and next to that, a chest of drawers left open for socks to crawl out.

The signs of a man living without a woman were in every corner; the smell, *La Opinión* newspapers spread around, the boxers, pants, T-shirts dropped here and there; no trappings like flaps of curtains for embellishment, no décor except for a calendar nailed to the wall. The room could easily depress Grandfather if he were forced to stay here. A suicide room. However, in the center, right in front of the cot, stood a brand-new—and in Grandfather's estimation, majestic—television console. The tail of an extension cord hung from the single lightbulb.

Take a load off, Obdulio invited, palm open to signal the cot, and Grandfather obliged, his eyes glued to the new television. He placed his lunch pail by his boots and sat and then Grandfather's buttocks almost hit the floor and he squirmed into a position remotely comfortable. His hunching back created a snail's-shell shadow, which bled into other shadows. But no matter, for he was eager to switch on the television, just as he was eager for Obdulio to switch on the room light a few moments ago. The butcher returned from his kitchenette holding two lukewarm cans of Tecate.

Lemon for Lady Luck, Obdulio said, squeezing the slice on Grandfather's can. But no salt to keep the bad luck away, compa, so we have to take our chances, eh? I got the high blood pressure. Obdulio kicked a pair of his boxers, flattened like a number eight under the cot, and then chuckled from nerves more than self-appreciating humor.

Obdulio's wife had been the one who kept their social life in order. She invited neighbors for Sunday get-togethers in their small home in Jerez, Zacatecas, and enjoyed such things as passing the cans of beer to their guests while he roasted corn on the open grill. Second nature to her, he missed her laugh and the toasted maize scent. They had lived separately for, what, more years than he cared to count—he with steady employment in the north, she thousands of miles away. Her letters always demanded something. *Claudia's vestido, de primera comunión, 162 pesos.* Always a demand. Their small house needed constant repair. In one letter she wrote, *El techo mucha agua. 400 pesos.* She had planned the get-togethers because life on the rancho was lonely and the fiestas forced him to talk to people, be a friendly man, and she did this, he knew, so that he could learn to be friendly to his five children.

When his wife had flipped up the line of the *t* in the words *vestido* or *techo* it was like flipping up the corner of her dress as she danced; and then when she brought the pen line around in a cursive flair, her dress whirling to cross the *t*, the tiny interconnection of crossbars which distinguished the *t* from a mere single line, Obdulio knew, he felt, the connection was an act of affection, a kiss for him. Her letters tried to keep him in the loop of his children's lives and she scribbled mundane occurrences and expenses that up until the accident, he rarely reread, that's how much he missed them.

Obdulio felt the fold of the letter in his back pocket and it was as thin as his wallet.

Well, I'll be, Grandfather said of the television, but somehow Obdulio thought he referred to his photograph which stood on top of the console. A very young man dressed in military uniform, Obdulio was mostly pleased to have once looked so dashing and full of dreams in the photo.

Thank you very much, Obdulio said, and he sipped small sips almost as a reminder that this is what one does with a beer in hand. Obdulio suddenly felt quite embarrassed for being an ungracious host. How could he not notice Grandfather thumbing the cloth of the speakers? It was the speakers of the console, the cloth spun with gold threads suggesting a real sophisticated elegance, that made Obdulio stop at the shop window for a second, then a third, fourth look.

Go ahead, compa, turn it on. Grandfather's hand itched to turn it on. Please, Obdulio said. Please, be my guest.

The colors amazed Grandfather. Dazzling harlequin colors. The brown of a horse was deeper than the real color of a horse Grandfather had seen growing up in the mining town of Metcalf, Arizona. Blue. Now, that was a true blue. He had seen that blue, that exactness, on the Gulf of Mexico as a youth on a fishing trip with other young scrawny, hungry men near the Isla de Tiburón, where they brought plenty to eat and drink; where they brought women much older than themselves to fuck. And before the butcher's voice interrupted, Grandfather swam in the memories of turquoise skies, floating on the shimmering of a woman's buttocks.

Did you hear about what happened last week? Obdulio downed the remainder of beer for courage to speak of it.

Grandfather gestured to show Obdulio he was listening, but tried not to take his eyes off the technicolors of the NBC peacock on the television screen.

May I share something with you, in full confidence, compa?

A man keeps his word, Grandfather replied. He slit his eyes because the incandescent colors blinded.

I am not a superstitious man, the butcher continued.

Yes.

I regret witnessing the accident.

A man is born with regrets, Grandfather said, deeply regretting the purchase of the black and white cherrywood-box television. With a color television, he could see the gold and purple satin of a wrestler's cloak. When he politely shot a glance at Obdulio, who sat on one of the kitchen chairs, the butcher's head cast a modest shadow over the bathing-suited woman pictured on the El Zócalo Fine Meats calendar. His pensive mood fed the shadows.

Do you believe in fate? the butcher asked. He worked his second beer now, a slight buzz teasing. He studied his thumbs, which rubbed the rim of his beer can. As he went up for his third beer, he asked,

Ready for another one?

Eh?

Ready for another beer?

No. No, thank you, compa. Grandfather had just emptied his Tecate can when an episode of *The Beverly Hillbillies* came on. He felt an affiliation with the cast of characters, a fish-out-of-water kind of feeling, but at least they had a million dollars. Grandfather only had one dollar.

What does this knob do?

It's to adjust the color. Like this.

Well, I'll be . . .

Obdulio politely waited until a commercial break to ask Grandfather if he needed another beer. What is a host supposed to do anyway but refresh a drink, make polite conversation?

Grandfather agreed, though the butcher's beer stuck on the bristles of his mustache and he wiped his mustache after he had downed the can and belched and handed the empty to the butcher. He liked it when Jed referred to the swimming pool as a "cement pond." Grandfather exercised an advantage in knowing the difference.

Do you believe in fate? Obdulio asked.

Excuse me? Grandfather bounced a glance from the television to the butcher and then back again to Granny's kitchen. What space-age appliances! His hunched back ached and he shifted the weight of his buttocks, stretching the metal springs of the cot. Obdulio handed him another beer.

Can I change the channel?

What was left for the butcher to say but, Please, be my guest, and Grandfather gladly flipped the channel, feeling the jerk of the knob with each turn. Grandfather marveled at how electricity ran through the cords to the glass tubes that transformed into millions of dots that created colorful structures out of thin air. A miracle, just like being dirt-poor and finding black gold, while hunting for a meal.

Grandfather rubbed his mustache after another swig. He hoped that Obdulio could stop his bone teeth from clattering for a minute and allow him to watch a television program in peace.

Knocked on the floor by Peter Gunn, a foreign spy bled a sliver of red ooze from the corner of his mouth. Obdulio the butcher knew this orchestrated bang and bump was not real. Real death wasn't neat and orderly, a penny of blood on a shirt, a drop on the corner of the lip. Death was piecemeal of blood muscle mesh, bones snapping as easily as desert ruts underfoot.

Bespattered with blood from the accident, he had to wear the shirt to the butcher shop. When he arrived at work, no one paid attention to the Rorschach blots, his fellow co-workers' aprons already soaked threefold.

His wife barely wrote. Each sentence amounted to three, four or five words. *The Lord is merciful,* her pen scribbling like chicken scratches in search of feed, *tu mayor, no se murió* . . . The *r* in murió rolled its tail like bait, a slight space between mur and ió, stopped at midsyllable as if she paused the pen in gratitude for their eldest son not dying. *El doctor, 562 pesos.*

Last Saturday, the sun, so damn spearing white, the sparkle of metal screeching and halting, lights changing into noncolors. No one paying attention to the boy except him because he'd received a letter that day and his wife wrote, *Hugo hold Pajarito across the flood. No se murió.* The blue ink from a Bic pen he had sent her, the stationery, puppies bordering the page, her handwriting, childlike. Punctuation so random, it charmed him.

Hugo was seven the last time Obdulio saw him and Pajarito only five months in his mother's womb when he left them looking for work up north. Now Hugo had carried his brother across a flooding river, and Obdulio thought it was a man's job done by a boy because his father wasn't there. The butcher imagined the blasting of sharp waters against his spiny legs, rising to his waist, to his shoulders. The risks his absence had put them all through. What flood? He assumed Pajarito was fine, but the house, the livestock? What flood?

Only a second, microsecond really, that was all it took. He watched the boy while he thought of his own son Hugo and only waited a second for the light to change because Obdulio wasn't one to loiter. In all the years he worked his way up at the butcher shop, he had never been late once, and so, in his white shirt, his armpits moist from humidity, he stopped only for a second to watch the boy inside a bubble of piercing haze, and he thought about the contents of the letter in his back pocket. Right before it was all truck metal, drained blood and people screaming, Obdulio swore he saw the boy lift off in midair before he struck the truck like an insect splattering on a windshield. Only after the flashing explosion did Obdulio realize that the larger boy was holding on to a smaller one and the smaller one was released, freed like an angel, leaving behind just a shell that looked no better than roadkill landing twenty feet away.

And then he recognized the anguish of a father dragging all the tonnage of sorrow off his red pickup, the door agape, stomping his desperate steps toward the flooding crowd of people.

The big boy, he was one of the bravest, Obdulio said to a reporter of the local newspaper whose name he had since forgotten.

Was the signal not working? the reporter asked. The driver to blame?

He tried to save the small boy, Obdulio said.

How?

Obdulio shrugged his shoulders because he didn't know the details. Whether Pajarito squatted on Hugo's shoulders, or rode piggyback or embraced his older brother the way he had seen monkeys do their mothers on some program. His wife barely wrote and so only recorded the essentials, leaving him guessing.

In answer to the reporter's question, he repeated, I saw that he tried to save the small boy. And Obdulio looked down at his splattered shirt and knew it wouldn't be good anymore.

After the accident, Obdulio became leery of handling cow muscle and sinewy flesh. He was not a superstitious man but the crack of chicken backbones or the scrap of pork guts now meant more to him than good employment. Why had he witnessed an accident of such magnitude? Why had Hugo crossed a flood? Was it a sign? Obdulio cut himself twice, and the other butchers kept him away from the meat grinder, lest he lose a finger. The sawdust on the shop floor stank of rot. He slept in leaps and bounds. What had happened to him? To a man his wife once described as having blood so sour, even the mosquitoes didn't bite?

He remembered a half dozen Sunkist oranges in the refrigerator.

Compa, the butcher uttered, may I offer you something to eat?

He remembered the salsa in the container from Tres Puntas.

I can't hear.

Obdulio repeated loudly, Are you hungry?

I can't hear the television.

Fate. All Obdulio wanted to do was go home, not here, to his temporary and exiled life in the Eastside, but to the house in Jerez, Zacatecas, with its perpetually leaking roof. And all he wanted after returning home was to sit with his boys, astonished they hadn't died. To go home now. Not tomorrow or the day after. This minute. Tonight. How could he explain this longing to his co-workers who sliced beef or goat with committed zest, or even to Rogelio Zumaya who sat with buttocks spread on the cot? He simply couldn't see himself returning to the butcher shop tomorrow and the day after and the day after that, because when he carried the dead weight of disemboweled carcasses on his shoulders, he felt he carried his own.

How do you make this louder? Grandfather asked. Can I put it a bit louder? But Obdulio was in the midst of planning, and did not hear Grandfather's request.

Grandfather noticed Obdulio's shifting mood. The butcher looked preoccupied. Grandfather read this as irritation, perhaps because Grandfather turned the volume knob a bit too loud or thumbed the color adjustment a bit too much. In his own house, he forbade the child or Grandmother from touching his television, but he supposed that since he was an invited guest of the butcher, and since they were both grown men with a mutual understanding of what courtesies that fact entailed, Grandfather felt entitled to change the channel, adjust the color and volume to his liking. He hadn't thought the butcher so small and petty. The butcher's silent sulking made Grandfather uncomfortable and he leaned forward to give his tailbone a rest.

To hell with him, thought Grandfather, reaching for the volume again. So small and petty, the butcher's head wobbled between his puny shoulders. After the Peter Gunn episode, Grandfather stood up and left without so much as a thank-you.

In the weeks following his visit to the butcher's room, Obdulio had soured whatever enjoyment Grandfather experienced watching his black and white television. Technicolor had entered the sixties to stay, and Grandfather suffered the same dissatisfaction as when the city replaced the streetcars with RTD buses. In the streetcar, Grandfather appreciated the surge of electricity zooming through wire cables, the buzzed and clicking speed of God the puppeteer steering the passengers home safely. But in a modernizing mood, the city purchased the sluggish Rapid Transit buses, which became overcrowded, standing room only, murder on his feet. Killjoy, that's what the RTD bus was, and the colors of people riding them were wrinkled gray, tired brown, faded red and certainly not the brilliant wondrous colors of the NBC peacock.

Having developed his foul mood on the bus rides, he returned home and washed his hands with vinegar, then rinsed them under the rush of cool water to relieve the burning. Grandfather dried his hands and became increasingly regretful about his television purchase. He spent the rest of the days following his visit to Obdulio's trying to land some blame on anyone except himself. He felt swindled by the sales pitch of the proprietor of the Black Cat Repair Shop, though he was a brother-in-law of his highly regarded compadre. He felt led completely astray by the butcher's petty desire to show off his new television—wasn't it the butcher who had kidnapped him at a very weak moment for a beer? But mostly it was Grandmother's fault because . . . well, she had cursed the purchase in the first place by saying it was bad luck.

He sat at the table, not saying a word to the child or Grandmother and picked at his refried beans, barely touched the homemade tortilla. Pushing his plate away, he settled down on his La-Z-Boy chair. Odd behavior, even for the likes of Grandfather, and Grandmother sneaked a palm on his forehead to see if his eerie silence and lack of appetite were products of heatstroke. While he allowed her to probe his forehead and cheeks, Grandfather noticed that Grandmother had placed a statuette pair of ballerinas on starched doilies in front of the rabbit-ear antennas, making his colorless television somewhat frilly and stupid-looking. Feeling weary, he didn't object. Prior to his visit with the butcher, this would have inspired him to rant and break things.

Nothing left to do but lick his wounds, pity all until it became tiresome and he sought to console himself. One afternoon, he took the 26 bus to Broadway, walked up to Temple Street and into Segunda Discounts. There, a primo of the brother-in-law of his highly regarded compadre worked as a vendor selling translucent green television sheets. If taped properly over the black and white television screen, the sheet was guaranteed to deliver color to a woman's lips as red as cherry Popsicles, return blue to a cowboy's eyes. At least that was what the vendor said.

Upon returning from the Segunda, Grandfather passed El Zócalo Fine Meats and was disappointed that Obdulio was not on the other side of the meat counter. Grandfather wanted to show off the tube of translucent green sheet which was rolled up so tight, it resembled a magic wand. But no matter. He returned home feeling disgruntled and unhappy, which meant he was somehow returning to his normal self.

He taped the sheet and turned on the set and yelled from his La-Z-Boy, Come see, come look at how vibrant the colors are! He ate his dinner in front of the television with renewed gusto, quite disgruntled with the world news, but definitely pleased with himself.

Color was not what Grandmother saw. She removed her specs and wiped them with the corner of her apron and then returned them to the bridge of her nose because everyone and everything on television was limited to one common color and strained her eyes. The washing machines, the contestants on game shows, the soap commercials, the panning camera of the Vietnam jungles. They all shared the color green. She stared at close-ups of the green Birmingham dogs unleashed and mauling flesh, their incisors as glistening as war planes on the nightly news. Green floated around her like cataracts.

It took several weeks before the child braved her first recess outside. Rather than swing on the monkey bars or play in the sandbox, the child leaned against the metal fence to look out at the wavering movements of life beyond the playground. The yelps and joyous cheer of her classmates behind her, the child studied the houses and driveways, the vacant lot on the corner, a woman hanging laundry, a station wagon being washed by a barefoot man, and felt a slow swelling lump of desire for Chavela and the blue house on First Street with its damp scent of tobacco and burnt-out matchsticks. The curtains of the screen porch were so old the sunlight sucked the beet and radish patterns dry. The child would curl up near the water pipes, which sagged like teats beneath Chavela's kitchen sink, the smells of earthy potatoes, moldy onions and the dusty twenty-five-pound sack of La Piña flour embracing her. The buzzard bell ended her first recess outside.

The child leaned on the fence every recess period after that, beholden to contradiction: her routine delivered solace and distress simultaneously. While her classmates exploded in rambunctious play, she noticed how the sun moved. Though she didn't know the names of the four directions as yet, the child realized the significance of witnessing time passing, just like the glossy eye clock over the principal's door. The forward hand-clip of a minute, the loud wink of its eye blink, the passing of time became a shadow constant behind her heart, a dark expanse as black as the tar-coated knees of her classmates.

She collected observations as one would collect ice-cream sticks: a youth riding a wobbly bike on the muddy shoulders of the street; a skinny cat roaming through the tall bird-of-paradise stalks; two comadres chatting between a fence; an old crooked bird man who fed his flock of pigeons daily. The desire to be on the other side of the fence, to run away from school and join them, was so strong, it startled her, just like the buzzard bell ending another recess.

She lagged way behind her blue-clipped classmates who had learning handicaps, or grab-bag capacities, non–English speakers, and who knew to fall into a line below the bungalow window at the end of each recess. A pink Spalding ball trailing its bounce, the set of abandoned swings still swaying, a red multicolored sweater sleeve swooning on a bench, the children emptied out of the playground just as rapidly as they emptied out their milk cartons, leaving the child to cross the ghostly tar-coated playground alone, her head loaded with confusing contradiction.

The trance effect of crocheting leveled her respiration and blocked off Grandfather's snoring, a guttural struggle so profound, it shook her eardrums. Once the limp latticework was completed, it would be soaked in starch and dried, and then ironed stiff and flamboyant, into a wreath as hard as sculptured wood. After a day of colossal heat that hindered movement, Grandmother welcomed the evening's breeze. She sat under the lamplight at the edge of their paisley couch closing her day by crocheting with skilled but uneven arms, the tip of her tongue between her teeth in concentrated effort. Her grandchild safely tucked away in sound sleep, Grandmother rapidly hooked loops and pulled from a thick spool, making a webwork of knots that caught the slippery insomniac hours. That is, until the arrival of the television.

Grandfather insisted on its volume, his loss of hearing worsening, and the television droned on, even as his lips suctioned scratchy grainy air once the newscast appeared. One evening Grandmother paused in her crocheting, a loop undelivered, a knot unresolved, and she stabbed her needle in a spool and listened to the English drone reportage of the country's collapse. Green jungles and green faces and green dogs. She removed her specs, licked them and then rubbed each lens with the corner of her apron, only making matters worse, the sinking feeling more pronounced, because things were crystal clear. Greenish Atlanta and Birmingham where greenish Negroes and gringos broke windows, the greenish heat of their discord firing their greenish blood to a pitch boil.

Night after night, she stopped crocheting. Would the color of the daily news ever change? No longer consoled in her spool and hook needle, Grandmother squeezed one hand with the other to get the warm rush of blood flowing. The spool rested beside her as Grandfather fought off nightmares some nights, his fist rising, his shoulders jerking, while other nights he slept soundly.

Wake up, Rogelio, Grandmother demanded, desiring his company. The La-Z-Boy had a salad-bowl depression molded to accommodate his hunched back and he slept more soundly on his recliner than in their matrimonial bed. She rose from the couch and lightly tapped his shoulder to arouse him, then pushed him harder, and he slurred, groggy, raising his fists to make contact, and then closed his mouth and slept some more.

To escape the television news, Grandmother wandered about the house, wringing her hands and searching for a peaceful space where the attack of the nerves would not find her. If she turned off the television, he immediately woke to brimstone and fire for reasons unbeknownst to her. If she paced up and down the hallway, the repetitious groans from the loose floorboard reminded her she was entrapped. If she looked out the window, the freeway construction bit endless trenches into the earth that resembled a moat, fortifying their safety from all that furious violence outside. No sooner would her sense of consolation override any panic than she realized the construction of the freeway was ridding the neighborhood of everything that was familiar to her. The memory of who lived where, who buried their children's umbilical cords or grew lemons the size of apples, done away. Grandmother thought about how carnivorous life was, how indifferent machinery teeth could be, and all these murky thoughts swirled the dust and tar and heat into a speeding meteor gathering strength.

She paced in her bedroom, the overhead fan chopping strenuously, the shoes lined in the closet, the shirts ironed and hung, boxers folded in quarters in the top left-hand drawer of the bureau, see? There they are, tucked as you left them this morning—some things change and some never do. Run water in the bathroom to drown out the grave voices of reporters warning of the escalating threat of nuclear destruction. Japan was only a photograph an ocean away, but Cuba so close she could hear the Russians speaking Spanish, and Watts, right there, sitting in your living room.

If she entered the child's bedroom, the hallway light fell on the photo, surprisingly unrattled from Grandfather's ever-present snoring. The man looping his arms around a woman's waist and resting a playful chin on the woman's shoulder, her daughter, Inez. She said her name finally, after promising never, never to say it again. Inez. Grandmother studied her daughter's faded laughter, her Inez in the photo, against the gurgling of her slumbering granddaughter.

Grandmother's uneven arm extended to touch Inez's face. What if the child turned out just like her mother? What if, what if.

A few sweaty hairs stuck to the child's temples and Grandmother pulled away the fleece lion head blanket from the child's broiling body. How a child's body could generate so much incredible heat was beyond Grandmother's comprehension, *but this is how you remember your daughter Inez. As you fold the blanket over the lion's incisors, the child moans and turns her head from side to side, causing you to jerk your hand away as if you have been singed by the heat.*

And this child was what was left of Inez. *The daughter whose small palm rested on your cheek as she suckled your breast. The daughter whose eyes welled wide with hunger. The daughter, your daughter, who fooled you into thinking that her vagina would not crave enough to risk birth. The daughter, your daughter, who convinced you that the belly of her heart would never become so gluttonous. The daughter, your daughter, whose dreams would be as big as revolutions that never thought to include you.*

Your mother's love was so blasphemous it deserved to be punished and you're not surprised when your daughter vanished in the hyphen of the Mexican-Guatemalan border. Death is finite but disappearance is not and so you see her face everywhere: in this granddaughter so full of heat; in this morning's oatmeal or in the glass window you gleamed yesterday with water and lemon juice; on the walls where you turned away from the fluorescent greenish glow of the television to watch the long wavering shadows flicker against last night. You squeeze one hand with another while you watch the child whose custody you requested against your husband's wishes, whose presence has cost you a million worries. You become aware, standing in the shaft of hallway light, that you cannot protect her from a world whose largeness invades every corner of your house. You cannot protect her even from the wilderness of herself.

And this fact will mangle you, mangle you into sleeplessness. Would you do it, have the courage to smother the child's breath once and for all? Let the meteor land softly over her head as you watch the child sleep, her lips making bubbles of air, small little glass bubbles of breath, and it scares you enough to flee the room, quake the rafters of your ribs, because right this moment, now, you ask, clenching your fist to your mouth, you ask:

How can you be a mother a second time when the world is so big and love is so, so small?

To avoid questions, Grandmother waited each afternoon at the end of the corridor rather than outside the bungalow like the other parents. At 12:35 p.m., Miss Eastman held the child's hand and walked her past the low water fountains, the bathrooms, past the equipment shed, past the school playground and through the long hollow corridor.

Under the shaded corridor, Miss Eastman's skin shone shoe-polish black. While the child slipped out her hand from Miss Eastman's chalky one and took hold of Grandmother's, Grandmother believed Miss Eastman was tarnishing darker from one day to the next, like clouds assimilating a storm, charged, electrified.

Vocab review, and the children quickly sat on mats circling their teacher. A pile of flash cards lay on Miss Eastman's lap, and the mole of her chin smiled friendly at the right answers. **DOG. RED. FISH.** Sitting next to the child, Moses discovered his chapped lips were useful in forming questions and not just at spitting paper balls.

You married to the cookie man? Moses blurted out. He couldn't read, but he could put two and two together. Even the four-fingered girl, who scratched the stump of her missing finger, looked up in utter amazement at the boldness of the question. A titter of nervous giggle ignited the circle into blazing rollick.

Moses wants to marry Miss Eastman, Rini chimed in. She leaned over to Milagros, and repeated the phrase as if she transferred important information, her bush and tangle of hair filling Milagros's vacant stare. Lollie pulled her sweater sleeves down to her wrist and in her most authoritative translator voice ordered Moses to shut his trap. Miss Eastman and Moses sitting in a tree, **K-I-S-S-I-N-G** . . . sang another boy, whose name the child did not know.

Quiet, now! Miss Eastman requested, the growing disorder of thirty-two children increasing. The flash cards nearly tumbled to the floor off her thick lap. She held her hand up, signaling silence. Bodies immediately became rigid, backs erect, and Miss Eastman's face was serious business. The teacher surveyed the circle of their faces with a stern teacher stare, and when the students were able to gather up their excitement and put it away, Miss Eastman proceeded with vocab review. She picked up a flash card.

Moses, first tell me what this word is, then I'll answer you, honest to God.

The birds, the air, the children were as silent as scripted dialogue forgotten onstage. The palms of Miss Eastman's hands were always powdery white with chalk. She flipped a card and pointed to the word written in black marker: **THINK.**

If the students disliked Moses because of his bawdy behavior and temper tantrums, chapped lips and bullying, they rooted for him to read the word so that they could hear the answer. **THINK,** it said to some of the students whose arms shot up, their bottoms lifting up excitedly. Now more than ever, the students wished that Moses, standing in front of the card, one eye shut in concentrated effort, had not been hit by a car as a toddler and that parts of his brain had not stopped working. **THINK.** They needed to know the answer, Me Me Me, they whispered, because some of the students wanted reassurance that no family existed, that Miss Eastman did not have a life outside of Bungalow Three. Indeed, it was unimaginable to see her outside of the classroom. **THINK THINK THINK.** That Miss Eastman belonged willfully and solely to Bungalow Three and to no one else.

Miss Eastman gently read the word: **THINK.** And a math-oriented but language-deficient Moses sat down again to think about the word.

The very next morning, Miss Eastman wrote **ERMILA ZUMAYA** on the blackboard, and for the rest of the day, the child would look up from her workbook and see it, imposing and neon-bright under the date. She admired it while sharpening her pencil or returning from re-cess, there it was to behold. By the end of their day, the child received a cupcake in a pastry box as a merit award. A feeling the child was not accustomed to washed her cheeks. The folds of her ears singed, her chest ached as Miss Eastman handed her the box for completing her workbooks and alphabet. The child knew her lips couldn't hold the huge smile, which burped out of her tummy loudly, making her class-mates split sides with laughter.

A bespectacled Grandmother didn't see the child lift the box to show off her award. The sunlight scarred her vision, and Grandmother couldn't quite discern the child holding on to Miss Eastman except for the white teeth of the teacher talking to the child as they walked the dark corridor to meet her. Grandmother had watched the escalating heat rising each and every day, the glass thermometer bursting, its red mercury spreading infectious green-tinted rage. Miss Eastman grew larger and darker, and the child swung her pink gift in the shaded hol-lowness of the corridor. No longer immunized, Grandmother knew it was only a matter of time before the roaming packs of Negroes would claw out of the television's own green guts, riot-rush to lift and over-turn cars and set fire to all the neighborhood had worked for, to any-thing flammable on the living side of First Street. Though the teacher passed the child over to Grandmother tenderly, Miss Eastman ap-peared so black, she was green.

The icing on the cupcake didn't stand a chance. Grandfather made grumpiness a full-time career. The child opened the lid to display her reward and even as the cupcake with blue roses and pink sugared lace melted into a lopsided lump inside the box on the kitchen table, the child expected him to acknowledge her sweet achievement, to say something even remotely kind. Instead, he left the table for his La-Z-Boy, a hint of vinegar lingering long after he was gone.

Grandmother followed him into the next room and sat down on the couch, fanning herself with a Blue Chip Stamp book. She wasn't one to ask for advice, but an increasing sense of anxiety began to build up in her, heat exhaustion perhaps, television fatigue maybe, world-weariness, and she began to ask her husband in a roundabout way. She believed like many others, not just her, that the heat was ultimate and would evaporate the waters and dry the land into dust bowls of drought, making the earth crack and quake. She gazed down at the basket of spools she hadn't touched in weeks, and asked if Grandfather believed in Judgment Day, and could he please lower the volume because she couldn't hear herself think, she couldn't hear herself think, his hellish box that miserably loud!

The child poked her finger into the whipped frosting and tasted the sweetness of hard work over the arguing voices of her grandparents. Mixed in the cement, a tumble of the fears and accusations. Sledge-hammers competing with Grandmother's heartbeats. Mixed in with the buzzing and farting of the earthmovers and the long cranes resembling dented kitchen utensils, Grandmother's inquiry—Is the child safe?—meaning either her granddaughter Ermila or her daughter Inez. Her question buried in the new pavement, her hands so soft and malleable, they were incapable of shaping her daily chores.

The playground's tar coat pumped the mighty hotness right through the thin rubber of the child's sneakers. A smog alert in progress and the child walked over to the shade of the handball courts while Memo, Stella, Lollie and Rini and her other classmates sat on lunch benches under an awning to play checkers, old maid, caroms or Chutes and Ladders, other raggedy old board games. Since physical activity was prohibited, the sixth-grade recess monitors worked double-time to keep the children from using the drinking fountains to douse themselves with water.

At the diamond wire fence, the child stared at a man shoveling dog turds into a bucket, two comadres talking by a stake-and-post fence, a fire truck speeding off. She anticipated the arrival of the old bird man, just as the pigeons did, gathering on the dilapidated roof of his house in numbers the child could not yet count. The pigeons cooed and fidgeted, awaiting their seed meal. Though she stood within the shade, the child felt her feet blazing, as if the heat came from the fiery core of the earth and not from above. Even the pigeons sought relief and flocked to one side of the roof where a leafy avocado tree hung over the house. Watching them huddling, it was easy for the child to consider their little pigeon claws burning painfully just like her own sneakers.

Upon the appearance of the old bird man, the pigeons fluttered in agitation. His broken body almost folded over in two as if the bucket of seed he carried was too heavy, and his unbuttoned shirt fluttered from the excited flap-flap of the numerous excited wings. As he placed the bucket down, gray feathers showered around him and this greeting made the bird man smile a smile so wide, the child was sure she could see it in his shadow. He picked up his bucket again and scuffled his slippers to the center of his clay-packed driveway and grabbed handfuls and scattered the seeds on the driveway like generous cups of water offered to thirsty soil.

Immediately a wave of wings swooped down and surrounded the old man's ankles in rolling, cooing, feathered pigeon bodies. His arms were skinny gnarled muscles of sea-wracked driftwood and some of the pigeons briefly perched on them before landing on the driveway. And it was in that moment, when some of the pigeons stretched their wings, while others pecked with their nervous beaks and pinhead eyes the crowded area of the driveway, that the child saw sizzling sparks. The candied-apple-red car was so polished, its doors so glossy, the sun danced sparks just like Chavela's sizzling matchsticks lighting her cigarettes.

Though she thought of Chavela, her eyes spied a thin, short man the color of maple syrup emerging from the automobile. The syrup man looked small, almost the size of Stella, who seemed as large as her heart. By the way he pursed his lips, he must have been whistling a song as he stuck his key into the trunk of the car. He wore a velvet blue vest and his long white sleeves were rolled up to his elbows. His sunglasses glinted here and there until the color of his car reflected red on his glasses when he closed the trunk with one hand. In the other, he held on to a large pink box.

The child recognized Miss Eastman, and when she greeted the man, he seemed stunted by her largeness. The child stared so hard, her gaze so intense, she didn't hear the buzzard end of recess, nor the rush of noisy students emptying the lunch tables. Miss Eastman fingered the strings of the box and then the syrup man laid the palm of his hand on Miss Eastman's cheek gently while the old bird man continued splashing seed on his driveway as the child saw how their lips touched briefly, brushing their breaths into one another's mouth, and then behind them she saw another wave of pigeons spread their wings in midair, expanding and filling space completely.

Pigeons in her belly, the child wanted to release them by opening her mouth wide. The feeling fluttered from her root-tangled intestines and traveled up through the tree trunk of her throat to the branch of her tongue, and there it perched, waiting for a listener. She turned to the lunch tables to seek out one of her classmates, but the playground was long ago empty, and she returned to Mr. and Miss Eastman, who had also vanished, and the child began to doubt what she had witnessed. Against the smoggy day as smoky as fog, the pigeons became a mass of feathers and wings, surrounding the old bird man. The loose shirt on his back billowed like a sail on a broken mast.

As the summer approached, the child tried to draw the kiss, **K-I S-S-I-N-G,** but the sketches of lips resembled the parakeet beaks knocking against one another. She crumpled several attempts into balls. Sitting in a tree . . . The parakeets pecked and screeched and bumped beaks and clung to the sides of the cage with their little claws and chirruped and fought and fell into naps that lasted long enough for the child to draw them. Birds kissing and dancing and eating and sleeping and Grandmother bird and Grandfather bird and teacher bird and cookie man bird and the old bird man and they all kissed and kissed. She wrote the letters **K-I-S-S-I-N-G,** tasted the sugared word on her lips. Clutching the sheets of sawdust paper at the end of the day, the Zumaya child ran through the playground bursting in bright sunny light, and then through the long dark corridor, and out from the other end of hollow silence.

EIGHT

A few summers before the summer of Renata Valenzuela's disappearance, there was the tent, and before the tent, there was Tío Angel lugging three quarts of Schlitz beer in paper bags twisted for easy handling. And before that, there was Turtle's Amá cleaning out the old O'Keefe stove, tearing it apart, leaving nothing intact except for the pilot gas flame that shook like fear.

And before Tío Angel knocked on the door of the house on First Street accompanied by his third common-law wife, Mercedes (or Aunt Mercy for short), and her younger brother, Cross-eyes, who stood behind her, Amá had soaked the oven knobs in Ajax and water, scrubbing the O'Keefe brand name so hard, the Brillo pads peeled the metal paint off.

And before all of this, the letter's arrival said something awful about Antonia and Luis's father, right before Antonia became Turtle and right before they became part of the McBride Boys por vida till death do us part. Meaning the letter said something like Frank, whose real name was Francisco, was dead, or worse yet, wasn't dead. Turtle would never know which one would make Amá hysterical enough to call Tío Angel and then chase them outside with the pretense that they had her permission to build a tent in the backyard as long as them two promised no funny business.

And that's just the way she said it, the words hissing through the gap of missing teeth, No funny business, sabes? Because that old man

Zumaya neighbor kept accusing them two of tampering with his tool-shed (which was true but wasn't true).

And so Turtle was dragging blankets and sheets out of the door when she spotted Tío Angel's arrival on the porch with his plaid short-sleeve shirt unbuttoned; and Turtle watched him place one amber Schlitz quart next to his combat boot so that he could knock on the screen door, Aunt Mercy right behind him holding a carton of Lucky Strikes and Cross-eyes behind her and on the lowest porch step, carrying a greasy bag with tacos from Tres Puntas. And before Tío Angel knocked on the door, Turtle swore that Cross-eyes's lime-green suit glowed a Friday party special. His side-zipper boots were the same color as his loud yellow shirt and he held the bag out so as not to get grease stains on his clothes.

And Turtle didn't think twice about dropping the bundle of blankets and rushing over to greet her favorite uncle and Luis Lil Lizard called her bad words for abandoning him so easily, for not showing loyalty. And after Tío Angel stroked Turtle's face, and after Aunt Mercy frowned mean at her shaved head and said, Why did you let your brother do that to you? the two entered the kitchen to investigate the letter that had made Amá weep. Cross-eyes stayed on the porch.

Turtle didn't know quite where Cross-eyes directed his glances. He seemed to stare at Luis Lil Lizard, though he handed Turtle a taco wrapped in tinfoil, and she sat down right next to him on the porch steps. She wore a pair of blue-jeans cutoffs and the bag of tacos rasped against her bare knee. The taco, stuffed with carne asada, onion and cilantro, kidnapped Turtle's hunger. She finished the taco in two bites and scratched her prickly short hair because she wanted to do something with her empty hands. The nickel sun busted out of the broken windows of the condemned houses on First Street and the tall metal cranes grew shadows as lengthy as giraffe necks across the walls.

Cross-eyes looked or maybe didn't look at Turtle. She clawed the top of her itchy head. The stubble felt grainy.

Want another one? Cross-eyes asked, and Turtle thought he asked Luis Lil Lizard, who ignored him because her brother was too busy be-coming something else like twilight becoming night. Like cutting off a lizard tail with rusty scissors as he did when he was younger, and growing another lizard tale for himself with the title of McBride Pride. Cross-eyes delivered another silver-bullet taco on Turtle's lap. She unfolded the foil and the corn tortilla was rubbery as only cold corn tortillas can get.

Whenever Tío Angel returned from the place he never talked about, he enjoyed a long, hot, steamy shower until his skin was polished bronze and his tattoos looked black instead of purple. Before he dressed for his homecoming parties, he wrapped a towel around his waist and partially covered the *Last Supper* tattooed on his belly. His girth accommodated all twelve apostles including Judas, whom Tío Angel had wanted to exclude, but the tattoo man said no, it wouldn't be for real if there wasn't a Judas. In consolation, the tattoo man tattooed Jesus' angelic head above Tío Angel's heart, and that was why he never buttoned up his shirt.

Turtle had visions of Tío Angel's appearances. The grown-ups never told her where he returned from. Never. So when Tío Angel appeared, it was twelve noon or twelve midnight, a frajo clinging to his bottom lip. He brought an aura behind him as bright as La Virgen de Guadalupe but also somber as Judas of *The Last Supper*. There was something holy and fearful about Tío. In her dreams, Turtle opened the door for him, and either brightness or darkness blinded her.

Amá had planted nopales around the rim of their small patch of grass in the back of their rented house on First Street, and it was the only plant that seemed to thrive in their yard. One could tell where their yard ended and the Zumaya yard began because the old hunchback Zumaya mowed and watered his lawn, manicured his shrubs, trimmed his avocado and peach trees with committed fervor while their own neglected backyard grew weedy and brown like an empty lot. Near the back of Amá's yard, and not far from where some corrugated tin leaned into rotting wood pickets left by the last tenants, there was a wire laundry line suspended between two poles where them two Gamboas had pitched their tent before.

The tent was always assembled with great precision between the

T-poles: layered sheets on each side, heavy quilts for the bedding, since the dawn mist made the brittle grass damp and cold. Clothespins were used as nails, Simon bricks as support pegs and the door flap had to be large enough to see the stars at night. Alone on a campout, they smoked frajos and conducted farting contests, burned plastic toy soldiers to see how long they took to melt and made fun of just about everybody over fifteen with the exception of Tío Angel.

Luis Lil Lizard would often stuff a pillow under the back of his T-shirt and above his shoulders. He hung his arms with apelike awkwardness and acted like Quasimodo, like the hunchback Zumaya himself, and they laughed until their bladders burst and they peed behind the Zumaya toolshed. Turtle tried to pee like a man, standing up, legs apart, and peed in the darkness like her brother, who stained the back plywood panels of the toolshed. They stayed awake until it was so dark they couldn't see the front of their hands, until their eyelids hung heavy and her brother had filled her with scary cuentos. Like the discovery of human skulls. While the construction men were building the freeway, they found bones. Telling no one, they just threw the skulls into the wet cement and kept on working. Only after getting Turtle's full attention, Luis Lil Lizard would say, Hey, you hear something? Tick-tocking? Don't you hear it? Outside the tent? Right behind you!

Yea? & Right & Fuck You! Turtle said, but tried to stay awake until the nighttime noises became exaggerated and sirens sounded like the long arm of La Llorona, until she succumbed unwillingly and finally slept so close to her brother Luis, they became one instead of two.

Cross-eyes teased Turtle, called her a cabeza de melón because of her shaved head, and Turtle was pleased when he spilled red chile on his yellow shirt collar. The stain looked like splats from a bad shave.

¡Ay qué la chingada!

God punished you, Turtle said, poking the last bite of her taco into her mouth.

¡Ay qué la chingada! Puta madre. Cross-eyes scraped a finger to remove the spill off his Friday night shirt and then he didn't know quite what to do with his finger. Su madre. Fuck me, he said, maybe to Turtle's cabeza de melón, maybe not.

Luis Lil Lizard almost said something with his almost-man voice. Instead he let out a bumpy, robust burp.

Brand-new too, Cross-eyes said, still pissed at his chile stain. He balled up some tinfoil and threw it out and sat back down to finish his meal.

Turtle smelled Cross-eyes even though the tacos carried a thick onion smell. Cross-eyes smelled of Zest soap and Old Spice cologne. All three of them ate quietly on the porch steps until Tío Angel screeched the screen door open and stuck his head out to see if they had enough tacos.

Need more? he asked in a voice like a man who really meant it, like someone who genuinely cared about them having enough. And Luis Lil Lizard skillfully opened the paper bag with one hand because the other held a taco dripping of salsa, and he gestured to Tío Angel with a slight lift of his chin, barely acknowledging his question.

Hanging with the McBride Boys, Luis was learning how not to talk, and it was all about learning the unspoken for him now: the downward three-finger signal meaning *M* for McBride-Marijuana-Muerte, Que Rifa; the confident badass walk protecting a nation of city blocks claimed by McBride; the khakis and Pendleton uniform por vida, the spit-shine wingtips polished, the haircut readied for battle; the one-of-a-kind McBride handshake—finger bullhorns ramming; the middle finger pulled erect like cannons to shoot out a Fuck you, y qué? A slight lift of chin to gesture, You ain't worth the trouble if you ain't part of McBride. It was all about unquestioned loyalty that only familia could understand.

And Tío Angel understood. He read the missing words and he slapped Luis upside his crew-cut head to get a word out of him. Speak up, he ordered, one combat ass-kicking boot coming out of the door. Hey, badass, you got enough to eat or no? Tío Angel asked again, his Jesus of *The Last Supper* tattoo peering out from between the curtains of his shirt. Luis Lil Lizard raised a shoulder to reject him, hate him, grabbed his third taco from the bag and finally uttered:

Yea, yea, yea. Enough already.

I don't take shit from nobody, sabes mi'jo? And Tío bent a little more to rub the spiky section where he had Three Stooges–slapped Luis, regretting his outburst.

Later, after quarts of beer and the lapses of grown-up conversations, Tío called Luis over, said, Ven pa'cá mi'jo, we need to cross some words, man to man.

Coming from the washroom, Luis approached him holding a bag of clothespins for the assembling of the tent. He stood in front of Tío Angel, out of respect.

Where's your other half? Tío asked, cupping Luis's face with the callused palms of a man unafraid to go to war or prison. Luis felt foolish holding Amá's knuckled cotton sack of clothespins, more foolish because of the attentive affection of another man. Tío Angel kissed him, a beery sloggy kiss on Luis's cheek, because he loved him like the son he never had, or he loved him because he saw himself in Luis and was reading the missing words like a book.

Luis Lil Lizard pulled back to reject his kiss, but not enough to prevent it.

You been hanging out too much with men, ése, Aunt Mercy said, a tumbler with flat beer in front of her. She wore a striped halter top, and her breasts cushioned her crossed arms. Aunt Mercy had a two-faced jealous edge to her that started getting sharper once you crossed her, and when she crossed her arms, it warned Luis Lil Lizard to get out of the line of fire. Luis walked past her still holding the clothespins, the slop of his tío's kiss lingering wet on his newly stubbled cheek.

Wash my clothes too, would you, tuff homeboy? Aunt Mercy continued, because she thought humiliation captivating.

There was something holy and fearful about Tío Angel. Amá and Frank were the only grown-ups that Turtle had seen duking it out until Tío Angel returned, and then the brawling added up to Amá and Frank and Tío, and then another time, two grown women slugging it out over Tío Angel and one of them was Aunt Mercy. Luis was still Luis and she was still Antonia and they were still quite young and it was at a barbecue. Frank was still their father and he leaned close to Amá, her shoulders hunching under the bulk of his cradling arm. It must have been a family gathering to celebrate Tío Angel's return from the place he never talked about.

At the barbecue, the grown-ups acted silly and light-headed. The music boomed loud from the RCA Victor turntable console inside the house. They had started the barbecue with easy listening music—Los Duendes' "Boleros para Enamorados," and then came the mariachi serenades in hi-fi stereo gritando mucho gusto drinking music. The charcoal smell, unique to cookouts and mixed with family gatherings and summer air, wavered in and out of the open windows of the houses up and down the block.

Frank never acted up at parties; he pressed close to Amá's cheek to speak with her over the music. He acted like a proper gentleman incapable of becoming a man who could knock out Amá's teeth so that she would have to cover her mouth whenever she smiled; a man who could throw a punch so hard, the thumps shattered the glassiness of her eyes; a man who used an ironing cord to whip Turtle, fists for Amá and for Luis Lil Lizard when he tried to interfere. A man who lived with such crazed fury, Turtle almost felt sorry for him.

But Frank acted proper at the barbecue, which began at two p.m. and continued into the late afternoon and the children already had their fill of potato chips and chili hot dogs and pork & beans and Kool-Aid. Before the children became grown-ups, the summer air was so sharp, it cut open the twilight like a cracked watermelon, and they lined up for slices as crimson as a twilight smile. And before the male children were old enough to be drafted into the Vietnam War, and before the female children became widows and single parents or caretakers of their husbands' maimed souls, they were carefree children, every one of them, at the barbecue celebrating the return of Tío Angel. They bit into the watermelon with unequaled joy and they removed their shoes and ran around the front yard barefoot, playing tag, playing hide-and-seek, playing fist-ball, never thinking of war or death or sorrow or nightmares and only thinking about what to play next.

Turtle and Luis received a scolding when they turned on the hose and flooded the rosebushes and Frank debated whether them two should be punished or be left alone and finally the be-left-alone opinion won out. Turtle hid until she was sure he wouldn't change his mind because Frank was a man incapable of remembering promises. She waited, and man, she hated waiting, before she reappeared at the barbecue again.

Someone brought out lamps connected to extension cords, and someone else removed the lampshades and switched on the lightbulbs in the driveway that eventually attracted circling moths. Chili sauce dried around the rim of the pot, and the remaining hot dogs burned into charcoal crust atop the forgotten grill. Watermelon rinds joined the paper cups and crumpled napkins, and empty longnecks were shattered everywhere. The music and the conversation, the dancing and the spilling of liquor rose in volume as the sun set and the night dropped.

Frank bowed in front of Amá, Fred Astaire–dramatic, and extended an invitation to dance. Amá coyly rebuffed his hand until the compadres and comadres urged her to accept, and after a slight hesitation, she agreed, and allowed Frank to lead her to the middle of the makeshift dance floor, which was really the cement driveway. She wore a sleek beige dress with pale gardenias and white high heels. Compadres and comadres pushed themselves out of the way to give these graceful dancers some room, to spotlight their youth and potential, and Turtle jostled around the bodies to see the shadows of her parents shuttle before her.

Amá held her head erect, her eyes ready to anticipate every improvised move of her partner's steps. Turtle had never seen Amá focused so hard on one thing. An arrogance unfamiliar to her face, Amá wore a sultry expression. Frank raised his arm and twirled her like a jewelry-box ballerina and Amá's white high heels seemed a blur. When they stopped they were tightly wound up against one another, and they stared at each other. Years rolled off Frank like the sweat he wiped away with his free hand. They were two bodies so tightly pressed against one another, one would think that nothing could come between them.

The nopal cactus was the only thing that thrived in their small rented house on First Street. The walls had absorbed so many years of disappointments, bad plumbing, strife, arguments, electrical shorts and temper outages that the wallpaper became unglued, the tiles fell from their grouting, the toilet chain in the water tank busted. Amá was part of the house, carelessly repaired with cardboard and duct tape like her cracked windows. Frank was part of the house, a loose, exposed wire ready to electrocute anyone who touched him. And Tío Angel was Frank's younger brother and a part of no house.

Before Angel was an ex-con, he was a Korean War hero, and his army portrait was hand-brushed at Veloz Photography to accentuate his long, dark lashes. And before the portrait glass was shattered one Christmas Eve, it stood on a doily on top of Frank's beloved stereo. A sure cause of another one of those fights that struck with mysterious force, it pulled out all the fear in Turtle, and her lungs fell useless like empty pockets pulled inside out. She took refuge on top of the house to escape the knowledge of how easy flesh tore, how fragile bone was, and her stomach and cheeks rasped against the sandy shingles of the roof. Her hands trembled so hard, it was difficult to keep from slipping from the angle slant downward.

From the nowhere of the night, Tío Angel appeared, his blue Buick skidding into the driveway. He sprang out, motor still running, headlights beaming, and jumped on the porch, rushing inside the house to discover Amá holding up her bloodied broken mouth, Luis Lil Lizard semiconscious on the floor of the kitchen. Turtle nowhere to be found.

Tío Angel lunged at his brother Frank, and after the bump and break of furniture, the fall and jingle of Christmas tree, the grind and gravel of glass shards, Turtle heard the screen door screech open. Turtle dug her fingertips underneath some shingles, terrified of falling, and she peered over the roof's edge and saw how awkwardly the scuffling shadows flew into the nopales.

The big men thumped their cold reptile chests and tangled their arms and stomped on the nopales like two huge dinosaurs destroying a city. Tío's knees finally pinned Frank down on the mat of dead grass. Amá headlocked Tío Angel, trying to pull him off, but Tío took little notice and his hair wildly thrashed against his own forehead. The headlights of the blue Buick stabbed the darkness, and Turtle could see Amá straddling Tío's bucking back while his fists sucked and sucked and sucked blood from Frank's face as red as the pulp of nopal fruit.

Luis was leafing through the wallets, slipping out dollar bills or lifting cigarettes or pocketing Certs mints from the purses belonging to the guests at the barbecue. He glanced out from the bedroom window and caught sight of his father Frank leaning forward, left shoe pointed out, to gently balance Amá's curved crescent moon back with the palm of his left hand. A handful of coins slowly dripped from between Luis's fingers. The secrets his parents kept.

Frank slowly drew in Amá and her body closed up against his. The song ended and his parents collapsed into each other's arms laughing, while guests enthusiastically applauded. Amá fanned herself with her hand, then covered her smile to conceal her missing teeth. She returned to her seat, her gardenias wilting at the folds of her waist.

Luis tore into his thievery with greater conviction. He emptied out a purse, carelessly scattering its contents in front of him to inspect the valuables. A lipstick, a few pennies, a broken comb, and some ripped pieces of paper impossible to put together again. Nothing of value. Nothing worth keeping.

Turtle had completed most of the tent assemblage by the time Luis Lil Lizard returned holding the sack of clothespins. She needed one more sheet to peg with old bricks, a few more clothespins to secure its place, and asked her brother to pass her some. Luis Lil Lizard simply threw the sack on the brittle grass, and the pins spilled out. Turtle muttered bad words under her breath and prostrated to retrieve the wooden pins, which were barely visible against the approaching night.

Luis squatted on his haunches to smoke a frajo on the other side of the sheeted wall. He wanted to be left alone and Turtle didn't ask to share the frajo. Was he still angry at her for having been caught shoplifting at the Val U Mini Mart? Was he ashamed of her? She pinned the last clothespin and saw his defined silhouette on the other side of the sheet, a figure of total boredom, distant and someone else. From this night on, he would refuse to help build a tent or spend time with her because he busied himself in becoming someone else. Turtle should have known that Luis would leave her tonight.

Tonight the McBride Homeboys would claim Luis Lil Lizard by searching out the freshly laid cement of the freeway bridges and sidewalks in order to record their names, solidify their bond, to proclaim eternal allegiance to one another so that in twenty, thirty years from tonight, their dried cemented names would harden like sentimental fossils of a former time. The huge slabs of concrete would provide inviting canvases for the boys, an exhilarating challenge of the best kind, beyond anything else offered tonight, and Caltrans would try not to lay cement over the weekend, too many vandals destroying property, too many warning signs that justify menacing threats, more sheriffs patrolling, giving the boys a hit-and-run game of tagging, spray-painting all over the signs in laugh-out-loud violations, becoming the Caltrans contractor's worst nightmare. On a Monday morning the workers would find:

MR SPEEDY x POOR x SIDE; BROOKLYN DIABLOS c/s; RUEBEN, ERNIE, RALPH; EL CHINO JOCKEY x Lote M/ LIL LIZARD, SANTOS x McBRIDE QUE RIFA; RUDY LOVES LA CAT BERNIECE POR VIDA.

The boys would never know that in thirty years from tonight, the tags would crack from the earthquakes, the weight of vehicles, the force of muscular tree roots, from the trampling of passersby, become as faded as ancient engravings, as old as the concrete itself, as cold and clammy as a morgue table. And in those thirty years the cracks would be repaired here and there with newer patching cement, making the boys' eternal bonds look worn and forgotten. Not even concrete engravings would guarantee immortality, though tonight they would all feel immortal.

Right after he finished smoking his frajo, Luis Lil Lizard's shadow would rise and reappear as a McBride Boy, an infinite part of the freeways. Tonight, even before Luis was out of sight, Turtle would start missing him.

Before Mercedes became Aunt Mercy, there was Rosie with corn-silk hair who accompanied Tío Angel to the front yard barbecue. Shortly before their arrival, a police cruiser patrolled the street and threw flashlight beams on the guests. It was barely eleven on a Saturday night, and one of the chota was a primo of a cousin of another primo of the host of the barbecue, and so the police officer gave them one hour to bust up the party. As soon as the police car departed, the compadres' bravery rose in an alcoholic fog and they told the phantom officers to go fuck themselves.

By this time, two compadres had carried out the RCA Victor home console stereo with as much care as taking out the trash cans on a Thursday morning, and the hostess just about fainted seeing her prized Moorish-style cabinet propped on bricks. Someone else had plugged it into an extension cord that ran through a hole in the screen window, and the hostess planned to get her husband for this after everyone was gone.

Someone had requested "King of the Road," which played about a thousand times, and someone requested "The Ballad of the Green Berets," which brought tears to the war veterans of the families. Finally, some real dancing music played on—rumba line, mambo madness, polkas de Los Broncos de Juárez, Grupo Paso Del Norte.

By this time, the younger children fell asleep in their mamas' arms. By this time, the comadres wanted to go home because they didn't want to have any trouble with the chota; yet the barbecue was turning into a full-fledged blowout. There wasn't a clean plate or cup in the kitchen. With the arrival of the guest of honor, los hombres wanted to blast the music for Tío Angel, forget about those pinche shot glasses and take direct swigs from the tequila bottle. By this time, little arguments broke out between husbands and wives, between children and mamas, between host and hostess, while someone had vomited in the bathroom and had made a feeble attempt to clean the mess. By this time, full-grown men cried over lost loves or haunting old wounds, and everyone needed strong coffee. Some of the women were simply fed up and started walking home, children in tow, and some stayed behind because, hell, this was, at the very least, a night out.

Talk became freer under the security of tequila, and everyone spilled secrets. Turtle overheard one man tell another compadre in the silence between a record ejecting and flopping down on the turntable, *Angel will always love her* in Spanish, and Turtle understood it because Spanish was not yet deeply buried in the middle of nowhere. The man then pointed, not at Angel's lovely date, Rosie with the corn-silk hair, who seemed amused by the staggering red-faced compadres trying to lift Tío Angel onto their shoulders, but to Turtle's Amá, who pulled her gardenia hem over her crossed knees as she sat near the garage door.

The other compadre propped his lopping drunken head with his cigarette hand and didn't reply. Before the needle skipped on the groove of the album and another polka played, which sounded like all the other polkas, Turtle heard fizzling, the lit cigarette singeing the drunken man's salpimienta hair. Its sizzling, burning noise sounded unlike anything she had ever heard before, and Turtle wanted to cover her ears.

Before someone pulled out Luis's draft number, and before the McBride Boys stole him away, Turtle needed to listen to someone speak and so went into the kitchen. Tío Angel sat at the table shirtless and Amá had stopped crying, though her flattened nose glowed red, her eyes almost punched swollen. Amá looked so tired. The soft fleshy lips that once appeared in her wedding photograph were now chafed slits where she inhaled her cigarettes. The whites of her eyes were pinkish as if the pain flooded even the smallest of veins. Turtle almost felt sorry for her.

The cigarette smoke lingered in the curtains, the chairs, their clothes, and Aunt Mercy stopped talking when Turtle entered. They all glanced in Turtle's direction. There was a small fan on the table to which Amá had tied strips of wet cloth so that they cooled the air and the fan's swirling noisy blades drowned out the radio's vacillation between stations. The letter regarding Mr. Frank Gamboa sat unfolded near the butt-filled ashtray.

Turtle opened the refrigerator and removed a metal ice tray and then cracked the tray, feeling their silent eyes drilling the back of her shaved head. Turtle removed some ice cubes and dropped them in a glass jar. She remembered the viejita then, the one they called Chavela, and remembered the way her cigarette hung from the corner of her mouth while cracking a tray of ice cubes on the porch railing of her blue house, which was the same way Tío Angel's frajo hung from between his lips. Turtle returned the ice tray and then filled her jar with water. Doused with Ajax, the stove knobs in the sink full of water bobbed like apples. Turtle wanted to ask about the letter, which was about to flutter off the table from the breeze of the fan, and Aunt Mercy, acting fast, placed the ashtray on it.

What about—

What about what? asked Aunt Mercy.

What, wha . . . where'd Cross-eyes go? Turtle asked, relieved to have thought of a question.

Don't call him that, Amá said. She pinched her nose with a paper towel and thus sounded nasal.

He's been called worser, Aunt Mercy replied.

Tío Angel's shirt hung on the back of his chair, and Jesus of *The Last Supper* peered over the table.

Where's your other half? Tío asked, and Turtle shrugged her shoulders. She looked over the rim of the mason jar as if drinking iced water were the most important thing in her life.

What's with the shaved head? Aunt Mercy asked Amá, though Turtle stood right in front of her. Aunt Mercy had a way of excluding people from a conversation. She had a way of making people like Turtle feel invisible though they were maybe two feet from her. It made what prickly hair remained stand on its ends, and she rubbed her head, a custom that she was slowly acquiring.

What about it? Amá replied, her words scraping against the gravel of her throat.

You 'member Chuy's daughter? 'Member her, Angel baby? Mercy asked. From Humphrey Street? La malflora who did her old man in, 'member?

Aunt Mercy dug a finger into her ear, her face crunching. She inspected her ear wax.

Chuy was a drunk, Tío Angel said, gulping from the amber quart of Schlitz. The bottle looked small in his hand. He took a long drag from his frajo.

Drunk or no, he didn't deserve to die like some pinche perro on the street.

Tío Angel's words Mercy, mercy, mercy floated on the exhaling puffs of cigarette smoke. Amá slowly wrapped a raggedy paper towel around a finger.

La pinche malflora stabbed him cold, man. I 'member you could see the police chalk marks where he just laid there like a dog. Dead. The malflora was bad news all around.

Bottom-line it, Tío Angel replied. Get to the point of your chisme.

Bottom line is la malflora shaved her head. That was the start of going bad.

Then Aunt Mercy crossed her arms and glared at Turtle. She had bottom-lined it to the max and this accomplishment pleased her.

The start of going bad, Amá repeated, sighing.

Turtle loitered in the kitchen hoping they'd forget about her and slowly resume their conversation about the letter. She wasn't thirsty, but without the other half of the cold-blooded Gamboa brothers, she didn't know what else to do. She sipped from her jar and hoped they wouldn't ask her to leave. The word "malflora" sounded so sad to Turtle, it was a word you shouldn't be left alone with.

Why she getting so tall? Aunt Mercy asked, as if there were something defective about Turtle's size. While leaning on the back of her chair, Mercy looked at her common-law husband. I guess it runs in the family.

Fix the radio, Tío Angel said, weary of Mercy's long-winded commentaries. His growing, smoldering cigarette ash hung tight.

What else do you want? Amá asked Turtle.

I was thirsty.

And now you're not.

Turtle became suddenly aware that she held a mason jar containing a trace of melted ice and she didn't know what else to do and just stood there listening. She tried to decipher the voices on the radio as Aunt Mercy swiveled the radio knob, the voices dissolving into unintelligible static. What could be worse in life than a bad flower? Turtle meekly placed the glass jar on the sink counter and tried to think of another question, stalling.

Well? Amá asked.

Jesus, man, Turtle said. Okay.

Tío Angel pulled in his girth, and Jesus appeared over the rim of the table like a sun rising.

You rang?

Unable to withstand Aunt Mercy's guffaws, Turtle left. Because she didn't know what else to do with herself, Turtle sat on the same porch step Cross-eyes had a few hours before. She looked out into the endless field of the construction. By Monday, the earthmovers would be running again, biting trenches wider than rivers; the groan, thump and burr noise of the constant motors would weave into the sound of her own breath whistling the blackened fumes of dust and crumble in her nasal cavities. And this sound would only disappear at night when she held her breath or when she looked out from her porch steps as she was doing now to see the blue house like all the other houses disappearing inch by inch just like Chavela and all the other neighbors. In its place, the four-freeway interchange would be constructed in order to reroute 547,300 cars a day through the Eastside and would become the busiest in the city.

But tonight, on the porch steps, Turtle stared at the incomplete on-ramp bridge being constructed above the boundary of the Chinese cemetery. It resembled a mangled limb, as if a monster dinosaur had bitten into it, and a mesh of electrical wires hung out of broken cement like arteries dripping mounds of heaved-up rubble.

At the barbecue, Rosie two-step slow-danced with Tío Angel, her long corn-silk hair under Tío's cologned chin, her arms wrapped around him, her ear and cheek pressed against the buttons on his chest, feeling his muscles below and then his heart beating through the eye sockets of Jesus below that. Rosie closed her eyes tight to feel him and Tío closed his eyes tighter to feel her feeling him. They barely skimmed the driveway, forgetting that they were among a whole crowded group of slow dancers. The crooning ballads slowly wound down the party. Most of the children had gone home and a bored, sleepy Turtle leaned on Amá, working herself into a cantankerous mood. Where Luis had disappeared to was anyone's guess.

Before Luis Lil Lizard had shaved Turtle's head, before she started going bad, Turtle had shoulder-length chestnut hair, and Amá absentmindedly wrapped Turtle's hair around her finger. And this gesture, so soothing a gesture, disarmed Turtle's grumpiness and she leaned heavy on her mother, sleep victorious.

It happened in early morning that was still the night before. Mercy arrived wearing rollers, her chenille robe flying open like a cape as she ran across the street, the curb, the lawn, to the driveway in fuzzy flip-flop slippers. Someone had phoned her from the barbecue and tattled on Angel, and Mercy didn't have time to paint her eyebrows, put on some shoes, remove her rollers. This was a real emergency needing an immediate response. Fuck it if she never before went out of the house without drawing her eyebrows.

Mercy tore into Rosie before Rosie even knew what hit her. Mercy grabbed a handful of Rosie's hair like one would grab corn silk when husking corn, and jerked her head away from Angel's heart. Then she pulled her elbow back as if it were an arrow and released a bull's-eye punch on Rosie's nose, splattering blood on Angel's plaid shirt.

From the gentle strokes of her mother's hand to the explosion of expletives and blood, Turtle was startled out of her sleep. Chairs fell to the ground, comadres began to scream, beer bottles broke as light-bulbs popped and someone yelled that Mercy held a knife, which turned into a revolver, but was really only her clump of keys. Stray fists and fingernails broke the skin on Angel's face as he tried to ref-eree between the two women. Losing his balance, he fell backward on the stereo, and the crooner's voice skidded to a stop. Rosie reached for Mercy's rollers and the bobby pins flew out in all directions like a porcupine trying to defend itself. Amá pushed Turtle out of harm's way, but Turtle struggled against her mother's grasp and pushed her-self between the grown-ups who stood by useless in halting the fight. Their faces pleaded, their gazes filled with car-wreck gawks, horrified and serious except for Frank. He was hysterical at the sight of two grunting mujeres wrestling over his big-time hero brother, their cheeks burnt red, neither of them easing an inch on the driveway. Stubbornly locked, there were actually moments when the two small women fisted each other so tightly, they froze, each one afraid to lose ground.

Finally a few comadres hollered and tried to pull the two women apart. Breasts hung out, blouses shredded, fleshy open wounds bled and in between the arms and noise, Turtle caught Rosie's face. Puffed, bright red, losing her grip on Mercy, her nose bleeding everywhere. And then Mercy losing, her once-rolled-up hair now matted in coagu-lated blood like a cheap dye job. Rosie losing and then Mercy losing, and Turtle felt she watched a mighty building blazing, forks of flames bursting from the windows, the powerful heat forcing the walls to col-lapse onto itself. A Judas of the worst kind.

A lone car passed on First Street and hours passed before Turtle heard another. She lay alone in the tent and listened to the muffler and then listened to the flutter of the tent and then heard the absence of sound, no radio, no fan, no conversation. The silence was as spooky as the absence of a heartbeat. A dog barked in consecutive yaps and then stopped, and then a choir of crickets rubbed their symphony of legs. Turtle waited for Luis to return.

Turtle looked up at the darkness between the wire lines and clothespins and observed the shadow play of the beavertail opuntia cactus on the sheets and thought perhaps they had, the nopal and she, something in common.

Cool went straight to her bare feet, and the breeze picked up from flutter to flap and it was a while before she heard the crushing dried weeds of footsteps. She hunched in the corner of the tent, pulling her knees to her chest, and waited for whatever was out there to go away. But the footsteps continued, and Turtle pulled the tent door aside and peered her shaved head out to see a twisted branch from the old man Zumaya's avocado tree scratching a window. Perhaps the wind strummed the laundry lines.

Luis?

Turtle. Her name sounded like a metal lid of a trashcan against some empty street.

Who's there? Luis?

Turtle ticktock.

Stop it, you fucker.

What are you waiting for? Come on, no one said.

The overgrown and brittle grasses, which grew between the back door of the house and her tent, played the shapes and shadows of the trees and resembled La Llorona's long fingers. All the lights were out in the Zumaya house.

This ain't funny, Luis, Turtle said. The winds loosened the edges of the sheets and lifted up the corners. Had it been a warm sunny day, the wind might have been a friendly breeze, but since the night grew empty of friends, Turtle didn't wait for the ticktock. She rushed out of the tent. Without a full moon, she groped for the back door of the house in a stumble. The winds blew the tall weeds like hollow flutes.

Turtle couldn't believe her mother had bolted the back door even though she knew they slept outside, and so Turtle tried to open the side windows. Amá had kept them shut tight because of the construction noise and dust, but sometimes she would crack the windows open to let the night air in. Turtle crushed her cheek against the window and pushed her fingertips between the windowpane to hoist, scrape the window up and open and be saved. The unsuccessful attempt delivered waves of frustration and terror. She rapped on the window. Everything remained dark and locked and silent.

Turrrtle, no one said. The more she tried, the greater her desperation became. The night became darker, loneliness more so. No one said her name. She ran around to the front door and reached for the doorknob and began banging on the aluminum screen door and her heart hammered like her knocking—long, rapid, unanswered.

Turtle worked her fingers into a small hole in the screen, and then yanked the screen enough to get to the doorknob of the front door. It was then that she heard a siren howling, which was long, urgent and routine in the Eastside. She refused to look up at the ghost houses and abandoned machinery and the trenches being readied for a mass burial. Her heart drummed inside her skull and she fisted both hands on the flimsy, loosened doorknob as if it anchored her against the blinding dark. The siren was unending and operatic. Turtle felt her bare feet begin to lift like the corners of the tent sheets just a few minutes ago. She held fast to the doorknob, her whole body lifting by the coalescing force of the siren's vacuous mouth. She held on for dear life, not wanting to be drawn in by the shrill, but the ribbon of its wailing was wrapping around her ankles and lifting. The siren's mouth opened wider and Turtle felt her sweaty fingers slipping from their clasp, suctioned at once and forever into the prolonged length of the street's mournful plea.

PART III

NINE

The morning drone of freeway woke her, the communal heave-ho electricity of working people gathering, loading, preparing for, in departure of, en route to their place of employment. And on this balmy dawn hinting rain Ermila asked herself: Why even bother? Why bother to lift her head from the pillow, sit on her bed to stare at the dog scratching ticks, pull on her robe and march past the living room where Nacho snored on the couch and straight to the kitchen to holler out her guts at Grandmother about the dog, why even try?

Why bother to remember Nacho's lips or glance at her alarm clock, and then place her feet on the hardwood floor and wrap the cinch of her robe into a fisted knot and crack the window slats to see so many people walking down First Street it could easily be six in the evening. People began cranking up this clunky machinery of human enterprise while others ended their workday by dawn. The El Gallo bakers had baked all night and by morning they had dusted the last batch of pan dulce, the sweet warm scent trailing her all the way to school. Too, the grocer of the Val U Mini Mart had already unloaded his selection of the freshest vegetables and fruits from the downtown docks where first come first served was the golden rule. And then there was the QA ever so vigilant and their cohorts the shooters. Peering from between the slats, the curfew roadblocks were suddenly stacked and stored and out of sight, delivering the streets to normal as if nothing had happened during those a.m. hours, though something had. And she knew it but couldn't put her finger on it and now she was down to five because she had one injured hand and Ermila sadly regarded her fingers wiggling from the awkward bandage like a family of foreign tentacles.

Why did she make it a ritual, a habit, a routine to pincer the slats apart each morning and observe men wearing their butcher whites, others with paper-boat hats or baseball caps, passing her window alone or in pairs? Four freeways crossing and interchanging, looping and stacking in the Eastside, but if you didn't own a car, you were fucked. Many were, and this is something Ermila always said in her head: You're fucked. Though this morning she said, We're fucked, as the men passed her window to gather on the corner for the Rapid Transit 26 bus where the women already waited, all ready.

Each morning Ermila saw them from her window: several women in several sizes and ages who carried with them the weight of a family or two or three, their backs slumped over as they sat on the bus bench, their sweaters draped over their shoulders for protection against the morning chill. They toted their history of muted desires packed tightly in the bags under their eyes, and carried with that the poker face of their responsibility, a grimace left over from their splash of cold water on their cheeks each morning.

The five-thirty bus took the first set of female passengers to the Westside where, *if* they spoke English, they worked as nannies for hire (and did the ironing) or, if they didn't speak the language, they worked as housekeepers (ditto with the ironing). The second set of women took the six o'clocker and traveled downtown, where they operated speedy sewing machines in the garment district or worked as hotel maids or worked as nurses' aides in nursing homes. But all of them journeyed out of the neighborhood and outward into the massive un-known to become a part of the city's working migration. It might have strained lesser believers, might have broken their profound belief in hard work, were these women not made of gut and grist and a gleam of determination as blinding as a California sun.

They sat on the bus bench, canvas bags beside them, filled with the day's essentials: fearlessness scrambled with huevos con chorizo and wrapped in a tortilla as thin as the documents they carried to prove le-gality. Neatly packed burritos in a container bought at a Tupperware party hosted by a co-worker or a cousin or the boss's wife and so they felt obliged to buy. Some carried jars of cool tap water con canela as Lollie's mother did (for cleansing your bladder from infections caused by not being able to get up from the sewing machine to "make waters"). Others carried embroidery projects or knitting for the one- or two- or two-and-a-half-hour bus rides that took them away from their families and familiarities from sunup to sundown.

Why bother looking at the bounce of purposeful step, their bus timetables tucked inside wallets, these men and women who hastened to their destinations feeling a sense of commitment, compelled to believe they held the world together with the glue of their endless sweat? They carried everything needed to assist them in holding up the operations of commerce, and carried it all onto the bus except laziness. It made Ermila tired just looking at them pass her window at six in the morning, though she wished it were already six in the evening and she could see Alfonso and forget everything. And mostly Ermila stared out the window, bothered by why there wasn't much else to look forward to in her life other than seeing the likes of Alfonso.

Ermila wanted no part of this morning, just as she wanted no part of last night. A fretful night, a fraudulent sleep, a troubled morning. The clock on the bedstand read 6:12. She heard the phone's muffled ring in the hallway and didn't have an ounce of desire to move from the window. Groggy and uninspired, Ermila wanted to slip back into her bed and feign an illness, cramps, rabies, flu, but Nacho knocked on the door and then rattled her doorknob and she was relieved to have locked it last night. The call was for her, and she opened the door and immediately caught coffee vapors, onions sweetening in lard spittle, and walked to the telephone and said with annoyance, Hello. Nacho returned to the couch and punched his face deep into a pillow theatrically to let her know of his inconvenience. It took Ermila moments to recognize the voice.

Rini?

Listen, what you doin' today? Rini's lips must have been tightly pressed against the mouthpiece. Her voice sounded submerged as if her tongue were too large for her mouth.

Whatta you mean? Ermila yawned. Her bare feet were cold on the hardwood floor. Same as you. School and after, I dunno.

No you're not.

No, I'm not?

I needed to do this more early.

Do what?

This thing.

You know—Ermila yawned, looking through the arch and into the kitchen where she noticed Grandfather sweeping the floor—quit jiving me.

I needed to call more early. Rini's grave tone rattled Ermila.

Call for what?

Not here. Rini's voice lowered, as if she'd turned momentarily away from the mouthpiece. The mom, she said. Him. Can we meet somewheres, like, now?

Oh, man, Ermila said and glanced at the couch. Was Nacho overhearing? But the radio in the kitchen was on the KWKW Spanish station and how could he hear her conversation over the music?

Grandma's gonna bust a gut if I ditch again, Ermila pleaded. She's on the warpath.

'Mila, please.

Lookit. I can't.

'Mila.

Shit's hitting the fan over Alfonso. But the soft muffled sobs forced Ermila to acquiesce.

Okay. Okay. F-troop it.

The letter *F* meant four, which meant Rini should call Lollie and Mousie, but they disagreed on where to meet. Rini wanted to meet at the Top Hat but Ermila thought their full-view presence during school hours was a risk. At last they settled on Concha's not-really-a-beauty-salon, though Lollie would be hesitant.

Nacho turned on his stomach and peered out from the pillow coyly, and it was that gaze which rekindled her irritation. Had she been wearing her slippers she would have taken one off and walloped Nacho into one of those sprawled bludgeoned bodies in his ¡Alarma! magazine. Instead Ermila headed for the kitchen, clutching the lapels of her robe close to her collar, battle rising in her gaze.

What's wrong with you? Grandfather commanded in a labored voice, his vinegar scent strong. He halted her with a shaky palm. Go put on some shoes! There's broken glass, can't you see? His good hand clutched the shaft of a sorry-looking broom and he directed her glance to the glass shards scattered on the floor. But Ermila was in no mood to listen to anyone, least of all her stroke-impaired Grandfather, and she proceeded straight to the stove, where Grandmother reached for a kissing Dutch boy shaker and sprinkled pepper on the sizzle of wet potatoes, then grabbed the kissing Dutch girl to sprinkle salt, the hot lard spitting. She returned them to each other, back to back, their lips puckering into thin air.

How come you put a dog in my room? Ermila asked. The heat of the burners and her temper rose like color scalding her cheeks. How come, Grandma?

And then Ermila pushed her bandaged hand into Grandmother's view. All words equally angry.

See? See what the dog did? Grandmother stirred the potatoes until they browned and absorbed enough lard to roll them into burritos for Nacho's lunch. But Grandmother's thoughts were somewhere else, far away perhaps, a hike of sorts, the sizzle of potatoes sounding like gravel underfoot.

Dog? Grandmother replied wistfully, poking a spatula into the skillet. What dog? she asked, as if the word made little sense.

Are you even listening to me? The ground had shifted under them and the earth had breached, creating a rift between the two women that began, one could safely say, at puberty, but truly began ten years before when Ermila first arrived on their doorstep. Although Grandmother's big ears sprang out from her thinning gauzy hair, she could barely make out what Ermila said from the other side of the bluff.

Dog? Grandmother repeated.

No dogs are permitted in my house! Grandfather said and then cleared his throat. A stroke had left his lungs filled with asthmatic fluid, reducing them into useless sogged tea bags. His hunchback seemed flattened, malleted by Grandmother's fists to loosen his phlegm. He often spoke to himself, low gummed conversations because the stroke had produced an insatiable hunger to speak, though his wife often turned to him at times with bitter repercussion, resentful stares jolting him into silence. Grandfather slowly brushed the grainy shards into a mound with focused precision as if his managed rescue from the tiny glitter held great importance.

Nacho appeared and disappeared abruptly, and now Ermila saw

him leaning under the vaulted arch between the kitchen and living room. He tried to remain as unobtrusive as possible, especially when Grandfather swept near him with a broom so old, it shed across the checkered floor, leaving more debris than it collected. Nacho opened the funnels of his nostrils to breathe in the breakfast scents but knew well his manners and waited until Grandmother invited.

Look, demanded Grandfather. Look at me, he said to Nacho, holding the dustpan with one unsteady hand. I'm not afraid to work.

The tilting dustpan sparkled with particles of fine glass. Nacho wore his undershirt tucked beneath the waist of his paint-splattered jeans. He crossed his arms and waited under the arch for the invitation. His appearance silenced Ermila, and she felt the sudden dread of dishonesty. Wasn't Ermila the one planning to trick her Grandmother today while accusing Grandmother of the same? Though one would expect the dawn to spread light at six-thirty a.m., this morning captured her mood—the storm clouds had darkened the kitchen, making the beginning of the day seem more like its conclusion.

What happened, Abuelo? Nacho asked, in reference to the broken glass. He repeated the question because Grandfather wore a hearing aid box in his front shirt pocket connected to a thin white wire plugged to his ear. Most of the time, though, the batteries were spent.

Another earthquake condenado, Grandfather replied. Things keep breaking.

I think it was last night's helicopters, Nacho shouted in Spanish. I don't think it was an earthquake.

Ah, Mi'jo, Grandfather sighed as if exasperated by a hardheaded apprentice. Ay.

Yes, Abuelito, I—

Go put on some shoes, Grandfather yelled at Ermila. Ermila ignored him.

Tell her to put on some shoes, he instructed Grandmother, but she ignored him as well. Grandfather's leather belt was pulled to its last notch and the thin extra belt leather dangled as he continued to sweep the glass into a dustpan.

Ermila scraped out a chair and glumly sat down. She stared at the yellow windmills of the blue tiles, debating. The commercials on the radio were working their way under her skin.

Are you deaf, Rogelio? Grandmother bumped a plate of scrambled eggs and papitas on the table. Come and eat, I said.

And you! Grandmother jabbed the spatula at Nacho. Don't come in here with that T-shirt. Whereas two minutes ago Grandmother hadn't paid much attention to Ermila or the voices on KWKW, now it seemed a spit of hot lard had slapped her awake. She meant business. Nacho quickly responded and returned buttoning a wrinkled shirt. Grandmother dolloped oatmeal into two bowls and then pointed to one of them and said his name and Nacho gladly complied. He pulled a drawer open, picked a spoon and forgot to close the drawer. He bucked the chair closer to the table's rim and then tore his toast in pieces as if it were a tortilla, which he dipped into the porridge. Ermila noticed he didn't shovel his porridge down. As he chewed, he smiled across the table at her, and the smile made her take hold of her robe lapels.

The following moments were so quiet one could hear Grandfather's gritty sweeping and the mucus argument between his lungs, making greedy demands for oxygen. So quiet, the flame of the burner Grandmother had turned off gasping its last breath. So quiet, nothing was left to fill the silence between the sound and its echo except for a puny voice on the KWKW station.

Ermila brushed her oatmeal aside and rose and pulled out a box of cornflakes from the pantry while Grandmother squinted an evil eye. Ermila poured the flakes awkwardly to emphasize the injury, the disability of a dog bite, and then poured nonfat milk that resembled dirty white water. The milk warm, the flakes stale (Ermila knew well Grandmother's disgust of cold cereals and was surprised to find the box still on the shelf), she ate spoon after spoon as if she relished the breakfast. Nacho crunched his toast, Grandfather wheezed and Ermila requested again to please get the dog out of her room. The flakes sloshed around in her belly.

Grandmother said she was crazy and turned to the stove and began making the burritos.

Abuela, should I go to see if there's a dog?

Stay out of my room, Nacho, Ermila said. Six-forty-five already and then Ermila remembered her date with Alfonso. She wondered if Alfonso even remembered. When he called her last night, he was higher than a kite, slurring his *I love you, baby* like a damned pendejo.

Grandma, I got my check to pick up after school.

What time you coming home, then? Grandmother asked, without looking up from her burrito tinfoil-wrapping work.

I dunno. Ermila slurped the last of her milk trying to give a resemblance of youthful cereal abandonment.

Late?

Late.

Tell me, Grandmother said. What time?

What time?

What time.

I dunno.

You dunno?

I dunno.

Before curfew?

Maybe.

Maybe?

Mr. Salas might want me to do some work, Ermila lied. She got up from her seat and placed her used bowl on the sink counter.

Ermila, Grandmother said, looking point-blank at her. I don't deserve your lies.

Where's my food? Grandfather asked.

Be quiet, Rogelio, Grandmother said with such bitterness Ermila thought she was going to throw the spatula at him. Don't you tire of using your mouth? Grandfather looked confused.

I was just—

And get the clothes off the clothesline before the rains start up again.

Do you need help, Abuelo?

Don't ask, just help, Grandmother said, slamming the spatula and turning her back to all of them. Nacho shoveled his last piece of toast and porridge into his mouth, grabbed the empty clothes basket and the clothespins can and followed Grandfather outside. He left his bowl on the table, the chair pulled out, bread crumbs everywhere, inspiring Grandmother's hope for Nacho's speedy departure.

In the hallway Ermila couldn't hear Grandmother's stony words. They loosened and clattered, spiraling down the deep chasm. By the time the words reached their steep drop, no sounds were caught.

Did you hear what I just said?

Did you hear what I just said? Ermila mimicked her Grand-mother's words, already turning up the volume to the noise of the planned activities of her day. She pushed the blank of the bedroom door in and went to her bureau and heard the low, vibrating growl warning her. When she gingerly opened a drawer, the dog snapped so close to the hem of her robe, she felt saliva flecks on her ankle. Startled and angry at its unprovoked viciousness, she chose to use the bath-room down the hallway to dress for school. She hugged her bag of cos-metics with one arm, her jeans, mohair sweater and a T-shirt top drooping over her other arm.

On the chipped plasterboard wall, the medicine cabinet mirror hung over the bathroom sink. Its plastic arabesque trimming had been painted a clumsy gold by Grandfather's good hand. Ermila applied her makeup in sections; powdered one eye, then the other, nose, chin. Cover Girl stick to erase the deep lines under her waning eyes, and eyeliner, one eye, then the other; smooth one eyebrow, then the other.

Already perspiring from the humidity, Ermila released her robe and it tumbled to the tiled floor. The lotion, Jean Naté powder puffs, a squirt of perfume. She could feel the ruptured flesh on her hand swelling. She discarded the old gauze and rinsed the wound, bending over the rim of the bathroom sink.

While she was intently studying her hand under the rush of the faucet, Nacho raised himself on a wooden apricot crate he had hidden behind the rash of prickly rosebushes for the occasion of staring into the high bathroom window. He could hear the rain begin pinging against the tin coffee cans holding the geranium seedlings. Torn by his own discretion, his shirt dampened by the rain, Nacho gripped the slippery pane of window with groping fingers and lifted himself to catch a brief glimpse of flight. He watched Ermila bend over the rim of the sink to pour some iodine on the wound, then swath her hand with gauze. In spite of himself, Nacho marveled at the wingspan of gliding buttocks stretching against the material of her white cotton slip, and he stiffened, no longer feeling like a man. Nacho felt like a shameful beast, and in spite of his shame, he trembled with the catch of fresh smell, the hair in his nostrils spiking.

* * *

Concha's Beauty Salon was housed near Boyle and Brooklyn, right in the middle of a residential area, the back entrance well hidden by an alley. So narrow was the stairway leading down to the salon, you could stretch out your arms, as Ermila was apt to do, and touch both walls while descending to the airless basement where the ossified breath of tobacco smoke and Black Flag roach spray intermingled with the chemical stench of hair dye. The shop itself consisted of a triptych mirror, one pumped-up beauty chair, its bruise-colored Naugahyde seat X'd with silver duct tape to cover holes—making it look like a discard from Gene's Barbershop—and a sink winged with two wide counters. An assortment of clippers, hair blower, hot rollers, combs and brushes snarled with knots of hair, and drawers of plastic rollers the size of toilet paper tubes were scattered on the counters like the ruins of a Kmart sale. Peroxide and beauty aids provided caulking for the puzzled cracks on worn faces, and Concha's was well stocked with industrial-sized bottles.

A cinder-block wall divided the shop from Concha's living quarters, the "backstage" area where no one was allowed to part the strips of plastic walk-through beads and trespass, where Concha would emerge, the beads rattling like a pair of maracas to announce her performance as a beautician. Indeed, Ermila thought of the whole salon as a sham, a mere prop. The real business, the one which held greater tantalizing promise, belonged to the other side of the doorway beads. Nonetheless, the wall of her shop was papered here and there, high and low, haphazardly with ads torn rather than clipped from various magazines and it wouldn't have surprised Ermila if the ads were stuck on with gum. Samples of women sporting hairdos like beehives dangled alongside stylish renderings of women relishing Salems, or the Miss Breck dye models for the months of June and December, April and February. For all the smells of seduction, the girlfriends found in the beauty shop a place both strange and disturbing, and they'd visited the beauty shop for a grand total of two emergencies, the last being Lollie's report card.

Not city-zoned for business, the salon stood on illegal legs and its lack of female customers made Concha an easy target for chisme. You could see Lollie's mother wagging her finger at Lollie to warn that once you choose to live on the corner of Gossip Street and Speculation

Boulevard, you're on your own. Admittedly, after all that had been said regarding Concha, the sight of an elderly customer slapping the glossy pages of a magazine while sitting under a cone dryer was a reassuring sight to Ermila. Yet, Concha's fall from successful restaurateur to illegal beautician had played out to the Eastside like a morality tale second only to the tale of Renata Valenzuela, a tale that grew like pressure in Ermila's ears. Lollie's mother cautioned against sneaking out of the house to go partying because you'll be bound to meet up with Renata. Next thing you know, she'll promise to take you to a dance at the Evergreen Cemetery where you'll vanish forever, and what kind of life is that for you?

For all intents and purposes, Lollie's mother had the presence of a ghost greater than Renata. Her stories followed the girlfriends like shadows and succeeded in haunting Ermila. *Oh?* Lollie's mother intoned again and again, crossing her pudgy arms tightly over her chest, one eyebrow arching skeptically. So you want to be like uppity Concha, who pulled up her skirts to moon the world? Well, guess what?

Of the four girlfriends, Lollie had the most to lose in riding the bus to the salon. Concha was her father's sister and the siblings had broken ties with one another after an argument never fully discussed, though Lollie gathered bits and pieces which came together like this: Concha was sucker-punched in love with a guitarist who got himself arrested in a contraband bust. Against her brother's pleading wishes not to, Concha put up her restaurant to cover the bail bond, and the *Well, guess what* went to Concha, who lost the restaurant after the guitarist jumped bail, fleeing to the unknown jowls of rural Mexico. The bits and pieces not only refused to come together, but for Lollie, the story also revealed glaring absences or no-fault inserts exploited by her parents.

The tale of loving sacrifice inspired Lollie to develop an immediate bond with her aunt. Forewarned against contacting Aunt Concha, Lollie had searched her out, since the restriction tripled her desire for intimacy. Not only had Lollie telephoned her slandered aunt, she also took significant risks in visiting Concha's shop on two occasions of great emergencies. And this morning, Rini's sobs over the phone confirmed a third one.

Full of youthful self-importance, Lollie thought to use her parents' constant cautionary tales like ladder rungs to mount an escape. But in fact the opposite was true. After Rini's F-troop call, Lollie had sat atop a pile of shoe-wear in the closet, tightly grasping a greenish phosphorescent plastic mold of La Virgen like a baseball bat. With five siblings in a two-bedroom house, the closet provided peaceful space if you breathed through your mouth, and she prayed to La Virgen about her impending visit to Concha's. Clearly, her loyalties were split thrice between her parents, Concha and her friends, which was why Lollie's hands shook the rest of the morning. In the overburdened bathroom, saunalike and towel-laden, a box of baking soda for toothpaste spilled on the soap dish, Lollie's hand trembled so that it was impossible to tweeze her hairy eyebrows into their penciled-thin arches. Time yelled to get moving, and she would have to face the day off-kilter, her eyebrows thicker than usual.

Jogging halfway down the city block, Lollie remembered the application form for the nurses' aide program, and she rushed home to retrieve it because this afternoon marked the deadline. Ermila had offered herself as a math tutor but Lollie's father insisted Lollie take on vocational classes after her dismal report card. Not wanting to disappoint him, Lollie had agreed, and now she maneuvered around the fold-away beds, plucking pillows, stepping over clothes, and scanning the cluttered kitchen counters. She uncovered the application form near the Aunt Jemima toaster cozy with her mother's signature and a thumbprint of what seemed to be strawberry jelly. Lollie ran to the bus stop, her shoulder purse strapped over a white turtleneck pullover, her full bosom bouncing like loose coins in her pocket.

The clouds were tight-lipped and tense after the torrential morning rain and her parents' disappointment felt like a chill so cool it made the tree branches shiver. Ay qué vida, her father had said last night, sadly, dreamily, a longneck beer leaning against the foot of the couch. Her mother watched *Hermanos Coraje,* a tittering of Spanish exchanges in the telenovela, and her father had buried his balding head on her mother's fleshy lap as if it were a hole in the ground. Ay qué vida, he repeated, his utterance possibly referring to her mother's comfortable lap, or perhaps a lament to his spent youth, a regret of what could have been.

Lollie had been writing her latest installment of her marriage to

Peter Tork instead of doing her boring history homework (she hadn't the slightest interest in learning about the Boston Tea Party) when she heard him. Belly down and ankles crossed on the carpet, she stopped writing in her diary feeling irritated more than guilty. Perhaps his sighing was an indication of sadness about her lack of academic success. The hollow self-defeating ring to his words sounded like a slow prolonged hissing of hope deflating from his chest. He said nothing after that, for her mother had traced a gentle thumb on his lips to hush him, lest he be tempted to continue a long-winded conversation after the commercial break ended and the telenovela resumed. When Lollie returned to her saga to count the pages she had written, a feeling as real and as false as every adolescent mood overcame her and she felt engorged by anger.

At First and Rowan, Mousie blew Bazooka gum bubbles while applying the last of her eyeliner over her lashes. A number of people milled around; no one sat on the wet benches. Having arrived just as the bus tires rubbed against the curb, Lollie tried to catch her breath and her breathing was as hurtful as waiting outside the door of Miss Flores, the girls' VP at Garfield High. Mousie snapped closed her compact, slipped it into a makeup bag, popped a gum bubble, zipped up her purse and then the two dropped in their fare and negotiated a hard-won space on the very crowded bus.

Minced between standing-room-only bodies, they flung from side to side as the rambling 26 ponderously resumed the downward slope of First Street, westward-bound. A passenger's perfume or hairspray, a blend of heavy funeral carnations, made Lollie's stomach wheezy. She poked a finger and stretched her asphyxiating turtleneck, tugging it to loosen its hold on her windpipe.

What's the big stink? Mousie said. She chomped on her gum until she felt warmth chafing against her bucket butt and her mouth froze. The groping really pissed her off because it felt like someone's hand was taking advantage of the compressed bodies. Mousie angrily turned, her hair whipping against Lollie's face.

Watch it.

Does this got to do with Jan? Mousie asked, spying out possible suspects who had copped a feel of her ass. Jan slept with Rini's mother, but apparently the creep wanted more than friendly kisses from Rini.

You got to ask?

The bus halted in front of the Hollenbeck Police Station, where black-uniformed policemen crawled in and out of the ant-hole entrance, and then the bus resumed with another jerk. Lollie worked herself into a frightening confusion. The swell of bodies began to push her under and she leaned toward the open windows of the bus to breathe. Over the heads of the seated passengers Lollie thought about consequences and the responsibility of facing mistakes as the bus passed Concha's boarded-up Los Jaliscos Mariscos Seafood Restaurant.

Do you know how that jaundiced woman supports herself with an unlicensed business? Lollie's mother once asked, as if Lollie's mother knew too well the terrifying answer. She's a nobody, Lollie's father added. He suspected that a larger appetite for something else replaced Concha's appetite for food, thereby reducing the soft flesh of her frame into lethargic thinness. But who knew the truth for sure? Concha's story of failure, of family betrayal, always led her parents to ask, Do you have any idea how much your sisters look up to you? Which only made Lollie feel as if she were destined to betray them, to pull a Concha.

Speechless, she smoldered, her hands flinging up in the air, as if pressing away the weight of being the eldest of the clan. Little wonder why she'd gone to Concha's after her report card, the failure cementing her future like the Del Gel she used to straighten her bangs.

The bus lumbered along, its speed barely topping thirty-five miles an hour. Lollie pulled up her sleeve and glanced at her Timex, a birthday gift. Homeroom over with first period well under way, and she knew her own seamstress mother was already at work in a large low-ceilinged room, her container of cinnamon tea near the foot pedal of her sewing machine. Smoky layers of lint obscured the windowless floor of the garment shop and the bombarding pinions of earsplitting stitching had left Lollie with degrees of deafness. This was because on quota deadlines, the manufacturer's demands increased, and her mother needed her assistance. She became a reluctant assistant, missing school to replace spools, pull trouser legs inside out, while wafts of lint dried her throat like cheap-brand cigarettes.

There was no stopping her mother's fingers splicing two strips of denim between the needle and bobbin in matrimony. Once, her mother had made a mistake, and as she pulled out the stitches, unraveling them easily, she said to Lollie, That's what can happen to you.

Before Los Jaliscos Mariscos Restaurant closed and its windows were boarded up and people like Lollie's parents fondly remembered the establishment, it was said to be the height of Eastside business success. The Anglo wrestler Freddie Blassie and the Hungarian champion Billy Varga frequented the restaurant, arriving without fanfare but leaving behind their legendary eating habits like having five orders of grilled garlic shrimp atop aromatic rice. An unsubstantiated rumor that Mil Máscaras patronized the restaurant every Thursday for the Tortillas de Cangrejo Special proved challenging, since no one could recognize his face; the Mexican wrestler always appeared in movies wearing his trademark ski mask. Subsequently, on Thursdays, customers became willing gaming participants in a guessing contest; they shot curious glances at one another suspiciously, smiled sheepishly, bought one another drinks with kindly pleasure.

On their first date, Lollie's father had commandeered her mother through the employees' entrance of the restaurant. Music from the jukebox played boisterously, and the scent of fermented spices hovered over the laughter and noise of so many conversations, they all jazzed into a tremendous humming scent. The couple sat in a U-shaped booth in full view of the kitchen's double doors, which swung in and out with the energy and pomp of spectacular service. Lollie's father had clasped her mother's hand over the Formica table, his fingers between hers, his thumb massaging her Jergens-lotioned skin.

Her father talked about the restaurant business. Before he explained how to drop live lobsters in boiling water, and before Lollie's mother cringed, Lollie's father ordered a piña colada for his date and a martini for himself. He tried not to stare at her sharp bra cones accenting her pink cashmere sweater as he explained the difference between freshwater and saltwater fish. Not many people knew the difference and Lollie's mother nodded an I-never-knew-that nod.

He pointed to his sister to make Lollie's mother realize he was serious in his intentions. Concha wore Elizabeth Taylor eyebrows and sat at her puzzle table near the double doors piecing together hundreds of jigsaw puzzle pieces of the Eiffel Tower. She'd periodically rest her cigarette to scrutinize a shape, until she found the matching curvature, and then she would gently press a piece into its place and then rub her finger back and forth to make sure the fit was absolutely right.

Lollie's mother saw her hold up another piece, puff her cigarette and then glance away from the puzzle in time to enjoy the comings and goings of the men she employed. Men who worked with a crisp delight in rushing from booth to booth, their celebrated efficiency well tipped, men like Jorge the waiter, whom Concha detained, snagged, tugging on his black velvet vest as he headed for the bar. He bowed into her slightly tilted, peroxided bouffant as if he were accustomed to her interceptions and pointed a finger to a blank spot where he thought the piece Concha held would fit. Concha flirted a pair of lashes so lumped in black mascara, they would seem impossible to lift on any lesser eyes. Larger than life, Concha seemed scary to Lollie's mother, who'd had to borrow her best friend's sweater top, the one with the pink stitched sequined flower, for her date. Lollie's mother didn't even own her own toothbrush.

The vodka began to spin her father's words over the chatter of customers, and over the vindictive ballad sung by a local self-declared musician who often sang for his supper. The guitarist claimed to be the last member of the Trío de Los Panchos, his crude guitar strings coiling and bonging from his battered instrument. He stood behind the microphone and introduced himself as such and then spoke of earning thousands of dollars playing backup for Eydie Gorme with his two other partners. To prove it, he began to sing boleros like "Sabor a mi" and "Solamente una vez," which were mainstays on any jukebox worth its weight in salt. The tired man sang without conviction in a voice as spent as his alleged record royalties, and he paused between lyrics routinely, as if his other two nonexistent members filled the silence with their melodious chorus.

Right before Jorge the waiter came to deliver their appetizers, Lollie's father finally released her mother's hand to mimic two handfuls of shrimp being tossed in the imaginary pot of boiling water and Lollie's mother jumped back to avoid imaginary scalding. He grabbed her hand again and held it and tenderly kissed her knuckle bone and said there were secrets he wanted to share with her and he gestured a V with two fingers to signal another round of drinks and then he revealed one of those secrets: ice cubes tossed into the boiling shrimp. I never knew that, Lollie's mother said. She became impressed with his firsthand knowledge, his take-command attitude and, make no mistake about it, his this-will-all-be-mine-someday, complicit air. The hot and cold concept so captured her imagination that she hadn't noticed the waiter palming a tray of refreshing ceviche picante. Lollie's father dipped a chip and fed her, the ceviche tingling her lips without waging war against her tongue. She fanned herself with a napkin because the booth's trapped heat caused her cheeks to glow with arousal, her chilled lips to frost as she sipped her crushy colada.

After the restaurant had shut down, it continued to remain an anniversary marker of Lollie's parents' first date. That's the night your mama gave it up, Lollie's father had said once as they drove past the boarded-up restaurant, its front gardens dried up and as dead as its business. Only traces of its grand past lay in the cascading stairs. Lollie's mother punched her husband's arm hard, a knuckle punch to make it hurt, and her knuckles, having used a zinc washboard for years, were tough and hard. The punch was all that Lollie needed in order to confirm that she, Lollie, the oldest of five, was irrefutably conceived on that night.

Photographs were wedged between the thin metal rims of the triptych mirror of the salon to create a sepia frame. There were photos of Mexican film stars who had spent carousing evenings, often photographed at Concha's insistence, smiling down on their plates of food, relishing the moment. Over a crab salad, Dolores del Río wore dark shades, though the restaurant was dim with candlelight. In a black turban María Félix looked three times more stunning than her film posters, toasting the photographer with a flute of champagne.

But of all the snapshots, Ermila had only recognized three: Lollie's kindergarten picture taken in Eastman's class; another one of Lollie's tribe, an aura of innocence in their church clothes but a hint of cockiness in their smiles; and the third one, a snapshot of Lollie's parents circa the 1950s. Lollie had once pointed this particular photo out to the girlfriends. Lookit! Lollie had said, the convoluted strain of a bad report card in her voice. My mom and dad, and she tapped a fingernail onto the photograph, its edges serrated as old photos often were.

The photo preserved Concha and Lollie's father and mother in a restaurant booth. Empty glasses and traces of food on plates crowded the table. Lollie's mother resembled the girl in the classic teen flick *I Was a Teenage Werewolf* and Lollie's father, in pomade-wet hair, looked like a young Michael Landon before his hair loss. But Concha was someone else and Ermila had to ask Lollie for identification. The Concha in the photo wore a peasant blouse and her full bosom busted out of its low cut while a large gold crucifix leaned on the valley of her cleavage. With ratted, coiffure hair and eye makeup modeled after the Queen of the Nile style, her presence dwarfed Lollie's parents. To Ermila, she resembled a woman wrestler, full and strong, or an opera singer, dramatic and flamboyant. Concha had smiled fully, her painted lips so enunciated, they sang.

Mousie couldn't contain her laughter and told Lollie: Lookit, your mom's all, like, "I'm drinking beer."

Don't be like that.

Like, "I'm getting all peda."

Shad-up.

Like, "Look at me, I'm all pedotes."

The girlfriends had busied themselves laughing over the other photos, with the exception of Ermila. She sat on the chair, picking at some duct tape, and thought about time passing. Old age seemed a thousand years away from Ermila and the only reminder of age in the salon was the hair dyeing scent meant to bleach it away. Ermila sensed that something wasn't right. None of the adults in the one photograph were presently close to replicating their youthful looks and this realization blew her mind. Lollie's father's grew bald, and his eyebrows had disappeared from work-related stress. The best that could be said for him was that he tried to complete one semester of trade tech, and his good looks, while they lasted, delivered in him a sustaining feeling of entitlement. Lollie's mother was now as round and practical as a jelly jar and the best that could be said about her was her enthusiasm for sporting a challenge. What-doesn't-kill-you-makes-you-stronger type of bullshit, and if Lollie's mother wasn't so damned clairvoyant, it was possible to hate her.

And then there was Concha, the woman who slowly, gradually lost her shape without the slightest hint of worry; everyone, except her niece Lollie, slid right off Concha's glare. Only her smile, a smile so wide it cracked her stare whenever Lollie visited, had a resemblance of her old self in the photo. The best that could be said about Concha was her glorious indifference about the shape of things now. Clad in nun's shoes, a pair of flat threadbares she wore without nylons, she walked as silent as a burglar, vanishing behind the mysterious door beads to her private rooms to retrieve a carton of cigarettes. Barring the loose tassel clasps, teensy shreds of black leather that probably jumped and cheered with godly steps in another time, her shoes appeared utterly forsaken. If Concha felt any bitterness about the thunderous clunky noise of her downfall, she didn't show it. Her mannerisms, her Twiggy-thin look, seemed to be as cool as the menthol she loved to smoke.

Her fall from grace and her subsequent revival delivered upon her an authority that Lollie received without question. However, Ermila felt that Concha's advice clearly derived from an instruction manual different than the appliance and Ermila felt unsettled at seeing Concha pulling in a drag of her Salem menthol, then exhaling a forceful stream of smoke which looked thicker than her skinny arms.

About Mousie's drug bust, a joint found by her mom in her underwear drawer (their first emergency), Concha had said, While you're going out for the milk, your mom's coming back with the cheese.

Huh?

About Lollie's failing report card at their last emergency visit, Concha's eyes had darted around the salon for the motion of it, for making a point of it, and then replied sarcastically, It's not the end of the world.

Ermila had thought, What kind of fucked-up comment is that? She had stared at her reflection in the mirror and the bad lighting darkened the rings around her eyes, and then just over her shoulder, she caught sight of the lumpy hem of Concha's white coat gathered where the crooked stitches began and ended. Lollie's mother slowly filled up with the fatty tires of family responsibility while Concha emptied because of family abandonment and Ermila had thought, What kind of fucked-up options are these? She felt her chest collapsing to her stomach, bulking around the ledge of her waist like powerful menstrual cramping.

True, life goes on, but when Concha flipped the **OPEN** sign to **CLOSED,** and walked through the bony beads of her doorway and into the solitude of another year, was she startled to see the smoky image in the mirror of someone from another life? Or did she simply light another cigarette, flip off her shoes and sit in front of a puzzle and realize there would always be a jigsaw piece of puzzle missing, a vagrant reminder of an absolute absence? In doing so, knowing full well it wouldn't be the end of the world. With those thoughts tumbling and clanking in her head like wet jeans in the dryer, Ermila turned away from the mirror and looked up to the hole in the ceiling that she thought Concha's shooting smoke might be aiming for.

As passengers left the bus, Lollie and Mousie found seats behind the driver, right above the useless shock absorbers, and the two girlfriends bumped and jumped until it was their turn to exit. Lollie peered out the front-door exit, suffering a moment of indecision. The internal debate surfaced in the scowl of her face and her hands resisted the let-go of the steel rails. She could just as easily turn around and ask for a transfer from the driver and get to school by the beginning of third period and then turn in her application form, pleasing her father. Or she could disembark and run to Concha's with only one guarantee— she would feel exhilarated but shitty after the visit. The answer, it seemed, lay in her unwillingness to turn in the application form in the first place, waiting until the absolute deadline. A procrastinator? Nah. Who the fuck wanted to dump bedpans in the first place anyway?

Once Lollie's sneakers hit the slick pavement of Boyle Street, there seemed to be no turning back.

Trashcans, as dented as cans of stewed tomatoes at La Quebradita Market, stood guard on each side of the street. Loose papers flew and whirled under the tires of passing cars, liberated from the crows pecking at the throwaways. A pair of tennis shoes was lynched over a telephone wire. Lollie pushed her pullover sleeves up and rubbed the dots of her arm, especially around the elbow area, then pushed her sleeves down. Mousie rushed behind her. The champion bra Lollie wore was wired and fully cupped but just as useless as the bus's shock absorbers, and her breasts became the definitive bounce and jump. She ignored the quiver of her chest all the same. The two girls entered the side of a pale green house, and a mangy dog, whose muzzle looked grease-matted, barked from a torn window screen and Lollie yelled, Shad-up, and they cut through the driveway and around the apartment house and to the alley and opened the metal gate to the yard of the beauty shop, where they encountered Ermila. She leaned against the chain-link fence, two hands rubbing her eyes.

A strong paranoia was beginning to settle in Ermila's be-careful gut and she felt it impossible to disrupt a growing concern. Wintery-thin rosebushes crushed along the fence and thorned through the thick denim of her jeans, but the pricks were of little consequence. She had forgotten her math and geography books and this fact blew her mind. What had she been thinking as she bolted out of the house empty-handed? Surely Grandmother would find her folder and texts, then call the VP's office and find out she wasn't at school. Fuck!

Ermila's increasing anxiety while waiting for Lollie had concocted a range of nerve-wracking scenarios. Firstly, Grandmother's fury at the discovery of her truancy; secondly, her frustrating impotence in help-ing poor sweet Rini who now sat in the salon wiping her reddish nose with her sleeve; thirdly, Lollie's tardiness—no one seemed dependable anymore. And finally, meeting Big Al, the destroyer, later in the day, at Laguna Cliff for breakup or make-up, the decision left up in the air.

Two pitiful diehard trees across the yard looked defrocked and sullen. The corners of shirts pinned in a row on the laundry line next door lifted their sleeves in dismissive waves as her long black hair teased across her face in such silence, the strands stood like isolated threads, dissociated and twitchy. Ermila rubbed her eyes as Lollie called for attention, snapping her fingers, and Ermila became both an-noyed and grateful.

How come you're late?

I'm here now.

Mousie chewed her gum, pointing to Ermila's bandaged hand. What happened?

Nothin'.

What happened?

I told you.

En serio?

I told you.

I don't believe you.

Believe me.

So where's Rini? Lollie pushed her pullover sleeves up, glanced about in search of her while absentmindedly touching her arm hair. Three school periods from now the deadline would be over. She would tell her father tonight—she was better than a bedpan gofer. Ermila pointed in the direction of the salon's stairway and said:

Rini's in royal bad shape.

It's not the end of the world, Lollie responded.

Sez who?

We need to think.

YoYo would kick his ass, Mousie said.

For sure.

We gotta do something soon.

Mousie recommended spraying Jan's face with Aqua Net hairspray and Ermila rolled her eyes.

Come on, Ermila instructed.

Right, Mousie agreed. Someone got a gun?

Shad-up, man. This is for real.

It's gotta hurt royally.

A real bitchen hurt.

Cut deep, you know?

Yea. And then Lollie asked:

What kind of car does he drive?

Man, Mousie said, spilling over with excitement. Man, oh, man.

Ermila considered this and nodded. That's a start.

Lollie was downright inspiring. Why she flunked her classes remained a mystery, but Ermila, awestruck, had always appreciated Lollie's right-on sesos.

Okay, then, Lollie said, feeling sure. Let's go. And she led her friends into the salon. Back at school, the bell buzzard had summoned the end of fourth period, but this class at Concha's Beauty Salon was about to begin.

*   *   *

The girlfriends agreed to pool their money together sans their bus fare, which amounted to $3.54, and they headed for the corner mart to buy a box of steel wool soap pads. They carried with them four squirt bottles of industrial-strength acetone nail polish remover, Concha's contribution. From there, they walked a little over an hour to Rini's to save on bus fare, slowly accumulating a momentum of competence. Along the way they invested a dime for a Royal Crown that they passed to one another in a five-minute break. All the while they hoped it wouldn't rain, but the dark clouds above them were as unpredictable and untrustworthy as adults were. They wouldn't be surprised if the clouds would burst and plonk a bucketful of water on their heads, or they wouldn't be surprised if suddenly the clouds parted and the sun beamed through like the hand of God. Of course they hoped for the latter.

A street before Rini's house, Rini yelled, There!, halting as if she had fallen into a crack in the cement. And there it was, a parked Chevy Coupe. Metallic bronze, orange highlights not far from the Tres Puntas taco stand. The car was wax-sheen-polished like a warrior, the sun god, priceless. Ermila could tell that he had just arrived and parked because the air warped by the rising heat of the car's hood. As they approached the Chevy, Ermila glanced from left to right to see if Jan was stalking around somewhere. A U-Haul truck reversed, its rear lights flashing and parked directly in front of the Chevy, and the driver got out and winked at Lollie and walked across the street to join the line in front of the **ORDER HERE** small window.

Ermila said, I don't see 'im anywheres. The fact that Jan wasn't visible made her jittery.

Are you sure this one's it? Lollie asked.

Rini cupped her face and looked in the shotgun seat of the Chevy and studied it. At first her confusion made her judgment unreliable, a nudging doubt beginning to bloom until she saw it, the Hostess Snowball wrapper on the backseat floor. She had left it there to irritate him, a small subversion because the fucker was so anal about the cleanliness of his car.

Yea, she said. This one's it.

Real sure?

I'm sure.

They can see us, Ermila warned, already biting a thumbnail. Customers rimmed close to the taco building because the clouds predicted rain showers sooner rather than later.

We gotta move fast, Speedy Gonzales style.

He's like a cucaracha, Ermila continued. Hiding somewheres.

Should we wait?

I keso.

The girlfriends, dressed in straight boot-cut Levi's, staked a corner and waited a few minutes to see if Jan would emerge. They looked away from one another, each folded into her own thoughts, as they just began to understand the importance of what they were about to do. The magnitude hovered like the gray-and-silver-belly rain clouds ready for release. This was serious business, cosa seria, and what they planned to do held a moment of destiny in the ways of Concha (saying yes to the bail bondsman) or Lollie's mother (saying yes to Lollie's father on the first date).

Vendors arrived around four o'clock to sell to the congregating people at the Three Points. Ermila's heart pumped as she watched a corner vendor hold up a dollar bag of oranges while another sold flower bouquets at a price only someone in love could afford. Where was the cucaracha hiding anyway? The blue powder of the soap pad spread a steely tint on her bandages. A man set up his grocery cart containing Rex Lard canisters filled with his wife's steaming tamales under a hot towel, which he carefully lifted with a pair of tongs while a woman pushed a steel vat tied to a cart and filled with hot atole, calling out promises of the maize drink to relieve the "chills caused by the rains which come and go like a grown son." Lollie's hands trembled like they had this morning, as if they wanted to be plucked away from her body. Mousie was jumpy, but then again, she always was; and Rini's sweet face turned sallow. The blood from her cheeks settled like sediment at the bottom of an ocean floor, leaving her skin with a haunting serenity that one recognized in an embalmed face.

The girlfriends fought against their individual doubts and concentrated on one communal goal. Lollie repeated instructions and then they separated, holding two steel wool pads each, outlaw indias about to circle the wagon train. Too many vendors congregating, too many eyes peering, too many customers ordering from the menu, too many waiting at the **PICK UP** windows. Still, backs turned, arms extended, vendors selling, the U-Haul camouflaging, it was now or never.

From the east, west, north and south the girlfriends converged toward the magnet of their wrath's attention. There was no practice save for repetition of the task at hand and they knew the actual execution would have to take less than a few seconds. That's all they had. Each of them pulled out a squirt bottle filled with nail polish remover and each of them was assigned letters. They squirted the shapes of their designated letters with acetone, painfully stinging their open hangnails, and squirted until the last of the acetone resounded like farts relieved from their respective spouts. Onto the paint of the car's trunk, they scrubbed the liquid into the metal with the steel wool pads. Rini took the O's, because there was something therapeutic about circling and circling, and Ermila took the T's because she had one hanging on her wall and because Concha wore it years ago when she was a somebody. And Mousie took the U because the letter was in her name, and Lollie took the rest because she was good at carrying more than her fair share. They squirted and scrubbed and jumped on the bumpers to reach the top of the hood. And in not more than thirty seconds they were finished. **PUTO,** the hood said to him. The return address on the trunk, **LOTE.**

And just as they had converged, they pulled away in opposite directions slowly, sluggishly lest they call attention to themselves, not rushing to leave the scene of the crime, though it was a difficult task not to explode adrenaline all over the place. They had to silence the forcefulness of their delight, hesitating to acknowledge one another's glances. They strolled away in separate directions, carrying the flakes of metallic paint, bluish palms, the color of yams on their hands, barely containing their collective sense of invincibility.

Whatever laughter or disbelief, whatever overblown nerves Ermila had suppressed, now raised her spirit to the point that her steps felt buoyant and she felt an enormous craving for adventure. Jan was a coward who would never go after the badasses of Lote Maravilla and this reassuring knowledge, along with her wild inward exhilaration, delivered a sense of well-being, a motive strong enough to carry her smile to Laguna Cliff. Ermila reveled in becoming one of the winds of the four directions and just for a moment, a fleeting moment at that, she experienced a larger-than-life ability to soar over just about anything.

TEN

Outside of Cuero, Texas, the flat land of hard-packed soil grew scrub and cedar brush, mesquite. Mama and Tranquilina had pitched a tarpaulin in the center of a trodden field where hoof ruts baked in the ground and where earth dried enough to support the weight of chairs. With the rancher Stafford's kindness, they set out to work all day in preparation for the prayer meeting, raking away livestock paddies. In a moment of respite from the day's work, which carried the slight fragrance of freshly plowed earth, Tranquilina sat under an oak tree to listen as Papa Tomás practiced his sermon, a baritone voice inflecting words of compassion.

Not far from the field, pecan and ancient oak trees tussled as his voice rolled, a lovely voice, authoritative but melodious. As soothing as reading the Psalms. His voice lifted the drifts of soil, parted the bangs on Tranquilina's forehead.

Later in the day, she and Mama had hung beacon lanterns borrowed from the rancher Stafford on the tent poles with hooks made of wire clothes hangers. Tranquilina remembered how the trees wreathed the clearing, casting shadows on the tarp, and by evening the lanterns flared their golden lights and tinked against the steel poles in the warm evening breeze.

In the humid kitchen the amount of work involved to prepare for another services meal overwhelmed Tranquilina's sense of generosity. Unable to sleep, Tranquilina had pulled a hairnet down to her earlobes and tied on an apron the size of a curtain and worked alone in the kitchen for hours, barely conscious of her poaching grief. She had begun by washing all the pots and pans, all the bowls left behind from last night's service, her hands reddened by the scalding water, and then began preparing for tonight's after-services meal. Yet the work already accomplished betrayed the amount of work that remained to be done. Carrots soaked in the sink; the pile of dusty potatoes was already sorted, cleaned, now readied to be peeled and chopped; several heads of cabbage lined the kitchen counter and looked as if they peeked over a fence; a net bag of yellow onions sagged about on a chair, awaiting her attention. Tranquilina sharpened the paring knife with the whetstone.

Because Papa Tomás had lived for decades, she thought him deserving of permanence. Hadn't he lived a long venerable life up to last night? Hadn't he survived the assault in Cuero? Her self-delusion was punishable by a rage so gridlocked, it struck worse than the awful revelation of his death. The way she rushed to the telephone booth to call 911, without her poncho and barefoot, restraining a hysteria so close to erupting, she pressed a hand over her mouth while she ran; the way she returned to chase the slack-jawed children staring at his talons, as she tried to tell them he was in a better place. The way Mama carried on with the street woman without once rising to console Tranquilina or to respond to the morbid silence of the congregation who stood around Papa in disbelief, some in recognition of, others indifferent to, their own mortality. The only believer seemed to be Mama. In another world altogether, she embraced the woman, *Hear O Lord when I cry,* rocked her like a baby, *have mercy also upon me,* her voice the only rasp in the church.

The ambulance's siren had malfunctioned and persisted in its rotating melancholic howling. Before Papa was rolled to it on a gurney, Tranquilina had straightened out the knot of his orange tie and then slowly covered the hardened hooves of his feet with the gurney sheet, and then covered the purple clots that blossomed mysteriously against the aged translucent skin of his limbs, and then right before she covered the dewlap folds of his neck, and right before she covered her Papa's calmed face, she whispered into his ear, tear-crusted and mournful, a prayer of farewell, and then she kissed his grizzled cheekbone and realized, with all the indignities this holy man had to suffer, she had forgotten to shave him. His skin felt as rough as the whetstone she was using to sharpen her paring knife.

Her hands were stubborn and since there was no reason to sleep, there remained every reason to work. Tranquilina raised the knife with one hand and clawed a sullen cabbage head firmly with another as Mama entered the kitchen.

Where's Papa? Mama asked, as if it were crucial she know his whereabouts. She had already strapped her leather bag across her ample breasts like a bandolier and then ripped her raincoat from its hanger and closed the closet door. Had Mama forgotten that Papa's life was now measured in ounces of ash, to be reduced to a shoebox and marked with a number at the city morgue? Tranquilina had filled out papers, accompanied Papa in the ambulance because Mama had opted to stay behind to bathe the woman, baptize her, pouring water over the woman's mane, her throat raw with the life-and-death grate of insistence.

Where have you been?

Where's Papa?

Mama, we have a lot of work ahead of us.

Where's Papa, I said!

He's resting, Tranquilina lied.

What garbage! Mama replied and then repeated the two words with sharpened rancor. She glared at the cabbage, its floppy leaves brown-rimmed, and then at the knife and then at Tranquilina. Her squat figure stood between the kitchen entrance and the alley and she fixed a gaze at Tranquilina with ferocity that had no comparison.

Forgive me, Mama, her daughter shamefully replied. Outside, the Pangaea clouds broke against a blue-gray light generous enough to give shape and form to everything, and the clouds cracked into continents against the downtown skyscrapers. But the dawning light was absent in Mama's glazing eyes. Her eyes held the dark chill of pin-precise pupils, and as Tranquilina locked into her gaze, she felt the raging wind of Mama's hand slapping against her own, forcing the knife from her grasp to fall between the sink counter and the edge of the stove.

Mama, Tranquilina muttered in astonishment, a hint of disbelief, of confusion. Mama?

Mama pushed her flesh into the envelope of her brittle raincoat as if she were already drastically late.

Know ye not, Mama said, fixing her crinkly collar, that the friendship of the world is an enemy of God? Whoever therefore will be a friend of the world is the enemy of God, James Chapter Four. Mama buttoned hastily, and she conducted the mindless buttoning with trembling hands, saying, All this garbage has nothing to do with God!

And then Mama took hold of Tranquilina, and tried to wake her daughter from this slumber of false belief, to make her comprehend that they did not belong to this world. Mama shook her until she loosened her daughter's tears. And before Tranquilina could embrace her, a tight consoling embrace that she needed just as much as Mama, Mama had pushed her aside and marched into the foggy hiss of air vents and toward the conquest of souls.

Tranquilina prostrated herself, her skirt and cook's apron under her knees, and reached between the two fixtures to search for the knife, barely touching the greasy dust balls where the knife had landed with a visible zinc thud. She could almost see Mama storm the entrance steps leading to the doors of the Little Brothers of the Poor, testifying to the elderly who used crutches and dented tin walkers to arrive closer to Jesus Christ.

The knife had landed beyond Tranquilina's fingertips. She took a broomstick and rowed it like a paddle between the fixtures. From the nursing home, Tranquilina guessed Mama rushed to the corner of First and Hastings, where workers loitered in hopeful search of employment; after they had gone, she'd knock on the doors of the Chinese cemetery caretakers, who would try to dissuade her, gesticulating wildly since they didn't speak Spanish.

Tranquilina's broom made contact and she swished the mucky knife toward her along with curdles of rubbish and food crumbs and other garbage that had settled on the floor of the thin crevice. If water from the spigot no longer purified and if food no longer provided sustenance, what else would Tranquilina possibly do? Numb, she grasped the knife and turned the spigot on. As she rinsed it under a trickle of lukewarm water, someone knocked loudly on the door.

Clad in her poncho, Tranquilina crossed the silvery pavement to reach the working pay phone, and the trail of boot prints, a bluish aluminum shine on the oily asphalt, vanished under the speeding tires of an orange and green truck. Next to the pay phone a man whose chin grew long squiggles of beard busied himself by building a shelter in a vacant parking lot. Like all those she had encountered, he had risen from the ash of neglect, the smog of passing cars, and now he had appeared; she had not remembered him the night before when she had used the Bakelite telephone to report Papa's death. Sometimes he disappeared behind a sheet of aluminum siding, only his two hands and two bare feet visible, and sometimes he disappeared altogether under a newfound board. In the frenzy of his activity, it seemed the ropes of his beard often caught in the splinters or nails of the board and he pulled with exasperated fits and gestures, sometimes whacking his own beard as if it were disobedient, a nuisance. He moved about with great purpose until he noticed her.

What you think you looking at? the bearded man yelled, cupping his hands around his matted mouth as if he were summoning farm hens. You got a problem, cuz if you don't, I can give you one right now! And he punched his fist with the mitt of his hand.

Tranquilina thought twice then to approach the man on a day like today. She stood by the Knight's Bail Bonds' neon and thought better of using the phone. She tried to ignore his rants.

She saw the QA from the top of the hill where the lone phone booth was located, where the bearded man suddenly stilled, eyeing her suspiciously. The Quarantine Authority officers stood knee-deep in the flooded pool at the incline of the intersection. Dressed in fluorescent vests, they went about collecting the bobbing orange cones, which looked like the old carrots Tranquilina had left soaking in the ministry sink. Bearded man or not, she crossed the street.

The box of the Bakelite phone contained initials engraved over digits scratched over words Tranquilina ignored. The coolness of the phone receiver always stunned the cartilage of her ear and when she attempted to slip the grimy dime into the slot, the coin stuck between the whitened tips of her fingers. The phone rang and rang, though Tranquilina guessed Ben's sister was already on her way to work. Two men, their names stitched above their shirt pockets, waited for the light to change, and as Tranquilina ignored the hollow ringing of the phone, she overheard them comment about how bad the sweltering heat was without the rain, or how bad the Noah's ark rains had been without the sun.

Yes? Ana answered, harassed and out of breath. She had just locked the deadbolt, thrown the keys in her bulging purse, where they sank to the bottom as the phone began to ring.

Yes? Ana never said hello, as if she knew whoever was on the other line would ultimately require something from her.

Ana? Tranquilina asked. It's about your brother Ben.

Ana's not-again breath sifted through the receiver. So what else is new?

But there is something else.

I doubt it.

The landlord can't find him, so he came to me.

Ben left the apartment?

He attended our service yesterday. I intended to call you, but I had . . . Tranquilina faltered. She looked beyond the dirty Plexiglas of the phone booth, grasping the same phone she put to use to call the ambulance for Papa. He's gone, Tranquilina whispered, and by this she meant her father. He's departed, she continued, noticing the light. Days must have passed without it because this morning it seemed so dazzling.

Sweet Jesus.

The landlord tried to deliver the eviction notice and—

Eviction notice? Ana asked, surprised but not surprised. The bastard was gonna throw him out cold?

People kept complaining.

I was afraid something like this would happen. Sweet Jesus.

I know, Tranquilina said softly. She had no words of consolation and little energy left to pump the well of comforting. A few strappy crows pecked on something in the wastebasket not far from the pay phone, pulling wormlike stuff from a paper bag with their stubborn beaks. There had been just one or two crows at first, cawing like barterers until another two or three arrived by invitation, wings spreading wide, and then there were enough swooping in to cause a dispute among them. Each time an orange and green truck drove by, the crows that had strayed out onto the asphalt sported their intimidating large wingspans and issued earsplitting caws.

He should have stayed at the hospital.

We can't change that now.

God, this is all so tiresome.

I understand.

It's this policy report . . . I have this stupid meeting.

Crows swooped in on the rim of the overflowing wastebasket and then more swooped down on the man's shelter and the crows barely flinched at the boom and wobble of the aluminum siding collapsing, inspiring a loud diatribe from the bearded man.

Goodness, Tranquilina said.

It sounded like a car wreck.

Yes, she said without thinking. Tranquilina watched the man replacing his roof, angry shouts and scolds. Yes, a car wreck.

Well?

I promised the landlord that I would call you.

I mean, did anyone get hurt?

Hurt?

From the car wreck.

What car wreck?

Tranquilina?

Yes.

I just thought of something, Ana said. Ben's out looking for her.

Can you speak up? I can't hear you.

I said he's looking for her.

Who?

Ben. Damn. I'm sure he is.

I meant looking for whom? Who is Ben looking for?

It's a long story.

They grew quiet, each waiting for the other to speak. Black netting of crows laced over the trashcan, on electrical wires, on the curvatures of the buildings. Tranquilina couldn't help but think of the little girls wearing their black crow skirts at yesterday's service. The frontage of store windows appeared to shimmer its reflection, the faint bluish fluidity of water reflected against the slick pavement, a double negative. Tranquilina said, He's not safe, is he?

Ana didn't know how to respond: Ben's not safe, as he is not *in* a safe place, or he's not safe, as he *is* dangerous.

Listen, I'll try to get to the church as soon as possible, okay?

And then?

Can you help?

You know where our church is, right?

How could I forget?

God willing.

Here we go again, Ana said. Round two.

In round one, Ben's previous breakdown had elicited action at once missionary and forceful. Round one had called for a united effort, and Ana leaned on Tranquilina for help with her brother since their father had given up long ago. Even before Tranquilina had opened the church door, she knew it was Ana who knocked because Ana's cologne clashed in the air like wind chimes. Still dressed in her shoulder-padded jacket and a miniskirt matching the chalk-white color of her painted nails and dangling earrings, Ana contrasted in appearance to Tranquilina, who wore her long black skirt, red poncho and galoshes. Ana's stiletto spikes pecked loudly through the alley, while Tranquilina's liver-colored galoshes quietly skimmed the glaze of moisture left by the factory vents. Tranquilina hid her hands under the shield of her poncho, a fact Ana found most irritating as she slid behind the steering wheel of her used sedan.

The clunky elevator of the Hotel Hobro opened at the fifth floor and the two women strode down the hallway, walking in and out of rows of dim yellow ceiling lights; strobes slid on and off their faces. Ana fished out a ring of keys from a purse bulging with items and tried key after key in the keyhole until there was a noticeable click and then Ana shouldered the doorjamb open and tumbled a stack of cassettes. Ben? Ana called. Ben, it's me. The stench was overpowering. It was as if razor blades had gashed the air, making all the many smells of waste bleed together. Ana led the way through the well-worn canyon of stacked newspapers and books and Tranquilina followed, ignoring the stench by not commenting on it.

Ana found him hunched in a deep corner of his bedroom, and Tranquilina looked over the crest of Ana's padded shoulder to see Ben tightly wound up in a cocoon of army blanket. Ana tried coaxing him, but it was Tranquilina who inspired his trust, and her hand emerged from under the poncho and she whispered, Posterior dorsal view, see, Ben? Anterior palmar, here. And what is this, Ben? Ben took her nervous hand cautiously, and he whispered, his breath foul and hostile. Knuckles, he said, looking up at a familiar face. Your basic knuckles. Leading him to his bed like a somnambulist, Ana covered him and then went about the apartment in frantic motions to find the telephone and call the Psychiatric Emergency Team.

Ana refused to speculate, got to work immediately, to-get-this-damn win-dow-oooooopen! And the scrape of swelled windowpanes, the flakes of rasping dried paint, sounded like fingernails shirking against blackboard. The open windows diluted the smells of the room while Tranquilina filled the kitchenette sink with the rush of hot water and sudsy dish soap and then began to wipe the garbage off dishes with a limp sponge, filling the trashcan with remains that had festered for weeks in the sink. She worked diligently, her fingers a frenzy of activity. Her two hands were jittery but not helpless, and as long as her fingers remained unfazed by the cluttered reminder of isolation, they possessed in their assurance a hope she struggled to maintain. Tranquilina smashed cockroaches with her bare hand, and then proceeded in washing, rinsing, drying and stacking. A saucer already cracked slipped from her soapy grasp and shattered.

Ana heard the dish breaking from the bathroom and hoped it wouldn't agitate Ben, who lay way too quiet in his bedroom. Breathing through her mouth, her own throat feeling a hot surge to upchuck, Ana gripped the handle of a short plunger and then plunged into the brown, slushy liquid of the toilet. Her beaded white earrings slapped violently against her cheeks. After a few flushes the toilet threatened to overflow, and Ana almost gave up her composure. She let the plunger sit like a thermometer in a wide mouth, and she rested on the rim of the bathtub to inspect the runs in her nylons. These new panty hose were too expensive for her meager salary. The emerging overflow of the toilet slowly sloshed around the spikes of her heels. We all only have one life, she thought, gazing at the soiled specks on her white miniskirt, why would God want to give such a cannibalizing disease to her sweet brother? To her? Ana heard another pounce, this time a tinny hollow bang of a pot, which was followed by a blunt, almost soothing, SHIT. Coming from anyone else, it would not have been so funny, but since it came from the lips of the saintly Tranquilina, the word took on such a renewed and refreshing meaning. AH, shit! Ana repeated, smiling. Lots of it.

Heartened, Ana plunged again and flushed again until the waste was sucked away by the drainpipe, and then Ana dumped and dumped Comet into the bowl. With a bristle brush, she scoured the bowl and then flushed and repeated and then flushed again, a third time, a sixth time. Stray ginger hairs stuck to her pasty sweat-sheened forehead. Ana hadn't realized how much elbow grease she'd put into scrubbing the toilet until she completed the task, and her shoulder, right up into the base of her neck, ached enough to convince her she was growing too old for this, though she was only twenty-six.

She was on a roll now, and she removed her jacket, and then removed the black mold in the tub, Pine Sol liquid smelling like cough medicine. She broke a fingernail scrubbing the crud under the thick rims of the small sink and chipped most of the white nail polish while swiping the tiled floor and lastly wiped the silver mirror without once looking at her reflection.

Ana finished cleaning the bathroom convinced that her business suit would have to be dry-cleaned, another expense she couldn't afford. She found Tranquilina in the living room sitting on Ben's reading chair without the shield of her poncho. Ana dragged a box opposite Tranquilina and sat and flipped her spiked heels off. Her nylons had sprung runs around her big toe. She spread her flattened feet against the floor luxuriously. They sat for a minute, but only for a minute, and it felt so soothing to sit and simply rest. Sirens, horns, the din of speeding cars, such racket of steel and gas and industrial innovation and the ingenuity of imagination all reduced to freeway traffic.

Ana wiggled her toes.

Say it again, she encouraged.

Tranquilina studied the boxes next to the armchair.

Excuse me? she replied.

Oh, come on! I want to hear you say it.

Say what again?

The word SHIT . . . Come on.

Of course not. Tranquilina smiled. Are you joking?

Loud and clear, Ana teased, cupping her ear. On the count of three—

Okay, then, Tranquilina said and rose from Ben's reading chair. Shit! And then Tranquilina pressed her hand to her mouth to cover the delight or perhaps to suppress another vulgarity and Ana couldn't help but laugh and Tranquilina joined her until the laughter reached its end and only a trace of a smile remained on their faces. It was time to get back to work.

Tranquilina moved the boxes away from the windows to make a clearing in the living room. Earwigs, silverfish and dust devils surfaced from the yellowed newspapers while she resumed the time-consuming task of sorting Ben's books, placing them in subject order. In the end and to save time, she decided it was best to stack them by size alone.

The scent of cleansing carried into the vinegar and old lemon juice squeaking against the window glass. Ana buffed the window rigorously, even the far-reaching corners, the tail of her blouse pulled out from under her skirt. The job rewarded her with a diamondlike glint. Ana noticed the curtains wrapped around the curtain rod and then twisted into a ball. She undid each and Tranquilina stopped her book-sorting to watch a thousand little sailboats cascading down the faded blue, crumpled ocean. A thousand little sailboats, their wings of snapping sails rising and falling on the gusty furrows of the open window, at once glittering like knives or sunk in the roll of blue waves. Right before the Psychiatric Emergency Team arrived to take Ben to the General Hospital, Ana and Tranquilina admired the thousand little sailboats, whipping across uncharted waters, the random way they sailed bravely and capsized all the same.

Outside of Cuero, the lifts of summer's breeze played with hats and one could hear the tiny singes of burning moths near the heat of the lantern's glow. Hallelujah. Away from the tarp, fireflies sparked chaotic like atoms. The tarp taunted and the lanterns squeaked their rust loose. Amen. In front of them, Papa sang his glorious runway to heaven in praise and in gratitude of God's brilliant beauty. Yes yes yes.

Tranquilina kept repeating Papa's words so as not to forget their inflections and their meaning, not to forget his gravelly voice. After the phone call to Ana, she returned to the church, her thoughts on the bearded man. Her boots suctioned as she walked, the stepping sounds discordant in her ears, another double negative. Once in the kitchen, she resumed her work, to bury Papa's death in routine.

Tranquilina held another cabbage and focused on where the knife was to split the two halves when she heard the approaching footsteps and knew full well who it wasn't because she knew it wasn't Mama. But Tranquilina could smell. Even over the cabbage and the simmering pot of leftover meat bone and the Dumpster outside, she could smell the street woman. The woman's odor blended many smells into something else altogether, something similar to Ben's apartment, something indistinguishable and solid but distinctively hers and sharp enough to cut into Tranquilina's breathing. The burden of skid row arrived with the homeless woman, and it seemed unfair, Tranquilina knew, to associate her with such consuming stink because Mama had scrubbed the woman's papery skin to shed the sin, *cleanse your hands, ye sinners,* the wafers of dried skin flakes falling into the baptismal waters. Mama had brushed out the dandruff from the woman's tangled hair, *purify your hearts, ye double minded,* trimmed her nails until her hands were immaculate and when the woman had left the church, walking through the alley and to her special place, she wore a psychedelic-colored muumuu frock Mama had found on a Salvation Army rack.

The woman timidly knuckled the door open, resistant hinges thirsty for lubricant. Gripping her straw bag, she entered the kitchen and stared at Tranquilina. Their latest apostle had returned wearing her same clothes, the muumuu discarded completely. Less than twenty-four hours, and the woman returned in a rumpled condition, only this time, without her hats, owning a stink that arrived before she did, a smell so profoundly hopeless, Tranquilina couldn't bring herself to say a word. Crestfallen and focused, Tranquilina slammed the cleaver to split the cabbage in two.

The robust steam of the blackened pot rose and cracked the ceiling paint a little more. The woman shuffled the insides of her straw bag while Tranquilina looked up from the split halves of the cabbage to draw in drafts of air permitted by the small window propped open, to dissuade the woman's smell from entering her lungs again. Tranquilina stared out the window. In the alley, curls of fog drifted, condensed strokes of moisture above the air vents, misting as if water splashed on dry ice. Slowly rising, the moisture had already buried the wheels of the Dumpsters. Tranquilina turned and greeted the woman with a terse, polite hello.

The woman placed her straw bag on the table and continued to shuffle the insides until she pulled out a large balled-up object. It resembled strips of cloth wrapped into a ball. Because the fog was swallowing the steel of the Dumpsters and because things were no longer what they seemed to be, Tranquilina knew the woman's ball was anything but that.

The woman hadn't allowed the small lacerations on her wrists to heal—she took to picking at them once they scabbed. It was these fleshy lesions all over her wrists that Tranquilina watched as the woman peeled away the layers of the ball. The leaking spigot pocked one drop at a time into the soaking carrots as the ball grew smaller and smaller until one egg appeared, nestled in the strips of cloth, then another and a third one. The last egg appeared as animated and as perfect as the shape of a soul. The woman placed each egg inside a bowl, gently, proudly.

Tranquilina rubbed her bare foot against a bare ankle to consider the egg thievery. She wondered if she could afford it in their overdue account with God. Tranquilina's smile was not what it seemed. She slammed the cleaver and quartered the cabbage halves and threw them in a strainer.

Can you help with the meal? Tranquilina asked, but didn't even wait for a reply. She handed the woman a peeler without so much as a thank-you for the eggs, or congratulations for a job well done, or even, please do not steal again. Without hesitation the woman complied and sat on Mama's designated kitchen chair, curling the first peel off a russet.

Did it matter that Tranquilina hadn't asked the woman to wash her hands? They worked in a silence that was eerie and nonexistent. There were plenty of sounds to go around—the buzz of a meaty fly caught in between the panes of glass in the window, the overspill of broth on the flames, the strikes of a peeler, the woman's breathing—but Tranquilina paid no attention. With every move came a labored breath from the woman, and with every breath came a shorter and raspy wheeze that

Tranquilina refused to hear. She felt as if the two of them were land-locked somewhere, surrounded by nothing else outside of the kitchen except the never-ending solitude of what began in Cuero, Texas.

The kitchen door quaked, tinkling drawn-out tremors, for how long Tranquilina didn't know. She expected Ana any moment now, but she recognized the insistent scratching of the begging dog. Potato shavings struck everywhere—on the floor, on the bowl of eggs, on the table, on the woman's arms and legs like brown leeches.

Tranquilina unwrapped a bundle of tinfoil and opened the door and saw the lethargic ghost of the dog through the wavering fog, its dry nose resting on its front paws. The sight of her brought its tail into speed-wagging and Tranquilina threw the bone out to the dog and apologized for not having more. Much to her relief, the dog limped over and snapped at the bone in renewed hunger. Once back in the sanctuary of the kitchen, Tranquilina searched for a good onion from the sack and then ripped out the button and began to slice it on the butcher board with her cabbage-smelling cleaver. Her eyes welled up in tears and she allowed them to drop, like the water from the spigot, until a tinny, cymbal-like boom banged underneath the kitchen window. A trashcan toppled, a challenging growl, low and menacing, startled them. Tranquilina wiped her tears with the corner of her apron and peered outside to investigate.

That evening outside of Cuero, Papa's words had suspended like a bridge between possibility and impossibility. She'd sat next to Mama, her eyes nearly shut, drowsy from a drunkenness of faith. The humming of cicadas was enough to make anyone believe in God's everlasting beauty.

The rancher's son-in-law sat two rows down and wore the clothes of most men of the area: soiled blue jeans, a baseball cap crowned with sweat-salty spikes. He had hardened callused hands that were no strangers to tilling, and accustomed to clenching the shaft of an ax to split timber into kindling. And Tranquilina could smell him. Fermented earth and corn bread. The moon was hidden and the lantern light danced shadows on their faces as they willingly listened. For hours after the meeting, she hovered around Papa's words and felt radiant, the light so blazing she had not taken note of the rancher's son-in-law approaching from behind. In a cluster of trees, as she had sought to squat

and pee, he slammed her so hard with a shovel, the impact sent her flying arms forward. Her face thudded into the muddy damp manure and
for a few moments she had no idea what was happening. Rot in her
mouth, muck in her nostrils, she couldn't breathe, and he dragged her
facedown by the ankles deeper into the innocence of pecan trees. She
tried not to feel terror and tried to recite Psalm 31:19.

A roaming loose-knit pack of dogs began to challenge the mangy
mutt for the bone Tranquilina had just fed it. She could hardly see
them, almost ghostly in the cataracts of fog lingering over the alley's
brick walkway. The mutt defended the meal with fierceness, arching its
back, hackles raised in anger. Its whole body took on a shield of de-
fense with its tail erect like a sword. Its fight-notched ears pointed forward and the battle scars revealed that these challenges were not new.
They were part and parcel of its survival and it knew instinctively to
glare defiantly at the largest challenging dog, to growl its warning to
stay away. The other dogs of various shapes and sizes circled the mutt,
nipping and snarling at its sore hind legs. They bared their fangs,
growled, waited for the bigger dog to distract the mutt from the bone,
one of them locking its jaws on a leg while a smaller one barked and
yapped, cowering whenever the larger dog snarled.

The woman listened to the dogs about to fight. Moments must
have passed, because a peeled potato oxidized and turned to rust in
her hand.

Tranquilina tried to raise her hand to pull out the filth caught in
her mouth. She suffocated, grasping, coughing, her lungs weighed
down by his body, the body that slammed her as hard as the shovel,
and he mounted her and he thrusted and grunted and she felt his
breath stale and dead until he exploded into her insurmountable pain,
an inferno of excruciating wet fire. Mama called, a disembodied wailing from nowhere and everywhere.

She heard the boy cruelly cursing and Tranquilina suddenly felt
pity, groping slowly, modestly to try and find the waistband of her underwear, her fingers clenching nothing except the dank compost of
chaotic vegetation. She drew in all the shreds of his smell, and the core
of it, the culmination of this boy's smell, derived its power from fear.
Tranquilina repeated the psalm—*Oh, how great is thy goodness, which
thou hast laid up for them that fear thee.* She could barely turn to her

side to see his figure, a man so heavy in his hate he made deep prints on the earth as he ran, a blurring outline of a man, shrinking into the dark until he became night itself. She lay in still wait as if the slightest gesture exasperated the pain, as if the terror would repeat itself if she called out to Mama's searching voice. Through the canopy rustle of the trees, Tranquilina tried to find her underwear (it was imperative she find her underwear), and her fingers blindly discovered the hem of her skirt and she struggled to pull it down. Mama's lantern light broke into an approaching glow as Tranquilina repeated, How great is thy goodness . . . How good is thy greatness.

Outnumbered and outmuscled, the dogs overpowered the mutt. The larger dog clamped onto the bone and ran off while the other dogs trailed behind him, whining and nipping at his tail. The smaller one lifted a leg to pee on the rumbled trashcan next to the body of the mutt, and then ran off to catch up to the pack. The mutt lay warm in his own blood, his breathing a quick succession of pants, his eyes obsidian-glassy.

Full of leeches, the woman held a rusted finger to her lips. She burrowed her birdlike eyes into Tranquilina.

Hush, now, Tranquilina replied.

The woman selected another russet from the pile and then poked out a tumor with great stabbing force. Tranquilina ignored her and continued dicing the onion. She went on like this for another three bulbs and her eyes stung so badly, she raised them toward the ceiling to stare at the tangle of loose wires where a ventilating fan should have been.

Tranquilina demanded, Hush!

The mouth of the spigot continued its drip. Just when Tranquilina took to studying the formation at the end of the spigot, the pear shape gathering condensation, translucence filling into another hourglass and then plonking onto the makeup of a million other water drops, and just as another tear began to fill, it was then, at that moment, that Ana knocked on the door.

Tranquilina and Ana circled the streets of downtown in search of Ben. The headlights of Ana's sedan were bright for hours until they shone jaundice, a warning that her battery was running low. Canvassing whole blocks, Tranquilina would return wordless of Ben's where-abouts, and instruct Ana to go up two streetlights more and make a left and then suddenly request for her to please pull over, beam some lights on that large Dumpster over there, and then Tranquilina would be off again, only to return again and begin anew.

The hours passed in this way. On the corner of Main and Olympic, Tranquilina recognized Mama. Inside a parachute of lamppost light, Mama stood surrounded by a few curious bystanders near a **Post No Bills** sign. Mama coarsely shouted unintelligible words, guttural utterances unfamiliar to Tranquilina. It hadn't fazed Mama that the on-lookers were already scattering as the drizzle began. Tranquilina pressed her worried hand against the cool car window glass as raindrops the size of rice plonked on the windshield.

Fulminating thunder. As the sedan drove on to another destination, Tranquilina stared at her mama. Papa's ascension didn't deter Mama from her mission. The divine and the real became one and the same to Mama. Tranquilina rubbed the silvery window to see Mama quote from the pages of her Bible. Strands of hair clung wet like fine cracks on her ruddy cheeks. No matter that it rained; no matter that she had lost her umbrella somewhere, no matter that she was completely alone. The reflection Tranquilina now saw in the side mirror was that of a preacher who believed the drenching downpour was her consecration, the hail itself a swell of zealous applause.

ELEVEN

She could read, Turtle wasn't stupid. The cross-outs, tags, new gang emblems trashed all over McBride's graffiti on the walls of the bridge—all bad news. Lote M had fingered out the McBride Boys big time, singled them out for a class-grade-A, full-blown showdown. Tearing off McBride balls, Turtle was thinking, when the street woman appeared, tick-tocking from nowhere, and tripped into Turtle's funnel of lamppost light. Something inside her straw bag tick-tocked. Years of street instinct murdered by fatigue and Turtle jumped, jumped, can you believe it?

The Lote M vatos meant business and crudely chiseled away at the calligraphic tags—**Alfonso aka Big Al, Sir Santos, Palo, Lucho Libre, Luis Lil Lizard, Turtle, McBride Boys Que Rifa.** Perforating new conquerors over old ones with a blunt hammer, the remaining tags erased, shitted on, with strokes of red runny spray paint. Bold, ballsy headlines, Turtle was thinking, staring at Luis's old sketch of a lizard, a blueprint for his tattoo, now effaced under red initials from Lote M. That's exactly what the Maravilla vatos planned to do on the bridge, send a dispatch announcing erasure. And then the woman tick-tocked and Turtle aimed her stare at the owl eyes sunk deep into the woman's skull. Check the feet, Turtle said to herself, but her words crossed-voice with Luis's. Check out the feet to see if she's for real, or a cemetery apparition.

Luis Lil Lizard, so good in telling stories to Turtle, about the start, how it started, this thing with the ghost, no lie, the guys working the freeways, the bulldozers biting chingón bites too close to the cemeteries, chewing up coffins. And who knows, but that's how it started, no kidding this ain't a joke. The guys, they stand around, like, Look what I found—checking out the skulls, no lie. Man, oh, man, they don't know what to do, you know, just a bunch of jotos, and one of 'em says, Hear something? No, okay, so anyways, they're behind schedule so the bola de pendejos say, Fuck it, keep plowing and acting like it's no big deal, sabes? I swear to God. Who cares? Like it's nothing to throw in the skulls and bones and shit into the cement mixer, act like they never found the bones. So now all those little bones tick to find the rest of their family bones to tock, you know? So when you hear the ticktockingticktocking. Hey, you hear it, Turtle? Outside the tent! Right behind yoooou!

And just as Luis Lil Lizard had warned, the death mask tripped and her bag of bones tocked and Turtle froze, scared shitless, shitless, can you believe it? Just death and Turtle inside the round bright jar of lamppost light, nothing else surrounding them but night. Turtle inflated her chest, straightened out her shoulders so that she loomed asskicking larger and threatening. But all the woman had to do was press a bony finger to her lips to make Turtle shrink, to make Luis scream in her head, Check the feet, Check out the feet to see.

Turtle crashed out of the glass of light, splashing her sneakers in the raw, murky oil of the gutter overflow, grasping the jacket collar tighter around her throat to shield it from the woman's burning gaze. Escaping between two warehouses, Turtle emerged on the other side of the alley, relieved. The squiggling blur of taillights traveling the freeway became somehow comforting. Rainwater wrapped around her sneakers.

After two hours of walking, she arrived in the Eastside late. Turtle tried to avoid both the QA and the lengthy line of worn-out people waiting at the quarantine checkpoint. Wooden sawhorses as big as Clydesdales. She took Third Street once again, and walked under a long row of palms bordering the Calvary Cemetery. It was a major boulevard, so Turtle knew to be careful, since Lote M vatos probably cruised Third Street looking to bust any McBride Boy, so she turned on Eastern. Turtle vaulted over the short brick wall of the first Serbian cemetery, where she walked in a rumor of lamppost light past the engraved markers with names like Radulovich, Babich, Bezunar, Mijanovich. In a fenced-up country, the names were exotic, safely protected from the outside of the living, from the spray-painted names like Gallo, Spook, Lencho, Fox, BamBam, Wilo x *Con Safos*. After stomping on an old wiry gate enough, Turtle hopped out and jogged across the severed deserted remains of Second Street, and then climbed the wire-mesh fence of the second Serbian cemetery. She stood under an ancient eucalyptus until she was sure the coast was clear.

The Interstate 710 below her, Turtle sprinted, Go, Go, Go, across the bridge, and then slammed and scaled the tall chain-link fence, up and over, dropped into the Chinese cemetery like a load of stolen goods. She leaned on the brick crematory chimney to catch her breath and then caught the charred scent of wet incense, strong and penetrating. Heavy ice-block feet chilled in her dampened sneakers as she waited for her bones to settle back into their rightful places. After the encounter on the bridge, Turtle didn't dare sit, though powerful cramps quivered her thighs.

S for *Size up the situation*, Luis's voice instructed. Or was Turtle imagining his instruction? She adjusted to the darkness and then sized up the area. No way could she hide here; only an old chain-link fence and nothing else between Turtle and despair, not even chapels or crypts or large mausoleums to hide or sleep in, no suitable place to rest in peace. Fortunately, the cemetery was right below the Interstate ramps and except for the distant lights on the freeway, the cemetery's obscurity provided a few hours of temporary shelter.

This was her neighborhood, the one she grew up in, right across the street from where she stood now, and yet this particular cemetery had always remained a mystery. She touched the crematorium and remembered smoke from the chimney blowing ash over their games of stickball, and remembered too the fireworks and the grieving brassy orchestra playing mournful songs of farewell. The music, the scent, the mystery, had begged for Turtle to press her face against the fence like the other neighborhood kids had done, as if the Chinese funeral pageantry were created for their childhood curiosity.

Her vision infiltrated the graveyard. Food offerings, right there. A few families had apparently picnicked with their dead and left bowls of dried rice and softened fruit by the headstones. Hungry as she was,

Turtle didn't go for the food, didn't touch a grain of it, and instead checked her pockets for a something, anything even remotely edible. She fished out a sorry-ass frajo she had discovered near the Soledad Church steps, possibly from a priest taking a smoke break before looking for real currency, before jingling for change from the pink purses of his altar boys. A few puffs left and that was all she needed, and she puffed, drew in deeply, lustfully. The tobacco's soothing glow was like the scorching relief of whiskey, making her light-headed, dizzy. If only she had a joint to relax her or some black beauties to wire her up, but if-onlys were just as empty as her pockets. She chided herself and smoked the frajo down to its biting filter until it simply burned out on its own, and then she flicked it away and waited. Patience, man, it's Frankenstein.

U for *Undue haste makes waste.* She let an hour or maybe two pass, sat on her haunches for another hour and probably dozed off, the kind of dozing off which means you don't know you're sleeping until something like your cheek slapping against the dampness of chimney brick awakens you into getting your shit together. Turtle rubbed her whole face, palmed the shape of her head, shook hokey-pokey all around. Her jacket had grown loose, weight vacated, and the biting chill moved in. The cars no longer speeded by with the same frequency of rush hour, of everyone heading home or not home. Above her, silent skies. No stars to blindside or curtail the helicopters and their midnight sweeps. Turtle wasn't stupid. Her fists punched in her pockets. She had to make a move soon before the sweeps or else get stuck like a zoo animal in a cage, and so she began to step over the malleable humps of the muddy graves.

R for *Remember where you are.* Wasn't this the spot where she was jumped senseless, here, to be initiated into McBride? She could never forget that night, didn't want to relive it and tried to get the hell out of the memory. It was too damn dark to see the oval bowl of rice she kicked or the slippery deep mud puddle that gripped her sneaker, held on for dear life. Her heart startled and she yelped, a sucking gasp, and was surprised it came from her, and then she cursed herself—what a fucken girl she was—and pulled her sneaker out and continued across the cemetery.

If there was one thing she didn't want to do tonight, it was remember, and despite herself, she stared through the diamond wire fence at their old house. Of course the years would change it, the history of various renters, a family or two, but except for Turtle's landmark, the Zumaya house next door, their old house was hardly recognizable. Cars parked in front of the porch like some wrecking yard. And the house was painted a god-awful baby pink. Diapers hung on the old laundry line between the T-poles in the backyard where she and Luis used to build their tent. The new screen door and a warm glow of porch light burning for someone's return made Turtle wonder who lived there, who cooked guisos and refried beans with spoons of bacon fat on the stove where the O'Keefe name was scrubbed off. Whatever happened, she wondered, to all those nopales Amá had planted? All but one small cactus remained to give Turtle such an aching prick.

One RTD bus passed, two or three passengers maybe, autos and people thinning out. Guessing late night. Like a cheap T-shirt, their old house had shrunk, dwarfish, but the Zumaya house stayed snapshot-same except for the avocado tree chopped to a stump and a wooden fruit crate leaning under the bathroom window for no apparent reason. The hunchback's toolshed stood intact and his lawn remained lovingly trimmed, which assured Turtle the hunchback was still alive and kicking.

It had been years since, and no, Turtle didn't want to remember how careless they were to the house and each other. Broken windows veined with duct tape, Amá's broken bones, tiles eroded and fallen to the ground like teeth, Luis's locura, paint peeled, Frank's explosive temper and the stink of a thousand regrets like an old discarded refrigerator lingered in their rented house. But a home? You only realized you had one once you didn't and Turtle began to know a thing or two about rent. Up until she went AWOL from the McBride Boys, it seemed she had rented her life for real cheap.

Traffic finally thinned enough to guarantee time to hoist herself over the fence and then dump-fall, spring up to rearrange her squat and look normal. Hands behind her in full view, she walked westbound, strides long enough not to look like a run. She turned back, looked over her shoulder at the old house, now a pebble, a grain, nothing. Blank.

Crossing Hastings Street, Turtle walked to loosen ideas or hoped for intervening fate like accidentally bumping into a classmate of pre-McBride days, a jangling of charitable change in her wallet. Better still, discovering a dollar bill near the cantinas, right there near the fire hydrant, a panicked drunk trying to count his money before heading home to tell the wife and seven kids he was working overtime when the thief pulled out a gun. Walking, listening for brakes of rubber tires, the motors of the helicopters. Come on, no one said, and Turtle walked on.

She spat out a clump of phlegm. Soreness, cramp here, there, her knees jerking like a puppet on a string. Amá had given up, caved in and moved out of state to who knows where after Tío Angel's knifing, and Turtle refused to go even if she had been asked. She stayed behind with Luis Lil Lizard until her brother was drafted, and then stayed behind with the McBride Boys until she went AWOL, and then she had no familia to stay with, nobody, not a one, can you believe it? The parasitic chills sucked up whatever internal warmth her baggy jacket provided, and she decided to jog past the First Street Store, trying to break a sweat. Downward and upward the paved hills of First Street went, steam licks rising from the manholes.

Turtle reached Evergreen Cemetery. It was the oldest cemetery citywide, and four tall cinder-blocked guard walls kept the neighborhood from spilling in. An ancient chapel stood right smack in the middle of the grounds, and there were so many marbled mausoleums and vaults, Turtle had only to choose. The best way in, two chain-link gates facing the living side of First Street, and Turtle deliberated whether the break-in was too much of a hassle. On one of the brick pillars, which held the gate hinges, Turtle saw the old wash-out tag: **McBride Boys Controla.** Yea, old news to Lote M Homeboys.

All she had was the Workman screwdriver. Turtle guessed she could probably spring the gate pipes open enough with sufficient pressure to slip through and then wire it back in place. With a quick glance over her shoulder, Turtle plunged the screwdriver between the gate pipes and pushed. Swift and silent, breaking and entering professionally, an effort as easy as slicing soft butter. A felony performance. She tuned her ears to the gravel of tires halting, jiggling of keys, static of radio waves, her two locked fists on the screwdriver as if it were an oar. Her peripheral vision caught any porch or headlight, her nose readied for the agitated scent of police leather's strong testes musk over tobacco, her sneaker pushing.

Assault and battery to the gate, giving her all kinds of attitude, metal pipes screeching a challenge. Rusted flakes showered on her knuckles and Turtle grunted a full muscle weight, pulling the screwdriver forward, pushing a sneaker backward to pry the poles apart. Unhinged, rehinged and totally uncooperative, stubborn old metal gate mocking her. Fuck you, she whispered to the gate, motherfucker. Out of sheer determination to sleep in the chapel, Turtle tried again, and then again until her ears trapped laughter.

Turtle leaned into the shadow of the brick pillar, quiet and invisible, holding the screwdriver behind her. The source of the noisy conversation she heard came from four customers leaving the Happy Times Cantina. Turtle could see their outlines: one of them was stocky, one short, the other two so drunk they slumped their shoulders, camouflaging their height, their heads wavering with exaggerated weight. If only she had been able to open the gate, she would have been safe. Now she had to deal with four drunks who were slowly coming her way.

Their laughter grew boisterous, a joke or comment busting them up with rowdy disregard as they approached the brick pillar. Hiding in the shadow, Turtle clenched the handle of the screwdriver. Adrenaline rising to a boil, thawing the ice of her skin, fingernails clawing her own palm. Exhausted or not, she had to deal with them. Stab the short one first, because the smallest ones were always the meanest and he'd be the sharpest opponent; and then strike the stocky one in the leg to incapacitate him; the other two would be easier because they were staggering drunk and would be slow in reacting. A kick to the purses, a fist in their sloshy stomachs and when they're down, stomp their faces to make sure the perpetrator is unidentifiable in a lineup.

Uproarious laughter at a phantom story delivered by one of the four. Shit, shit, why hadn't she been able to bend the gate pipes? This fight, all fights, muddled her head. Fighting to stay conscious after the last guy was down or fighting to keep enough blood in her to make it to safety. Ya no más—put that in your **U.S. Army Field Manual 21-71** survival book—no more. One of the men pushed another to make it known it wasn't respectable behavior to laugh in the presence of death, and they quieted. The light must have reflected off the screwdriver in her hand as she lifted her arm to wipe the sweat from her forehead, because one of the men, the stocky one, pointed directly to her.

V for *Vanquish fear and panic*, and the only way to do just that was to believe the opponent, the enemy, was more terrified than you. Bola de pendejos, Luis would call them, and the four men quickly sobered up, a kind of cop-halting-you sobered up, and she saw them whisper among themselves. She scrutinized the high brick pillar, the barbed wire on top of the cinder-block ledge. How could she have let herself be cornered? How could she keep her breathing from sounding like blasting car horns in a tunnel, and how long could she keep this up? Her sweat smeared against the leather of her jacket. How and How and How did it come down to this, to Turtle wishing she were safely inside a fucking cemetery?

What are you waiting for? Come on, Luis had said. She hadn't seen him in days, which didn't seem strange anymore. No questions asked. Even as she hurried to put on her shoes, he was already out the door, already crossing the dead end, a rippled silhouette in the late afternoon. He strutted with admirable confidence along the wire fence of the Chinese cemetery. Once she caught up to him, once her shadow bled on the back of his unbuttoned Pendleton shirt, he turned and pointed an accusatory finger and said:

You walk like a pinche turtle.

Turtle said, You're cold-blooded.

A McBride Homeboy now as permanent as the purple initial **M** tattooed between Luis's index and thumb, he waved to Turtle to follow. They walked along the embankment of a huge wide man-made channel where, a few years back, houses stood as abandoned as her memory of them. Following Luis's rapid pace, Turtle found it hard to keep up and to keep quiet without asking questions like where were they going. She was taller than Luis, taller than all of her classmates, taking after their father Frank. Years sprouted inches and the only gifts Turtle received on her birthdays came in the form of length and width. Today was her twelfth birthday, and she could clearly see over Luis's shoulder.

Luis stopped. See these? he asked, pointing to sticks, little orange flags attached to the top of them, hundreds or more of them lined along the embankment of the endless channel, the kind that Caltrans surveyors used to indicate who knows what.

Yea, so? A show of disinterest, contemptuous, but secretively grateful; a show-me-something-I-don't-know look. Luis pulled one, then another, and then flung them into orbit across the channel.

Fucking with 'em, he said, uprooting them like carrots, farmworker style.

She didn't get it. No questions asked, but he wanted her to come out for this? And Turtle joined him, javelin-throwing across the channel as wide as a river, a huge straight artificial river naked of water, and discovered the channel was wider than her arm throwing strength. Luis looked out, quiet and somber, at the openness of the earth, the muscle split. He gazed at it like a boy/man enthralled by his own wound.

Turtle tried to look where Luis stared. No cement or asphalt or water, as far as she could see. Nothing but a gouged-out canyon of dirt and dirt and more of it. And more to this than stick-flinging, bootdusting. At first Turtle thought her brother had slipped, stones hurtling downward to the bottom of the dry riverbed, and she yelped and chided herself—what a fucken girl she was—and then she saw Luis sidestepping, riding the curvature down, arms out for balance, pony-dancing, causing dust clouds to rise around him. Turtle realized it was an entrance, a makeshift path, and Luis was riding down, surferenvious moves keeping his balance. She plunged in, catching a momentum downward, clumsily at first and skidding her ass, then springing up before Luis noticed, knocking her knees to a halt on the machine-packed bottom.

She swiped at her cutoff jeans, banged her palms to get the red clay dust off her T-shirt. This took a few moments, too many for Luis's patience, and he yelled, What you waiting for, you turtle? The words already riding on his annoyance.

But Turtle smelled the belly of the earth. Cool and dry, dark and rich, flat. Dead and alive. Another planet, a crater of another world mixed into her real world all at the same time. To the right and left of her, the walls resembled legs sprawled apart. Her sneakers stood beneath miles of earth that had been heaved up, plowed aside, carted off and carried away in preparation for the rolling asphalt of the Interstate

710 Long Beach and Pomona freeways. Severed tree roots jutted from mud walls. It was another planet altogether and she gazed above her at the high ridge and marveled at how far down the tree roots had grown. Except for the horizon being erased by the night, she saw nothing above them. Out of sight, out of mind, and over the embankment, everything was forgotten. Nonexistent.

Turtle stood alone, turned three hundred and sixty to look for Luis. The night stalled above her; arriving this far down took time. She saw his distant figure heading toward the crotch of the channel and ran to him, angered at his impatience; his bringing her, then losing her, whatta joto. She ran toward the only spark of light in the night, stomping over dried mud grooves of tires and boot prints. She ran toward the narrowing of walls and spotted him approaching a nimbus of light.

The McBride Boys congregated glassy-eyed in a semicircle, a garbage can blazing. The red and pumpkin flames brightened the sides of their faces. Hearing footsteps, one of the boys broke out of a trance and saw Luis and jutted his chin in recognition and then fed the fire with surveyor's sticks. The plumes of flame fought one another.

At least a dozen of them. McBride actively recruited toughened unimaginable lives. A few sat on the bulldozers, the Caterpillar tires landlocked in hardened mud. Others on their haunches, at the margins of the semicircle, and the rest so close to the fire it made their faces shine sweaty. Turtle joined Luis and hooked her thumbs on the belt loops of her cutoffs. The blaze ate itself with brilliant efficiency. Nothing except the walls of packed earth, and the darkness closed in from all sides, making the fire luminous, mesmerizing.

Thick smoke, tobacco, sagey smell of marijuana as familiar in the neighborhood as Old Spice cologne. Orange flares of fire reflected in their eyes.

What the fuck do you think you're doing?

No one flinched except for Turtle. The boys understood that this question belonged to Luis and Luis understood the same. But he didn't have to answer to anyone, and he pinched a joint handed to him by another homeboy and torched it with his Zippo lighter and then inhaled and held the expanse of his lungs until it was impossible not to breathe. The voice came from beyond the firelight, somewhere even beyond the margins, out of the darkness.

¿Qué hubo? Luis Lil Lizard said, studying the fire, the others re-lieved that he spoke. This is Turtle, Luis said, my family. In a tone used to buy fruit, a pound of apples.

Pinche jolly green giant, teased another voice that hadn't made a decision yet to be a man's voice or remain a boy's voice. The tension getting to everyone.

Say it to my face, pendejo, Turtle demanded, her uneasiness need-ing an excuse to erupt. She yelled the challenge again, turning toward the dark. The bulldozers resembled great ships. Come on, puto, what you waiting for? The heat was fueling her courage. Say it to me. Tenta-tive laughter, a few lazy chuckles. The joint came around to Luis again.

Nobody said you could bring 'im.

Who died and made you jefe? Luis said without rancor or anger, plain and simple, asking a question where the first rule is, no questions asked. The fire shadow played on his face.

He's not McBride, ése.

I ain't gonna tell him that.

He's not McBride.

And who's gonna tell him he ain't?

Eh-eh-AN-Y-vo-vo-vo-LUNTeers? asked a stuttering voice.

Only the chomp and snap of the fire responded. Luis held down the three-finger sign to create M, Trece M: Muerte-Marijuana-McBride. And then a dozen M's flashed all around the bonfire. Turtle was no longer a who anymore, but a what belonging to a new generation of firekeepers.

Luis Lil Lizard took a second hit of the joint. Happy birthday, he uttered, knotting his lungs to hold in the fumes, releasing and landing, and then Turtle's brother passed the torch to her.

Being in close proximity to the cemetery unnerved the men, to the point of spooking them enough to investigate. Turtle hoped they wouldn't get nearer than they were now, she could smell them, their sour beer yeast and cigarettes. The screwdriver went from one hand to another, her palms too sweaty for a good grip. The men's heated de-bate was interrupted by the first of the nightly helicopter sweeps, and Turtle sighed. She saw the short one sprint double-time across the street, abandoning the others until they regained some sense and broke up in different directions, swaying and stumbling, but managing to get the hell out of sight. Turtle relaxed her grip, waited for the spotlight of the helicopters to noise up another street. Out of sight, she began to work the gate again.

The gate poles finally gave way enough. Turtle had lost so much weight, her thinning body slipped through, her metal zipper xylophoning against the pole. A loose wire hitched her jacket and she jerked out of its grasp and gave the gate another good fucking kick, found herself on the other side.

The gravel trail to the chapel slowly appeared once her vision adjusted. An odd comfort accompanied her crunching steps. At the fork of the trail, Turtle discovered a spigot with a trough near a trashcan, a place where people dumped their old flowers, got water for their new bouquets. Turtle wasn't aware of how much she missed washing her hands and face until she felt the wet sensation of water between her fingers, a tub full of water belonging to another time. She bent to drink directly from the spigot and then rinsed her face one more time, for the aliveness of it, the cleansing of it, ducked her whole head under the spigot, rubbing her fuzzy growth of hair. After she was done, the studs of her ears were mirrored in the gray muzzle of spumy water like blobs she spit out on the sidewalk.

The toe poppers in the gook fields embodied surprise. Detonated at the slightest contact, the hesitation of a boot above them, the hovering of a body, barely a shadow to activate an explosion. Surprised to see a pinkish mist of skin and boot and testicles in front of you and surprised to see that grounded flesh had once, not more than a few seconds before, belonged to you. Even more surprised to realize that you survived in part when the guy next to you had not. Land mines were what obsessed Luis, an all-consuming subject in the barrack showers, in the training films where the narrator's voice wobbled, the film tread bare from sheer use, because having balls was what Luis was all about.

Ése, your huevos get blown off, Luis said. His sleek biceps were absent of fat and flab and looked like wires tightly twisted, and he raised his wiry hands and formed a kaboom, saying, Fuck, in disbelief, then cupping his crotch with his tattooed M hand. He couldn't resist laughing.

He sat between Turtle and Lucho Libre at the Greyhound bus station, smack in the middle of the derelict town, the walls of the depot held up by the homeless asking for a spare dime, the ceiling trapping an explosive mix of solid smells: armpits, tobacco smoke, carbon monoxide, and if exhaustion had a smell, that too. Inducted, boot camp, now heading off for a tour of duty, Luis wore combat Vibrams spit-shined, extra shoelace wrapped and secured around the collar of the boots. Whenever he moved, his lizard tattoo scurried up his bicep and hid under his rolled-up T-shirt sleeve where he kept his cigarettes. Inside the leg cargo pocket of his fatigues rested his **U.S. Army Field Manual 21-71, SURVIVAL** issued by the Department of the Army Headquarters, and probably the only book Luis ever read. For the last ten days, Luis blasted his veins out of style, trying anything to put him into a stupor that resembled R&R, taking out the manual at odd times, on Big Al's porch one day, after a no-sleeper another night, whipping it out in agitation, like a pistol out of the holster of his fatigue leg pocket. He repeated the lines frequently to Lucho, to Santos, to the puto who sold him a nickel bag of heroin so pure, it made him puke and made him hunger for it again. **S** for *Size up the situation*, Luis said so many times his words crossed-voice Turtle's and made her loca.

Ca-ca-ca-come BACK with your NUTS, Lucho Libre stammered.

That's the plan, Luis said. An image in his head made him quiet. He shivered his leg.

They grow back, pendejo, Turtle replied sarcastically. Don't you know?

Co-co Nuts, maybe. Yours, maybe, Lucho said to slug Turtle back. Con safos to you, girl. The boys knew Turtle was the only McBride Boy lacking, as in **S** for *Sin* huevos and Lote M knew it too. Lucho puckered his chapped lips, blew her a kiss. All this while Luis sat silently between them, an image in his head.

Fuck you.

Lucho asked about the time, and then hunted for a clock. Only when the stutter took over did Lucho's face fiercely distort. His words spluttered, his left eyebrow crunched, his cheeks spasmed and his lips opened to unmoor the sticky utterances from his mouth. A lifetime affliction, a cackle that never caught, was said to have been the result of his father's joke. Anybody in their right mind knew not to fuck with Lucho's stutter.

You could tell time? Turtle asked.

Wha?

You know how to tell time?

This, this what you said, Lucho said, frowning, ain't funny.

Can't take a joke, ése? Turtle leaned forward, her hands spread flat on her thighs. Waiting, man, she hated it. She had been wired for a few nights, strung out like Luis, and sat, her head cockeyed, her eyes pinkish, lids narrow. She lit a Camel, smoked, and when she placed her cigarettes back into her pocket, the new leather jacket she wore sang its taut newness, its badness, music to her leather-loving ears. Another stud on her ear in commemoration, and she defended her earrings to Lucho and Luis—Hey, pirates wore earrings, y qué? Her head freshly buzzed, and then shaved, looking tight, round and clean. Right before entering the bus depot, the three torched up a few more joints in the parking lot and were feeling mellow. People passed, sideways-glancing, but she had been feeling so good having her brother home, she ignored their gawks, gazes, fascination, fear.

Wha Wha YOU looking at? Lucho said to a depot employee, a pasty-faced eleven-to-seven-shifter who swept. Take a pitcher, maybe.

Out of his stupor, Luis began to mimic Lucho Libre. Ka-ka-ka-kant you talk better? And he laughed so hard, his bony shoulders jerked violently and he had to wipe away moisture from his eyes. Turtle wasn't hearing right. She turned to her brother and told him to lay off Lucho, not for Lucho's sake, but for his own. Luis was smarter than this, better than this.

Carnal, this ain't the way to act, Turtle said. Lucho's mood shifted from pissed off at Turtle, to being pissed off at the gaunt, broom-clasping baboso gawking at him, to getting really pissed off at his best friend Luis for fucking around with his words.

Luis, geared up and ready for action, stopped shivering his leg.

Come on, Luis, Turtle said, lay off.

As if a land mine of realization blew up behind his forehead, Luis Lil Lizard's mouth fell open. He had forgotten he had a pussy for a brother. No matter how many asses Turtle kicked or how bad, how really bad she was, Turtle was someone he hoped never to become. Better to return in a body bag than become a pussy.

The PA system blasted off slurs of times and destinations and gate numbers. Ticketed people slowly rose with a weariness that shone like colors. Zombies scuffling to their respective gates.

Your draft number in, homes? Luis asked, letting the high bounce of his laugh lose its dribble. Right before Lucho responded, right before he geared his tongue to answer, Luis got into it again.

Wahwahwah, Luis imitated, as if Lucho were a Baby Huey wailing. Wahwahwah, Luis uncorking, hitting the walls, the ceiling. Tonight he found the stutter the most hilarious thing in the world.

Edging frantic, the show out of control, Turtle said, What the fuck is wrong with you, carnal?

Lucho's father had once been a semiprofessional wrestler who worked at the Olympic Auditorium between main bouts. The father had arms like hams, which was dangerous. He was in love, and a jealous strong lover at that, of a substance they didn't even have a street name for at the time. Speeded him into a wisp of burnt-out matchstick, but inspired him to prank around with his small son. He had grabbed Lucho out of bed, after losing to an ass-licking prick, a Freddie Blassie wannabe, and carried the boy to a freeway construction site. The incomplete overpass looked like a concrete pier, and Lucho's father held him at the edge, threatened to let him go for the fun of it.

The screams that Lucho screamed that night were distinct and everywhere. His pleas to be released rose up from the borderless mass of confusion between safety and harm, between fun and terror, between hatred and love, and the shrill sounds escaped from his throat but caught on his two buckteeth. Just as Lucho had tried to twist and spasm out of his father's grip, so did all the words the boy wanted to cry out. When his mother returned home from a bartending shift, his father denied the act, and then fessed up only to say that it was a joke. And it was a joke, the way something funny happened to Lucho's voice after the bridge incident, his words snagging on his set of teeth like tattered pieces of clothing on barbed wire.

Worse yet, as Lucho's facial muscles struggled in moments of increasing anger, his stutter spluttered out of control, leaving him with locked fists.

You ga-ga-ga-ga-ga-GOT a problem? Lucho muscled out, eyes blinking as he rose, boxing-glove fists tight, his father's hams flexing, and Turtle rose and Luis rose, bouncing off, the threesome surrounded by overflowing trashcans, rows of plastic chairs, the transient and temporary huddled in one-hour sleep intervals, under a burnt-out lightbulb.

Luis chose the time and place for the McBride rites because those were the rules. And what did Turtle have to lose anyway, seeing as how she could now be and belong? Don't be stupid, Luis Lil Lizard whispered to her, which meant, be careful. His voice neutralized her fear. Turtle was ready. Two things Luis said to instruct her, but she only heard the first and began to run toward the Chinese cemetery and—she bolted, no problem, scaled the fence, slammed down, pulled her sneakers out of the mud, pumping her legs, avoiding the gravestone obstacle course bumping into stones, tripping into others, her palms out, ready to break the fall. Then she felt it, a presence, a breathing living presence, and took off into another urgent sprint until she slipped again, skidding and scraping a knee all the way to the bone of her kneecap. This is fucked-up, Grade-A fucked-up, she muttered, and she heard it now, the breathing and footsteps that she knew were not hers because she sat on her swamp-wet ass clutching her knee to her chest.

A cool hand crept around her neck, and she froze. From out of the grave someone grabbed her ankle, and from the cemetery night, a full-sized palm slapped her facedown, the metal-cold fingers, the bagman's hands, and she wasn't about to let it happen again. Turtle sprang up, limping. She swung, blind awkward swings, frisks of air blows, making contact with nothing, nothing, and then a vato hollered with an angst big enough to drench the thirst of what was to come, screamed, ¡La Llorona!

Then fireworks in her head, behind her eyelids exploding, mushrooming white light going dim, no room for a plan. Turtle swung her fists like mallets in order to contact flesh, but the others were the ones making contact, hundreds of bullet-speed shots to her head, stomach, legs, and then when she saw an opening, sensing it, seeing it, suddenly her mind thought otherwise and her body folded as a respite from pain. Turtle collapsed on a sodden grave, while she saw another self run away, another Turtle jumping the gravestones like a gazelle, feeling the wind running through her hair like fingers, running faster and out of this pain.

Her body jelled together with mucus, sweat, defeat and the grave site she fell on soaked up enough of her blood to turn flowers into red poinsettias. Coming to, Turtle heard the winds of her own breathing rushing through the passages inside her head. She smelled the muddy smell of swamp and grass. Heard the trumpeting of her own voice blasting, Luis, Luis, though to the McBride faces hovering over her, it was only a delirious whisper.

Turtle, you up?

Her vision distorted, one eye swollen shut. She barely nodded yes, a ton of bricks banging her forehead. Her lips felt like the size of her pain.

You can take it, ése, Luis said. Turtle tried to find his face, but all the boys blurred into one another. She tried to raise her torso, pull herself up. Luis Lil Lizard came forward and hooked his arm under one of hers, hoisting her upright. Her legs wobbly, her broken ribs a useless ladder of support, she felt like a sack of shit. She collapsed against her brother.

Clocked you, man, it's a record, Luis said, not looking at her face, her arm over his shoulder. Slaps of congratulations on her back, and her head vibrated spectacular pain as Luis dragged her away, her toes leaving slick trails. Turtle pulled Luis closer and whispered in his ear.

What's the second thing? The two Gamboa brothers were almost outside the Chinese cemetery.

You say something?

Turtle nodded, tried the question again as they crossed First Street.

Louder. Luis struggled with her lethargic weight and held Turtle up as best he could while opening the door of their rented house.

Oh, yea, the second thing, Luis said, the second thing is you don't tell nobody who did this to you.

Turtle lay sprawled on the couch and she viewed everything as one would in a shallow pond, blurred and fluid. She craved a glass of water, her lips feeling a million years of drought, and turned slowly to Luis to ask for water, her head massive against a small pillow. But Luis seemed only a breath in the vague light coming from a distant moon, a smeared stroke of charcoal transfixed on the wet blots of blood on his hands. Keeping her thirst to herself, Turtle didn't know what grieved him so.

Quit this bullshit, Turtle demanded. She stood between the two, a barrier. But Lucho had detachment in his eyes. Detached from his friendship, from his loyalty. He worked on detachment from everything that made him who he was, until his eye sockets were empty holes. Turtle recognized the gaze, the practice of coming out of your body, so that the pain wasn't yours; that's how you outlast them all.

A golf ball rolled against Luis's boot, averting his attention. A child, barely four, approached him, a cautious and mischievous look on the boy's face. Luis bent and took the ball and then gave it to the boy.

Lucho, baby, Luis said, as if the name were melodious, Lucho Libre, and he affectionately slapped the big man. Can't take a joke, homes?

Luis shouldered the strap of his duffel bag and walked to the gate, knowing Lucho and Turtle would follow behind him, because that's what they always did. Before he went through the tunnel, Luis delivered a straight-up stare, and Turtle knew this was serious. Luis signaled the three-fingered Trece M and Lucho returned the honor in a salute. Luis Lil Lizard's tattoo reassured Turtle. Her brother knew all about survival. He would return. Spin the plastic globe or search the flat maps of the street guide and all the roads led back to McBride.

And you ése, which meant Turtle, don't be stupid. Luis Three Stooges–slapped Turtle on her shaved head, half with affection, half with resentment, and before Turtle could embrace him, her brother was already across the threshold and a million miles away.

A large overgrowth of bougainvillea vines crawled up the brick walls and meandered in and out of the window grids of the Cremain Garden Chapel. The grids were new, protection against vandals, and Turtle had to stand on her toes to pull out the ivy and then tried out each corner of the metal frame for a loose screw, for an unlocked bolt, any indication that the grid could open into the warmth of sleep on one of the wooden benches. Stubble from the vines drew out blood, a sting as annoying as a female mosquito, and Turtle's stinging fingers traveled each corner of the frame, unbelieving of her luck. Luck was as scarce as money and all the grids were locked and double-locked, and she thought, Isn't this fucken illegal, a fire trap, and the chapel so airtight-locked? The drizzle began and Turtle said, Fuck, and then the helicopters began and their hurricane gusts of wind forced a column of palm fronds to beat against one another angrily, and Turtle stood unbelieving of her luck, the discarded vines tangled all around.

I for *Improvise*. What next? Unsuccessful at finding one grid unhinged, Turtle sought out an accommodating marble crypt that had overlays where she could shelter herself from the rain. Turtle crossed her arms over her chest, stomped back to the main gravel trail. Plugs of gunfire carried over long distances and over the cinder-blocked walls. Turtle was dead tired. That was how she said this in her head, I'm dead tired. Did Luis say that? I'm dead, somewhere in 'Nam, bullets whisking by, did she just hear him?

The lone rapid crunches of gravel footsteps, she passed the stone tree-trunk monuments, the broken rods, the columns and pillars and the statues on the gravestones that she couldn't make out, a bust of a lamb here and there, an angel or two darkened further by the wet of drizzle. Turtle arrived at the fork in the trail and thought about what else to do to keep warm and find shelter. She lifted the trash lid near the spigot and stuck her hand in for old and dry bouquets. Withered, brittle bunches, once tossed inside the casket of the tin can, now exhumed, and Turtle stuffed the bunches inside her jacket until her body was round and padded with the rasp of the expired.

Turtle felt the prickly barbs of baby's breath against her chest like claws, but they did their work. They kept the warmth trapped inside and she began to walk as the drizzle began to rain. Under a willow, Turtle sat dead tired on a marble bench to rest and thought about how hurtful bad flowers can be and then she thought of Chavela and the potted ferns and her hibiscus flowers. The raindrops fell through the holes of tree branches and puck-pocked on her jacket. V for *Value living*. Living was made up of a bouquet of details. Chavela's warm towel carried the fragrance of Dove soap. She wiped Turtle's face and the moist cleansing made her feel refreshed, lovely. For some reason, the viejita liked Turtle and tweaked her chin and gave her lemonade because as far back as Turtle could remember, she always had an unquenchable thirst.

But let's face it, if Turtle knocked on Chavela's door right now, a Grade-A cold-blooded malflora with studded ears, smelling like vomit from the trash she had been forced to eat, would Chavela welcome her? Would the old lady offer Turtle a shower, sudsy Dove foam for her chest, hips, her thighs? Offer a meal? A bed?

Turtle left the bench, not caring to avoid the puddles on the gravel trail. She spotted a crypt through the lashing rain, and detoured from the path, heading toward it pell-mell. The majority of the names engraved on the mausoleum and on the large marble staffs were those Turtle recognized as street names: Hollenbeck, Lankershim, Van Nuys, Bixby. John Edward Hollenbeck was born in Hudson Valley and died in 1885. Yet on Crawford's marble crypt there was only the name, no dates or birthplace. Turtle discovered a marble-gated crypt that belonged to Robert E. Ross, who was born in Clarke County, Ohio, on August 15, 1836, and died March 31, 1884, in Los Angeles, California. It looked livable. Slabbed walls, a roof, and a floor that was completely dried. A for *Act like the natives*, accept and adapt. Turtle pushed the rusted old gate in and entered the Ross crypt.

The roof was low, forcing Turtle to hunch. She felt relieved from the assailing rain and unzipped her jacket and let the parchments of flowers tumble to the floor and all around her ankles. Bunches and bushes of old carnations and roses and gardenias and magnolias and baby's breath, reduced to their brittle bone stems, still carried a trace of transient perfumes. All of the bunches together, the petals and leaves and stems, created enough padding for a bed. L for *Learn basic skills*.

Reclining over the dried flowers, Turtle snuggled the small of her back against the white marble overleaf engraving: **Asleep in Jesus, Blessed Sleep.** It was almost like sleeping on burnt grass in the tent. Yawning, she crossed her arms and bent her knees a little, curled her back. Palm fronds like frightened plumage of hunted birds brushed against one another in intervals of wind bursts. As Turtle inhaled the perfume of decomposing gardenias, she wondered about Robert E. Ross. She nestled her arms tighter and closed her mouth to savor the full meal of sleep. Right before she drifted off, Turtle wondered what possessed this old white man named Ross to die so far from home.

TWELVE

First there were the bluish and yam colors from Jan's car, which remained steadfast on the bandage from this afternoon. Then Ermila had pressed her palm on a crinkled, weatherworn billboard to slip off her shoes and the ass-colored peachy flakes of the Coppertone girl smudged Ermila's bandage as well. The second she saw her hand on the little girl's bare ass, Ermila attempted to erase the colors, to eliminate the ass sensation by rubbing her palm against her Levi's.

She headed down to the sandy shore of Laguna Cliff, dangling her pair of shoes and walked directly under the lifeguard booth. A few scavenging seagulls trailed not far behind, mistaking her shoes for a bag of bread crumbs. Wheeling pelicans hovered over the heads of two die-hard fishermen who dipped and cast their rods at the edge of the blackened pier, the choppy currents of water against its wooden pillars. Except for the fishermen and the seabirds, Laguna Cliff was deserted.

From the time Mrs. M. had brought her for a visit, she had begun to plant herself in this beach, this shoreline. The waves furrowed near her bare feet, small saline scribbles on the sand. Ermila inhaled a sea breeze so condensed, she felt its weight and muscle of ice. Strands of hair lashed about her face as she strolled, bending to retrieve a concha to give to Concha, stopping to watch the crabs scuttling to safety once the waves receded. Out in the horizon, the hazy sunset lost its dusky glow, and still there remained no sign of Alfonso. Near the poles where, in better weather, a volleyball net would extend, Ermila sat on a sand dune and pulled up her knees to her chin to wait for him.

The call from Alfonso and later the dog in her room were not coincidental. Did Grandmother think Ermila stupid enough to allow the dog to sabotage her plans to meet Alfonso? Grandmother's denial only proved her guilt. She inspected the soiled gauze of her bandage. It smelled of acetone and she pulled at some loose threads absentmindedly. Frothy salt water indented the shoreline before her but in other places the waves slapped against the jagged rocks or chased the gawking seabirds with its whiplash kelp. The dusk faintly blushed like the color of Strawberry Hill wine Alfonso would dilute with fruit juice to make it tolerable for her ingestion.

It had been an eventful day for Ermila and she lay on her side, the molding of her body pressing against the clammy, sandy chill to rest. In a contemplative repose, she propped her head with an elbow while resting her injured hand on a hip. Soft licks of salt water reached closer to her bare feet, informing her of its rising tide. Slow-moving layers of tumbling fog rose from the expansive glacierlike sea and moved toward the shoreline. Alfonso was late as usual and as the drowsy evening wore on, the temperature began to drop.

Under her yellow mohair she felt goose-bumpy and the ocean slowly disappeared under fog and then everything disappeared until the sand stung like a slap on her face. She stood up immediately, unconvinced that she had been napping, that she was unaware of her dreaming. She rubbed the back of her neck and shook the sand from her hair. In the short amount of time it took for the vague sun to set, the fog had spread a sheath of whiteness over every object, disguised every form. The lighthouse became a winking yellow cyclopean beacon. An avalanche of vapor mist had overcome the wooden pier.

Out of the fog two sudden arms lunged forward. Ermila felt the weight of her shoulder blades crushing against Alfonso's chest. You wait long, 'Mila? His voice damp and toasty in her ear. He covered her eyes and his fingers were sticky and citrus-scented as if he had just peeled an orange. Having a strong dislike for surprises, Ermila never reacted well to them, and her immediate response was to jab a hard elbow into his ribs, which she did angrily.

But to her amazement, Nacho, of all people, stood before her in ill-fitting jeans where Alfonso should have been. Huh? The hems of his paint-speckled trousers were raised inches above his ankles, revealing a pair of white socks, and his shirt, thin and worn was ripped at the seam of the sleeve. He had a dark bruise the size of a half-dollar on his cheekbone. His pathetic self multiplied her irritation.

You stupid asshole! Ermila pitched him a fastball shoe. What's wrong with you? The scolding seemed loud against the vacancy of the beach. The seagulls fluttered aside, more out of instinct than fear.

I don't mean . . . Nacho said apologetically and then let the futility of his explanation saturate him. Ermila's hair lashed about her cheeks.

You don't mean what? What?

Nacho appeared bewildered by her outburst. He bent down to retrieve her shoe and she tore it from him. He pantomimed his hands in gestures of speech but let the wordlessness do the speaking and leaned on the balls of his sneakers, a nervous habit.

Tell me! Did Grandma send you? Tell me now!

Nacho shook his head no and sheepishly slid his fingers into his pants pockets to bring out her identification card, the one issued by the QA to prove residency. The official photo captured her late hours, too much Strawberry Hill wine. In the distance, a foghorn moaned like a lonely heifer. The nearest lamppost seemed too far away to shed ample light on the card. If the fog had not been so dense, Nacho would not have had to thrust the ID so close to Ermila's face.

Nacho had discovered her card in the basket of clothes he had taken down from the laundry line as instructed by Grandmother. He carried the basket to the kitchen because Grandfather hadn't been able to do much more than open the screen door for him with his good working hand. Because the kitchen felt cozy and embracing, and the leftover breakfast scent lingered, and mostly because Nacho needed to separate his own clothes from the pile of clean laundry, he decided to fold the clothes on the table.

He noticed Grandfather's displeasure. Nacho's committed efforts to fold dish towels with imprecise angles made his old, grumpy Grandfather wheeze displeasure through his nasal passages with loud, noisy breaths. Is this what men have been reduced to? his milky stare seemed to ask. The sight of a healthy young male spreading a shirt with buttons facedown on the table and then handcuffing the long sleeves and then confining them behind some bad folds was too much to bear for Grandfather, and Nacho thanked God Almighty that he turned away.

But Nacho was confident in his full bosom of eighteen years and he crunched his pairs of briefs as if they were made of flour dough and thus had a dough's capacity to keep a balled-up form. He had dismissed how others thought of him as he folded clothes or painted holy figures on tin plates or read fotonovelas geared more for a female audience or whatever else he might choose to do because life was too short. His father thought him too strangely easygoing, which was why Nacho was sent up north in the first place, forcing his mother to fill jarros with tears. But his mother recognized this easygoing trait as an asset, which was why Nacho decided to return to someone who appreciated his strengths.

Nacho's mother had taught him how to cut up a raw fryer chicken, fold shirts, keep his nose clean of wicked women who always wore blood-red lipstick, who said words like "bebito" and "forever," but he was truly unprepared for the challenge of living with old people set in their ways. He respected them, though he knew they weren't crazy about his chronic unemployment or his takeover of the sofa and he often felt unwelcome. Despite what Grandfather thought of as his propensity for laziness, Nacho had secured enough funds with odd jobs for a one-way bus ticket back home, since his van, the piece-of-shit van, would not make it across the state line, much less across the Southwest. And so full satisfaction showed on the young man who planned for success in the not-too-distant future. Nacho continued folding the towels, pairing socks and aligning each pant leg of the stiff trousers with great pleasure.

The task of laundry completed, his clothes a pile of their own, Nacho saw himself as thrown off by his yearning for Ermila's attention; she was the only reason he had stayed this long. His eighteen years did not leave him without some hard-learned lessons and one of them was that a woman like Ermila would never appreciate a man, a healthy and talented man like him, at least until she grew older. He had warned himself against his strong affections—why should Ermila care for him simply because his feelings for her were staggering? He was only eighteen but already he knew that putting gasoline in a broken car was useless; it wouldn't go anywhere no matter how much wishing he did.

Nacho came to the last pair of trousers. The pair belonged to his cousin and híjole, they were almost doll-like in size. Folding the pair, he had noticed a piece of paper peering from the back pocket and then he remembered how the nylon of Ermila's slip spread tightly across her ass when she bent over the bathroom sink. If his smile could be measured in distance, he smiled kilometers. Since Grandfather had diverted his accusatory eyes into an unknown space, Nacho brazenly slipped his hand in Ermila's pocket and removed the paper, his fingers reliving the hump of her firm buttocks. Her identification card was crinkled and faded from the wringer wash and the discovery fueled his courage to declare his love. Knowing exactly where she would be and at what time, he would use the card as an excuse. Nacho planned to arrive and inform her privately of his feelings.

The anticipation of seeing Ermila later delivered a package of goodwill throughout the rest of the morning. Nacho whistled as he carried his pile of freshly laundered clothes to Grandfather's humid and dusty toolshed, which had not been used for years. The cracks between the bricks and wood where Nacho kept his traveling trunk in storage were green with mold. And no matter how much Nacho kept the door wide open to air out the dingy room, the shed held a captive trace of urine. He wired a heavy flashlight on one of the wooden beams and then he opened the trunk. Inside, he had already packed a few mementos (a Swiss army knife made in Hong Kong for his dad, waxed fruit for his mother, a paddle ball for Lupe and silk flowers for school chums' wives), which he had purchased at the swap meet where he sometimes found work on weekends hawking rubber flip-flops or previously owned eight-tracks.

He laid his clean clothes inside the trunk, gathered his shaving kit, a bundle of ¡Alarma! magazines, a few tapes, some of his favorite fotonovelas. Once he persuaded himself it was better to travel lightly, he decided to leave the fotonovelas and shelved them behind a bowl of nails. He packed his tubes of paints; large and small, brushy and lean paintbrushes; a journal of sketches; and papers, papers, more papers. He stuffed with difficulty, for the trunk was smaller than he had remembered it, a set of vocabulary workbooks from his English as a Second Language night class. No sooner had he enrolled in the ESL class upon his arrival than he dropped it. The language class was so basic, it made him feel stupid and small, and he was everything but.

A transistor radio that played more static than music was placed on top of the workbooks. Nacho was not a practitioner of efficient packing and ended up throwing things in. But the lack of luggage space did not sour his intentions; in fact, he had caught himself humming. His roots weren't deep enough in the Eastside for him to experience nostalgia and except for seeing Ermila alone tonight little else was comparable to the incredible thrill he felt staring out of the confines of the toolshed and into the endless possibilities of the open door.

But all did not go as planned.

You listening? Ermila hollered, or do you need Drāno to clean out those ears of yours? She tore the ID from his hand without so much as a thank-you, and then slipped it in the back pocket of her Levi's, and then thought better of that and slid the ID into her wallet properly.

Nacho turned nervously to the lifeguard tower. He heard a faint knock, claps against the door of the weatherworn booth, distracting Ermila. His hands were specked with bits of white paint that had chipped off the bloated wood panels. He hid them in his pockets.

How come? Ermila searched for Nacho's true motive in showing up. How come you came? Hands in his pockets, he shrugged.

I'm going, he replied.

Okay, she said. Go, then. Good-bye. How else should she respond? She knew he spied on her, ready to detail all her travesties to Grandmother. Pitiful. Her not-really cousin was pitiful.

No. I'm going back to Reynosa, Nacho said and then turned toward the horizon—the sun was blotted out completely.

Whatta you mean?

I'm going home.

You mean for good?

Nacho nodded.

I thought you were gonna learn English.

Nacho shook his head no.

Ermila fought back the questions: Why? When? How come? It suddenly occurred to her that Nacho had driven his piece-of-shit van all the way to Laguna Cliff just to give her the ID card and this thoughtful act alone saved her hours of interrogation at the checkpoint. She felt ashamed and stared at him.

I thought you wanted to stay.

He glared at her.

I hate it here.

So? Perhaps the haze between them had caused Nacho to appear bruised and beaten. The chill of the sea breeze pimpled his bare arms and Ermila noticed a darkening icicle forming under one of his nostrils, a nosebleed.

Your nose, Ermila said. She was taken aback, and her tone softened. I think it's bleeding.

Nacho touched his nose as if he didn't believe her and then when he felt the moisture he looked bewildered. He brought out a handkerchief and wiped his nose and then bent on his haunches to rinse the hankie in the ocean's froth. The water lapped around the ankles of his sodden sneakers and he seemed not to care as he swiped his face again with seawater.

He rose and stood closer to her, his body built with the strength of one who had physically labored since the age of five and the clumsy clothes, the fresh-off-the-border high-water jeans, the flabby torn shirt, betrayed him. Ermila began to wonder who Nacho really was.

You better split, Ermila rallied, or you'll get caught by the QA.

I am, Nacho replied, but he made no attempt to move. He continued looking out into the solid mass of fog.

You better, cuz Alfonso won't like this.

He's not to show up. Nacho thought for a minute. He missed a verb somewhere.

Buddy, you don't wanna mess with Big Al.

Big Al, Big Al! ¡Qué mierda!

Fuck you, Ignacio!

Nacho's skin pricked at the cool breeze, at the harshness, but also at the affection in her use of his full name. He pressed his arms to his sides for warmth and looked over at the direction of the lifeguard tower. What he did to procure his plan was purely out of a plot in a fotonovela, and just as unbelievable. He felt both proud and manly, and then doubtful of his action. If he had succeeded in making a big mistake by abbreviating Alfonso's rendezvous with Ermila, it held no regrets for him now that he was leaving for Reynosa.

Where he is now? Nacho asked confidently.

He'll be here.

No.

Any minute.

He's not to show up.

This time Ermila heard it too. Thumps from the lifeguard booth. They sounded like a rubber mallet against wood.

Did you hear that? she asked.

What?

I don't know. Like pounding. Nacho shrugged.

Something's not right. Ermila held her elbows to shield herself. There! There it is again!

Don't have fear. Nacho reached over and Ermila flinched, a childhood reflex, raising her injured hand in a symbolic attempt to block his. I don't mean— Nacho began, almost short of frustration, like the last attempt to shake pennies out of a coin bank. I mean, I don't mean to—

He cut himself off, knowing his power to explain was beyond his vocabulary, and he thought simply to show that he meant no harm. Nacho again reached over and touched the loosened strands of her black hair to glean the sticky mats of sand, the weaves of grains, which lingered still. The sand fell everywhere, sprinkling through his fingers like twinkling slivers of the tiniest glass. He did this with such gentleness she could feel his fingers trembling slightly. And then he showed her the glitter he had gathered from her hair.

You need a ride? Nacho asked, finally breaking the reverie. A foghorn guided ships to the harbor and they could hear it in between the thumps coming from the booth, the plashing of boats tied to the pier. The density of chilled mist enclosed them.

No one needed to tell Ermila about Alfonso. She knew all along he was and would remain an asshole.

Let's go.

Bueno. Okay. And Nacho pointed in the direction of the path's entrance, which was demarcated by the Coppertone billboard.

You sure your shit car works?

Nacho shrugged to indicate that her guess was as good as his. They clodhopped over the sand dunes quietly toward the parking lot. Ermila saw the billboard's patchy lights breaking through the mist. She castigated herself for not being more careful with things that really mattered.

Back at the billboard, Ermila swiped off the caked sand from her feet as she studied the pigtailed girl's reaction to the pup tugging at her underwear. Her unmasked and untanned buttocks embarrassed the girl and Ermila couldn't fathom why. Angry, maybe. Frightened, yes. But embarrassed? At a dog biting *her* ass? This just didn't make sense. The dog bite beneath the sandy gauze had begun a renewed throbbing as if Ermila's eyes reminded the wound of its pain. An account of today's experiences including the girl's ass had been deposited all over her bandage, and Ermila brushed her swathed hand hoping to erase the inscriptions and then carefully snuggled her feet into her shoes. Action completed, she gazed at the poster as if it were a fake landscape.

Nacho studied the layers of fog and wondered where its source of propulsion began, and then wondered about the ocean's source, from what blackness the ocean sprang. He considered this in a vague way until it began to form images that he would later record in sketches. Leaning at the edge of the billboard, Nacho considered the notion of all the world's water coming from one navel, one belly button, and so swept up was he in this one thought, Nacho didn't hear the slow deep jaggy pull of paper. The navel image was thwarted by Ermila, who had pinched a corner where the poster and the panel board separated and then ripped a paper strip with such rage, all she left behind was a cesarean incision that widened, then narrowed across the Coppertone billboard.

¿Estas loca, 'Mila? His hands, once inside his pockets, flew out to catch her before she ruined the billboard completely. Ermila's cheeks, the edges of her ears, glowed crimson. Somewhere in the closet of a childhood memory, Ermila recalled having done something similar.

Is it just me? she asked, and she crunched the piece of poster paper into a tight ball and then let it drop into the glutted range of litter clustering in the overgrown grass. Is it me? Am I the only one who thinks something's wrong with this picture?

He clenched her wrist and dragged her away hastily, not wasting a moment to see if somebody had witnessed the vandalism. Ermila let herself be pulled along to the parking lot and her wrist was so scrawny-thin it reminded him of the old spare water pipes Grandfather had stored in the toolshed. The light of a lamppost barely perforated the fog and a few parked cars were sporadically spaced in what was otherwise an empty parking lot. Nacho's hand, his chilled fingers, cuffed around her wrist and she noticed a couple twisted with urgent humping on the backseat of a red convertible.

Was that the way she and Big Al looked, shimmying the Impala like scratching pups searching for a mother's teat? She averted her eyes back to the shore, lagging farther behind. Was it her, or was the world going crazy? Somewhere in the dark, long stretch of parking slots, pranksters out for a good time tossed a thick amber beer bomb and its shattering caused a series of yelps and whoops. Ermila's head splintered.

Nacho had parked at the end of the lot so that his van (a miraculous piece of dented steel welded together without much more than a prayer) would not stand out conspicuously. The hood looked as if it had been worked over with a sledgehammer, its doors pocked like bad acne scars. There had been so many repairs that one could not tell what the original color of the van had been. Nacho untied the wire that held the passenger door to its hinges. As she waited, Ermila noticed an Impala very much resembling Alfonso's, parked near the **No Trespassing—Private Beach** sign. A headache's mirage, perhaps. She refused to search for Alfonso. After having seen the shimmying convertible, her blistering shame returned.

The door hinged opened and hung like a loose tooth and if it were not for the headache gathering momentum, Ermila would have burst into laughter. He prompted her and Ermila climbed in and then Nacho rewrapped the wire. She wiped away the condensation on the windshield with the knuckle of her bandage to see the glaciers of fog drift apart, whitish and nomadic shapes hovering above the glass of ocean.

Nacho sat behind the steering wheel. Bueno, he said, prayerlike, and then turned the ignition. The engine of the van missed a few times, then caught and sputtered in a drawn-out fashion, and then went dead and refused to be resuscitated, though he tried time and time again. Accustomed to the van's misbehavior, Nacho then waited patiently.

The rapid beating of Ermila's heart created a disquieting pressure between her ears. The avenging buoyancy she had carried to Laguna Cliff seemed to disappear in the fog, engulfed by uncertainty as thick and soupy as molasses. Just as Chavela had predicted, Ermila's world was beginning to crack from under her. No solid tierra firme to stand on, nothing to hold on to. I gotta do something soon, she kept saying to herself as she sat in the passenger seat of the van.

The red convertible had quieted its rocking. The increasing swell of guilt became a warning to Ermila to steer clearly away from what she was feeling now as Nacho's hand slipped between her arm and breast. She fixed her gaze on the side of his face, which wasn't shaded; his ear-lobe had dried blood crusted. Had Nacho been in a fistfight recently? Ermila swallowed the bulky sea chill, inhaled the sent of car uphol-stery so old, its tales rang full in her nostrils. Nacho held her shoulder blades gently and began to press her against his chest. Crumpled maps and Jack in the Box food discards compressed between their bodies on the front seat of the van. In whatever areas his hands made contact with her skin, she molted sweat. The sense of longing in Nacho star-tled Ermila, and when he pressed his mouth to hers, a deeply long and fitted kiss, she actually felt the force of her own desire.

I can't breathe! She pulled back. It was true. His kiss suffocated her. I can't breathe, open the door.

I thought . . . he said, and trailed off. She began to squirm in his grasp. You're hurting me.

No, Nacho protested, but had not realized until he saw his own knuckles whiten that, in fact, he was grasping her very tightly. His face hung, and his protest dissipated. He unfastened his grip but not fast enough.

Open the door. Open the fucken door now!

Her eyes followed Nacho as he jogged around the front bumper, shoulders stooped, T-shirt torn and flapping against the sea breeze. Condensation fogged the door window from her rapid breathing. Nacho couldn't jimmy the wire fast enough. Ermila hadn't realized how much she had pressed herself against the side of the door until the door became unhinged and she almost fell out.

Already tossing the words over her shoulder, she yelled, Go home, Ignacio!

¡Estás loca, 'Mila, muy loca!

Go home or don't. I don't care, she shouted, running through the parking lot. I don't care what you do! Trashcans appeared before she could avoid bumping into them, her head splintery with pain. Empty parking slot after empty slot, Ermila passed the billboard, the chill freezing her lungs. She heard the high yaps of a dog, and her heart flurried and pained. As she reached the main boulevard, cars speeded by and her sneakers crunched the gravel shoulder where the bus-stop bench was located. She sat there, her head cracking like ice.

Quiet, Peppino! an ancient Anglo man demanded. Bad dog, Peppino! And he choked the chain of the frantically yapping Chihuahua. Are you okay, missy? His question carried the tinctures of cough elixir on his breath and when she peered from her hands, the Anglo man seemed straight out of a Béla Lugosi film, complete with a fedora and a vintage tuxedo rank with mothball cologne. He was cast in a ghastly light that made his face appear spectral, and his voice suggested fragility.

I'm okay, Ermila said. She glanced to make sure Nacho had not followed her. She felt the hot breath of the little bat dog near her blue-jeaned ankle and was ready to kick it when she looked down to see that the dog wore a little top hat fastened by an elastic strand and a tiny coat, complete with a red bow tie for a collar. It was so ugly, it almost looked cute.

Missy?

For real. I'm okay.

I was just thinking that myself, the old man said. I was thinking, this crazy world is falling apart, but me and Peppino are doing A-okay.

Yea.

And what about all this fog? the old man asked as if they had had a long protracted conversation regarding the weather.

Can't see a thing, Ermila replied.

The length of the wide dizzying boulevard seemed endless, its swift wind of cars slapping her hair about. She pulled loose threads away from her lips and then, as if enough composure were gathered, rose from the bench. The eastbound bus stop was on the other side of the broad boulevard.

Well, Ermila said, I gotta get home.

You sure you're okay?

Yea, mister. Thanks.

Be careful!

You too, Ermila said.

Missy, you don't know, the old man said, what riffraff is out tonight! He tipped his fedora like a gentleman while the Chihuahua tugged its leash.

Peppino's dignified trotting bounce, his tail wagging as he worked toward the shoreline, made the old man's rubbery lips smile. At the entrance of the beach path, Peppino raised a hind leg on the torn Coppertone billboard, and then scratched his ear, jostling his little top hat. The Chihuahua sniffed about the weeds for other urinary telegrams. The vandalized poster didn't surprise the old man. For years, things in this city had been getting out of hand, falling apart, and he hoped Peppino would be finished with his peeing business soon and they could head for the safety of home.

However, the dog had another thing in mind. Peppino discovered a thrown-away hamburger. The scavenging seabirds, city rodents and other preying mammals hadn't uncovered the treasure and it had Peppino's name written all over it. The dog gouged into it greedily. Consumed in his thoughts, the old man didn't notice the dog chomping and gulping, contrary to the manners of a tux-clad pedigree, and once finished, the Chihuahua continued to nose through other litter buried in the weeds. The dog searched with such vigor, his little top hat had gotten pushed way back off its ears.

Come on, Peppy! the old man said. Finish up!

The shifting weather was, to the old man, akin to the aches of age. He woke each morning with a new foreboding ache, a sharp cramp, another piece of himself losing its predictability. After all these years living near Laguna Cliff, the old Anglo man had never witnessed such an ambush of climate, surprising and merciless. The man followed the tug of the leash through the fog. Once the fog turned into drizzle, the old man resisted being led against his will and wrapped the leash around his fingers as reinforcement.

Enough, Peppy! No sooner had the old man decided enough was enough than the drizzle froze into pebbles and then into sharp pins of hail. The man ambled, clunky in his old age, to find temporary shelter under the lifeguard tower. The wet sand inside his shoes irritated the old man, and he resented Peppino.

Now see what you've done? the old man scolded and choke-chained the leash to stop the dog's complaining. His finger dug under his fedora and scratched as Peppino began to whine at the hail spearing the booth above him. Angry deafening bursts of hail pelted all around him until it subsided and then the old man heard some thuds coming from above him, from the lifeguard booth. Peppino growled and then sprang in renewed barking excitement. The dog twisted from his leash, pulling, pulling, a don't-hold-me-back kind of pull.

Hello? the old man called out. Hello? He hushed the dog in order to hear a reply. Is someone up there? he shouted, if only a hint of tentativeness in his query. Truth be told, he really didn't want to know. He distinctively heard the thumps again.

All this seemed a clear omen to the old man. The thumps and thuds, the hail, this morning's buzzard perched on his small garden compost; Poe's "Raven" he had read the night before; tonight's young missy, who resembled a flighty canary with an injured wing. He read them as omens, but what the omens meant was a mystery to him. And as he thought these thoughts, the dog escaped, and the twitchy Chihuahua pounced up the plank leading to the booth, stumbling over his top hat, the leash trailing behind like a wobbly blue line. The bulge-eyed dog sniffed and whined and scratched the door. Cautiously the old man climbed the wooden plank.

A foghorn moaned sadly in the distance, and the lone moaning always meant loss to the old Anglo man, a longing so wide, it wailed for connection with something as solid and as faithful as landmasses. Hello? he repeated again, his heart as loud as the thuds. Hello? he said, his voice cracking. The pounding suddenly stopped, and the man was close enough to hear muffled words of distress. His rheumy eyes inspected the busted lock. Trembling, he pushed the creaking door open and Peppino rushed in.

PART IV

PART IV

THIRTEEN

The large chain-link cage where Ray stacked the bottle crates was situated in the back of his store and each time he heaved a crate higher on top of the others, Turtle could hear the bottles clunking like marbles slam-dunked into the rim of an empty mayonnaise jar. From across the street, Ray resembled a caged man, unhappy in his hard work. Crate-stacking pinched Ray's old face under the single, functional lightbulb and he puffed his clean-shaven cheeks as if there weren't enough air around him to suck into his lungs. He had shoved his .38-caliber stub-nosed handgun in the back pocket of his trousers, and every time he bent down Turtle noticed the outline of the cuete even as the cars sped by between them.

Everyone in the neighborhood called the Japanese store owner by his first name, Ray, and they could set a watch to Ray's bottle-stacking, which was the last thing he did before closing the Friendly Shop. The tinking of soda bottles was as dependable and reassuring as the evening clanging of the church bells. Members of the Hernández family, who lived close to the store, looked at their clocks or watches whenever they heard the glass and crate, and used the opportunity to make a point to a child plagued with tardiness or a husband who never acknowledged promptness as a virtue, to show how a trustworthy constant was a huge comfort against life's randomness. Under the shadow of the Hernández family's palmilla tree, Turtle knew it was 6:50 in the evening. Exactly.

Before the Val U Mini Mart came in and nearly ruined his small business, Ray sold bologna for ten cents a pound and the neighborhood got to eating bologna in tacos or scrambled with eggs or placed between two Wonder Bread slices with sour cream and salt. At Ray's, for a nickel, kids purchased plastic wedding rings, a variety embedded in greenish sponge. Under his counter, chocolate candy bars lay side by side like Christmas gifts ready to be unwrapped. Ray sold special lollipops that might have a sticker with **YOU ARE A WINNER** attached to them, in which case a free lollipop was in order. Five cents bought two packets of Kool-Aid, one you could selfishly pour into your mouth and mix with spit, while saving the second one to stir into a pitcher of water with enough to share all around. At Ray's you always found what you needed.

Turtle loitered under the Hernández palmilla thinking about the items inside Ray's store. The cold sodas in the red Coke machine, the candies, bologna and bread loaves swirled around Turtle like the pinkish pigs' feet she loved to eat. Hunger began eating at her cramping muscles and she found herself watching Ray from across the street, relishing the memories of fried bologna and a taste of blue Kool-Aid on the tongue. Ray's white windbreaker crinkled every time he lifted and heaved and strained. He stacked the red crates of empty soda bottles inside his storage cage and the jacket crunched like footfalls on slushy gravel. Turtle waited for Ray to complete the last pile of crates before she crossed the street.

Ray noticed the tall figure approaching. He wasn't a fool and had worked side by side with a generation of young Spanish-speaking boys just like this one coming directly toward him. In the beginning, the young boys arrived at his store boisterous and excited and impossible to defuse as they exchanged deposit bottles for Bazooka gum or Hostess Sno Balls or marbles. Ray knew how to handle them and then sold them their penny desires. Unafraid to scold, he scooted them out, admonishing them for their noisy curses as they busted out of his double screen doors with great gaiety.

But times proved unpredictable and the neighborhood had changed. The cigarette-smoking boys returned to his store and demanded, in mangled English, Ripple wine on credit. Ray was less apt to scold and refused to sell liquor to minors until he saw them turn into hoodlums right before him, saw their eyes, bloated and jell-like eyes, turn into raging red tentacle veins of men who simply used the five-finger discount to liberate anything they wanted from the store. Ray could do little more than buy a gun. When he saw the figure crossing the street, Ray patted his trouser pocket to make sure his .38 was within easy reach.

Turtle deliberately removed her hands from her leather jacket pockets so as not to jolt Ray into using the cuete she knew he packed. She let a smile surface, a sepia smile in the dusk, and she could feel her face muscles cracking through the dryness of her weather-exposed skin. How many nights had she roamed the streets? How much more could she take of this? Turtle saw Ray straighten up, saw him pat his back pocket, and then she raised her hands above her head, palms up. See? she tried to tell him with the gesture. See? Empty-handed, no cuete, no screwdriver, not a frajo, not a friend, not a pinche penny to my name, you got it? Harmless as a girl.

The chain-link cage door stood between Ray and Turtle. Within the shadows of the fence, Ray couldn't clearly see Turtle's face. Some hoodlum or other had kept smashing the row of lightbulbs that lined the back of the store and after a few weeks of replacing them, Ray had decided against encouraging the practice. He left the sockets busted and popped, except for one working bulb. Ray hadn't thought to regret such a decision until Turtle loomed over him, faceless. The two of them locked stares through the diamond wire, forgetting for a moment who was and wasn't in the cage. The absence of outside lights, the dim pellucid light of the lamppost and the reflection of rained-on asphalt steamed Ray's vision so he couldn't get a good look. He stared at Turtle with such intensity, if Ray had been much younger, Turtle would have mistaken the gaze for a challenge.

Ray finally recognized Turtle. Of course, and he knew his brother too. How much weight had this young man lost? But there was something different in his hollowed cheeks. He looked so young. His height, the jacket, the weird-looking haircut, the queer stud mutilations on the ears, and the way his dilated eyes were blank like those of a cat coming in from the dark, as if his irises expanded to absorb all of him, inflated Ray's fear. Ray's face reddened like mercury filling a thermometer, his blood pressure skyrocketing. It made Ray feel that Turtle was too close for comfort. He jerked his thumb back and said, Get lost.

Turtle didn't move. After a moment's beat, Turtle asked for a quarter and then promised to get lost if he paid her off, and Ray didn't know whether the young man was serious. He checked behind Turtle, looked around to make sure Turtle's presence was not a diversion, not a trap, since his kind always traveled in packs. By this time, darkness prevailed and Ray had to convince himself that all would be okay. The work of bottle-stacking and the fear of getting ripped off again had made Ray perspire underneath his insulated windbreaker. A pair of headlights lanced Eastern Street and disappeared.

Don't be late for dinner. Ray's promptness was a meaningful commandment upheld by his wife. His watch ticked away and Ray still had to lock up the doors and then drive to Monterey Park and find parking. The wife would say the food is cold, go warm it up yourself. His chest burned like a leaf of paper, a sliver of ashen air, charcoal rising up to his throat and making his mouth powdery like dust. He caught himself wishing for the cops, the QA, but the Quarantine Authority sounded just like the War Relocation Authority and even though they all had promised protection, Ray knew it was a bunch of hocus-pocus. The diamond-shaped grids shadowed across Turtle's face. Time ticked on and Ray didn't want to go there, back to the memory of tarpaper and dust, of sentries standing guard. Spanish for apple orchard? The newspaper made the camps sound quaint, like a vacation. No, he refused to return, and Ray realized that if the young man had planned to rob him, he would have done so by now. His breathing settled. Ray acquiesced and jiggled out some loose change from his pocket and pushed a quarter through a metal diamond.

Thanks, Ray, Turtle said. You're ah mero mero, carnal!

Customers addressing him by his first name did not offend Ray, nor did the familiarity surprise him. But hearing the unmanly timbre of voice slowly lubricated Ray's hold on fear and he let slip a sigh of relief. With a bit more confidence, he repeated his Get lost, and said it—made sure to say it—with a tone of familiarity as well.

Turtle, full of plan, strutted around the store, and Ray heard the screen door open and then snap shut. Ray couldn't believe it; he felt betrayed by his own kindness. Uneasy at having to open the cash register in front of this boy, he tried to remember if he had loaded his .38.

He looked at his wristwatch but couldn't see the time with only one dimly lit bulb and he damned himself.

The wife had complained incessantly about the gun and had made him promise not to load bullets into its small cylinders. Ray had promised the wife more to shut her up; but now he couldn't remember if he had reloaded it. His chest began thudding with a pain the wife had been worried about; his hands shook nervously and increased his difficulty in clamping the curved hook into the padlock. That done, Ray ran to the front of the store as fast as his achy back would allow him. He found Turtle leaning against the Coke machine, awaiting service on the customer side of the sturdy oak and glass counter.

The aisles of scattered wares the age of the small building, the dinginess of two lightbulbs suspended from the ceiling, made the Friendly Shop anything but friendly. And yet Turtle sensed a sudden flood of welcome. The red Coke machine buzzed and its engine clicked and then hummed as it had in her youth; the faithful refrigerator had always kept the Hires root beer or strawberry or Fanta orange or RC Cola sodas sweat-cold. Two large glass vats sat on the thick oak counter right next to the cash register—their positions had never changed. Floating chile peppers and pigs' feet swam in their own placenta of vinegar in one vat while another contained beautiful pickles the size of salad cucumbers, the size of genitalia described by Ray's male customers, who still laughed at the oldest joke in the book. Turtle stared at the pigs' feet with hungered recollection.

Ray's heartburn increased. He tried to burp out a gas bubble as he rushed around to the other side of the counter without taking his eyes off the tall boy. He wanted the transaction, whatever it was to be, to be done as soon as possible. A bundle of keys bulged from his front windbreaker pocket like an abnormal growth. He glanced impatiently at his watch. The anticipation was killing him.

The countless transactions carved a trail on the countertop; countless exchanges, from penny purchases to countless credit line stories, had grooved the wood. Turtle pointed to the box of Big Hunks inside the glass case and Ray grabbed the candy bar and slid it across the counter to Turtle and then Turtle slid the quarter with one stiff filthy thumb toward the owner. Not wanting to open the cash register, Ray simply pulled out fifteen cents in change from his pocket and slid the coins back to Turtle. A fast, suspicious and distant exchange played out on the worn groove of the counter. The humming of the refrigerator halted abruptly, leaving an oppressive silence. Turtle ripped the paper and bit into the candy with such a desire, Ray realized he had not witnessed such hunger, though he had lived too long a life to deny its existence outside of the store's double doors.

Having read about the incident in the *Eastside Tribune* the very next day, Ray said he came forward because the wife had thought it was the right thing to do. It was true that the wife and he were of two minds about it. He never trusted men in funeral suits. False teeth in their mouths, he had said to the wife. No, no, the wife insisted, *insisted,* and so here he was in the police station, more to shut her up. He found himself sitting across a desk owned by a man in a blue suit who scribbled Ray's dictated words with a pen the man shook every once in a while because it was running out of ink. Ray had advised the man, burn the tip of the pen with a lighter to get the ink to run smoother; but the man continued writing the report and shaking the pen as if Ray were a dunce and didn't know what he was talking about.

First things first: Ray wanted to correct the newspaper typo, the misprint of the name Antonia. No, it was Antonio, with an *o* at the end, brother of another Gamboa. Yes, he knew the brother of this Antonio too, didn't he just say? That one, Ray would never forget. He was an outlaw, a gangster, a real son of a bitch, excuse the profanity. The brother had a nickname like a reptile. Iguana? Snake, maybe, he couldn't remember. Ray had once caught the brother burning a girl with a match behind his store and told him to get lost or he'd call the police.

First things first, the man repeated, nodding his head in agreement, and then asked where Ray was from and the wife patted Ray's shoulder to calm him, to say to him, The good man didn't mean it, and Ray replied angrily, without humility, that he wasn't closing his store for the morning to be asked such stupid questions. He wasn't a foreigner, if that's what the man was insinuating. He was born here, in this country, a U.S. citizen, no more a foreigner than him. Ray's palms began to sweat and he placed them over his kneecaps and rubbed the moistness from his lifelines.

Except for those years at Manzanar, Ray had lived all his life in Monterey Park, just a twenty-minute drive from where the incident occurred. Didn't the man know what Nisei meant, wasn't the word even in the man's vocabulary of citizenship like the word Jap? If the man didn't believe him, just give him a map, Ray requested, for proof, and he'd point to **YOU ARE HERE,** point to the blank spaces of erasure, the unrecorded topography where things happened, tears shed, injustices, that would shrink the man's fleshy neck over his shirt collar back to size. Things in the shaded areas boxed in between the blue, brown and gray lines that only residents who had lived there all their lives would know. If the man needed proof, then give Ray the city map and Ray would tell him, decipher things for the man. Could the man do that? Could the man claim a thing like that?

No. This was not what Ray meant when he said first things first. The young man Ray encountered the evening before the incident was a boy and not a girl. There. That was all he wanted to say. Truths had to be told and Ray was well aware that the newspapers made constant mistakes and always made false things up. He instructed the man to read the headlines and Ray pointed to the man's steno tablet, as if the pause in the man's writing made it seem he was unbelieving of Ray's words. Listen, Ray assured the man; he may be on in years, yes. No doubt. But that didn't make him a demented fool, and then Ray dropped his palm, heavy with perspiration, onto his kneecap again.

This Antonio boy stood as close to him as the man, and Ray described how scared he was of the boy, who wouldn't be? His heart wasn't healthy and the fact that his pipes kept clogging like a sink drain worried the wife. They'd been married for . . . for . . . Ray couldn't remember. Twenty-nine, the wife reminded him, smiling, and then Ray told her, begged her, to please go sit outside the office where the cigarette machine was located, and she bowed her head in close to his and whispered in Japanese, a quiet murmur of discretion, and she shook her head NO.

Why did Ray do what he did if he was so frightened? What was he thinking that night? Who knows? Why do people do what they do to each other? Why does the sun come up only to go down? Maybe if Ray had been one of *their kind,* you know . . . How else was he supposed to answer that question? Ray wasn't an old fool and so he wouldn't speak with humility. The man paused to shake the pen.

Look, Ray wasn't sitting across the desk of the policeman to argue. He didn't close his store to waste his time arguing. Whether he was a she or she was a he, it was of no consequence to him anymore, understand? Because the youth that came into the store was so hungry, Ray seemed surprised that the hoodlum hadn't shown any inclination to kill for a taste of another candy bar. And when things were going nuts all over, this said something.

The white taffy and chocolate disappeared in a few bites. The Coke machine started up again with a tremor that shook the floor and then the vibrant humming followed and they could feel it underfoot. Ray zipped up his windbreaker, looked at his watch and then turned off one of the ceiling lights to prompt Turtle to leave. Turtle licked the candy's paper and then she licked her sooty fingers and then crumpled the candy wrapper and tossed it into the trashcan near the empty bottle rack.

Ray walked with haste to the customer side of the oak counter. He wasn't cognizant that he carried within his hands a long metal chain accompanied by a padlock the size of a heart. An automatic routine so embedded in his behavior that Ray had no memory of opening the bottom drawer under the pigs' feet and no recollection of scooping the thick chain and padlock to lock up the front doors of the store, and then no recollection in having carried the chain dutifully to the entrance of the store. Such was his closing practice of the day, each and every day.

Maybe the reason grew from the weight of the chain he carried; Ray remembered looking down at his hands and the chain was limp and drooped like a small drowned body; or maybe it was the achy spasms of his back as he approached the double doors. Maybe it was his bad heart, or maybe his good heart. Maybe he wanted to be kind, or maybe employ one of their kind. Maybe he thought about dust and how he ate it at every meal, slept with it between sheets, had breathed in the dust storms like smoke. Maybe because Ray understood way too well how everything could be taken away in one signature, one Executive Order Number 9066, and all that was left were the clothes on his back, and nothing, nothing else except perhaps for someone's kindness, a memory which still made him weep. Maybe, just maybe Ray felt a sliver of pity for this starving boy. Out of courtesy, he shouldered the door open for Turtle.

You looking for a job? Ray blurted out and then regretted the offer immediately. Ray hadn't the slightest idea why he entertained the notion. Offering this hoodlum a job? The wife would give him hell and would tell him, Go ahead and kill yourself. Why should I care!

Come tomorrow in the morning, Ray said. Maybe I give you a job.

Turtle wiped her nose with her leather sleeve. She heard the crisp of Ray's windbreaker against the chinking chain. They both stepped through the doorway and stood under the store sign. Turtle said:

What time you want me here?

Turtle caught Ray by surprise. Ray lowered the chain because of the dull ache of his forearms.

No joke.

No joke, what time? Turtle waited for an answer.

Seven a.m. Exactly. Ray was a man who went by the clock and everyone knew it, including Turtle. He bolted the double doors and needled the chain in and out of the door handles and repeated:

Seven a.m. If not, Ray said, don't count on me.

Turtle nodded. Ray's handgun resembled a fat wallet slipped in his back pocket. His hands moved swiftly to secure the padlock and then he tested the chain to make sure that everything was bolted absolute. Turtle waited until Ray completed the lockup before she extended her hand. Ray hesitated and then understood and the two shook hands.

The wife kept nodding in agreement at Ray's depiction of the evening, and this surprised Ray. She hadn't been present to see the strange kid, hadn't touched his hand or smelled his rotten flower smell. Ray pulled out a handkerchief to wipe the sweat from his palms and asked her why she nodded, because he was the one who had retained the sticky press of the boy's handshake, not she. Whatever object Ray had touched after that, be it the steering wheel of his Rambler or the knob of his front door, Ray embossed the boy's microbes and germ contagion on everything. No matter how much Ray washed his hands, no matter how hard he wiped and rubbed the sweat off his palms, his hands couldn't forget the boy's lingering stink, like flowers left way too long in a vase of putrid water.

Yes, Ray finally admitted, tucking the handkerchief away in his back pocket, he did make mistakes. Just the other day, Mr. Marmalejo came into the shop to buy a loaf of Weber's bread. He gave Ray a five and Ray returned change for a twenty. And Mr. Marmalejo said, You're wrong, and Ray said, No, you're wrong, until Ray opened the cash register and saw the five under the change rack where he kept the twenties. Well, Ray wasn't perfect and he knew that the man wasn't perfect. Didn't he make innocent mistakes too? So all right, Ray finally admitted, he may have been wrong about the boy. Was that what the man wanted to record, Ray's mistake?

But isn't all of this a mistake? Ray asked, looking at the wife. As the man shook his pen, Ray looked at his own palms, the fingers, the nubs of appendages that worked hard to deliver food to the wife's table or provide her with a home that no one would be able to take away again. And Ray gazed down at his pair of hands that hadn't touched the wife's naked flesh in a long time and yet the boy's handshake came between him and everything else now. When the wife asked if Ray was feeling okay, Ray didn't know he was rubbing his palm over his heart to quiet the burn. Ray wanted to get back to the shop and told her so, told her he was wasting precious time. Ray had a lot to do: unchain the doors, slice open the delivery boxes, price the merchandise, finish shelving the cans of Campbell's soups, slice bologna, keep ahead of the Val U Mini Mart competition and keep his hands so busy they'd forget about the boy.

The man's pen didn't even work, and Ray knew the man would miss the important words, skip them and blame the ink. Ray knew it and the nod and bounce of the wife's head annoyed him. He stood up without humility and knew he would never again talk to the policeman whose pen was running out of time. The wife pulled him back to his chair. She pressed the sourness of the boy's handshake and Ray broke off her grasp to walk out, his belly full of knowing. Make no mistake about it: the man in the funeral suit would take Ray's statement and crumple it up like a snowball; toss it under **TRASH** or maybe file it under **WHO CARES?**

Turtle moved swiftly, side-jumped a low picket fence and went straight to the garden hose neatly spiraled near the spigot and drank deeply, the chocolate and taffy producing a gagging thirst, and then she replaced the hose as she found it. Turtle worked her mouth to scrape the last savor of the candy bar. Not far from the palmilla, two plastic decorative flamingos dawdled on the lawn, useless and remarkable to the eye. Turtle blew into her hands and jammed them in her pockets and felt the screwdriver as she watched Ray get into his dented black Rambler. The start of the engine initiated a pop of muffler, and Turtle watched Ray make a sloppy U-turn, the Rambler's headlights sweeping over the houses across Eastern. The muffler left behind the palest trace of exhaust.

The rains had succeeded in washing the city's grime, leaving a polished veneer to everything in sight, except for the skeletal trees, their very roots thrashed about in the storm unmercifully. Even the wet pavements shone with tinfoil gleam, and the flamingos glowed pink in the darkness. From the temporary cloud breaks, Turtle saw a few stars shine into a constellation of fortuity. A little money sounded promising, an employment opportunity as strange for Turtle as having two stupid lawn flamingos keeping her company. What had gotten into Ray anyway? Ray had looked as serious as a heart attack and scared shitless when she approached him and then ended up offering her a job. A job, can you believe it? Maybe all that bottle-stacking was tiresome, or maybe it was just one of those strange nights when actions no longer needed motives, and Turtle decided to shut off the questioning, the how come, the why now, the what if, and leave the wondering for another day.

No reasons needed for actions tonight. To prove it, Turtle suddenly reached down to remove the wire legs of the flamingos. She bent their thin-ass wire legs into a bulky metallic pretzel and then sent them rocketing until the metal landed with a thump on the roof of another house. Behind her, a window lit up inside the Hernández house; someone arrived and Turtle had to make a move.

She needed a plan for tonight and considered Evergreen again, but what about an alarm for waking up? Ray's words were serious. Seven exactly. And Ray stuck to his word like he stuck to his black Rambler when everyone knew he could easily afford to drive a new Cadillac. Chale, no way. Turtle couldn't risk oversleeping. Not for this once-in-a-lifetime opportunity, her first job.

Where to go, where to go? she asked herself, jumping up and down in a little exercise for body heat. Turtle pulled out the fifteen cents from her leather pocket. The possibility of riding the RTD bus all night was out of the question. Her eyes did a slow sweep across Eastern. A row of lampposts brightened. Cars pulled up in small driveways. The scent of lard-spitting dinner pork chops and nopalitos, tortillas toasting on the comal, dinnertime and the smell of another workday ending.

Turtle decided on two things: not to go too far from the store, and not to sleep tonight. A job meant a little cash flow, money in the pocket, food on the table, a pig's foot, maybe even a bus ticket to wherever Amá was living. And the store was located on McBride territory, which meant Lote M would think twice about the hassle. This was shaping up well and looking better all the time. The long night became ablaze with house lights. Pairing the pink torsos of the flamingos side by side, Turtle left them hollowed out and false, land-born and immobile, unlike her. She walked with purpose, invested with a plan for the night.

Returning to the anonymity of the Chinese cemetery, Turtle huddled near the crematory chimney and tried to stay warm and awake for one more night. The weather had become so strange that the barometer of her body was no longer reliable and if she guessed right, all she had left was nine hours until daylight. Turtle had confronted worse than chalking up some time. Way too easy. The rains began again, flooding the minutes into puddles which stormed into hours and then into the gutter overflows and then the rains turned into assaulting pebbles of hail and then halted just as rapidly. All she needed to kill was a few hours and be at the Friendly Shop by seven in the morning to say: Mi carnal, Ray, how much you gonna pay me? To stay awake was to keep moving, sharklike, and Turtle jumped the fence onto the living side of First Street.

Turtle chose to move north on Eastern to avoid the roadblocks altogether. Eastern Street curved around the ancient lomas, and the nopal cactus and chollas sprouted throughout the crevices of the hills. Wherever earthquakes had pulled rock apart from rock, the slopes opened up with shallow, earthen mouths to catch rainwater, and then dried out in terraced clumps to grow beds of blond weeds so thick, they pricked like unshaven beards. Compact framed houses were embedded as much as the exposed boulders of the hills themselves. Their makeshift terra-cotta walls once teemed with families rambling around the kitchen table or around the television, blue tint from the windows. But now the houses were as quiet as an owl's wingbeats; as silent as the glittering porch lights turned on for the night, soundless and dominant as stone.

When she was young, the lomas she now passed seemed like magnificent split bellies of rock torn out of the flesh of the earth's skin. Luis Lil Lizard filled her with stories about the lomas. Once upon a time they had tried to jump-start the bulldozers because Luis believed and convinced her to believe that if they bulldozed the hills on Eastern Street, they could reach a region called New Mexico. It was the only thing she could recall that Luis ever desired with a bad, committed ache and she never knew what he searched for but helped him just the same because she loved him worse than herself.

Up the darkened path of a hillside driveway was the entrance to Sybil Brand Institute for Women, nestled like a natural outcropping of granite up high on one of the hills. She crossed the street to avoid the entrance but felt the mist of sorrow like a ghost late at night. Turtle walked in haste, the zoom of dreary cars passing, passing houses and makeshift fences and every once in a while she passed a fellow pedestrian who tottered home from swing shift. Every so often a dog tied to a porch pillar would bark at her shadow, tipping over its pie plate or spilling a Cool Whip water dish, bark so that the porch lights switched on and off and neighboring eyes made security checks for possible escapees from the prison. Once Turtle reached the top of the hill, she spotted a column of lights surrounding a university parking lot across the great divide of the 10 Interstate freeway. The fuzzy glow of lights against the blank night seemed as distant to Turtle as the glare of the moon.

At the freeway bridge, she turned and walked southward and then climbed a small winding side street. Woolwine Avenue narrowed into one car road, where Turtle discovered a vacant lot used for old furniture discards. Leg boards and cloth material and wire lay exposed like old bones. She sat on the remnants of a mattress and stared at the university lights and her head, too heavy with drowsiness, began to cave in between her shoulders. Her instinct alerted, Turtle realized too well that if she remained still for much longer, exhaustion would pull her into a peaceful, weightless catastrophe of sleep. She willed her body into motion and rose from between the boarded box springs and turned right around to descend the lomas once again. Hands in her pockets, Turtle stitched over her earlier watery footprints, uphill and downhill, coming and going to nowhere and back.

FREEZE! The word a loud commanding shout like a military order.

A group of dogs answered one another in triphammer barks.

Motherfucken jura, Turtle thought. Can you believe it? The Lote M vatos gave no warning, so it must be the cops. The voice was to the back of her and Turtle placed her hands slowly behind her neck to say, See? Harmless. Her leather jacket hung like skin about to shed and her khakis flapped so loosely on her hip bones, they could slip right off at a moment's notice. If the jura had stopped to interrogate her a few nights ago, Turtle's heart would have been hammering enough for her ears to deafen. But tonight Turtle barely felt a murmur, her heart too uninspired to accomplish fear. Nonetheless, she made sure not to make any sudden gestures and held her hands in holdup position.

I'm not doing nuthin'.

My ass you're not, the male voice replied. Turn around slow-like, vato.

He used the word "vato." Maybe Gang Detail, the worse kind of cop. Turtle turned cautiously to discover a familiar pearl-peach Pontiac Bonneville idling near the curb. Santos's pride and joy, the car's gold pinstriping and chrome-gold hubcaps shone under the dulling light of the lamppost like a ripe peach picked right off the tree. Other than the cracked rear window, the car looked *firme.*

Long time no see! Santos yelled from his driver's seat, his voice hinting betrayal.

You got me, fucken puto! Man! Relieved it wasn't Gang Detail, Turtle moved toward the car, painfully conscious of her legs jerking. They both knew Turtle was AWOL, but Turtle refused to show any remorse and as she bent into the Bonneville's open window, she acted as if it were a Sunday afternoon and they were just chillin' at the park.

Qué la, vato, Santos said, disbelieving. He was installed in the driver's seat, sitting on the pristine leather biscuit tucks. You knowed I find you. Even in the dark, te noté, man. I knowed it was you. Santos lowered the volume of Ralphi Pagan crooning "Hey There Lonely Girl." Turtle cocked her head into the rolled-down window, disturbing the side mirror.

Watcha my mirror, ésa. And Turtle closed her right elbow in. So where you been?

Santos was all primped up in his sterling white T-shirt, a navy blue wool beanie pulled over his forehead to cover his eyebrows. Wearing driving gloves, he knuckled the chain steering wheel with the assurance of a man who commandeered his vehicle, the pilot in charge of his aircraft, the one and only jefe of the dash and panel knobs which adjusted sound and speed and escape. As he sat there in a posture of staunch control, Turtle could not possibly imagine Santos anywhere else but behind the wheel of his pearl-peach Pontiac Bonneville.

She answered Santos's question with another one, What went down? and thumbed the broken rear window. The lowriding Pontiac had been tarnished by the sin of broken glass and the temporary repair consisted of a piece of cardboard held with duct tape.

Hilda, Santos replied. Fucken Hilda, man. The music, the scent, the rosary hanging from the rearview mirror, nothing had changed. Santos fondled the beads of the rosary gently, forlornly.

I crashed her heart and so she crashed my car.

You deserve it, puto, Turtle replied. You ain't no saint. The sameness, oldies-but-goodies playing, the crème leather bucket seats as inviting as velvet, as smooth as vanilla ice cream, the mix scents of Santos's cologne against the veiled trace of high-grade Acapulco gold—all of this was a memoir from way back, a fervent pulp of another youth. Turtle found herself flexing her nostrils to inhale an almost forgotten sanctuary, and she drew it all in until her chest inflated with maximum memory and it was then that she released a sigh, an exhale so long it resembled sadness. Santos ejected the Pagan tape and slipped another one in and Thee Midnighters' Little Willie G. sang "Whittier Boulevard." The song played out ancient invocations. Turtle touched the unoccupied passenger bucket seat.

Man, you look like shit warmed over.

The cold turd herself. Turtle reached over the seat and the two slammed fists.

You stink like one.

Fuck you, ése.

Santos took off his beanie and ruffled his hair. He had a weakness for diamonds. Under his gloves, Turtle noticed the stud diamond ring on his pinkie. Santos slipped the beanie back on, and the two listened to the boom of Midnighters brass for a while.

So you didn't answer me.

Whatta you talkin' about?

Where you been holding up, homes?

You my parole officer, o qué?

Where?

You writing a book? Turtle spit sideways to let Santos know she wasn't interested in his questions. Santos leaned over the bucket seat to unlock the passenger door.

Let's go for a ride.

No way, man! Turtle shook her head. You think I'm crazy? She knew the rules—Santos would take her to the others so as to beat some sense into her good. Beat her something fierce. She only trusted Santos as far as she could throw him. The screwdriver felt reassuringly heavy in her pocket. And with the promise of a job, Turtle didn't want to fuck up the opportunity; not even for McBride.

I'm gonna ask one more time—let's go for a ride.

Nah, Turtle replied. She scanned around nonchalantly. You gotta give me more credit, homes. I ain't stupid.

It's me or them QAs.

Nah, I got some urgent business.

Business? Qué la . . . business?

What's it to you?

We're familia, homes. Santos's knuckles rested on the chain of his steering wheel again. You're not one man, pendejo.

I'm a ghost, ése. Act like you never seen me.

Too late, man. Get in.

You gonna make me?

You heared me.

Did I hear right?

Just get in, homes. Santos reached over to unlock the door a second time. He had bad luck tattooed all over him. Turtle resisted the temptation. The last time they had hung out together, they were arrested for vandalism near the Friedman Bag Company off the 101 Hollywood freeway. They were detained at the California Youth Authority for tagging the walls and it was for this violation that Amá decided to give her up to the courts. Turtle cupped her hand over the lock of the passenger door, preventing Santos from unlocking it.

But damn if tonight wasn't a strange night of opportunities. Maybe Turtle could talk Santos into buying her a hamburger. God, the thought of fat hot french fries was tempting. Little Willie G. singing from the flickering light of the tape deck, the rosary so long it dangled over the dash. The seduction was working its way into her muscles. Standing still, Turtle's achy leg muscles reminded her of the full night ahead.

What time you got?

You mean you got somewhere to go? Santos asked sarcastically.

And you do?

Yea.

Okay, you tell it to me first.

Heading to Alfonso's canton. Now you.

Heading to hell.

They slammed fists again.

You need a bath, man.

Didn't you quit hanging with that motherfucker? Turtle asked.

Big Al got jumped, man. Got saved by a fucken little rat dog. Santos crossed his heart solemnly. I ain't lying.

En serio?

I swear on my jefita's grave.

It had been a long time since laughter had arrived like chunks of food between her lips and Turtle laughed so hard, she felt her knees buckle. Santos joined in.

A Chihuahua dog?

To top it off!

Oh man oh man. Turtle leaned her head closer to the passenger bucket seat and laughed until her ankles wanted to collapse. She wiped the tears from her eyes.

Oh man oh man. Their laughter leveled off and they listened to the intoxicating music until a siren ripped through the night. If it's one thing that the Eastside never lacked, it was the constant howling of a siren. Ambulance? Fire? Police? QA?

They were quiet once more until Turtle asked:

So what's going down?

Big Al knows who jumped him, knocked him down and locked him at Laguna Cliff. In a booth. Makes you inspired.

Lote M boys?

Nah, Santos replied. He stroked the rosary beads as if the stroking delivered a form of comfort. Over a fucken girl, can you believe it?

Yea, I can believe it.

Over pussy. Now we're just gonna pay the FOB a little visit, tú sabes, so's he knows not to mess with the McBride Pride!

Fuck Big Al, Turtle voiced in conviction, and she removed her hand from the door lock. No longer interested in spilling her blood over someone like Alfonso, she straightened her back, cracked her neck. She rubbed one damp sneaker against the other for warmth. Turtle continued:

The motherfucker don't know the real enemy. Lote M is tearing balls left and right and Big Al's worried over some FOB. Lote M is out, vato, full force, fucking up all of our terrain, and look what's important to that motherfucker. Turtle's runny nose mucusy from the chill. Fucken Big Al no vale la pena, homes.

You're a pussy, man, Santos said over Thee Midnighters' song "That's All." . . . A big fat ugly dark dripping pussy.

Yea, ése, whatever. Fuck you, Turtle replied. She straightened up, removed herself from the window of the Bonneville and looked to the hills. Her eyes followed the long serpentine street to the top of the lomas and her ears keened in on the low whine of mosquitoes, a growing reverie of buzzing. Fuck, she murmured. Fuck.

From behind the lomas, the high tower searchlights of a helicopter swayed in the sky. The metallic locust descended swiftly and invaded Eastern Street with its bright spotlights, its whooshing blades spinning with storm-force speed. Clothes on laundry lines snapped and a dog howled as the tempest of the whirlwind drew closer. The winds ground the air beneath its plated runners. Ice-cream wrappers and Skippy dog food cans and dry tree leaves and orange rinds and discarded Clorox bottles rose in a vacuous stir. The copter circled in on the Bonneville in a military maneuver, blinding Turtle with the fluorescent explosion of iris-burning light. The uninterruptible torrent of light gushed all over Santos's shiny hood like white acid.

You don't just stand there like a lame duck in target practice. Fuck that, and Santos turned the ignition key, revved up the engine and then punched the accelerator. No debate on this one, and Turtle clicked the car door open, dove headfirst into the Pontiac Bonneville, which was already in motion, already in a U-turn two-tire wheelie. Santos's pride and joy speeding off, the car skidding and the passenger door flying open. Then, with a thump and screech, the Bonneville landed on all four Goodyear whitewalls. The force of the Pontiac's downhill speed slammed the door shut and then the car roared away with the godspeed assistance of gravity.

FOURTEEN

Pomona 60 West versus the QA roadblocks—both options held equal disregard for Ana's time. Her boss, Mr. Peters was the same—he delivered on her desk a folder of Northern Mutual Insurance documents just a few minutes before closing the office. She was lifting her purse, pulling her jacket from the back of her chair, thinking about the search for Ben, when Mr. Peters appeared, placing the one-inch-thick folder on her IBM Selectric typewriter. His sports coat on, his watch a hunk of brass and gold, he glanced at the time as if she were the one detaining him. He told her, You are my lucky lady, referring to her poker face and to the pair of cubed dice earrings she wore that morning to complement her business attire, a strict office dress code uncharitable when compared to the amount of her paycheck.

Of course, she said, as if it were an oversight on her part, and by the time she completed proofreading the small print, the fly-turd print, two hours had already passed. Her eyes were pink-rimmed and squinty from exhaustion, from proofreading, red pen in hand, insurance policy documents day after day in faint office light. Her optometrist had predicted bifocal lenses in less than a year and more out of financial restraint than vanity she held back their purchase.

QA roadblocks were enforced by the time she got off work, causing the side-street traffic to squeeze into a sluggish bottleneck. Ana idled, sweating buckets with the hope her car wouldn't overheat. She thought about Ben and then thought about the search for him as the mambo line of traffic moved in slow rhythms. The temperature gauge on her dash began to rise and her impatience began to surge. As soon as the QA directed her through, she floored the gas pedal to get to the first free intersection. Relieved to be this far, she slipped off the dice earrings and tossed the pair onto the dashboard.

So what else is new? she had asked Tranquilina, and meant it. Sooner or later Ana found herself in search of her younger, brooding brother. Years before, he was easy to find, since he had one private space and not a city of caves to hide in. She often found him on top of the roof, his supine body studying the stars that shrank in receding pulls of heaven. Once, she had found him morose, his face bloated from having cried, though he cried no more. Their mother had gone and their father had called her a slut and Ben rested his head on the palm-pads of his hand, by now accustomed to Ana's intrusions. Right beneath where Ben lay, their father watched television, a small fan tipped toward him to dry the perspiration of a day's work off his face.

Benny, Ana had said, his name curled forward by the rising Santa Anas. She made her way down the roof slant, barefoot and cautious. Some of the shingles were so damaged, the grit had worn down to the tar and she tried to avoid those craters so that Father wouldn't hear the pressure, so that Father wouldn't think there were rats in the attic. Ana had ducked her head beneath the television's metallic antenna and then crouched close to him, her knees to her chest. His old sneakers were unlaced, thready holes at the toes, pointing to the sky. No choir of crickets tonight. Only the vibration of the antenna's undulating humming, its audibility dependent on the pitch and brush of the Santa Ana currents.

She knew Ben disbelieved her words about God's little eyes, his gestures unchanged and unconvinced. He lay on the thin grit of shingles and gazed at the pinpoints of drowning light. Her words barely made a dent against the black sky.

Prove it, he said, to challenge such nonsense, to listen to her explanations rather than the humming above him, or the muffled voices of the television below, but Ana acted as if she didn't hear him. When she wasn't frowning and when she tilted her chin in the right way, Ana resembled Father and her ginger hair weltered in the breeze.

You're not understanding, Ana finally replied. Nothing but the wrong words came out of her lips in explanation. She held no scientific proof. She didn't know how to convert the mysteries into something solid or organize the Scrabble-game alphabet into make-sense words. Faith couldn't be sculptured for Ben; couldn't cradle him like the San Gabriel Mountains guarding the inhabitants of the city. Ana gave up, and sat in silence.

I don't believe you, Ben added.

So don't, Ana stated, and meant it, stretching out her bare legs, the grit scratching against her calves. She heard the canned laughter from the television. Counterfeit in its merriment, the noise rose from the heat vents that resembled little tin houses on their roof. Something as simple as metal fish-bone receptors had transmitted images into waves and then back into images and Ana looked up at the antenna and then marveled at the fish-bone shapes of all the other antennas on all the other rooftops.

The antennas quaked and careened with the strong winds like a school of airborne fish. Invisible gusts of air agitated the fluttering hem of Ben's T-shirt, and compelled the tall palm trees of the Calvary Cemetery to dust against the dullness of the dark or whipped her own hair against her lips. Ana had wondered how wind needed resistance to make its invisibility felt. She held her own palm up, bucked her elbow and spread her fingers, wide and open, as she did when she painted her fingernails or assisted a young Ben in tracing his hand to make a turkey on a paper plate for Thanksgiving. The warm and very dry winds bullied her, and bent and darted the metal ribs above her. Strands of her hair spiked with electricity. She heard more canned laughter. The wind laden with desert dust and tree bark rose and beat about the rooftop.

You're a liar, Ben said, now wanting to pick a fight.

I give up.

Ana tried to keep the static shock of her hair away from her forehead. Disrupted by a jolting rake of fingers, a scoop of a palm, Ana's hair became wild wires in cilia motion, the circuit of sparks catching, once, twice.

It's so windy up here.

Whatta you expect? Ben snapped, relieved to have something to snap at.

You better come inside now.

Leave me alone.

You're gonna get a licking.

What's it to you, anyway?

At least I'm trying, Benny. At least I'm doing that.

Moments later the television went off. It must have been late, because Father dragged his taxed feet over the old wood-swell creaking floor where Mother had placed a cilantro-green rug to lighten the sounds. Father's habit was to turn off the television and then tread to the bathroom, where he would urinate, then flush the toilet. The water would clunk against the ancient pipes as Father moved his feet to check their room to make sure they weren't sleeping together. If they were, if he caught them, he would arouse Ben with a press and shake of shoulder, get him out of her bed and scold him with army-trained discipline. But silence flowed out of the roof vents, and Ana knew that any minute now, Father would be searching for the two of them like some hide-and-seek game, ready to holler their names once he realized they were not in their bedroom, and not under their beds. Not even inside the house.

Ana waited for that moment when Father would realize they were nowhere to be found. She could see him shake his fists at the Santa Ana winds, hear him shriek like a maniac and then vise his head with his hands once again, certain he had been abandoned a second time.

Ben seemed everywhere. Ana thought she spotted him under a storefront awning, or there he was selling a bag of oranges at the street corner. But worse than these sightings, worse than the harsh humid air that blew through the fan vents of her used sedan, was the possibility of arriving at the church too late for Tranquilina's help. She might think it unsafe to search for Ben at night and this dread deepened Ana's anxiety, which was why she risked taking the Pomona 60 West in the first place. She grasped the steering wheel, dented the moistness of her palms with her polished nails and turned left after clearing the QA checkpoint. On Soto Street, she caught the I-5 freeway entrance and, in her freeway savvy, knew this would hook her up to the Pomona 60. Ana had maintained a driving strive onto the multiple-lane freeway until the cars were trapped into files of gridlock.

Stuck behind the bumper of a mammoth Mayflower moving truck and unable to see what was ahead, Ana tired of seeing the driver on her left picking his nose, the driver to the right applying lipstick on her mouth. Motorcycle riders, mere flashes on her rearview mirror, slalomed in between the stalled, throbbing stoppage of cars, hundreds, thousands, filed in neat rows. The cars and trucks began to crowd her until a wild impatience moved her to set her signaling blinkers on and aim the car in a crawl toward the closest runaway exit out of the Pomona 60 West.

She exited and ended up in an unfamiliar city block of boarded-up warehouses. One radio song, then two, and then commercial blather, Ana still remained lost in the maze of downtown streets. She drove beneath the overpass at the edges of a no-man's-land where a single eucalyptus tree stood tall and slight, an anomaly of nature. Otherwise the deserted area revealed the congealed remnants of squatters like scabs on a wound. Ben-like people bequeathing cold and blackened wood chips to campfires; abandoned makeshift cardboard beds; forsaken newspapers. They squirreled away bundles of clothes or bottles collected for deposit money inside the concrete catacomb of pillar and girder. Everywhere, Ben appeared.

The city lampposts began to shape a downtown skyline. Ana drove past Fred's Furniture & Income Tax and realized she was too far east and immediately made an illegal turn into a one-way directive, a big mistake she tried correcting with another illegal U-turn, the bombastic horns of other cars shooting her with insults. From one turn to another, her pair of dice earrings rolled on the dashboard as if the cubed numbers had been tossed onto a craps table.

Tranquilina's voice had not caught Ana off guard, because every time the phone rang, it was mostly bad news that became worse throughout the day, a chokehold she tried swallowing, along with Mr. Peters's constant requests for unpaid overtime. Time had shot forward in her anxiety to look for Ben and it took her precious minutes to unlock her car door, to ignite the clunky used engine, to put pedal to the metal, to rush to Tranquilina's church, only to get lost in the one-ways of the city. And was this the second or third time she had driven past La Malinche Passport Fotos/Yerbería? Her white ruffled Paul Revere blouse was sweat-drenched. Completely disoriented, she peered over the horizon of the dashboard as if she had hoped the church would send off a banner of light to direct her, when suddenly a dog dashed in front of her. And then there followed a whole pack of asphalt jungle dogs, overwhelming the boulevard, rushing between the forest of bumpers. The assembling mass of dogs followed the alpha dog who, no doubt, was the leader, the confident come-on type, its jaws clenched on the spoils of his bone hunt. Ana stomped onto her brakes, a mighty shrill, forcing the contents of her purse to fly off the passenger seat and scatter all over the floor of her sedan in a burst of aspirin tablets, Certs mints, pens, Kotex, Kleenex and other items kept for necessity's visit.

Surrounded by honking, the alpha dog jumped up between bumpers and taillights as if the pavement were griddle-hot, while the others in the pack clawed bumpers or climbed on the hoods of cars in an attempt to cross the street. By their very number and size and colors, by their nervous scrambling tick of paws on the hoods, the pack became an unusually startling sight. Astonished at the fact that she might have scattered much more than just her purse entrails, Ana pressed her car horn and joined in on the cacophony of beeps.

Bigger dogs leaped from hoods to trunks, sliding and slipping, while the smaller ones trampled between the bumpers, biting tires. A few dogs jumped on the roof of her car, and she heard the ticks of their claws right above her. All of the dogs howled and growled in devoted vengeance in response to the hooting and catcalls from the drivers who found themselves in their own gregarious herd of cars. And the challenging noise of the two assemblages continued until the unstoppable pack raced out of sight.

Slowly the cars loosened spaces between the bumpers and began the dance of the side-street crawl. Just as rapidly as her hot tears had appeared, they disappeared, leaving only grayish slivers of mascara under her eyes. The Kleenex was not within reach, and she had to make do by carefully wiping her eyes with her finger. The last thing she needed was to splotch her good white blouse with mascara stains.

Ana inspected herself in the rearview mirror and then looked over her dash and immediately recognized the loading zone space between a Wonder Bread truck and a blue VW beetle. Right there, all the time. How stupid could she be? She signaled and parked and thought she had lost her mind.

Ana hastily threw her personal items back into her purse and then entered the alley. She had not seen the carapace of the dog until she felt something crunch like eggshells underfoot. The dog, a furry sack of meshed muscle, lay saturated with flies near a toppled trashcan. The crunch of step stirred up the anger of buzzing flies and Ana covered her mouth. Stepping through the obstacles of scattered trash, Ana knocked at the church door. A lone bulb hung low and radiated little light over the kitchen table and then spilled over the threshold of the door as Tranquilina answered the knock.

I had to work late, Ana said by way of explanation, as an excuse for being this tardy.

Come in, Tranquilina replied, swatting a few flies away from her face. Ana scraped the muck from the bottom of her heels before entering the kitchen, and Tranquilina shut the door behind her.

Any word from Ben?

I wish I had one to pass on.

Ain't this some bullshit? Ana asked, attempting sarcasm, a slight mocking, to show what one must put up with for family. Flies were already zagging on the quarters of the cabbages in the strainer. Potato peels were splattered around a simmering pot and yet the room did not hold the mélange of steaming consommé or the well-intentioned hum of an honest day's work. On the contrary, the stench of trashcans scattered like roadkill all over the alley, the dim lighting in the room and the sheer texture of heat entrapped between the boxed walls made Ana feel worse than ever. Nauseated, she checked to see if the small window was propped open.

Would you like a glass of water? Tranquilina asked, noting Ana's paleness.

What I need is your help, Ana replied, her voice breaking one word at a time. But I see that you're preparing for services.

Javelins of flames shot out from under the neglected pot. Tranquilina raised her palm for Ana to say no more and then proceeded to retrieve her liver-colored galoshes from the closet where a lone hanger hung empty without Mama's raincoat. Tranquilina removed her hairnet and tucked it in her apron pocket and then removed her apron as Ana watched the street woman peeling potatoes, her sclerotic face gazing up at Ana suspiciously.

To Ana, the woman was one of many, a spoke in the wheel of Tranquilina's traveling ministry. The woman momentarily stopped her peeling, her arms tattooed with scabs and scars and open wounds, to study Ana's face, her shaky hand clutching the handle of the peeler. Ana smiled uncomfortably, a smile made to order, stiff, unreal, like the smile she pasted on her poker face each and every Northern Mutual Insurance morning.

The squeaky hinges of the closet door, the patter of lid hissing from the boiling steam, the buzz of flies, and the resuming clean whittle, whittle of one potato after another. Tranquilina lifted the sack of onions off the chair and then sat down to pull on her first boot. The simmering pots complained with the lips of their lids and the combustion of the small kitchen felt as if the rooms would explode any second, and Ana wiped her forehead with the ruffled sleeve of her blouse. How does Tranquilina get from A to Z each day without going bonkers, Ana thought, without being shredded apart like the dead dog near her doorstep? Ana's anxiety amplified just as much as the singe and scold of boil, just as much as Tranquilina's patient pull of her second boot.

We have to go out for a while, Tranquilina said to the woman, pausing between each word in order to avoid any misunderstanding. Please stay here and tell people to come by tomorrow. The woman looked up at the ceiling while her lips wrestled furiously with ideas on what to do. Moistness beaded above her lip and half-moons of dampness darkened under her armpits. In a resigning gesture, the woman flopped back down on her seat, the fluff of her worn clothes ballooning somewhat. She began to pluck the scabs off her wrist.

Don't do that, Tranquilina said, in a tone unfamiliar to Ana. Stop it.

The woman stared at Tranquilina, her lips gummed with an effort to reply, but it was Tranquilina who finally spoke. I'm sorry, she said. *For my life is spent with grief, and my years with sighing, and my bones are consumed.* I'm so sorry if I have been unkind, but can you please stay here for a while?

Tranquilina rose in practiced repose and then tromped her galoshes to the stove to turn off the burners, her red-tasseled poncho readied for the cool night.

Seek and we shall find.

All right, Ana said. Yes. She was prepared to tread over the unraveling ribbon of the night all night if need be. Let's do it.

They drove again and stopped again until Ana saw the woman preaching on the corner despite hail so firm, the icy pebbles hit the windshield of her sedan like marbles. Ana thought about the burden of faith. The traffic light finally turned colors and Ana guessed that Tranquilina had recognized the figure, because the sigh Tranquilina sighed so deeply was one Ana knew well. They continued their drive, slowly, methodically, until Tranquilina requested that she stop. Once parked, she instructed Ana to stay in the car and high-beam the darkness between the warehouses while she entered the alley to disrupt the nocturnal, the squatters, the no-men people. Tranquilina approached their darkness with an aura of light behind her and to Ana, she became someone else, some*thing* else altogether, a stenciled gray dazzling figure.

Ana rattled her dice earrings in one fist and then felt the dice in the open palm of her hand as if to access the weight of its numbered prediction. Finding Ben was all a matter of chance, and yet every time Tranquilina entered the alleys Ana entertained—no, allowed herself—the privilege of hoping that Tranquilina would emerge from the darkness with her younger brother Ben. She studied the dice and Ana blinked to keep her tears from having their way and then slipped her dice earrings back on her earlobes, a mundane and familiar thing for her to do.

The moisture of her breath fogged on the window. She examined her vacated hand and turned it over and suddenly it became a delta of lifelines and then Ana spread her fingers in memory, and her hand became an antenna receptive to electrical charges. Ana looked over the sun-cracked dashboard of the sedan and into the mouth of the alley. The headlights faded, and just beyond its reach of light, Ana saw murky movement between the swiping windshield wipers. A snap of someone's face, a reflecting glint of bottle glass, a flash of cloth against the liquidy darkness. Ana shaped her hand into a cup empty of water.

Ana's alabaster shoulders stung sunburn-pink as she sat between her parents on the edge of the man-made pond at Belvedere Park not far from the **ABSOLUTELY NO FISHING or SWIMMING** rules painted on a sign as big as a patio table. To the left, her mother dipped her feet into the colored, treated water, the rim of her mother's seventh-month pregnancy well hidden by the large ruffles of her swimsuit. To the right of her, Ana's father sat piercing an earthworm on the safety-pin hook of his makeshift fishing pole. He did this most of the afternoon in order to catch a goldfish for her fifth birthday, and the worm wiggled and lashed about against the green tint of his aviator sunglasses.

It was only a matter of time, her father said, sipping whiskey the color of his hair. The sheer boredom of watching a fish line dipping in the water developed in Ana a slow agonizing dread as powerful as drowsiness. Ana paddled her toes in the water until a cluster of children, a noisy, riotous group, piqued her curiosity, and she ran off to investigate.

The circle of children, faces she didn't recognize, names she didn't know, huddled close to the picnic bench in a secret circle. She stared up at one boy in awe of his audacity. Without the least bit of remorse, the boy yanked off the legs of a huge moth, its antennas flittering furiously. The others, like her, watched in astonishment. Then the boy answered a holler, and discarded the maimed insect, tossed it high into the pond and then ran to his picnic table, the others rushing close behind.

She had stared at the floppy set of wings and hoped the moth would flutter away, an ascension into heaven to sit on the right hand of God; but the moth simply wrapped its wings around itself like a shroud, causing a slight ripple in the water, its antennas falling limp and still. It began to float away, and Ana followed the moth's path, padding her feet on the mossy rim of the pond until it was carried away to some nearby dreg of fallen leaves. Struggling weakly, the insect tangled itself and then untangled itself and then drifted away, moving slowly, fusing in the ripples created by Ana's mother entering the pond.

Mother waded farther away from the rim of the pond and the ruffles of her swimsuit inflated like elongated balloons. She stretched her arms out as an invitation for Ana, who gladly accepted. Mother held her in the water and Ana's feet floated. There was no ground to touch; all the better. Who knew what was at the bottom of the public pond? Broken glass to prick your heel, grease to slip on. Satisfied to be buoyant, she looked down to see Mother's blurry feet, toes warping and rooting until Mother bent her knees gently and their two heads submerged underwater.

Hair expanded like wings above them, myopic eyes opened under slightly bruised water. Silvery minnows winnowing around her, Ana released a row of bubbles from between her lips, large pearls of glass rising, an amazement cut short by something floating into her mouth. She felt something trip on the rug of her tongue, perhaps the dead moth, perhaps a microscopic insect. Choking, Ana squeezed her head into her mother's belly, latched on to Mother's pregnant hips while something bristled in the deep end of her throat. The pond water had made Mother's toasted flesh rubbery and Ana pulled and scratched at her bathing suit straps until one of the straps unfastened. Ana finally swallowed and then thrust her head up to break out of the veil of malachite waters, gasping.

Little wonder she became frightened of calm seas or stormy rivers after the incident. Since then, bodies of water had created in Ana a terrific anxiety. Ana grew up to have many fears but none was as strong as her fear of water; her lungs had proven to deflate like defective life preservers, useless. She remembered swallowing whole mouthfuls, a paralyzing sensation, water spilling over the hauls of her open lips, sinking her downward. The moment embodied all of what was to come, her intuitive struggle against suffocation, all that she grew to mistrust especially in love because her mother had stood motionless, the incapable savior, her naked aureole so darkly purple her nipple resembled lava rock.

The sedan's battery was dulling and Ana felt her bursting anxiety about to dash her one remaining hope. She closed her eyes and breathed again, recovering the muscle memory of relaxation. The windshield wipers produced a squeak-and-squawk cadence, which accompanied the steady gale of rains. In the screen of her eyelids she imagined Tranquilina moving about the murky alley, her poncho wrapped around her.

The young hoods like those on Figueroa Street would never harass Tranquilina because they knew she was penniless. They would allow her to search inside a cardboard shelter or permit her to ask in her all-knowing voice, Have you seen a friend of mine?

She would hold a hand or two and speak kindly of Ben by saying He might cross the street instead of passing close to you.

The homeless women like the ones near the public library would recognize the respectful tone she used to inquire of Ben and their hands would pull at her poncho, kneel before her, kissing her black skirt, asking her repeatedly, Will the rain ever stop? Their sooty fingers clasping for a definite answer, each hand reaching to be saved.

When there are stars, Tranquilina might say, it'll stop raining.

Who ate my time? another would ask.

Cannibals, Tranquilina might answer.

Stay here, they would plead, stay with us.

God will never abandon you.

Ben would recognize the suction of Tranquilina's galoshes and watch her mythic figure. He would hear her asking the tecatos through their delirium of vomit and diluted heroin for a young scar-faced man in a voice stern and gentle, objective as water. And Ben would reach out to her from depths of the black ocean. He would say to his savior:

I am drowning.

FIFTEEN

Right before the first of two buses arrived to take Ermila away from Laguna Cliff, the weather pounded her with buckets of hail. Wet as the word "rain," her yellow sweater sagged over the contours of her thinness, making her look more bony and defenseless than she cared to convey to the listless bus driver. A jingle of coins dropped in the glass box, a punch-hole on a paper transfer delivered, Ermila swayed all the way to the back of the bus, shoes sloshing. She plopped on the long vinyl seat covering the grind of engine vents because, having experience riding the buses, Ermila knew the vents provided much-needed warmth for her ass and thighs.

As the bus jerked forward, strong heat blew out of the vents, warming her ankles. She pulled the edge of her sweater and wrung it, a small puddle spreading on the rubber flooring. Her jeans were plastered on her, cold compress on her thighs. The other passengers returned to their lethargic viewing out the window. A black man, cotton-haired, lobbed his head to and fro in committed sleep while a child relaxed his lumpy body beside him.

Ermila sat fuming, the kind of furious heat which emitted from the countless odometer miles accumulating on the overused, overheating bus engine. Nacho's constant attentions were fodder for her rage, and Alfonso, the big-time idiot, left her stranded at Laguna Cliff with barely enough in her wallet to make it back to the Eastside. As if she needed more heat, she began to list things like Chavela's reminder notes taped to the wall: **Jan,** one said, for fucking up Rini, and **Rini,** for not telling her mother. **YoYo,** for not being around to kick Jan's ass. **The war.** It took all the good ones away. Fucken **QA** culeros—enough said. And then Ermila rode it and rolled the long rush litany of angry, outrageous injustices: at her mother and father for dying and at being left behind with grandparents as backward as roots and at her grand-mother's dog biting her. And at the Fine Meats calendar, and the em-barrassed pigtailed girl in the Coppertone poster, and how about the fickle weather that rained and stormed and cleared up and hailed at such merciless moments as to happen right before the arrival of her first bus?

Ermila pulled back her cascade of wet hair and wrung out the wet and let her fury work its tumble dry magic. By the time the bus reached her midway point, a downtown bench in front of the botánica and Knight's Bail Bonds, it was after nine. Miserably damp, Ermila disembarked, fol-lowed by a bright-green-hot-pants-wearing woman, and the old black man who moments before slept enough for two people, and who stepped off the bus followed by the boy. The man and the boy vanished around the corner almost immediately but the lanky-limbed woman leaned a hip on the drugstore window and the Knight's Bail Bonds neon light flashed against her bare thighs. The woman fired up a cigarette between her pouting lips as if she were born to do this. Even with her tangerine nail polish on long nails and the ridiculously spiked heels, the woman looked as harmless as the bearded man did across the street. Relieved to have the spidery woman for company, Ermila nonetheless kept a nervous watch for the anticipated arrival of the 26 bus.

What you chicks looking at? the bearded man yelled.

Nothing, you prick! the spidery woman replied like guttural spit. Lifting her cigarette to her mouth and then blowing smoke, she didn't move from her spot near the neon light. Her tangerine nail polish matched the glowing ash at the end of her cigarette. In response, the bearded man ranted, waving a rag around as if he were shooing birds away. Ermila hoped the bus would arrive soon and watched a produce truck pass, a white lengthy limousine pass, and then two cars and a not-in-service Yellow Cab.

You don't get it, do you? the spidery woman asked Ermila.

What?

Don't you get it, maaannn? She chain-smoked, her smokes inside a Peruvian cloth bag.

Ermila nodded, feigning recognition, though she hadn't the faintest as to what the woman meant. She continued to keep a vigil. A bus that wasn't the 26 passed and then a wasted-looking woman who carried a bundle of clothes as if she had planned on visiting an all-night Laundromat stopped to the ask the spidery woman for a cigarette. The spidery woman replied her regrets and then pointed to the bearded man and said, I got the cigarette from that nice man. And the woman with her bundle crossed the street. No sooner had she arrived than she held a shouting match with the bearded man which was interrupted by the arrival of another bus that wasn't the 26, and the shouting ended with the woman throwing the bundle of clothes at him.

Too much, the spidery woman said, finding the whole scene very amusing. She used the end of her cigarette to light another cigarette and then smashed the butt under her menacing heel.

Ermila had noticed a car, a four-door vehicle with two passengers, passing a second, then a third time, and she began to harbor a profound desire to get home as soon as possible. What would Lollie do if a car were stalking her while she waited in the barest bone of streetlight? She crossed her arms defiantly and considered her options. There was a phone right across the street, next to the bearded man. She had already rehearsed the scene so many times where she told Big Al to fuck himself, she was convinced it had actually occurred and so didn't want to waste a dime calling him. The last resort was also the best. She would wait for the bus.

What do you want? the spidery woman shouted, and at first Ermila thought she was responding to the bearded man. However, something about the way she said it made Ermila guess this wasn't right. The car passed them in its fourth orbit, its turn signal blinking right. The spidery woman emerged from her silhouette and then turned to Ermila and poked her nest of hair; it was really a wig because it moved en masse when she scratched it with a fingernail.

They're bastard narcs on the cruise.

Narcs, Ermila replied innocently. What do you mean, narcs?

Narcotic cops, maaann, she said venomously, and then she stepped off the curb to flip the car off with her middle finger. The drizzle didn't have committed direction, shifting from one faint slant to another as the car drove under a lamppost, its windshield wipers sluggishly swiping. The two women in the car didn't look like cops, but then again, Ermila hadn't the slightest idea how narcotic cops were supposed to look. The taillights of the circling car dissolved into the fine mist. The spidery woman fixed her wig as if it were a hat, pulling it from right to left. She tip-tip-tipped back to the curb, her thin bow legs unstable, and continued:

What a fucking police state, maaann! She said the word "man" as if it were a hot, scorching iron pressed on linen. It's the MAN, maaann, don't you get it? Clearly frustrated by Ermila's naïveté, the woman savagely rummaged inside her Peruvian cloth purse until she pulled out a Marlboro pack. After lighting her own, she suddenly offered a cigarette to Ermila in a moment of forgiveness. Ermila said no, thank you, for reasons she wasn't quite sure.

After the spidery woman finished smoking one and lit another, she asked Ermila, What happened to you? She was sucking the cigarette contentedly. The tobacco perfume of the woman's Marlboros made Ermila's nose itch like Chavela's cigarettes and she had rubbed it with her bandaged hand the full time they waited.

It's a dog bite, Ermila replied.

Wild! the woman said as if the answer pleased her immensely. She approached Ermila and Ermila noticed the red pimples on her forehead, the old mascara crud in the corners of her eyes. She carried an aroma of stubborn tobacco like the kind that clung to motel walls, courtesy of Big Al; like the dead breath of junked refrigerators left on the curb for the taking. The woman picked off a yellow puff from Ermila's damp sweater. With her tangerine-polished pinchers she let the puff feather down and watched it until it reached the slick sidewalk.

Wet and wild, the spidery woman said. I dig it.

The bearded man sat on the bundle of clothes as if he were nestled in the down of Buddhist contemplation. He stroked one rope of his beard, a gesture that implied he wasn't thinking as much as plotting. Ermila's hope was that he wouldn't get it into his sesos to cross the street. The way he stared at her, as if she were a sugared marshmallow Easter chick, made Ermila lean closer to the struggling zaps of the Bail Bonds light. Determined to look hell-bent, Ermila uncrossed her arms and stared right back at him. Her indignation proved to be good armor against the chill of Broadway Boulevard.

As the drizzle turned a notch closer to rain, the bearded man held up a shirt to shield his head. If Lollie were here, what would she do? A bus transfer in her back pocket, Ermila pushed her damp mohair sleeves up and then pulled them down again and she resolved to protect herself, a notion that somehow never occurred to her so clearly as now. She attended a decision to lean firm and steady against the window with the neon sign like the spidery woman, fully aware of the MAN, her shoulders cooled by the slab of glass. She pushed her sleeves up in defiance until finally, finally, the massive pair of lumbering headlights of the number 26 moved toward her almost two hours later than scheduled.

Friday night and Whittier Boulevard, the cruising, happening place, was virtually deserted, compliments of the QA. Everyone either stayed home (fat chance) or found a whole other party to go to because these stubborn QA culeros were unyielding in upholding safety. Fifteen, count them, fifteen officers worked the checkpoint, twelve of them leaning on the orange and green trucks sipping hot coffee, chatting and chilling, grazing in the grass, so to speak. They seemed to have multiplied from yesterday, from the day before, looking official enough to intimidate those who hadn't had run-ins with them before.

They bulked, all of them, not from the muscle of workouts or academy-regulated exercise but from the loads of cartridges and pistols they carried in their waistbands, plump with the weight of batons and flashlights, choke chains, handcuffs and Mace spray. They made noise whenever they moved. Their leather creaked and their nostrils whistled and their lips quaffed hot coffee. Their walkie-talkies spit and spewed and they sneezed, laughed and exchanged anecdotal gossip about stubborn inhabitants and hick wetbacks, illegal aliens caught in the process of interrogation. They considered themselves protectors of lives, procurers of security, guardian angels of the quarantine, and five of them managed the rows of vehicles while six of them held up flashlights as thick as pipes, spotlighting the queue of people who looked just as haggard and distressed as Ermila.

Just over the heads of the forty-eight people in front of her, forty-nine if you counted the sniveling child in his mother's embrace, was Grandmother's porch on First Street, the five steps leading up to the door, the door which opened to the hallway and which led to the fullest moon of her warm, dry bed. She seemed as close to her bed as the scent of pomade belonging to the man in front of her. Before tonight, escaping Grandmother's constant tallying of wrongdoings had become Ermila's main goal in life; but now everything around her somersaulted upside down and Ermila's one desire was to get home as soon as possible. This new-sprung feeling arrived as much as a surprise to Ermila as her disappointment in having to wait yet again, and she stood in line shivering. The curfew provided one more bitter screw that twisted in her skull, and waiting once again became as unbearably nasty as the toddler in his mother's arms.

The line of waiting people hadn't moved an inch.

Hey, what's the holdup? Ermila blurted out. We all wanna get home! The neighbors who stood in front of her turned from their quiet conversations because she said it loudly, flippantly, a rabble-rouser stirring trouble, and suddenly they had opinions and whispered between themselves. Then several heads turned to see the reaction of the nearest QA officer. If the officer heard, he showed no sign of it and he hooked a finger to let a man through. The toddler began to cry in his mother's arms, a fatigued exasperated complaining sob and his mother tried to soothe the child. One stocky officer walked over to Ermila, wheezing and creaking, and the neighbors followed the noise with their eyes. They unconsciously separated themselves from Ermila.

The officer was an oldish man with grayish sideburns and his nametag read **Ulysses Rodriguez.** He was dark-skinned like Grandmother, the color of cocoa, and Rodriguez's arms busted out of his orange vest, engorged with the fat of authority. He chewed an imaginary cigar.

Say what, now? Rodriguez challenged, and he leaned on one black-tipped boot. The wailing of the child reached such a pitch it was enough to make anyone edgy. Once or twice the child choked on his own sobs, and he struggled to breathe, as if the wind got knocked out of him. His mother kept bouncing him harder and harder until he let out another wail, harsh and phlegmy.

Someone want to complain to me, he said, not as a question but a statement.

Okay, Ermila replied, a weak tremor in her voice. I wanna get home, okay? The neighbors in front of her and the others behind her nodded tentatively. Ermila shivered, her mohair sweater holding in the day's entire dampness, but she was too exhausted and too giddy to stay silent.

Rodriguez wasn't tall but he was muscular, and when he hooked his thumb on a belt loop near his holster, his biceps bulged tight against his uniform short sleeve. His leather belt spoke as his stomach muscles contracted.

He fingered Ermila out from the line of people. ID, he ordered. Rodriguez's gaze followed her bandaged hand as she pulled out her wallet from her back pocket. He studied the card for several seconds, studied her face and then studied the card photo again. Having been through the wash, the ID looked worn. She tucked her bitten hand into her back denim pocket hoping he wouldn't ask about the injury.

You think I like to do this? Rodriguez asked.

I don't know, Ermila replied.

You think I like this job?

You don't look miserable, whispered one of the neighbors, and another guffawed and then cleared his voice.

The scrutiny added to her weariness. This was the end of the line. Hold back. Self-preservation kept pulsing in Ermila's head. Shad-up, she instructed herself, don't say another word. The child was whimpering, pausing to gather another lungful. It occurred to Ermila that the child might be ill.

You think you're doing me a favor? he continued, eyeballing her in a straightforward, you-can't-get-away-from-me-now glare. You think rabies is a good thing?

Ermila responded with absolute silence. Rodriguez scratched his chest as if he debated what to do next and the leather of his belt whined. He glanced at his watch.

You're in violation of curfew.

Ermila was about to respond when Rodriguez raised his palm as if to halt her from speaking. Now, before you talk—he paused and inhaled—think about it.

I had to work overtime.

Come on, Rodriguez said, holding the corners of the ID with his thumbs. Give me something better than that.

Having trouble, Uly? one of the officers asked.

Nothing I can't handle, Rodriguez shouted back to his coffee-sipping colleague. Now, come on, honey, I don't want to hear lies.

Why would I lie? Ermila continued. And in sheer boldness, she blurted, call the Salas Used Cars dealership if you want.

Who, now?

Ermila felt dizzy with the exactitude of his pinpoint starch-ironed white shirt. She bowed her head hoping Rodriguez wouldn't notice her deceit. Why did they have the need to fuck with people? she thought. Why can't they leave us alone? Rodriguez flapped his ear with a finger.

Who did you say?

Salas.

By God, that crook still in business?

Yea, Ermila said, relieved that his attention shifted from the interrogation, and then not so relieved that Rodriguez seemed to recognize the name. She tried sounding neutral when she added, Yea. He's my boss. Mr. Salas.

Unbelievable. Salas? Rodriguez laughed while thumbing the corner of her worn identification card to see if the lamination was fraudulent. I bought my first junker from him. He smiled the smile of a man who might have just come upon his own yearbook photograph twenty years later. Rodriguez sighed deeply with middle-age nostalgia. The pits of his wrinkly eyes softened in memory. Yes. Cream-white, bucket seats, AM/FM radio . . . a real piece of work, but I loved that Mustang. The neighbors nodded in commiseration. Before returning the card, Rodriguez flipped it over to see if any alterations had been done. Satisfied, he pointed beyond the wooden roadblock, clearing her up to go. Get moving, he told her. And tell Salas there's a curfew in effect.

Okay.

He'll get a hefty fine.

I'll tell him.

About to sprint toward her house, Ermila heard the child once again burst into grueling sobs. The violent chaos of an unknown sickness rattled in his throat. One moment the child was whiny and complaining, the next moment he let out a wail of rocking bronchitis which caused him to struggle for breath.

Let her go, Ermila said, pulling up her sleeves and pointing to the mother. The ill child rested his head on the crescent of his mother's neck in resignation, a thumb between his lips. His eyes and nose were mucusy. I'll wait my turn like everybody else.

Go ahead and wait, then, Rodriguez said.

What's the holdup? a colleague shouted.

Lay off, Rodriguez shouted back.

He directed the mother out of the line as if he were directing traffic. The mother quickly complied and Rodriguez checked her papers, and then checked the child's papers, and then the mother rushed off. The leather of Rodriguez's thick-soled shoes creaked with its own wheezing infection as he returned to the head of the checkout point. The strips of fluorescent yellow on the back of his orange vest seesawed up and down. Ermila watched the child, who laid his crimson cheek over his mother's bumpy shoulder and sucked the thumb of one hand while the other flopped round her neck. Ermila's fingers waved good-bye before the child closed his eyes.

Ermila ran the remaining blocks and soon discovered, as she stopped to catch her breath, that Grandmother had left the porch light on. She saw it from the corner of the street and the faint yellow bulb seemed to stretch across the starless night. A gold tooth in the solemn mouth of midnight, a reminder of this day thankfully coming to an end.

Nacho's junker was parked in front of the house and Ermila hadn't noticed that the back door of the van dangled like a thirsty dog's tongue until she got close enough to inspect it under the lamppost light. Inside the van, Nacho had begun to pack his belongings. Three boxes wrapped in string, and a cluster of cardboard tubes that Ermila guessed contained his sketches, though she had never requested to see them. His abrupt decision to leave unsettled her and it was partly out of this resentment that she didn't offer to help him.

He dragged his huge trunk out of Grandpa's toolshed and was pulling it across the lawn, its stubborn weight halting in short stops on the lawn. He seemed not at all surprised to see Ermila standing near the rear door of his van and he asked with a grunt, You can help a little? Nacho hadn't realized that the yellow sweater she wore had a row of brassy buttons until now. They glinted under the vague lamppost light.

I'm damaged, Ermila said, lifting her filthy bandaged hand, but had a change of heart when she saw that Nacho continued to trudge the trunk across the thick pad of lawn. Using her good hand, she grasped the second handle of the trunk and was only able to lift it up a few inches from the grass. This lack of muscle seemed charming to Nacho.

Do you got a dead body in here? The weight of the large suitcase, the poundage, strained her shoulder. Nacho sprung a smile.

Be a strong man.

Fuck you, Ignacio.

You can do it?

Ermila nodded affirmatively. On the count of three . . .

And the two heaved the trunk onto the bumper and then they pushed it with united force into the van like a coffin into a funeral hearse. Nacho slapped his hands together. After giving pause, he rerolled a strip of canvas and tucked the roll in between the trunk and spare flat tire. He looked around. Nothing left behind; nothing else to pack. He shut the back door and secured it with another piece of wire.

Now you gonna tell me what you're up to?

Like?

Why you going so fast?

Ah, he said. So that was what she meant. He replied, The bus goes . . . Nacho pressed his lips in search of the translated word and then it came to him: It goes in two-thirty. For his traveling, he had changed from his torn T-shirt and jeans into a presentable cotton white shirt which he wore untucked, a pair of black loafers and for once he didn't lean on the balls of his feet. Except for a wisp of hair on his forehead, his hair was palm-greased and combed smooth.

Did Grandma let you go?

Sure.

Nacho fixed his renegade wisp. He surveyed the area to make sure nothing was forgotten. The bruises on his cheek rose into welts, and he pulled his face away from her touch.

Why do you have to go now? she asked.

Why I need to stay so long?

Under the lamppost the two turned toward the helicopter in pursuit. Nacho caught a flash of metal screeching on Eastern Street and he thought how these gangs of cholos made it worse for everyone in the Eastside. He could easily live without all of this. He was glad to say good riddance to the helicopters popping bullets like corks; adiós to the concrete and cars, hasta la vista to the cholos, and mostly good-bye to those enormous disturbances of the heart.

As for Ermila, she turned to see if she recognized the car chased by the beams of the helicopter and wondered about Big Al. He was never the pursuer, but always the one being pursued.

Bueno, Nacho said, prayerlike. He stared at her chest expanding against her buttons and then caught himself and he felt her gaze against his cheek almost as if it were a sharp press of her palm. In instantaneous shame, Nacho realized that his folly at Laguna Cliff was his outright thievery. He tried to steal a kiss. A lesson learned but not well enough to halt the want of kissing her, to give her a gentle kiss on the corner of her tender lips, just this one and only time. To say good-bye.

Ermila, Nacho said, stretching his nostrils, can I give me a kiss?

What? Ermila asked, confused.

Everyone had warned Nacho. He had made a major mistake at not having persevered in his ESL class. How stupid he felt and yet he wanted to bust out in laughter. He repeated his question to himself incredulously, Can I give *me* a kiss? Me? And then he thought, Híjole! The spell of the so long, the imagined scene of farewell, the final bon voyage, was broken like a stone disrupting still, moonlit waters. It only worked in fotonovelas, pendejo!

He looked down at his too-tight loafers, but this time only for a moment, and then he looked straight at her, then at the porch of a house that wasn't his home, and he smiled from ear to ear. He smacked a few kisses on his fingertips in jest and blew them to her and before Ermila could say another word, he was sitting behind his steering wheel.

This time the van didn't need coaxing. One try and the engine ignited promptly. Ermila remained under the lamppost and watched as Nacho ground the gears to shift from first to second into a metal-crunching third. In the side mirror, she saw him wave good-bye to her, sweetly, lovingly, just as she had done with the sick child at the roadblock. Then the rickety van turned left on Eastern and vanished.

Ermila looked into the gray traces of van exhaust to find the shapes of things missing. Who was it that told her everything went up into thin air but never quite disappeared? Something always remained behind, like the photograph of her parents, like the formidable mass of oil on the asphalt where the van had once been parked. Ermila wiped her nose with her gauzed hand and then turned her back to First Street. She crossed the thick slab of lawn to the porch.

As long as she could remember, Ermila had dreaded the accusation of possessing too much of her mother's blood. Now she realized as she pulled her key chain from her pocket that she hadn't possessed enough. Her mother had been brave; her mother had fled into the night unafraid to leave a place of locked doors and police chases and quarantines and all the other things that made her desperate to escape.

Ermila pushed in the key to unlock the bolt.

The doorjamb released the lock and darkness spilled from the hallway into the lit porch. What would it cost her, what would she have to sacrifice, what hearts including her own would she have to break, Ermila soberly asked, in order to have her mother's courage to leave the very house she so willfully chose to enter? The door slowly cracked opened and from where she stood, Ermila noticed Grandmother's vague shadowy figure on the couch stirring from the noise of the prolonged and squeaky hinges. As usual, Grandmother was waiting up for her, and though Ermila swallowed, she was not prepared for what was to come.

Inez? Inez? her grandmother quizzed from the silent obscurity. ¿Eres tú, mijita? A tone as tiny as a cumbersome pebble rattling in an empty shoebox, a baby-shoe-small voice filled simultaneously with relief and anger. Shrouded in nightmarish confusion, Grandmother had uttered the mistake and Ermila suddenly felt the rushed transfusion of disappointment. How she wished she were someone her grandmother wanted her to be.

It's me, Ermila whispered sadly. The sudden blast of loud explosive laughter slapdashed the dark walls of the hallway, a wicked laughter, alive and rudely beautiful, and the racket splashed Ermila as she stood under the threshold of the door. As loud and constant and noisy as the long squeal of the front door's rusty hinges, her mother's laughter no longer spilled like ink from the photograph which hung in her bedroom, but arrived from the hungry belly of Grandmother's strongest desire.

SIXTEEN

The police report filed on Sunday morning after the incident read: Reliable informant Mr. Edward Janson a.k.a. Jan reported vehicle vandalism and cited possible gang retaliation activity between Lote Maravilla and rival gang McBride Boys. Air Patrol proceeded after Quarantine A. [*sic*] clearance to investigate suspect Santos Bermudes a.k.a. Saint believed to be armed and dangerous, in metallic peach-colored Pontiac Bonneville, California license plate UVN 456, rear window damaged; suspect rendezvoused with Antonio Gamboa a.k.a. Turtle at 23:07 hours, corner of City Terrace/Eastern. The two suspects' known gang affiliation of McBride evaded investigation and proceeded down Eastern at 117 mph, ran red light on Floral and Easten [*sic*], entered freeway Pomona 60 at 23:16 hours, eastbound, Third Street entrance. Radio contact to Highway Patrol overridden by report of collision with alleged fatalities off 101 N. Sunset Blvd. exit. Thereby forced to abandon pursuit at 23:25 hours. Reported and signed by . . .

Adrenaline pumped the chambers of Santos's heart just like the fuel pumped into the Pontiac's eight-cylinder 303-horsepower engine. The chase was on until the stunning white jets of spotlights suddenly lifted up and pulled away, a miracle, and, like anything close to miraculous, Santos found it hard to believe.

It's a fucken trick, Santos yelled over the roar of the engine. They just offed the lights. They done it before. The rosary that hung from his rearview mirror banged against the dash as Santos navigated the swerving acceleration of the Pontiac on the freeway, tight-fisting with his leathered palms the metal chain of steering wheel. Turtle rolled down the window and stuck her head out to make sure this disappearance wasn't a cop trick.

Cause for celebration, she whooped and screamed in delight and inhaled the icy air of victory. Astonished, Turtle rolled the window up. Can you fucken believe it? she asked again and again, rocking.

It's a fucken trick.

I tell you, they split.

Santos didn't ease on the gas pedal until he was absolutely sure, and he finally slowed down to sixty-five and then checked the gas gauge, just in case. He steered the Pontiac onto the Beverly Boulevard exit.

Easy, easy, Turtle said, rocking back and forth.

Santos let the shock cruise out of his lungs. This called for a high-five hand slam at the intersection.

This baby is the sweetest, Santos said, stroking the Pontiac's dashboard. It cost me my left ball, but it pays to have four pumps on the cylinders.

Can you believe it?

Que rifa McBride.

Que rifa!

Santos's gloating unrestrained, he cruised the Pontiac down the boulevard. The words to tell and retell the story were already crackling in his head, a story worth telling for a thousand and one nights. Best yet, Santos had a witness, a collaborator. Santos couldn't believe his luck, and he punched his partner on her leather sleeve. Turtle responded by yanking Santos's wool beanie and then whirled it around her finger like a party favor. It was all too unreal and Santos turned the volume loud to blast the speakers, to let Little Willie G. announce their badASSness.

Lookit! Turtle said in disbelief. She pointed to the back window. The duct tape didn't even come off!

McBride controla!

¿Y qué?

Turtle side-ached from laughing. La vida loca! Too much, this was all too sweet, and she slowly relaxed her body on the biscuit-tuck passenger seat. She yawned and thought an hour of cruising wouldn't hurt; maybe two hours tops to glow in the sweetness of feeling good for once. No problem to keep awake for three or more hours after that because tonight could be clangorous with strange opportunities.

Bored with the music of Thee Midnighters, Santos ejected the eight-track and tossed it in the backseat, then reached over to the glove compartment. The door dropped and hit Turtle's knees (watcha your right knee, your left knee, your weenie), and then Santos pulled out another cartridge, too agitated to keep calm, his pleasure too huge to contain inside the car. He inserted his trustworthy favorite tape of all time (no lie) into the eight-track and thumbed the bass volume.

Man oh man, Turtle thought. Not the cowboy.

But it was. A Gene Autry track, Santos's mother's favorite, and he played it only when he felt surreal like he was feeling now. Autry's fuzzed, whiny voice sang while Santos's palms kept a beat against the steering wheel. *Out there, where a friend is a friend.* Turtle didn't care much for Santos's selection of music, but music was a sacred thing, and she had simply to stomach the cowboy twang, the back-in-the-saddle bullshit, because people like Turtle who knew Santos knew not to mess with his mother's favorite all-time singer.

Jack down the windows, Santos instructed.

I'm iced.

No offense, homes, but you stink like my nalgas.

Nah, carnal, YOU stink like ass.

Santos yelped a grito and then laughed as Autry continued his chorus. I love, I mean I love this part, Santos said, turning the volume to maximum: *Where the longhorn cattle feed, on the lonely jimsonweed, I'm back in the saddle again.* Santos inhaled his dominance of the boulevard. Tucked away under the visor mirror was a skinny marijuana joint laced with PCP. Santos bit his glove off to pull out the joint he had been saving for a special occasion and handed it to Turtle, who now rode shotgun as if she knew nothing else.

My jimsonweed.

What is it?

Angel wings, ésa.

I'm ready for takeoff, Turtle added without hesitation. She ignited the joint, small ash flaking, and then she deeply inhaled. The warm fume of marijuana thawed her lungs. Her face burned like a first snort of cheap whiskey down the throat, and the gruff shock forced a succession of coughs. Turtle hadn't remembered feeling this spirited in such a long time. She howled and then sniffed the air, breathing in all this refreshing bedazzled good fortune.

Santos pinched the joint from Turtle's fingers while he joined in the Autry refrain: *Riding the range once more, totin' my old forty-four, where you sleep out every night, and the only law is right, back in the saddle again.* The track played on, clicking noisily to the next song. Turtle was afraid the song would stay in her head. She gingerly turned down the volume as they continued to smoke the joint until the roach end burned her chapped lips.

Autry, Turtle thought, her head fogging up with gathering cottony clouds, wasn't all that bad.

They cruised outside of the QA roadblocks, detouring up and down Spencer Street where Santos's ex-girlfriend Hilda lived. Santos turned onto the side streets where porch lights glowed like halos of silver and where people slept behind drawn curtains, minding their own business. After some cruising, Santos felt bored and restless and more than angry that Hilda wasn't home.

Where could she be?

She crashed your car, ése, Turtle reminded.

Yea, but where's the bitch now?

Who cares?

Where to? Santos asked.

Forget 'bout Big Al, ése.

Then where to? Santos was impulsive, a big minus to Turtle.

¿Qué traes?

I asked you, where to?

Fuck off.

Where to, pussy? The two remained silent while Autry sang "You Are My Sunshine."

Finally Turtle said, or thought she said, The falls. Let's hit the falls.

Santos cruised easy on his Goodyear whitewalls, obeying the speed limits all the way to Monterey Park. He turned down the music, the moment souring, and rode the side streets, driving past the white framed houses up on the hills, lovely Southern California spreads with long rolling lawns and hedges trimmed in perfect rectangles like movie sets. Off of shortened El Porte Street, the two reached Cascade Waterfalls, a turquoise and exotic man-made pyramid staircase built on the side of a hill.

Years ago the water cascades and lights and Roman-columned balcony had spawned a generation of lovers who parked at its base. Grapefruit-sized lightbulbs had bordered the stairs and by nightfall the lightbulbs would imbue the water with a deeper aura of melted glass. The last tier flowed silvery, and a couple might get out of their car and sit on the tiled rim and then a young man might splinter the reflection of his beloved in the mirroring water just by touching it.

Now the falls had been shut off to repair a pump piston, which apparently took years to order from the city to the county, from the Department of Recreation to the Department of City Facilities, and the utter absence of burbling water gave the falls an emptiness. The falls had fallen into disregard and disrepair, and lichens and spray-painted graffiti, including a few placazos belonging to the McBride Boys, were splattered everywhere on the flaking turquoise concrete. It was anyone's guess when the falls would be returned to their once-glamorous state.

Santos parked under a row of eucalyptus trees to shield the car from sky surveillance and had second thoughts about the risk factor. It pained him to leave his ride, his only beloved, under a tunnel of raggedy trees. Once dried, bird shit was lumpy and difficult to remove, and it would ruin, completely ruin the metallic paint of his Pontiac. Even before he turned the ignition off, Santos asked Turtle if birds crap at night, but the shotgun seat was already vacant, and Turtle was already three-stepping up to the balcony, to the apex of the pyramid.

Turtle reached the balcony in zip time. She didn't even feel the concrete steps under her, her sneakers bouncing, leaping into thin air. Standing between the column replicas, Turtle admired the lights of the nearby hillsides and waited for her heart to quit beating. She whistled and when Santos turned, she waved at him, her cloudy breath misty before her.

The first time she had come to the waterfalls, Tío Angel had brought her. The falls cascaded in full glory, breathtaking and unreal. He had bought her a Coca-Cola, and told her she didn't have to share it with anyone, and even then she was too awestruck by the falls to sip.

Tío Angel had parked in the approximate area where lovers might have parked; where Santos was bending over, burning a match for light, his head buried in the Pontiac trunk to retrieve the .38-caliber ammunition for the .357 Magnum revolver he had hidden under the spare tire. As the years passed and the water pump broke and the purchase order for the pump piston was lost, the lush growth of trees began to overlap the sidewalk and so Turtle could barely see Santos's matchstick flickering through the leafy branches of the trees where Tío Angel had once parked his Ford.

In her memory of a memory, Turtle began to hear the slippage of the falls. She saw herself getting out of Tío's car and dipping her fingers into the water and the water falling, falling water, and then she drank from her privately owned bottle of soda. Chlorine-scented and pristine-polished, the falls cascaded down and then down and then down again. The border of wavering lights had glittered like a sleek serpent. Tío Angel had purchased a bottle of Coca-Cola then and she drank it then, the sinful drink then, the falls like glass then. Turtle saw her young self then, her face bouncing back then, surfacing then, falling back then, to the bottom then, and back again.

The family, Big Al's family—he was Alfonso, to his mother—had lived in the small house on McBride Street for twelve years and when they first bought the house, Alfonso, who was no more than six or seven at the time of mortgage-signing, had stood beside his father to watch the people across the street eating at El Rey's Tacos. Under the protecting overleaf of the porch, father and son had enjoyed the restaurant's mascot, the neon-flashing burro, its tilted sombrero hovering over its lazy eyes, a colorfully lit serape for a saddle blanket. This was their television—his father and Alfonso entertained by the flashing of the burro, of people congregating around their tacos, before his father lost the first of many jobs.

Shortly after they moved into the house on McBride Street, Alfonso's mother had bought a new couch on a two-year layaway plan from a man who owned Howard's Furniture on Whittier Boulevard. Mr. Howard's tenacity to stay on Whittier Boulevard, while the other Anglo shop owners began to flee, was more of a testament to his drinking, as some have argued, than his loyalty to a small group of working women who paid on installments, reliably, religiously, their bimonthly payments. His small shop was squeezed in between Leeds Shoe Store and the Candy Cane Baby Clothes Store, and the same items, a telephone stand, a rocker, a magazine rack, always remained on display in the window. Regardless of what they said about his drinking or fondness for Mexican women, Mr. Howard kept many a house in the Eastside furnished and there soon came a time when Alfonso's mother had the couch delivered to McBride Street.

His father refused to toss out the old couch because he was never good with changes. The day the new couch came, Alfonso and his father took the old one and moved it to the porch. While his mother worked very hard to pay the mortgage (in the garment district downtown, and then on Saturdays cleaning the bottoms of childlike old men at the Little Brothers of the Poor), his father had worked very hard in making the couch accustomed to flexing its seat cushions to his moods. Though the springs pricked the seat of Alfonso's pants, and the cushions sagged and clumped hard in places, his father always found purpose with throwaways, and he placed the supple couch on the porch, where he sat almost every Friday afternoon before he changed jobs yet again.

Years had passed and nothing had changed. His father's chronic employment failures continued until one day his father left to pay the water bill and then called his son from somewhere and said he would be home in a week, leaving behind a yard full of throwaways. Alfonso waited three years. They got to not talking about his father, his mother and he, and like things that were endlessly repeated, the silence surrounding the subject of his father became a ritual, a routine. His mother's constant rise to meet the demands of two jobs continued to cause her absence from Alfonso's life.

Never changing, the old couch remained on the porch while his mother's new couch was still cloaked in the warehouse plastic protector. Except for the holidays when someone would replace the burro's sombrero with a Santa's hat for Christmas, or cover the long muzzle with a Zorro mask for Halloween, the burro's lengthy flop of ears remained the same. Streets remained dead-ended, schools remained disputed territories and all of it left Alfonso with a sense of want so hollow, there was plenty of space for many things except happiness. Nothing ever changed on McBride Street.

The head principal of Belvedere Junior High described Alfonso as "incorrigible." The last straw was the last draw. Alfonso had hated Mr. Fango, who taught seventh-grade mechanical drawing, or Mr. Fango hated him. Either way, the animosity had exploded on one hot and humid California spring day, which was no different than a hot California summer day in the basement of an earthquake-damaged building.

The young boy and older man began to tussle—over what, none of the witnesses were sure. The other boys (only boys were assigned to drafting classes) shouted for help, a looter's screaming, unconstrained and gathering strength from the sheer unleashed excitement of disbelief. They saw everything but nonetheless were confused: half of the boys saw Mr. Fango throttle Alfonso's neck with his two drafting hands, blotches of perspiration on the thin spine of his shirt back, while the others witnessed Alfonso throttling Mr. Fango right above his tie knot. Whatever the story, both teacher and student became a two-headed monster choking one another until they salivated, until their faces were beet-red.

Despite bloodcurdling screams earlier, the students remained silent during the inquiry that followed, never trusting any school official enough, much less the head principal, who, they felt, hated every last one of them. Alfonso was taken to a room—to cool his heels—where, wouldn't you know it (and you wouldn't, because the principal had elected not to include this in his file), Alfonso began to sob. The badass nowhere boy folded his arms to shield the tears of vulnerability, of bewilderment, of, let's say it, fright, as the head principal sat across from him filling out forms for suspension.

Alfonso spent the next seven years trying to live down that humiliation. Never, ever let someone see you scared. Mr. Fango was transferred to another school and somehow no one missed the fact that Alfonso stopped coming to school after his suspension was over. At first, when the Caltrans people unfurled the freeways, he had whole abandoned blocks to get lost in. But after the freeways were completed, Alfonso opted to sit on his father's couch the greater part of the day. He invited his McBride Boys to couch with him. That's the way the word took on meaning.

Couch it at Alfonso's on McBride, someone would say, or Let's get couched at Big Al's. Dead-end safe, burro-endorsed, his empty house empty from dawn to dusk. And so Lucho Libre came next, and then Luis Lil Lizard and Palo, and then Santos, who babysat his baby brother PeeWee, and then Turtle and a dozen other boys with a dozen other nicknames, and all were invited to sit on the couch abandoned by Alfonso's father. All wanted either to live up to their badass-nowhere status or live down some stabbing humiliation.

We're couched in it, Lucho Libre summarized, which meant to the homeboys within earshot, We're up to our necks in this one. To be couched in it meant McBride Boy action had to be taken. No other option was available, especially when one of them had been assaulted, humiliated and especially when it happened to Alfonso. They had been waiting for Santos to deliver the cuete and while they waited, Lucho Libre, PeeWee and Palo dropped newly bought Quaaludes and washed them down with swigs of discount whiskey. With the exception of Alfonso, the boys sat slumped in a stupor buzz, heads heavy, eyes the color of red gel. Alfonso was already numb with agitation, hopped up on revenge. His knuckles bled broken skin; traces of red crust dried around his nostrils, a cheek swollen and purple. He breathed through his mouth, his lip fiery thick.

He searched for Saint's Pontiac. That homeboy needed to learn a lesson on promptness—no more couch room for Santos. Alfonso promised to bust Saint's balls, knee his fucken pretty face. And to show how he was gonna de-couch Santos, Alfonso slammed his shoulders against the railing until the old wood cracked, until his neck and shoulder bruised like a space picture of the cosmos.

¿Qué traes? Lucho Libre asked. He sat on the lumpy couch with Palo and PeeWee. Sometimes Lucho thought that Big Al overdid it, became a hysterical pussy, always ranting, always wanting his own way. He lit a cigarette and sucked hard. But he never told Alfonso how he felt, nor would he. It wasn't about guts, having the guts to tell Big Al to go fuck himself, it was about . . . it was about . . .

The best part of getting couched was not having to think, and Lucho didn't want to ruin the buzz by doing so much of it, and so he lifted the bottle of Southern Comfort and gulped to quench a hum-drum thirst. His eyelids heavy weights but by no means shut, Lucho studied the space where Alfonso had transfixed his gaze. Alfonso stared beyond the **Dead End** sign and beyond the dull, expressionless snout of the burro. All they had between them and the enemy world was each other, and right this moment, this was the best that life could offer. Lucho burped and then relaxed and flicked the last of his cigarette over the railing.

Does your brother have the cuete? Alfonso asked PeeWee. Seconds passed before PeeWee registered the question, the comment directed at him in piercing bravado. Unnaturally knotty, the youth's Adam's apple shifted with a gulp. Lucho yawned in boredom with Alfonso's rants, his locura, his acting-out pussy style. He couldn't believe he was picking on PeeWee, little PeeWee, who was ten, maybe. Lucho was disgusted at Big Al's bony ass picking on a kid.

Sí-mon! PeeWee replied, his mouth dried and thorny as tumbleweed. He looked down at the pair of gray sneakers washed way too often. PeeWee believed in Santos, his older brother, his carnal, his blood, his hero. Of course! No doubt that Santos had the weapon. Stupid of Alfonso to ask.

Sí-mon que sí!

You sure? Alfonso didn't want to hear lies. This was a matter of life and death, and there was no room for lies between them. Er? But before PeeWee answered, Big Al slapped him across the side of his crew cut.

If Saint has the cuete, where is he?

I dunno, PeeWee whined, rubbing behind his ear.

Where is he?

I dunno! Alfonso's bulky ring, the one his mother purchased on installments, felt like a bullet when he slapped PeeWee's head. PeeWee held back and rubbed behind his ear, wounded.

Is Saint here or not, you fucken puto?

¿Qué traes, carnal? This from Palo, who sat between Lucho Libre and PeeWee on the old couch, and he grabbed the bottle from Lucho and took a long scorching gulp of Southern Comfort.

Yea, man, PeeWee agreed, pouting. What's wrong with you?

Ca-ca-cál-ma-te, Lucho Libre added.

Palo sluggishly brushed away the cinder ash of a joint that scattered and burned black pinholes on his T-shirt. He was a tall twig of a boy, and second in command after Luis Lil Lizard. He enjoyed such a strong buzz, he refused to get up from the couch to pacify Big Al. Palo blinked, and he swore his blink lasted an hour.

Santos is un camarada de aquellas, ése. You knowed that.

Yea, ése, PeeWee breathed. Cheeze.

Qué pinche jodida, Big Al declared and then slammed his palm on the loose porch rail. Santos was a fuckup, a big-time motherfucker, just like the other motherfuckers he was hanging with. His mother said that he was headed for doom because of these dead-end friends, street orphans she called them, and she made him promise to attend vocational school at the Job Corps classes downtown. He registered for upholstery training and showed his registration slip to his mother to get her off his back.

His mother slept in the side room with a wound-up alarm clock that ticked until it exploded every morning at three-forty-five. And he resented that she had to work so arduously day in and day out, without much to show for it except for this sorry-ass house across from the burro's observant expression and for her new couch, its colors splotched with the ugliest patterns of red roses he had ever seen. Her love for this furniture piece, her pride and joy, was probably where she got the idea that Alfonso should attend vocational school for upholstery. Alfonso's mother had kissed his cheek when he showed her the registration card. But she really had to be crazy to think he was gonna waste away doing stuffing and ripping and sewing someone's else's ass cushions when there was much better ready cash available out there beyond the borders of the throwaways.

Lucho offered the yesca joint and Alfonso puffed. A few cars drove in the small parking lot and parked and the passengers headed for El Rey's. After clubbing on a Friday night, the women slipped off their heels as the men swaggered toward the restaurant. Over the bent chain link fence, the boys watched the dating couples eating at the taquería tables, the burro's sombrero neon flashing on and off above its goofy ears. Maybe hours or maybe minutes elapsed.

How's the training class? Palo asked, as if he were Alfonso's father asking How was school? Alfonso would have let the stupid comment roll down like water off a duck's back, but Lucho, fucken Lucho got into it with:

Yea, man, upholster any new ca-ca-couches?

PeeWee didn't know better and chimed in, What 'bout fixin' this one? And he pulled out some cotton fuzz from Alfonso's father's old couch cushions. Palo began to quake into erupting laughter. On the dumpy couch, three pairs of shoulders shook with hilarity.

So I'm a joke? Alfonso asked, standing right in front of Lucho. He considered Lucho's thick wavy hair. Lucho barely moved except for a slow smirk on his lips, and he tilted his head because the tone from Alfonso sounded like an unmistakable challenge.

So I'm a payaso? Alfonso poked a finger into Lucho's ham arm. PeeWee dropped his laughter, averted his glance to his sneakers while Lucho narrowed his eyes. Lucho's lips became a straight flat line as he spread his thighs, pushed in the prickly rusted springs that came through the cushions and escaped between his legs.

'Tás loco ya madre, homes, Palo interceded. We're just riding you, that's all.

Stay outta this.

Just taking the edge off things, tú sabes.

Lucho realized he was chewing his tongue, his jaw muscles grinding his teeth, chewing full force. Got a-ah-ah-ah PROBlem? he managed to ask, his jaws not wanting to let the words go.

Chúpame! Big Al cupped his own crotch, gesturing his balls, and said, Vamos, you fucken joto. That's all Lucho needed and he leaped from where he sat. PeeWee jumped and bolted for the farthest end of the porch. Annoyed, Palo stood. He hated breaking up his perfectly fine-tuned high but had to, to deal with Big Al's locura.

Massive drum thighs apart, Lucho posed in an intimidating stance ready to pounce on the much smarter Big Al. Not doing something about the insult was unthinkable. If only Big Al would swallow that nasty smirk off his face, Lucho could sit down and get back to not thinking and relax his fists, which were strong enough to crush Brazil nuts bare-handed. He raised a palm around Alfonso's neck and then tenderly kneaded the brittle back of his friend's shaved head.

Say you're sorry, Lucho said, almost pleading.

Big Al returned his request with silence. Palo spoke, his voice arriving from far away, unintelligible. Lucho continued massaging Al's neck, and the sense of violent arousal a moment ago now landed on his lips like a picante, which made it more difficult to resist pressing his mouth forward onto Al's, to feel the scratch of Big Al's mustache. The drugs in his body, the feel of Big Al's flesh against his fingers, invoked the desire to release the stiffness of his erection in the wet hole of Al's mouth as he did yesterday, the day before and the day before that in the back room. Lucho's willingness for magic acts, for feeling Al's mouth full of fire, allowed him to ignore Alfonso's ambivalence.

Alfonso had always blamed the angel dust or the whiskey or the mota for his cocksucking because he wasn't a joto like Lucho. Alfonso even had a girlfriend he fucked in order to prove he wasn't a joto, never ever a joto like Lucho. Which was why Big Al deflected Lucho's gesture and shoved Lucho backward with all his might, baring his teeth in disgust.

Palo said, Wha the fuck! and readied himself for a war.

Unbalanced, Lucho stumbled, his arms flinging awkwardly. He would have fallen over the porch railing were it not for Palo, who grabbed his arm and kept repeating, Wha the fuck!

Because he was in love, Lucho struggled to control his overwhelming urge to crack a skull, snap a bone, and because he was in love, he kicked the porch pillar instead of Big Al's face, the wood splitting under the titanic blow. He wanted to cry, but that was no way for a vato to act, and so Lucho took to the steps, the stairs creaking under the weight of his steel wingtips. He turned his back on his family of men and walked away.

Where you going? Palo yelled.

Give me a frajo, Alfonso demanded, and PeeWee complied with nervous, shaky hands.

'Tás bien loco, ya madre, man. Palo stood disbelieving as he watched Lucho disappear down Third Street. Wha the fuck?

Let the pinche joto go.

You knowed what you did? Palo asked. Without Lucho, no way can we bang up that Nacho dude. Mira, this Nacho is kind of bionic. Look what he did to yous.

The downers, I told you. That's the only reason he took me easy.

I'm telling you we need another vato. PeeWee here, he don't count.

PeeWee, who lit Alfonso's cigarette, became indignant and told Palo to fuck off.

You're ten years old, pendejo! Palo booted the kid in the ass. Get the fuck home before Saint cuts your balls off! When PeeWee refused to budge, Palo wrapped his fingers like a hockey mask on PeeWee's face, shoving him down the porch steps. The scuffle, the shifting of body weight, the awkward and violent push, called for the patrons of El Rey's to turn and watch the happenings. They watched PeeWee hold up his scraped elbow and then watched as Palo faked one step toward him. Injured or not, PeeWee peeled off in the same direction as Lucho.

Palo said, Blow it off, man. Saint's a no-show.

Turning pussy?

¿Quieres algo conmigo? I'm the one who found out the vato's leaving on the bus.

Yea, he's leaving 'n an hour.

The only thing I knowed is Saint's not here and we'll be waiting all night for nuthin'.

Who's asking you to stay?

The neon sombrero on the donkey kept flashing its mantra. Alfonso joined Palo on the old couch and the two sat there like forgotten men sitting on a park bench, tossing life's regrets over the edge of the chain-link fence as freely as empty Coors cans. After finishing off the last of the whiskey, Palo shook his head from side to side. His head heavy, he began to nod off. Man, his eyelids slammed down hard.

They should call it a night.

Near the stairs of the porch, Alfonso's mother had planted a few rosebushes. It was his father's job to care for them and then when his father left it was Alfonso's, and he just forgot to care too and the poor bushes withered into brittle stems. Their browning leaves dropped like twisted bird tongues on the mud where a lawn once flourished. The throwaways, his father's collection of sinks and metal boxes and tires, gave the house a sense of random abandonment. Years of waiting proved to Alfonso that nothing in their yard would grow. Nothing grew on McBride Street anymore except the night.

Nacho don't know who he messed with, when he messed with me.

Fly him back to Tijuana packed in ice. Palo lanced his finger playfully. Cosa seria. He shook a frajo from a Marlboro pack and offered it to Big Al, lit his and then Al's and inhaled, wallowing in a renewed sense of camaraderie.

Al exhaled through his nose, studied the smoldering red ash of the cigarette, and then he took the lit end and crushed it against his swollen cheek with such force his eyes welled and the cigarette extinguished. The sizzle of his flesh startled Palo into wakefulness.

Man, 'tás bien loco ya madre, vato.

Alfonso scrutinized Palo's poor sorry face contemptuously. Palo regretted his gut reaction.

I was loaded on downers, Big Al said. A glaring luminosity of scorched flesh blackened and pinkish like an infected pox on his cheek.

That's the only reason he took me good.

Let's do it, then, just you and me, Palo said and rose from the couch, feeling aroused by the wild potential. Fucken yea, we can do it. We got the Impala, we gotta purpose. Man, just you 'n me.

What 'bout the cuete?

Palo felt respect for the homeboy. Al's face was all fucked up and it demanded respect.

Just you 'n me.

Headlights shone in the distance, and then brightened into the driveway. Relieved to see the Pontiac, Palo slapped Alfonso on the back. No words were exchanged between the two of them. They knew what had to be done. Alfonso marched toward the pearl-peach Pontiac, his Pendleton plaid slapping. Palo followed behind, flicking his cigarette in the dying rosebush, his heart a drum in his head. The engine purred and Santos turned up the volume of the eight-track.

Turtle turned to acknowledge the voices in the backseat. Someone slapped her on the shoulder, another said he was gonna kick her ass for AWOLing. But they all seemed light-years away, their voices cartoonish squeals rewinding. She forgot she sat in a car, someone's car, and was surprised to hear the voices coming from the backseat. Turtle smelled toasted meat and it struck her as funny when she looked up from studying the veins of her arm and hand to see Big Al poke his head between them to give Santos directions.

Turtle resumed pressing a finger against her rubbery green veins. Veins were the strangest things, squishing this way and that, squirming all over her body. The PCP bounced words off of Turtle's chest, the music of the eight-track too psychedelic for her head. As Santos reversed his Goodyears, Turtle found Autry's twang slithering under her flesh like greenish larvae pupating, wings incubating.

PART V

PART V

SEVENTEEN

A perpetual drowsy fog of gaseous fumes hovered over the freeway routes. Divergence and convergence, six freeways in Ermila's front yard, right across from her bedroom window, though she rarely had use for the delineated corridors. Velocity and trucks, vans, motorbikes, speed blasts, trailers and more cars, right there. But Ermila couldn't, even for a minute, imagine where to go but straight to bed.

She prepared for uncluttered sleep by removing her damp sneakers and jeans, puddling the heap of clothes on the bathroom floor. She discarded her filthy bandage, a scroll of colorful events, and then twisted on the faucets to a shower blast of hot water. Afterward, she slipped into a scented linen nightgown fragrant with the scent of fresh laundry-line breeze and then inspected the skin around the dog bite, which looked crimped and shrunken and therefore not in need of another bandage. Instead she swaddled her hair in a towel turban and walked into her bedroom. The dog answered an itching fit by plunging its teeth into its flesh in agony. It was too busy to bother with her footsteps, and she heard its claws against the honey wood floor.

Giving way to a numbed exhaustion, she lay on top of her chenille bedspread, unable or unwilling to exert any more effort to peel the sheets apart. The copter sweeps continued harassing the night. She remembered that she had failed to pick up her clothes and sneakers from the floor of the bathroom, which would prompt another scolding from Grandmother, and considered moving her legs back through the hallway once more to place the clothes in the laundry hamper. To make peace. She had finally figured it out. Grandmother's bitter anger rose because Ermila was *not* her mother and this one lone insight declared itself like pale but reassuring light against the strange echoes of night.

Ermila closed her eyes to the sounds of sirens bursting like fireworks then vanishing, a pair of chased footsteps on the sidewalk, the dog's scratching claws ticking beneath her bed. In the next bedroom, Grandfather coughed and then cleared his throat a number of times before silence occurred, a sign that he struggled with sleeplessness. Just as oblivion formed into an involved sleep, a man spoke from between the wrought-iron bars of her window.

Within sleep and not sleep, Ermila understood how Grandmother could mistake her for her mother, Inez. Dreams overlapped other dreams, which folded into other realities, and one never quite knew what was fake, what was real and what was the dream, and so the man had to repeat her name several times before she fully comprehended the existence of a voice. Ermila yawned and looked toward the window and then read her clock. It read 1:42 a.m.

Who's there? she asked, and when she spied a shadow, she pushed her shoulders against the headboard of her bed. The dog growled at the voice's mannish timbre.

They're gonna jump 'im.

Who's out there?

Gonna kic-kic-kick his ass.

Is that you, Lucho?

Ermila needed to get to the window. Her toes barely touched the cold floor before the dog struck, forcing her to jerk her feet up. She pulled her knees to her breasts, curving her back on the headboard once again. She saw Lucho's bulky ashen figure slicing through the blind slats.

Whatta you want?

Listen, I—

Whatta you talkin' about?

Let me—

You sound high, Ermila said.

Your—your—your cuz, man.

What about Nacho?

She heard Lucho mumble something that blurred into a low murmur just like the freeway vibrations. His voice sifted through the metal screen like a sieve.

I don't hear you, Lucho.

He tried again, but whenever he became excited it was incredibly difficult for him to speak calmly and without a stutter.

Kill time, Lucho managed to say.

Who? Ermila was on her feet now, balancing herself on the bed carefully because the rusted mattress springs coiled and groaned. Who?

Al, he replied. Alfonso.

Who's after him?

Na. Na. Na.

No?

Ermila looked around the room. The crucifix hung right above her and she leaned forward and slid the cross from its nail. The dog's growl crescendoed.

Wait up, she demanded.

Na. Na.

I'll be right there.

Disrobing, Ermila pushed her nightgown down to her ankles and then lowered her gown like bait, slowly dipping the lace hem until it tickled the dog and it sprang forth from under the bed, locking its jowls on the hem of the cloth. With a powerful swing, she whacked the side of the dog's head with the crucifix, forcing its jowls to release and its sausage body to wheel clumsily across the room. The dog whimpered, its claws dashing and slipping to find shelter. She ran to the window and crossed her arms, her nakedness shielded by the closed blind slats. Whatever Lucho was trying to tell her involved Nacho or Alfonso or both, and she spoke through the slats in a whisper reserved for confessions.

Lucho, she said. Lucho Libre, tell it to me slow.

Na, na, na, na.

Nacho?

Yea.

What 'bout Nacho?

Kill time.

Someone's out to get Nacho?

Yea, yea. Kill time.

Who's after him?

I gotta go.

Lucho? Lucho? But she knew he was gone and lifted a slat up to see. Little wonder why Nacho's face was bruised and why his nose bled. He had been in a fight, but with whom? Alfonso? No time to deliberate cause and effect because she had to get to the bus depot as soon as possible to warn Nacho. What the hell had Nacho done to warrant a death sentence? Calling the police was not an option, and forget telling Grandmother.

Nervously, Ermila peered out the door of her bedroom to see the bathroom occupied. Dammit. She donned her nightgown and waited until she heard the toilet flush. Finally, Grandfather emerged, his face pinched with sleepiness, and when he saw her standing near the bathroom door, he dismissed her with a wave of his good hand. Go to bed, he said. His bare feet shuffled sluggishly down the hallway floor.

He adjusted the sound of the black and white television above hearing but not enough to wake Grandmother and then reclined on his chair to watch a late-night horror film.

Once inside the bathroom, Ermila chewed a fingernail to think. It would only take a few minutes for Grandfather to fall back asleep. Okay, fine, just a few minutes. Ermila grabbed her mildew-damp clothes and dressed again. The cool sneakers were the worst, constricted and awkward and resisting her socked feet. She checked her wallet and then her pockets to reaffirm what she already knew: she had no money and thus would have to go by foot. The bus depot was on Fifth Street, that much she knew. Fifth and something. Run to Fifth and then turn right. Head in the direction of downtown. She was bound to run into it.

She peeked into the hallway to make sure the coast was clear but noticed Grandfather changing the channel. Nothing seemed to be going her way. She bit her nail again and then thought about what to do. The window. She had to sneak out of the house through the bathroom window. Using the bathtub rim, she heaved her torso up and pried open the bloated windowpane and then climbed slowly, inching her way out of the small, rectangular window.

The whoosh of the city's vehicles, the broken-up silence from far-away night, made her feel that they lived on an island, the freeways closing in on them like ocean waves, the tierra firme vanishing swiftly. The only plan she had was to run, run her sneakers like she did in gym class while reciting the Hail Mary, for the rhythm of it, the chant consuming her instead of the agony. Pray and run. Pray for the clouds to hold the rain. Pray her legs wouldn't fold. Pray that Nacho already sat on the bus. Pray that Lucho Libre hadn't known what he was saying. Pray the Hail Mary for the beat of each rosary bead to tease her feet into believing it was possible to reach the depot in forty-five minutes.

Ermila discovered that an apricot crate stood upright as if someone had anticipated her escape. Finally, with some luck, Ermila used the crate and leaped to the ground running.

The nighttime hours grew shapeless and huge, measured by the lengthy stretches of boulevards. The wipers screeched and pulled against dry windshield glass because the rain had paused, a slight reprieve, at least a half hour before, and the annoying swipes were extra loud due to the fact that Ana had turned off the radio to save on battery juice.

Ana, Tranquilina said. She had her arms under her poncho for warmth, and her boots seemed ineffective in keeping her feet from feeling chilled. The windows continued to fog and the wipers continued their god-awful scraping.

Yes?

You can turn off the wipers, Tranquilina intoned softly. Without the swiping rubber scraping, the silence made Ana feel worse. She drove twenty in a thirty-five-mile-per-hour zone and barely did fifteen past the Greyhound bus depot in a lethargic trance. The radio off, the heat off, the headlights of the car casting faint beams, the tank of gas reaching empty, the two women seemed absolutely fatigued by the endless search, though neither of them had wanted to be the first to admit failure. Their only other alternative was to go to their respective homes alone, and that was the last thing either of them had the urge to do just yet.

Where is he? Ana pined as if Tranquilina knew and refused to disclose his whereabouts. While Ana lamented, Tranquilina shifted her stare from the rearview mirror to side mirror, scanning, seeking. Not more than two city blocks away from the depot's double-door entrance, a small news and food kiosk stood open, and Tranquilina saw a hint of a face behind a grated window. A young man lingered outside the kiosk counter, munching on a pastry, its cellophane peeled back like banana skin, his hot coffee steaming on the counter lip of window.

On Central, Tranquilina asked Ana to U-turn and then instructed her to drive to the corner of the depot where the lamplight shone dreary blue and where a few dented drivers in dented taxis waited for a fare. She instructed Ana to lock the doors and keep alert and then, as she had done so often the last few hours, Tranquilina got out of the car to inquire.

She approached the kiosk and said to the young man licking his fingers, Excuse me, sir.

Nacho raised his eyebrows, his fingers in his mouth. He looked away in hopes that she was not addressing him directly and then sipped his coffee with serious and focused intent. This time, Tranquilina spoke to him in Spanish, and again he ignored her, as he was well versed in the trickery of immigration officers. He castigated himself for not having stayed in the depot. Instead, he gave in to his craving for coffee and as a consequence was confronted by this stranger.

Two in the a.m. on the dot and the man behind the kiosk window shut a wooden window panel and the bang startled them both. For Nacho this meant move it, and he picked up his cup of coffee and began to walk toward the depot.

Where you headed? Tranquilina asked. She spoke Spanish like a pocha.

He pointed his cup to the depot's double doors.

May I walk with you a bit?

Nacho studied her suspiciously. She seemed quite odd, which inspired a feeling of apprehension, but in the end he nodded his approval because she wore a poncho like his tías did back home. Her nose was almost as red as the poncho.

I don't have money.

I'm looking for a friend.

Taken aback, Nacho asked for a repeat. Was this a solicitation of a kinky prostitute? He puzzled over her request, genuinely amused.

Isn't everyone?

I'm looking for someone very special, Tranquilina replied. Nacho couldn't help himself. The lateness or the earliness of the hour made him light-headed and the caffeine hadn't induced any type of clarity. He said:

Could it be me? He felt a drop of rain on his cheek and looked up at the mass of clouds that blinded any star from shining through and for a reason unbeknownst to him, he smiled. The coffee cup he held was plunked with a raindrop. The two strolled down a block until they reached the intersection, and Tranquilina stalled the walk to make herself clear.

He's a student. That's his sister over there. Tranquilina pointed to the sedan parked up ahead, its windshield glossy against the muddy Yellow Cabs. Nacho waved to her as if that were what he was supposed to do by way of introduction, and Ana returned an abbreviated wave over the steering wheel. She ignited the engine and then drove to the intersection and idled the sedan and leaned over to unlock the door while Tranquilina slid into the passenger seat, immediately unrolling the window to speak properly.

We can't find him, Tranquilina continued. Nacho stood near the open window to better hear over the engine. And we're very worried.

Oh, I'm sure he's out having a good time somewhere. You know students, Nacho said. They're all the same.

He might hurt himself.

Ana stared at the dashboard for her eyes to have something neutral to do.

Why would he do that?

Tranquilina didn't have a concise answer. His flat nose and eyes lined with lovely lashes seemed radiant under the bluish gleam of lamppost light and his lips pursed as he asked such an innocent question.

Not knowing exactly how to respond to her silence, Nacho added, He must really be very unhappy. He threw the cup and its contents into a trashcan on the corner. Less than another city block back to the depot and then to the bus and then to home. Nacho couldn't possibly imagine being that sad. He rubbed his hands against his trousers in a futile attempt to remove the pastry stickiness from his fingers and leaned on the balls of his shoes.

Have you tried the cops?

What for? Ana replied.

Aren't they supposed to help?

His name is Ben. Ben Brady. He has a scar, Tranquilina said and traced a finger over her left eyebrow to demonstrate where the scar began and where it ended. Drizzle misted around him.

I wish I could help, Nacho said, but my bus leaves—he stopped to glance at his watch—in twenty minutes.

Where you going? Ana asked, suppressing a yawn, her eyes moistening. Nacho was eager to get back into the depot before the pour of rain and knew that casual conversations could go on forever. He wanted his answer to be curt and replied, Home, and when he said the word, he grinned in utter delightfulness because he couldn't believe it. He was going home.

I can't wait.

Large raindrops, just a few, hit the windshield of the car.

Not again, Ana whined in reference to the weather. She covered a second yawn and the yawning became contagious. Nacho yawned and then Tranquilina yawned.

Isn't this crazy? Nacho asked, turning his face to feel the titillating shock of water giving way to another pending storm. Nacho had to admit: one characteristic of this city he appreciated was its melodrama: his departure accented with rain, the odd woman in search of a lost man, her exhausted companion complete with old bags under such young eyes. Pure Hollywoodlandia. Would Nacho have tales to share back home! He took Tranquilina's chilled hand and squeezed it in a friendly handshake.

Go with God, Tranquilina said. Ana simply turned the ignition and the sedan U-turned and drove east. A flash of lightning blazed on the horizon of Fifth Street, camera-bulb, blinding light, splashes of brilliant white light on the chain of smooth metal bodies of parked cars linked bumper to bumper.

Nacho never knew what hit him.

Turtle saw herself vomiting. She was outside the Pontiac standing in the rain watching herself inside the car, her stomach nauseated and wanting to vomit again. She saw Saint push her out of the car, saw herself on her knees, the rain flogging her body, vomiting on her jacket, vomiting near the tar of tire. She had something of great importance she had committed to do this morning, but she couldn't remember what it was, and tried reaching out to help herself up. She looked at herself, cool vapors steaming from her nostrils. God, how she felt shitty and wanted to tell Saint, or Alfonso or Palo. But they were busy, staying in the car, staying dry, intent on watching what, Turtle didn't know.

That's 'im. Big Al said. What him, who's him? Turtle wanted to ask. Did she hear right? Soggy pellets dropped and yet Turtle wasn't in a hurry to get out of the rain. The doors all opened at once, and the McBride Boys jumped out. Turtle leaned on the hood of the Pontiac. Her body smoldered in the rain. She had trouble breathing and with each inch of body that moved, she heard a ripping of flesh. She was moving, her body moving to join the McBride Boys because all they had was each other. The movement made her nauseous again and she fell to her knees again to watch Alfonso stuff a boy into a crack in the brick wall. Startled winos fled from the alley, and like a disturbance cast into a tranquil horizon, they flew frantically away in different directions.

Turtle watched the boy's head burst, splattering liquid on the sidewalk. Arms and legs sprouted like one big insect cannibalizing another. This was a hard-core jump and another Turtle, the one not her, pulled out the screwdriver, her old faithful, the dependable cuete, the nonbetrayer.

A boot slammed against a pair of testicles, and Santos's face grimaced. Palo wrapped the boy's neck with hanging wire and then pulled to slice his skin like clay, while Alfonso's teeth clamped down on the boy's ear tearing it to leave a hole as deep as the boy's howling mouth. Lightning flashed; the lamppost above them popped, causing an electrical short, and it rained sparks like liquid sparklers and Turtle thought this was beautiful until the sparks died down into darkness. The boys' shadows turned to ghostlike haze.

Santos held what resembled a plastic toy gun, the kind that Tío Angel had once brought from the war. Turtle laughed at how stupid he looked aiming the toy gun against the boy's bloodied forehead. She didn't know why she did it, but Turtle kicked the gun out of Santos's grasp in a mass confusion of limbs. The gun flew quietly in the air, a million years of flying, and then landed somewhere in a trash heap. Santos turned and punched a rubbery fist on her lips, and Turtle laughed because it felt like such a small itsy-bitsy pinch.

Turtle wants to waste him, Alfonso shouted, his nostrils flexing, reveling in the smell of victory. He held Santos's fist from making connection with her face again and then pointed to Turtle's screwdriver. Turtle turned to his voice, the voice of blur, indistinguishable and slow, and she heard him saying within the hard percolation of the rain:

Turtle's thinking. She wants to waste him! Alfonso was sure of it and pushed Santos away.

Sí-mon, Santos replied. Let her take the fall.

Waste him slow, Palo instructed, pointing to the mutilated body struggling to escape. Turtle clenched her jaw because she no longer had a mouth to speak. Encircled by the McBride Boys, Turtle grew larger and invincible and she had to remind her lungs to exhale so that the suffocation she was now experiencing with the screwdriver in her hand could not render her motionless. Her instinct alerted, she willed her body to move in the direction of the brick wall, where the boy struggled to lean, a palm held out to stop her.

And Turtle lunged at the boy with all the dynamite rage of all the fucked-up boys stored in her rented body. Bits of flesh splattered on Turtle's face and it struck her as funny until panic set in like the freeze of cold rain. She pushed the screwdriver against a bone, felt her arm muscle thrust forward with greater force, then pulled back with all her strength. When she plunged the screwdriver in again, it went so deep through the pit of the boy's belly, it hit the brick wall and when she heard the snap-crack of bone, she took it to be the boy's rib and not her own wrist and arm bones breaking.

The torrential rains surrounded them. Tranquilina glanced at the sideview mirror as Ana drove away from the curb to see the young man completing his journey back to the depot. Instead, through the melting glassy rain of the back window, she thought the boy had fallen into a hole walled by contorted poses and slashes of rain.

Stop the car! Tranquilina yelled and then rolled her window down to stick her head out of the car. Her view remained distorted. The lamppost faulted, riotous light, then diminished to nothing, and she couldn't discern exactly what was happening.

What's wrong? Ana strung alert and tried to study her mirrors. Is it Ben? Is it? Where is he? Did you see Ben? She pulled over to the side of the road, her engine running on fumes, and Tranquilina jumped out of the car, one boot stumbling onto a sewer grate that swirled an eddy of water, forcing her to slip altogether.

Go get help! Tranquilina yelled over the tear of thunder. Do it, Ana, please.

Why? What's happened? Ana hollered.

I don't know, I don't know.

Ana drove off, no more questions, the car skidding.

Small pools of water sloshed in Tranquilina's boots as she ran. The storm fell like strong metal pins making the whole of Tranquilina's return to the intersection agitated and frightening.

Turtle clung onto the lamppost and staggered upward. Her hand hung limp from her jacket sleeve and she slowly let the screwdriver fall without a sound, without a thud or concrete clink. Her fingers began to swell and it bothered her that she could barely lift her palm. She stared at the screwdriver for a moment, but couldn't focus because everything was swaying as if she were on a ship caught in a storm. She closed her eyes to keep from falling again, reveled in the lull between thunder, the freedom of darkness. Frozen in wait, Turtle found herself melting from ice to water.

The water rose and spilled over the concrete curb, and she felt a vague tremor of pain begin to seep and enter the localized area of the bone breaks. The bones in her hand and wrist cluttered loosely in a sack of bruising skin. She wondered what time it was and if she should begin walking to Ray's store. Turtle opened her eyes and looked around and found herself abandoned by the McBride Boys. The Pontiac was gone, as was Gene Autry's voice, and she watched the black ooze out of the torn hole of the boy's ear.

And then like a déjà vu, Turtle recognized the woman who bent over the boy, removed her cape, a superman's cape, and pillowed it under the boy's mess of black water. Now the pain arrived, shooting up from Turtle's hand to her arm, her head. Breaks of white radiant lightning flashed one, and then another, and Turtle grimaced, her hand resolutely useless in shielding her eyes from such brilliance. Turtle thought at first it was the rain that had saturated her jacket, T-shirt, and trousers, but soon realized the black blotches were splatterings of blood.

Why? the woman asked Turtle, and kept asking.

"Why" was not a word that meant something to Turtle. The PCP was wearing thin and the invincible feeling slowly dissolved. Turtle's hand ached in rising volume, her lip the size of California. Why? Turtle forgot why. Turtle didn't know why. She didn't make the rules. Why? Because a tall girl named Antonia never existed, because her history held no memory. Why? Go ask another.

Turtle's lips weighted down to muteness. In answer to the woman, all Turtle could do was hold up her broken arm to show her. A crackle like burning wood pierced through the rain. Stunned, Turtle looked bewildered and then felt a sticky ball of grit push from between her swollen lips. Luis Lil Lizard had once told her that them two lived in a stay of execution. Only the pain, which overwhelmed, surprised her.

Don't shoot! Tranquilina rose, waving frantically. She saw the snaps of rifle sparks and emptied her lungs to repeat, Don't shoot! Don't shoot! Over the surging rains, a second round crackled.

Turtle's chest burned down to her belly. Although she stood in the shower of rain, her face flamed something fierce. She dropped to her knees, quietly, into a puddle of oily water. Someone cradled her, held her as tight and strong as her brother, held all of her together until sleep came to her fully welcomed.

We'rrrre not dogggggs! Tranquilina roared in the direction of the shooters. Stop shooting, we're not dogs! The words crashed into one another, rocketing into one big howl of pleading, demanding, a speeding blur of raging language blending in with the chaos of commands and shouts and orders and circuslike commotion coming from the shooters who stood in the darkness.

Spotlights beamed white and Tranquilina squinted, the harsh light burning and flooding over the rifled body of the young man she had held so as to protect him. His sneaker had twisted halfway off his foot, his soggy sock ridiculously dirty. Except for the beating pins of rain, silence now prevailed.

Tranquilina rearranged the boy in an effort to make him comfortable in his eternal sleep, just as she had done with the other boy lying a few yards away, the one she had become familiar with only a few minutes before. Absolutely drenched in the black waters of blood and torrents of rain, Tranquilina couldn't delineate herself from the murdered souls because these tears and blood and rain and bullet wounds belonged to her as well.

Sorrow so wide, it was blinding. Tranquilina vaguely heard commands, crazy shouts, confusing screams and searched out the dark spaces between the high beaming lights to discern the phantasmic figures of the sharpshooters, struck still at her gaze, their rifles cocked and aimed. A web of lights shot from every direction and Tranquilina tried to shield her eyes. Except for Tranquilina, no one, not the sharpshooters, the cabdrivers, the travelers dashing out of the depot, the barefoot or slipper-clad spectators in robes, not one of them, in all their glorious hallucinatory gawking, knew who the victims were, who the perpetrators were.

The sharpshooters steadied their barrels.

Tranquilina closed her eyes to hear her heart beating. She summoned the stories of Papa and Mama's miraculous escape. Shoulders back, Tranquilina raised her chin higher, as Mama had told her time and again, to fill up with the embrace of ancestral spirits. The rain on her face cleansed away the grievous exhaustion, and she ignored the command to place her hands on her head. Her arms by her side, her fists clenched, she would not fear them. Shouting voices ordered her not to move, stay immobile, but she lifted one foot forward, then another, refusing to halt. Two inches, four, six, eight, riding the currents of the wilding wind. Riding it beyond the borders, past the cesarean scars of the earth, out to limitless space where everything was possible if she believed.

ACKNOWLEDGMENTS

I am fascinated by the notion that readers may never fully understand how challenging it is for a writer to keep stable and constant the genuine vision of a novel when in fact a writer's life is in rapid motion, changing, evolving, expanding, decreasing. In other words, it is hard to keep your vessel afloat during the personal storms without the assistance, advice, encouragement, guidance, and love of family, friends, colleagues, students, and other writers way too numerous to name here. I extend my gratitude and heartfelt love to all of them for keeping the faith.

I would like to thank the Hedgebrook Residency; Michael Collier of the Bread Loaf Writers' Conference; Ted Kheel of Grupo Punta Cana; Ruthie Viramontes of the Victoria Apartments; and the Los Angeles Public Library for providing space that allowed me to work on the novel throughout the years. Julia Alvarez, Junot Díaz, sweet Manuel Muñoz, Brennen Wysong, Rosemary Ahern, and Marie Brown read early drafts of the novel, and I appreciated their keen observations, their sharp criticisms and honest commentary. La Susan Bergholz and future Nobel laureate H. G. Carrillo read the final draft, both calling me within days to let me know what they thought. Only rarely does one have friends who would put everything on hold, give up their precious time to read a novel, and I love them dearly for it.

From Bahrain to Brazil, from New York to Texas, from Ithaca to Irvine, all my friends have been extra special. I only hope they all know what they mean to me, but a few shout-outs anyway to Sandra Cisneros, María Herrera-Sobek (a.k.a. "La Jefa"), Ana Castillo, Ana Maria Garcia,

Yvonne Yarbro Bejarano, Paula Moya, Sonia Saldivar-Hull, Margarita Barcelo, Gabriella Gutierrez y Muhs, Lucha Carpi, Norma Alarcon, Rosaura Sanchez, Cherrie Moraga, Lydia Rodriguez, Mary Pat Brady, Norma Cantu, Margaret Dieter, Inez Versage, Elizabeth Gonzales-Towers, Genet Chavez-Gomez, and Nydia Hernandez, not to mention the IHC "girls"—Melanie, Martha, Elaine, Gay, and Valerie. All of them are my co-madres of heart, of survival.

To the students I have met and had conversations with everywhere, but especially to the lovely students at Mercy High School and Saint Mary's College, and the students majoring in American studies at the University of Bahrain, I will never forget you.

My gratitude to my editor at Atria Books, Malaika Adero, who was fearless in taking on a novel like mine with such dedication; it gave me much-needed confidence. People like Sybil Pincus, Johanna Castillo and Krishan Trotman at Simon & Schuster have been extremely thorough and professional.

Since the death of our parents, our family has become a huge web of relationships where cousins, nephews and nieces, in-laws and out-laws, brothers and sisters are so interconnected, no one member will ever feel alone. I am so proud, consider myself so lucky, to be a part of this extended web of crazy, hectic, miraculous, beautiful familia Viramontes.

I would not have been able to survive bicoastal family obligations and meet my professional ones without my patient, competent, efficient, and ever-so-vigilant agent, Stuart Bernstein, who is an artist in his own right, a master planner, a kind, compassionate man. His is always the first e-mail I open.

My colleagues in the Department of English at Cornell University, and especially those in the Creative Writing program, have been inspirational. Indeed, if there is any thoughtfulness in the novel it is due to the conversations between friends over a glass of wine, in the hallway of Goldwin Smith, or at Moosewood.

I sincerely thank my husband, Eloy Rodriguez, and my children, Pilar and Eloy Francisco, who have had to live with me for the crazed duration of the novel. I know this was extremely difficult and I tell them every day I love them.

And finally I acknowledge you, my dear sister Frances, who lives on fiercely in my heart for time immortal.